This book should be returned to any branch of the
Lancashire County Library on or before the date

D0589860

~~GRAVEYARD~~

WILLIAM C. DIETZ

THE MUTANT FILES
GRAVEYARD

TITAN BOOKS

THE MUTANT FILES: GRAVEYARD
Print edition ISBN: 9781783298785
E-book edition ISBN: 9781783298792

Published by
Titan Books
A division of Titan Publishing Group Ltd
144 Southwark Street
London
SE1 0UP

First edition: February 2016
2 4 6 8 10 9 7 5 3 1

A CIP catalogue record for this title is available from the British Library.

Printed and bound by CPI Group (UK) Ltd, Croydon, CR0 4YY

For my dearest Marjorie.
Thank you.

ONE

Sunday school teacher Misty Roker was having a nice day until her students found a body behind St. Patrick's Church. Roker was in her classroom, putting instructional materials away when sixteen-year-old Emily Stills burst into the room. "Miss Roker! A man is lying in the parking lot—and there's something wrong with his face!"

Sunday school was over, but the children's parents were still attending Mass, so Misty instructed Emily to remain in the classroom while she went out to investigate. A playground had been built behind the church and was surrounded by a fence. The children were gathered in front of the gate that opened into the parking lot, clearly looking at something. She clapped her hands. "Go inside, children . . . Emily's waiting for you."

When the children turned, Misty could see the worried looks on their faces and felt the first stirrings of concern. She had assumed that a drunk had passed out in the parking lot. That would require an explanation, but she could handle it. Now, based on the complete lack of chatter, Misty sensed that something worse was in the offing.

As her charges filed inside, Misty approached the gate. The man was lying a few feet away, eyes wide open, staring up into the bright sunlight. That was when the nurse noticed the facial discoloration, the swelling, and the hundreds of tiny stitches that ran around the circumference of his face. What the heck?

Misty opened the gate and knelt at the man's side. She felt for a pulse. The results were unequivocal. The man was dead—and had been for some time.

Misty fumbled for her phone, dialed 911, and reported the find. "My name is Misty Roker. We have a man down behind St. Patrick's Church. He's unresponsive, cyanotic, and I can't detect a pulse."

The dispatcher promised to send an aid unit and, as Misty waited for the medics to arrive, she noticed the white envelope. It was protruding from the man's shirt, and when Misty pulled it free, she saw that Father Benedict's name was written on it. Deep down Misty knew that she shouldn't open the envelope but curiosity got the better of her. So she took it out, opened the unsealed flap, and looked inside. That was when Misty saw the five one-hundred-nu notes and a single piece of paper. She read what was typed on it:

Dear Father Benedict,

This man has gone to a better place. His name is Joel. Please use the money to cover his burial expenses.

Thank you,
Alcmaeon

Misty frowned. *Alcmaeon?* What kind of name was that?

A siren could be heard in the distance. So Misty stuffed the note back into the envelope—and slid it back into Joel's shirt. The EMTs arrived a minute later, along with a police car. The medics went through the motions of checking Joel out, but he was dead, and all of them knew it. The envelope went to a patrol officer who was careful to hold only the edges of the object before sliding it into a larger envelope. Then, after taking Misty's name and contact information, he turned her loose. Sunday school was over.

* * *

Cassandra Lee and Lawrence Kane were looking for a condo. The decision to live together had been made during a recent vacation, and now they were looking at condos in Santa Monica, an area that both of them liked.

But they were very busy people, which made finding the time to tour properties difficult. And, now that Kane's home was up for sale, the task was that much more urgent. Which was why they'd toured two different possibilities that morning and were about to discuss them over lunch.

The restaurant was called Mac's and was located about a mile away from the famous Santa Monica Pier. It had large windows that looked out over the highway to a sandy beach and the pale blue ocean beyond. "So," Kane began once they'd been through the buffet line, "what did you think?"

Lee nibbled on a huge strawberry. It was delicious and gave her an opportunity to stall. Even though they'd been through a great deal together, they hadn't known each other for long, and she wanted to give him a considered response. "Well, the first place is the larger of the two, and I liked that. But it needs a new kitchen."

Kane had a straight nose, even features, and was wearing a white polo shirt over jeans. He nodded. "True . . . And the head chef needs a good place to perform his culinary miracles. It might be fun to do a reno. Then we could have the kitchen exactly the way we want it.

"How 'bout number two?" he inquired. "It's smaller but it comes with *two* parking slots plus a place to keep your bike."

Lee's Harley Road King Police Edition motorcycle was a problem, since most condo buildings provided only two parking places, and she hoped to keep the bike nearby. Lee was about to respond when her phone began to dance across the table. Kane made a face. But Lee was on call and had to answer. "Hello, Detective Lee."

"Sorry," Deputy Chief Jenkins said. "Life sucks."

"No kidding. What have you got?"

"Something weird," Jenkins said. "That's why I called you."

"Screw you," Lee replied. "And the horse you rode in on."

Jenkins laughed. "Somebody dumped a body in the parking lot behind St. Patrick's Church."

"Okay," Lee said. "But that doesn't qualify as strange. Not in LA."

"True," Jenkins admitted. "However, based on a preliminary evaluation by the coroner, this guy probably died as the result of a botched face transplant."

"That *is* weird," Lee agreed.

"Oh, but there's more," Jenkins added. "The dead man is *B. nosilla* positive."

Lee was surprised. The John Doe was a mutant! Thirty-one years earlier, back in 2038, a terrorist called Al Mumit (the taker of life) had turned a spore-forming bacteria called *Bacillus nosilla* loose on the world.

The bioengineered bacteria was delivered to *Kaffar* (unbelievers) all around the world by 786 *Shaheed*, or martyrs, each of whom had been selected because they had light-colored skin, were elderly, or only a few months old.

The results were even better than what Al Mumit had hoped for. Billions fell ill as *Bacillus nosilla* spread, and of those who contracted the disease, about 9 percent survived, with slightly better odds in developed countries. And of those who survived, many went on to develop mutations. Some of the physiological changes were good, but many caused disfigurements or were lethal.

"Patrol officers responded," Jenkins put in, "and they found a note on the body. According to the person who wrote it, the deceased is named Joel. But that isn't a whole lot to go on. Head over to St. Patrick's and collect what information you can."

"I'm on my way," Lee replied.

"Yanty will meet you there," Jenkins said. "I'll see you in the morning." Lee heard a click.

Lee looked at Kane as she put the phone away. "Sorry, hon . . . Gotta go."

Kane had been through it before. He smiled. "No problem . . . Let me know if you'll be home for dinner. If you had to choose between the condos we looked at today, which one would it be?"

"The larger one," Lee replied, as she took a final sip of coffee. "It had an incredible view of the ocean. There's a room for your office—and a kitchen reno would be fun."

"And your bike?"

"There's bound to be a storage unit somewhere nearby."

"That's very nice of you."

"I can be nice," Lee said as she got up from the table. "Sometimes."

Kane laughed. "Shall I get a box for your food?"

"Please," Lee said. "I'll call you." And with that, she left.

Because Lee was on call, both of them had driven to Mac's alone. Her vehicle was a so-called creeper, which was street slang for an unmarked car. Except that most creepers had not only been tagged a dozen times but often bore the letters TIACC. "This is a cop car." Her sedan was no different.

Lee's vehicle was equipped with a rarely used nav system. She'd gone straight into the police academy after college, graduated near the top of her class, and spent four years as a patrol officer prior to being promoted to detective. And, like most street cops, Lee knew the city like the back of her hand. She took 10 East onto National Boulevard, which morphed into Jefferson Boulevard, which delivered her to the church with a minimum of fuss.

St. Patrick's was a large building with a green roof and towers that were somewhat reminiscent of the Spanish missions only with a more modern aesthetic. *That's Kane talking*, the voice in her head said. *Since when did you care about architecture?*

So? Lee answered. *That's how it is when you have a relationship with someone. They rub off on you.*

Or they come to own you.

That's bullshit, Lee thought, as she pulled in behind the church. *Maybe you would like to spend the rest of your life with a bunch of cats. Personally, I'd prefer a man.*

"This is 1-William-3. I am Code 6. Over." There was no need to say where she was since the dispatcher could see the creeper's location on the computer screen in front of her.

Church was over, and only a few cars remained in the parking lot. The body had been removed by then, but a police cruiser was still there, as was the middle-aged crime-scene investigator everyone called "Moms." She was busy taking pictures of the area while the bored patrol officers looked on.

Detective Dick Yanty had seen Lee pull in and made his way over to meet her. He was balding, wore wire-rimmed glasses that had a tendency to slide down his nose, and was wearing the usual plaid sports coat. Technically, both of them reported to Lieutenant Brianna Wolfe. But Yanty and a detective named Prospo had been assigned to work with Lee on the Bonebreaker case, "the Bonebreaker" being the name the media had bestowed on the serial killer responsible for killing Lee's father and eight other cops over the last sixteen years. "Hey, Lee," Yanty said. "Does this suck or what?"

"It sucks," Lee agreed solemnly. "So what, if anything, do we have?"

"First there's *this*," Yanty said as he handed her a sheet of paper. "It's a copy—so don't worry about prints."

Lee read it:

Dear Father Benedict,

This man has gone to a better place. His name is Joel. Please use the money to cover his burial expenses.

Thank you,
Alcmaeon

"*Alcmaeon?* Who the hell is that?"

Yanty pushed the glasses up onto the bridge of his nose. "What did you do while you were in college? Everybody knows who Alcmaeon of Croton is."

"That's bullshit," Lee replied. "You ran a search on it."

Yanty grinned. "Yes, I did. It seems that Alcmaeon of Croton lived in the fifth century b.c.—and was one of the most eminent medical theorists of his time. Although he spent most of his time writing about medical stuff, he studied astrology and meteorology, too."

"So he was a nerd."

"Yup."

"That's interesting," Lee said. "And it seems to support what Jenkins told me."

"Which was?"

"The coroner thinks Joel might have died of complications following a botched face transplant. We'll know after the autopsy. But try this on for size . . . The hack who botched the operation felt guilty about Joel's death. So he dumped the body here along with some money to pay for a burial."

"And signs the note Alcmaeon because he or she identifies with the old goat for some reason," Yanty put in.

"Exactly," Lee said. "And how much you wanna bet that the perp is Catholic?"

"Perhaps," Yanty replied cautiously. "But maybe Joel was Catholic—and the doctor knew that."

"Good point," Lee said. "How 'bout video? Do we have any?"

"Yes," Yanty replied. "The church is equipped with a full-on security system, so we might get lucky. A guy named Mike agreed to work on that. Come on . . . Let's see if he found anything."

Lee followed Yanty through a small playground and into the church. They found Mike in a nicely furnished office sitting in front of a monitor. He turned to look over his shoulder as they entered the room. Lee assumed that Mike was a parishioner. He had mocha-colored skin, a buzz cut, and serious eyes. "I have it," he announced. "At least I think I do."

"This is Detective Lee," Yanty said. "You sound doubtful . . . What's the problem?"

Mike nodded to Lee. "They say a picture is worth a thousand words," he said. "Watch this."

So the police officers stood behind Mike as he started a black-and-white video clip. Lee could see a time and date stamp in the lower left-hand corner of the screen. It read: 05/12/69 04:12.

As the three of them watched, a white box truck drove into the lot behind the church, did a U-turn, and came to a stop. Lee expected to see someone get out, open the back, and remove Joel's body. They didn't. The truck drove away. And there, lying on the pavement was the corpse. "Damn," Yanty said admiringly. "That was slick!"

"The perp cut a six-foot-long hole in the bed of the truck," Lee said. "And it had to be left or right of the drive shaft."

"And that means he or she's done this before," Yanty

commented. "Or plans to do it again."

"Precisely," Lee said. "Mike, can you zoom in? If so, I'd like to take a look at the license plates coming and going."

It turned out that Mike could zoom in, and he proceeded to do so. The results were disappointing to say the least. There weren't any plates. "So we have *nada*," Yanty said. "Shit." Lee was in full agreement.

Lee managed to clear the crime scene by three and made it home by four. Except that the condo didn't feel like home after what had taken place there a few weeks earlier. But Lee was determined to ignore that . . . And Chef Kane helped her do so by serving cocktails, tossed green salads, and some crusty sole. Then it was time to sit on the deck and watch the sun go down. "We need a view like this one," Lee said as she sipped her coffee. "What a great way to end the day."

That led to a discussion of all the properties they'd seen over the last two weeks and how to rank them. Later, as Lee lay next to Kane, she thought about the way her life had changed. There were things to look forward to now—and a person to share them with. That was new, and for the first time in a long time, Lee was happy.

Lee had never been good at getting up in the morning and was often late for work until she moved in with Kane. Now, every morning began with a kiss on the forehead or a pat on the bottom, depending on what part of her was available.

As Kane went out for his morning run, Lee took her shower and got ready to leave. Then they had a cup of coffee together before going their separate ways. It was a ritual and one Lee looked forward to. So she was standing in the kitchen, and Kane's coffee was ready when he returned. He was dressed in a tee shirt, blue shorts, and running shoes. "You're right on time," Lee observed. "A shrink with OCD . . . Someone should write a paper about that."

"A cop who breaks all the rules," Kane countered. "Someone should write a paper about *that*. And maybe I will." They laughed.

Kane took a sip of coffee and gestured to the small flat-screen TV that sat on the counter top. "So what's in the news this morning?"

"It sounds like peace could break out at any moment," Lee replied. "The Aztec ambassador is going to meet with a representative from the Republic of Texas later today. And our Secretary of State will be there, too."

After the plague had struck, hundreds of thousands of people were declared communicable, some mistakenly, and herded into hastily organized "recovery" camps. Eventually, the recovery camps became "relocation" camps as untold thousands were loaded onto trucks and sent east. The sudden influx of mutants caused the "norms" in bordering states to flee west—and those who were B. nosilla negative were allowed to stay.

Other parts of what had been the United States went through a similar process, resulting in so-called red zones, where mutants lived, and the green zones, which belonged to the norms. It wasn't long before zones and collections of zones gave birth to nation-states like Pacifica, which consisted of Washington, Oregon, and California, and the Republic of Texas, which incorporated Idaho, Utah and Arizona.

Meanwhile, south of the border, a new Aztec Empire had been born. In many ways it was a long-delayed reaction to the Treaty of Guadalupe Hidalgo, which brought the U.S.-Mexican War to an end on February 2, 1848. Having won on the battlefield, the United States could dictate the terms of a settlement that allowed it to acquire more than five hundred thousand square miles of valuable territory, including what became the states of California, New Mexico, Arizona, Nevada, Utah, and parts of Wyoming and Colorado for the paltry sum of $15 million. A settlement that still rankled more than 220 years later.

And that was why the newly formed Aztec army had crossed the border halfway between San Luis and Nogales a few months earlier and had been slugging it out with the Republicans ever since. And there was the very real possibility that Pacifica would be dragged into the conflict since the Aztecs were determined to take California back. "I'm glad to hear that everybody's at the table," Kane said. "Maybe they can work something out. How about you? Will this be a normal day?"

"I hope so," Lee replied. "I'll call or text you if things go off the rails." Lee gave him a coffee-flavored kiss followed by a wave as she headed for the door.

Lee knew that there were a number of people who would like to kill her, including the Bonebreaker. So she was careful to scan her surroundings as she left the condo, entered the elevator, and rode it down to the parking garage. The car appeared to be undisturbed, but appearances could be deceptive. Lee removed a handheld GPS and cell-phone detector from her bag, turned it on, and circled the vehicle. If a tracker had been placed on the sedan during the night, the device would warn her. None had.

Lee got in, started the engine, and drove to a restaurant called Maria's, where she ate a breakfast burrito before completing the trip to work. The LAPD's headquarters building was known for its angular appearance—and cost $437 million old bucks to construct back in 2009. Unfortunately, the façade had been damaged by a rocket attack in 2065 and was still awaiting repairs.

Lee entered the ramp that led to the parking garage, paused to show her ID, and continued down until she located an empty slot. Then she rode an elevator up to the sixth floor, which was home to the Chief of Detectives, her staff, and about sixty detectives. All of whom occupied the maze of cubicles generally referred to as the bull pen.

Of the larger force, only twelve men and women were members of the elite Special Investigative Section (S.I.S.) charged with getting the city's most dangerous criminals off the street. That was the unit Lee belonged to—and she made it to roll call with a minute to spare. The conference room was about half-full, which was typical, since five or six detectives were out of the office at any given time. But both Yanty and Prospo looked glum. Probably because they knew something that she didn't.

Lee plopped down next to Prospo and was about to interrogate him when Jenkins entered the room. He had black hair, startling green eyes, and brown skin. He was dressed in a nicely cut gray suit. "I wish I could say 'good morning,'" Jenkins said soberly, "but I can't. All of you have met Cheyenne Darling—and are cognizant of the relationship she had with Deputy Chief McGinty."

Like Lee's father two years earlier, Deputy Chief of Detectives Ross McGinty had been murdered by the Bonebreaker and his body dumped next to the Hollywood Freeway. Most of him anyway . . . The Bonebreaker liked to keep his victims' extremities.

Furthermore, Lee knew that although McGinty and Darling had been lovers, they didn't live together because he feared for her safety. And McGinty, like her father, had been subject to bad dreams and bouts of depression.

"Darling was visiting friends yesterday," Jenkins continued. "And when she came home, a package was waiting for her. It appeared to be from her sister, so she opened it. And there, nestled in shredded packing paper, was Chief McGinty's left femur."

Lee heard expressions of disgust and anger from all around her as she remembered what had been sent to *her*. It was meant to hurt and had. Fortunately, with Kane's help, she'd been able to recover. So she knew what Darling was going through. "We need to find this asshole," Jenkins said grimly. "How 'bout it, Lee? Have you got anything new?"

"The Bonebreaker was active during the Vasquez investigation," Lee replied. "We know that because he was posing as Detective Lou Harmon. And we're pretty sure that he was wearing a latex mask that covered his entire head."

Harmon had been murdered by the serial killer years earlier, and by posing as the dead detective, the Bonebreaker was demonstrating his superiority over everyone in the LAPD. All of those in the room knew it. What they *didn't* know was that in order to prevent more murders by *another* killer, Lee had been forced to interact with the Bonebreaker. It was a decision that could get her fired.

"So," Lee continued, "we're in the process of contacting all of the companies that manufacture, distribute, and sell full-head masks to see if we can identify him that way. Odds are that the Bonebreaker has an extensive collection of masks, so who knows? Maybe we'll get lucky."

"Let's hope so," Jenkins said. "Meanwhile, the forensics people are going to run every test they can think of on the femur."

"How is Ms. Darling doing?" Lee inquired.

Jenkins made a face. "Not well. What about the face case? How's *that* going?"

Lee and Yanty provided brief reports and were told to "Stay on it."

Then it was time for other detectives to sit on the hot seat while Lee thought about the day ahead. She was working on another Bonebreaker lead as well. One she couldn't tell anyone about, because if she did, they'd find out that she'd been in communication with the very person she was supposed to bring in.

Finally, after the usual reminder to catch up on their paperwork, the detectives were released. Lee went back to her desk, where she worked her way through thirty-nine e-mails before slipping out of the office.

It took less than fifteen minutes to drive to Chinatown and the walkup apartment that Ebert Keyes called home. The relationship went back to the point when Lee had arrested Keyes for hacking into the state's social support system—and reclassifying himself as fully disabled. A change that increased the size of his monthly payment by three hundred nubucks.

He'd been released after serving six months of a two-year sentence, and now he was out on parole and working as a freelance "troubleshooter." Was he hacking on the side in order to supplement his income? Probably. But Lee hoped not.

Lee took advantage of being a cop by parking the creeper in a truck zone. Then she called in: "This is 1-William-3. I'm Code 6. Over." If someone, Jenkins for example, wanted to check on her movements he'd be able to see where Lee had been. But he had no reason to track her movements. Not at the moment anyway.

The response was a predictable, "Roger that, 1-William-3."

If the area hadn't been especially prosperous before the plague killed off half the population, it was even more depressed now. At least half of the stores Lee passed had faded for rent signs hanging in their windows.

But according to the neon sign out front, the Sue Yong nail salon was open for business and appeared to be thriving. Lee stopped in front of the nondescript door next to the salon and pressed the intercom button. There was a soft whirring sound as the camera mounted over the door zoomed in on her. Then she heard a click as a lock was released.

Lee pushed the door open and was careful to close it behind her. After that she had to climb a narrow flight of worn stairs in order to reach the second floor. Lee knew there was a freight elevator at the back of the building, but Keyes took pleasure in forcing able-bodied people to exert themselves.

Once on the second floor Lee was confronted by a steel fire door complete with a waist-high gun port. To say that Keyes was cautious would be an understatement. But that was understandable given where he lived—and the type of people he dealt with. Lee pushed another button, was rewarded with a click, and pushed her way into the chaos that was Keyes's apartment.

A winding passageway led through piles of electronic equipment. Some of the computers were intact and some had been gutted for parts. Eventually, she emerged into the open area where Keyes spent most of his time. He had an unruly head of hair and was seated with his back to her. Sunlight struggled to penetrate the filthy windows.

Though classified as a norm, Keyes had been born without legs. But in postplague Pacifica, people assumed that anyone who looked different was a mutant and therefore dangerous. That, plus an innate shyness, meant that Keyes lived alone. He was working at a parts-strewn workbench that ran the width of the front wall. "Have a seat," he said without looking around. "I'll be with you in a second."

Lee looked for a place to sit down. There was no option other than a toilet with grab bars on both sides. The rest of the furnishings consisted of an unmade hospital bed, the sliding power lift Keyes could use to hoist himself in and out of the chair, and haphazardly mounted flat-panel TV screens. There wasn't any kitchen, which explained why so many empty take-out containers were stacked on a table. Lee watched a cockroach emerge from a flat pizza package and make the four-inch trip to a box labeled, SHANDONG TO GO.

Keyes turned at that point and realized that she was still standing. He had a full beard to match the hair. "Sorry . . . I don't get a lot of visitors. . . You'll find a chair over there."

Keyes pointed, and Lee saw he was correct. A cardboard box full of junk sat atop an old straight-backed chair. She went over to retrieve it. "There," Keyes said, as she sat down. "That's better. So how's the law-enforcement racket?" The wheelchair made a whirring sound as it swiveled her way.

"It's never been better," Lee replied. "People are lining up to get arrested."

"But no Bonebreaker?"

"No. Not yet."

Keyes had a tendency to tug on his beard when he was thinking. "I'm sorry to hear that . . . Especially since I don't have any good news for you. I ran a reverse trace on the e-mail address you gave me but ENOB8 led to a dead end. It looks as though the Bonebreaker is making use of an onion router that directs traffic through a network of volunteer-run relays. Thousands of them. And that makes his e-mails impossible to trace. I'm sorry."

Lee's spirits fell. She'd been hoping that Keyes would pull a miracle out of his technological hat. "So that's it? There's nothing we can do?"

"No," Keyes answered. "Maybe the government could identify his real IP address. But I don't have the necessary resources—and for some reason, you can't bring them in on this."

It was a very perceptive comment, and Lee knew that her lack of an adequate response would confirm his suspicions. "Okay," she said. "What do I owe you?"

"Nothing," Keyes replied. "I'd still be sitting in the slammer if you hadn't gone in front of the parole board. So I owe you."

"That's bullshit," Lee replied. "But it's *nice* bullshit. Thanks for trying. Speaking of your parole, how's it going?"

Keyes grinned. "Are you kidding? Take a look around. It's perfect." Both of them laughed. After two or three minutes of small talk, Lee promised to stay in touch and left.

Having struck out on the Bonebreaker lead, it was time for Lee to turn her attention to the so-called face case. There were thousands of box trucks roaming the streets of LA. So Yanty had chosen to focus his attention on the handful of surgeons who specialized in face transplants. Was one of them moonlighting?

Were the doctors aware of any suspicious activity? And was anyone performing legit operations on mutants?

In an effort to develop leads, Lee, Yanty, and Prospo were going to interview *all* of the face-transplant specialists in LA. The first doctor on Lee's list was on the staff at the UCLA Medical Center in central LA, and Dr. Mary Kottery had agreed to see Lee during her lunch hour.

With that in mind, Lee wanted to be on time, so she pushed hard to make her way through the midday traffic. It had been worse back before the plague, or that's what the old-timers claimed, but Lee found that difficult to believe.

With only ten minutes to spare, Lee pulled into one of several parking lots associated with the medical center. Like so many of the city's structures the boxy buildings looked old and worn. Still, everyone agreed that the hospital was one of the best Pacifica had to offer. After hiking in from the parking lot, Lee had to pass through multiple layers of security before gaining access to the main building. And since Lee was carrying two pistols, she had to show her ID to five different people before being cleared through.

Then began the equally demanding task of going up to the third floor and navigating her way through a maze of hallways to reach Dr. Kottery's office. A receptionist invited her to sit down, and Lee had to wait for fifteen minutes before the surgeon arrived.

Kottery was a tall, thin woman, with wispy bangs and the precise movements of a bird. She wore baggy scrubs and was quick to apologize. "I'm sorry to keep you waiting, Detective Lee . . . This morning's surgery took longer than I thought it would. Please . . . Let's go into my office. Do you mind if I eat my lunch while we talk?"

Lee assured Kottery that she didn't and sat across the desk from the other woman as she tackled a complicated salad she'd brought from home. Another person might have found it difficult to scan the postmortem photos and eat at the same time but not Kottery. "That looks like a transplant, all right," the doctor said as she examined one of the pictures on Lee's tablet. "One that went horribly wrong."

"So do you know anyone who might do something like that?" Lee inquired. "Have you heard of illicit face transplants?"

"The simple answer is no," Kottery replied. "But you said that he was *B. nosilla* positive, correct?"

"Yes."

"Well, our ability to communicate with doctors in the red zone is somewhat limited," Kottery said. "But we know that facial disfigurements are common over there. So if one of our surgeons had some success, word of that would spread, and there would be a lot of pent-up demand."

Lee frowned. "So he or she might be performing such operations on a regular basis?"

"It's possible," Kottery allowed. "But remember . . . A transplant is a very complicated process. That means that the person you're looking for would have a lot of accomplices, including doctors, nurses, and technicians. And they would require all sorts of supplies, not to mention HLA typing, which is used to match the donor with the recipient. Otherwise, there's a possibility that the recipient's body might reject the transplanted tissue.

"Then the team would have to tackle the surgery itself. And since they would be connecting nerves, arteries, and veins, that would require a high degree of skill plus a well-equipped surgical suite. And this takes us back to what I mentioned earlier. Perhaps Joel died at the hands of a quack. But there's a second possibility, too . . . What if a highly organized group of people operated on two dozen patients? And had only one or two failures? That would represent a pretty good success rate. Oh, and by the way," Kottery added. "If this is a larger operation, then where are the donors coming from?"

That was a very good question and one that Lee continued to consider as she returned to the office. After entering the cop shop, Lee convened a meeting with Yanty and Prospo to share the essence of what Dr. Kottery had told her. Then all three of them went to work on the new lines of inquiry. What if Kottery was correct? What if Joel's death was the exception rather than the rule? That would mean that the people who ran the transplant business would be looking for donors. Where were they coming from? And what about the HLA typing Kottery had mentioned? Were the criminals using a commercial lab? There were lots of questions but damned few answers. So Lee was busy right up to 5:00 P.M., when she noticed the time and put in a call to Kane. "One hour," she promised. "I'll be there at six."

The whole notion of coordinating her life with someone else was new to Lee. It was confining in some ways—but pleasurable in others. She wasn't lonely for one thing . . . And making Kane happy made her happy. That was a revelation.

Lee left work and drove home. Traffic was bad, but she knew that drinks would be waiting, along with a pretty sunset. She made it to the condo in a little more than half an hour and was out on the deck shortly thereafter.

Once dinner was over, Lee took care of the dishes while Kane went off to return phone calls from his needier patients. Then it was time for some TV, a bit of snuggling, and bed. It took Lee a while to fall asleep. And when she did, there were dreams of thunder . . . Except that as she awoke to a bright flash of light, she realized that it wasn't a dream.

As Lee lay there, she heard a series of overlapping booms and wondered if they were part of a thunderstorm. So she rolled out of bed and made her way out onto the front deck, only to discover that something completely different was taking place. The Pacific Ocean was pitch-black except for flashes of light out on the horizon.

Then came the rumble of what sounded like a freight train passing overhead followed by an explosion off to the east. That was followed by *another* flash of light and a loud bang as one of the high-rise apartment buildings to the south took a direct hit. Part of the building crumbled into the street and flames appeared in the wreckage. Then Lee knew what she was looking at. Naval gunfire! Enemy ships were shelling the city of Los Angeles.

Kane appeared next to her. "Oh my God," he exclaimed. "The Aztecs . . . It must be the Aztecs. We're at war." Sirens began to wail, alarms began to beep, and the shells continued to fall. Suddenly, everything had changed.

TWO

Having been assured that the seven-ship task force sailing up the West Coast belonged to Argentina, and would remain well offshore, Pacifica had been content to let the armada pass. Now they were about to pay for their stupidity. Admiral Juan Carlos Barbaro felt the *Tenochtitlan* lurch to port as both batteries of the battleship's sixteen-inch guns fired. A flash strobed the blackness as six two-thousand-pound rounds were launched into the sky. Barbaro knew they would travel twenty-three miles before falling on the city of angels. Except there weren't any angels in the city, just norms, thousands of whom were going to die. And for good reason.

Los Angeles had been founded on September 4, 1781, by Spanish governor Felipe de Neve, and was made part of Mexico in 1821 following the Mexican War of Independence. Then, at the end of the Mexican–American War in 1848, all of present-day California had been purchased via the Treaty of Guadalupe Hidalgo, thereby becoming part of the United States of Mierda (shit). *Why?* Because Mexico had no choice, that's why. After being defeated, Mexico was forced to enter so-called negotiations. Negotiations conducted while troops from Los Estados Unidos controlled the country's capital.

The Treaty of Guadalupe Hidalgo established the Rio Grande as the southern boundary for Texas and gave the U.S. ownership of California, plus land that would eventually became New

Mexico, Arizona, Nevada, and Utah along with parts of Wyoming and Colorado. All for fifteen million old dollars. Just the thought of it filled Barbaro with rage. *Pero la venganza es dulce* (but revenge is sweet), Barbaro thought to himself. *Now is the time to claim that which is ours.*

But it wouldn't be easy. The beast that hid behind the name Pacifica was very well armed. And Barbaro knew that the first onslaught of shore-based aircraft was about to hit back. And there would be lots of them.

Unfortunately, Barbaro didn't have an aircraft carrier to support his ships. That meant the task force would be forced to rely on surface-to-air missiles and antiaircraft guns to defend itself. The night lit up in a dazzling display of firepower as a Vulcan 20mm Gatling began to fire. Then one of Barbaro's lesser ships took a direct hit from an enemy missile, and a momentary sun lit the night. The Battle of Santa Catalina had begun. Would Barbaro die before the *real* sun could rise? Quite possibly. But it would be worth it.

Lee looked up as a jet roared overhead. It was flying low and was gone a second later. Then a flash of light strobed the surface of the ocean, and she heard a distant boom as something exploded. *A ship?* Yes, that seemed likely as streams of red tracers probed the night sky. "Come on," Lee said as she touched Kane's arm. "Grab whatever is most important to you and let's get out of here. There's a good chance this building will take a hit."

"I hope not," Kane said, as they went inside. "That would be bad for real-estate prices."

Lee smiled in spite of herself as she went into the bedroom where she dressed for work. Her normal "look" consisted of a tee, jeans, and combat boots. She wore a .9mm Glock in a shoulder holster under her left arm—and a .357 backup on the back of her belt. She was about to close the dresser drawer when she saw the old .45 semiauto.

Kane was packing a bag on the other side of the room as she turned in his direction. "Here . . . Take this. And here's a spare mag. They belonged to my father. Every whack job in the city will be out on the streets, and you might need some protection. Where will you go?"

"I'll be at St. John's," Kane replied. "I'm on staff there, and they're going to need all the help they can get. Shrinks included. As for the .45, I'll take it. And thank you."

Lee smiled. "You're welcome."

"There's one more thing," Kane said as he shoved the weapon into his waistband. "Something I've been meaning to say for some time now."

The lights went off for a second and came back on. Lee saw the look in his eyes and felt a sudden stab of fear. She pressed a finger against his lips. "No, darling . . . Don't say it."

All of the people who had loved Lee were dead—so she was a bit superstitious where the "L" word was concerned. "That's nonsense," Kane replied. "*I* love you and refuse to die until I'm a hundred years old."

Lee entered the circle of his arms. "You promise?"

"I promise." They kissed, but not for long, as a shell landed somewhere nearby and caused the windows to rattle. As the embrace came to an end, Lee went back to packing. A second outfit, toiletries, and all the ammo she had went into an overnight bag.

Lee's cell phone chirped madly, and she knew why. Every officer the LAPD had would be called in to help cope with the crisis. Never mind the safety of their loved ones. They would have to fend for themselves. That went with being a cop.

Rather than drag things out Lee said, "Take care, hon . . . And one more thing . . ."

Kane looked at her. "What?"

"I love you, too." And with that, she left.

Once in the parking garage, Lee threw the bag into the backseat. Then, rather than take the time to check for trackers, she slid behind the wheel and started the engine. The next step was to switch the grill lights on and activate the siren before pulling out onto the street.

There were lots of cars, most of which were northbound. So many that some drivers were swerving out into the southbound lanes, causing head-on collisions. As Lee drove south, she saw that there were pedestrians, too. Some had nothing more than the clothes on their backs, while others wore packs or were pushing grocery carts loaded with belongings. Meanwhile, flashes of light lit up the horizon, and Lee could hear the dull thud of overlapping explosions as the dispatcher dealt with calls. "No, 3-Victor-4 . . . I can't dispatch backup to your location. I suggest you disengage and pull back. We have reports that enemy troops have invaded the Compton area. They are mutants, repeat *mutants*, so all units are advised to don class-one protective gear.

"Yes, 2-Mary-8, I have that. You are Code 6 . . . Be careful out there.

"No, 2-Ida-7, do *not* return to your station . . . The Los Diablos gang overran it fifteen minutes ago. There were a lot of casualties."

And so it went. Lee gritted her teeth as she weaved in and out of traffic, swerved onto sidewalks when that was necessary, and had to push a stalled vehicle off to one side in order to clear an intersection. The driver was out of his car yelling at Lee as she drove away.

Then the streetlights went out, traffic signals stopped working, and the already chaotic situation became even worse. All bets were off as drivers began to use their vehicles as battering rams or fired weapons at each other. Most of them seemed to be intent on accessing one of the freeways, which, based on what Lee had heard over the radio, were so congested that traffic had come to a stop.

After switching streets numerous times, Lee found herself on West 1st as she approached the point where she would pass under the 110. That was where she had to stop for a police barricade manned by four heavily armed patrol officers. A sure sign that a state of emergency was in effect. The county had plans in place to deal with every possible catastrophe, including plagues, earthquakes, and war. And all of them had one thing in common. The area between 101 to the north, South Alameda St. to the east, West 6th Street to the south, and 110 to the west was to be sealed off and to remain that way until further notice.

Among the buildings inside that zone were city hall, LAPD headquarters, the Metropolitan Detention Center, and the Department of Water and Power. All of which would be critical during the days ahead. Lee killed the siren and had to wait as the patrol officers refused entry to a family searching for a place of refuge.

As they were forced to turn around Lee was allowed to pull forward. The street cops were dressed in riot gear, which meant Lee couldn't see the officer's face as he came up to the driver's side window. "ID please," the policeman said politely.

Lee understood. Just because she was driving a police car didn't mean that she was a cop. She held her ID case up for the patrol officer to see. He nodded. "Where are you headed?"

"Headquarters."

"Yeah, that's what I figured," he said. "Don't bother. It took a direct hit. The survivors are moving over to the Street Services Garage."

"How many casualties were there?"

The man shrugged. "A lot . . . But it would have been worse during the day."

Lee thanked the officer, passed under the freeway, and entered an area of relative calm. There were no traffic jams or columns of terrified refugees in the secured zone. In fact, the streets were nearly empty.

Lee was only vaguely aware of the Street Services Garage and took two wrong turns before she found it. Her headlights panned across a stretch of chain-link fence as she turned into the driveway. That was where a police sergeant and three civilians stood waiting.

The cop motioned for her to stop and demanded to see some ID. He appeared to be fortysomething and looked tired. After eyeing her badge, he waved to a civilian. "Hey, Joe . . . Fill this vehicle with gas and park it with the creepers."

Then he turned back to Lee. "Leave the keys in the ignition. If you have personal items in the car take them with you. We're creating a car pool, and chances are that you'll get a different vehicle the next time out. How's it going outside of the zone?"

"It's hell out there," Lee replied as she got out.

There wasn't much light but she could see the concern in his eyes. "This will be hard on Francine and the kids," he said. "I sent them north. I hope they make it."

Lee swallowed the lump in her throat as she pulled the suitcase out of the car. "Thanks for being here, Sergeant," she said. "We'll get this sorted out."

He nodded. "I knew your father," the sergeant said. "He'd be proud of you." And with that, he was gone.

Lee was unexpectedly moved and had to hold back the tears as she towed the bag toward the dimly lit building. She could hear the rumble of a generator coming from somewhere nearby—and knew that the rest of LA's critical services would be running on backup power, too.

As Lee opened the front door and went inside, she found herself in something that resembled a madhouse. The lights flickered occasionally. The dispatcher she'd heard earlier had been patched into the intercom system, everyone seemed to be in a hurry, and there was no rhyme or reason to the way things were laid out.

It appeared that the Street Services personnel had been displaced by the police department. Entire departments were being run from cubicles, each of which was identified by a hand-printed sign. As Lee towed her suitcase down the center aisle, she saw sheets of paper labeled, CENTRAL TRAFFIC DIVISION, COMMUNICATIONS, MOTOR TRANSPORT, JAILS, and yes, PERSONNEL. To do *what*? she wondered. Handle vacation requests? Then it came to her: Someone had to keep track of all the cops who had been wounded or killed.

Lee paused at a desk labeled, AIR SUPPORT. A woman wearing a blue flight suit was typing on a laptop. "Excuse me," Lee said. "I'm looking for Operations. Specifically the Central Area's Detective Division."

The pilot looked up. She had short red hair and a spray of freckles across the bridge of her nose. "It's farther back . . . Just past the ladies' room."

Lee smiled. "The perfect location . . . Thanks."

A civilian was pushing a cart loaded with coffee and pastries down the aisle, and Lee marveled at someone's resourcefulness as she followed the wagon past a tiny first-aid station. Then, as the cart took a left, Lee spotted Jenkins directly ahead. Much to her surprise, he was dressed in a suit and looked fresh as a daisy. His face lit up as he saw her. "Lee! You're okay! That's wonderful. And you're just in time. Follow me. The meeting is about to start."

Lee was about to ask, "What meeting?" but was looking at his back by then. So all she could do was follow Jenkins to the end of the aisle and into a room labeled, EMPLOYEES ONLY.

It was easy to tell that the space was an employee lounge. Lockers lined one side of the room, an old refrigerator purred in a corner, and a huge corkboard dominated the wall on the right. It was home to a montage of safety posters and HR bulletins.

The fourth wall was made of glass and looked out onto a dimly lit parking garage filled with the trucks and other pieces of equipment that the Street Services people used to do their jobs. But more notable from Lee's perspective was the presence of Chief Corso who, much to her amazement, was wearing a pistol on his hip. *We're in some deep shit if he's packing a gun,* Lee thought to herself. *I wonder how often he goes to the range.*

Corso nodded to her, and as Lee looked around, she saw that Mick Ferris was among the ten or so people in the room. Ferris was normally in charge of the SWAT team, and the two of them had worked together before. He had a young-old face, a military-style buzz cut, and a lean body. He smiled. "Hi, Lee . . . And welcome to the team. We're going to need people who can handle a weapon."

Lee was about to ask for more information when Jenkins cleared his throat. "All right . . . Let's get to it. Chief Corso? Over to you."

Even with some stubble on his face Corso was still movie-star handsome and projected an aura of confidence as his eyes swept the room. "Okay," he said. "Here's what we know about the overall situation. The Aztecs invited everyone to a circle jerk down in El Paso, and, while that was going on, they sent a battleship and six other ships north to kick our asses."

"Where the hell did the 'tecs get a battleship?" a patrol officer wanted to know. "I thought they went out of style eighty years ago."

"So did everyone else," Corso said darkly. "Although I'm told that our government knew that such a vessel was under construction in Argentina's Tandanor Shipyard. And it's worth noting that Pacifica has an excellent relationship with Argentina. Or used to have one . . . Because what our Intel people *didn't* realize was that the Argentineans were building the ship for use by the Aztecs rather than themselves! So when the battleship and its escorts sailed north, they weren't perceived as a threat. Not until the shells began to fall on LA.

"Meanwhile the 'tecs leapfrogged the army down on the border by landing three thousand troops north of Camp Pendleton. It's a risky plan since it will be difficult if not impossible for the 'tecs to resupply the expeditionary force from the sea."

"So why do it?" Jenkins wanted to know. "Surely, they knew what would happen."

"It's a feint," Corso said grimly. "The *real* action is east of here in the Republic of Texas. That's where things will be decided. This attack was intended to put us on the defensive, to suck support away from the Republic, and to scare the crap out of the civilian population.

"And it's going to work because most of their troops are *B. nosilla* positive. All they have to do is mix it up with our citizens to inflict *thousands* of casualties.

"That's the *big* picture," Corso continued. "But while the military sorts that stuff out, we have to take our city back. And that's why you're here. At the moment, we control everything down to Slauson Avenue. But the area south of that, including Inglewood, Westmont, and Bell Gardens, lies inside enemy-held territory. Although we have reports the gangs from the Compton area are hunting the 'tecs down and taking scalps."

That produced a chorus of grim laughter, and Corso grinned. "Yeah, I thought you'd like that . . . Okay, let's get down to brass tacks. When the poop hit the fan, Mayor Getty was visiting a friend in Hawthorne. And she still is. The purpose of this team is to go down and pull her out before she falls into the wrong hands. Because if that happens, the 'tecs or one of the gangs will have a grade-A hostage."

Somebody said, "Oh, shit," and Lee agreed. There were some nice areas inside the community of Hawthorne—but there were plenty of rough spots as well. And that meant a rescue team might have to contend with both the 'tecs *and* the criminal element. All of which begged the question: What was the mayor doing in Hawthorne to begin with? Especially in the middle of the night? But if Corso knew, he wasn't saying.

"Here's the plan," Corso said. "The team will gear up, board a chopper, and fly south. You'll need to get on the ground before sunrise if that's possible. Two air force gunships will act as escorts. If you take ground fire, they will suppress it. Once you're over the LZ, you'll land, go after the mayor, and bring her back."

An alarm went off in Lee's head. "Bring her back?" From where? But before she could ask the question Ferris beat her to it. "So," he said calmly, "how far from the LZ will the team have to travel?"

"The LZ is located in a park three blocks away from the mayor's twenty," Corso replied. "But I'm told it's a nice area, so that shouldn't be a problem. Once she's aboard the chopper, you're out of there. It's as simple as that."

Lee looked at Ferris, and he looked at her. Both of them were thinking the same thing. Maybe the mission would be simple— and maybe pigs would start to fly.

The Bonebreaker awoke to a beeping sound. He was lying on his bed in what he thought of as the vault. He'd been dreaming again. Screaming, as they took his mother away. The beeping continued. The motion detectors! An intruder was inside the ossuary! He grabbed the long-barreled .22 off the nightstand and swung his feet over onto the floor. There was no need to get dressed because he habitually slept with his clothes on.

Cassandra Lee! It had to be Cassandra Lee. His heart was beating like a trip-hammer as he went to the door. Somehow, in spite of all his efforts to keep his lair hidden, the bitch had been able to locate it. But was she alone? Or was half of the LAPD flooding into his sanctuary?

The Bonebreaker opened the steel door and listened. He heard nothing but the steady drip, drip, drip of water into a nearby puddle. So he slid out into the tunnel with the pistol at the ready. Then he heard a distant clang. A door . . . Someone had closed a door!

With his heart racing, the Bonebreaker turned to the right and hurried toward the heart of his underground kingdom. That's where the security monitors were located, and they would reveal what was going on. Unless they found the power tap that is . . . Then they could plunge the ossuary into darkness.

The Bonebreaker was halfway to his combination workroom and control center when he heard a male voice. He was speaking Spanish. "Hey, Ruiz . . . Can you hear me? All I get off the radio is static. There's some weird shit down here. Bones and stuff . . . It looks like some kind of laboratory."

"I'm coming," a distant voice answered. "There's no need to get your panties in a knot."

The Bonebreaker was too late. One of the invaders had found the workroom, and another was on the way. But why would members of the LAPD converse with each other in Spanish?

The question went unanswered as the Bonebreaker slipped into a shadowy alcove and waited for Ruiz to pass. It wasn't long before the beam from a headlamp appeared, followed by the man it belonged to. The Bonebreaker could see that the intruder was wearing a helmet and a pack. The silenced .22 produced a pop as the Bonebreaker shot the man through the left ear. Ruiz staggered, brought a hand up to his ear, and had just started to turn when the Bonebreaker fired again. The second bullet pulped one of the soldier's eyes and entered his brain. He fell in a heap. The Bonebreaker listened as the first man called out again. "Ruiz? Get your butt in here. Where's Lopez? We need to clear this place and move on."

By that time, the Bonebreaker knew he wasn't dealing with the LAPD. So who the hell were they? Not a gang . . . Because gangbangers don't wear helmets and packs. His thoughts were interrupted as Lopez answered. It sounded as if he was close. "I had to take a pee. What a dump . . . These tunnels run every which way. Uh-oh, what's that? Shit! Ruiz is down!"

Lopez was kneeling next to Ruiz feeling for a pulse when the Bonebreaker shot him in the leg. That was the only target available given the way the soldier was positioned and the protection offered by his pack and body armor.

The soldier swore and turned. He was faster than Ruiz had

been and managed to fire a burst of bullets. They passed over the Bonebreaker's head and hit the concrete ceiling. But the Bonebreaker was ready and triggered three shots. Two of the slugs missed but the third struck Lopez in the forehead. He collapsed on top of Ruiz.

The exchange of gunfire was followed by a roar of outrage as the surviving soldier fired down the corridor. Bullets bounced off concrete and buzzed every which way. But the Bonebreaker stood untouched. *Thank you, Lord,* he thought to himself. *I live to do your holy work.*

He shoved the pistol into his waistband and ran. Or *tried* to run. Unfortunately he tripped over Ruiz, stumbled, and fell. A second burst of automatic fire flew over the Bonebreaker's head as he scuttled away. He was on hands and knees as bullets struck all around. Then he arrived at an intersection and took a turn to the right. The maze! He knew every inch of it, and the soldier didn't. *Hide,* he told himself. *Hide and strike back.*

The Bonebreaker was able to stand at that point and make better time. How many shots had he fired? Was it five? Or was it six? If the latter he had four rounds left. Not enough to deal with a soldier carrying an assault weapon. So there was a need for something more, and he knew where to get it. The costume room was the enclosed space where the Bonebreaker kept the wide variety of clothing required to create the disguises he needed. But it was a repository for weapons as well . . . Most of which had been acquired from his victims.

So he dodged from tunnel to tunnel, fully expecting to shake the soldier. But his pursuer proved to be very good at following him. *Too* good. And the Bonebreaker knew why. The soldiers were wearing helmets equipped with night-vision gear. That meant the man chasing him could see better than *he* could!

The Bonebreaker swore, turned a corner, and made a run for the costume room. The door was heavy, and considerable effort was required to push it open. Once inside, the Bonebreaker hurried over to the cabinet where the guns were stored. Then, with a new weapon clutched in his right hand, the Bonebreaker hid behind the half-opened door. Would the intruder enter? Of course he would. The outcome would come down to surprise, skill, and luck.

The Bonebreaker heard his pursuer before he saw him. First came the scrape of a boot, then the clink of something metallic, followed by the sound of heavy breathing. The soldier entered with his rifle at the ready and paused to scan the room.

The serial killer cleared his throat, causing the intruder to turn and exposing his badly disfigured face. The Taser jerked as two barbs shot forward. One of them destroyed an eye while the other hooked a scaly cheek. A fraction of a second later, twelve hundred volts of electricity surged through the leads and entered the mutant's body. The soldier uttered a grunt of pain, lost control of his muscles, and fell.

That was all the Bonebreaker needed. There were handcuffs in the cabinet. Lots of them. And once the soldier's extremities had been secured an injection of Ketamine would render him helpless. Suddenly, and much to his surprise, the Bonebreaker was having fun.

Sergeant Luis Alvarez awoke to find himself living in a nightmare. His left eye was blind, and he couldn't focus the right one. And when he attempted to move his right arm, it refused to obey. So he tried the *other* arm, followed by both legs, only to discover that all of them were immobilized. So Alvarez began to blink his remaining eye in an attempt to restore his vision. The strategy worked. Bit by bit, his surroundings rolled into focus. That was when Alvarez discovered that he'd been stripped of his clothing—and was clamped in a contraption made of metal and wood.

A stainless-steel table was positioned about ten feet away. And there, on the other side of it, sat a normale wearing a mask. The gringo that fired the Taser into his face? Yes. The miserable *pedazo de mierda* (miserable piece of shit).

The gringo nodded politely. "*Buenos dias*, fuck face. And welcome to LA. Judging from the markings on your uniform, and the ID card in your wallet, you are an Aztec. So that's a given. What isn't so obvious is *why* you're here—and what you hope to accomplish. Please enlighten me."

Alvarez summoned a gob of spit and launched it into the air.

His command of colloquial English was quite good. "Fuck you."

"Oh my," the Bonebreaker said mildly. "I'm such a lucky duck. It happens that I have a thing for men in uniform. You'll tell me, oh yes you will, but only one of us is going to enjoy the conversation."

Alvarez tried to remember. Ruiz? Dead. Lopez? Dead. But what about Camacho? He was the last man in. Would he step into the room and blow the normale away? Or was this the end of the road? All Alvarez could do was wait to find out.

A blood red sun started to rise as three helicopters flew south. Preparations had taken the team longer than Chief Corso had hoped for. That meant they were visible from the ground and immediately drew fire. It seemed safe to assume that at least some of it originated from the well-armed citizens of Los Angeles, who believed they were shooting at the Aztecs.

The rest of the fire was almost certainly from troops who had been put ashore south of Los Angeles and were raising as much hell as they could. But since the LAPD helicopter was only lightly armed, and the gunship pilots were supposed to protect it rather than chase ground targets, all of the ships continued on their way.

Cassandra Lee was seated on the port side of the helicopter with both hands on the pump-action rifle that was resting muzzle down on the floor. She was wearing an LAPD ball cap, a headset with boom mike, and a tac vest loaded with gear. The weather nerds claimed that the citizens of LA were going to have a hot day. With that in mind, Lee was dressed in a black tee shirt and baggy pants. A pair of combat boots completed the outfit.

But the forecast was for later on. At the moment, cold air was pouring in through the open side doors and caused her to shiver. Or was that due to the fear that was crawling around in the pit of her stomach? Was Ferris scared? He didn't *look* scared. But that was part of his job. Never show fear . . . Maybe your team will believe it.

The ad hoc team was made up of six people—four besides

Ferris and her. They included a hulking SWAT team member called Bear, a taciturn patrol officer named Collins, and a firearms instructor named Quigley. An uptight sort of man who most people referred to as Shithead behind his back.

The sixth officer was a porky desk jockey named Worley. There had been a limited group of people to draw from—but Lee knew that Ferris had chosen each person for a reason. Even if she didn't know what that reason was. "We're two out," the pilot said over the intercom. "Stand by."

Lee felt an additional jolt of adrenaline as the helicopter lost altitude. From where she was seated, she could look past the starboard-door gunner and out at the sprawl of houses beyond. It was a residential area for the most part—although Lee saw what might have been a mall flash by. Black smoke was pouring out of it. Had it been looted? Yes, with no cops available to stop them, the locals were "shopping." And since the fire department couldn't respond, the fires would have to burn themselves out.

Suddenly, Lee heard an insistent pinging sound as bullets struck the helicopter's unarmored fuselage. One slug in the wrong place, and the chopper would be forced down in what was enemy-held territory. That caused the door gunners to open fire. Each machine gun produced a stream of empty brass that jumped, tumbled, and rolled around the deck. Lee couldn't see the air-force gunships but assumed they were busy prepping the LZ.

If things went the way they were supposed to, the LAPD ship would land in the park, the extraction team would go after the mayor, and zoomies would keep the chopper safe. The fly guys only had so much fuel, however—so there was a limit on how long they could linger.

And if things *didn't* go as planned? Then, as Ferris put it, "We'll fake it." The skids touched down without warning, and Ferris began to yell. "Out! Out! Out! Form on Worley . . . He'll lead the way."

Lee couldn't believe what she'd heard. "Form on Worley?" *Why?* That question was still rattling around Lee's head as her boots hit the ground, and she waited to get shot at. But if there had been any bad guys in the zone, the zoomies had been able to chase them off.

The park was barely large enough for a crude baseball diamond and some decrepit bleachers. It fronted an arterial and was surrounded by houses on three sides and an elementary school on the fourth. The helicopter's rotors continued to turn as Worley lumbered away, and the rest of them followed. Lee found herself in the five slot behind Shithead.

Rather than follow the arterial north the way Lee expected him to—Worley led the team into the maze of houses opposite the north end of the park. During the first couple of minutes, they passed through side yards, crossed an alley, and climbed over a fence. The latter being difficult for Worley—who required help from Ferris in order to roll over the top.

But by that time Lee had a full appreciation for the method behind Ferris's apparent madness. Worley might be out of shape, but he knew the area the way only a kid could. Had he grown up there? Lee was willing to bet on it. And because of that, the team could not only stay off the main streets but conceal which way it was going. Assuming that Worley didn't have a heart attack and keel over, that is.

They had entered a large backyard when Lee heard a menacing snarl. She turned just in time to see a pit bull charge out of its doghouse and go for Worley. Shithead had a submachine gun slung across his back and a pistol ready to go. He fired left-handed without so much as breaking stride and nailed the pit bull in the head. It performed a somersault and landed hard. Lee was good with a pistol, but not *that* good. Now she understood why the firearms instructor was on the team. His job, like hers, was to provide security.

A zigzag path took them past a car sitting on blocks into the gap between two duplexes. From there, it would be necessary to cross a residential street to continue. "We'll pause here for a moment," Ferris said. "Collins, guard our six. I don't want to take a bullet in the butt. Lee, watch the left flank . . . Worley, you have the right."

So saying, Ferris raised a pair of binoculars and began to scan the far side of the street. Lee was down on one knee next to a short flight of concrete stairs. She eyed the row of mostly occupied houses to the left and the church at the end of the block. Everything appeared to be normal, but an eerie silence hung over the neighborhood. What noise there was came from a long ways off. It consisted of the pop, pop, pop of rifle fire followed by the clatter of an automatic weapon. Aztecs fighting citizens? Gangs fighting gangs? Both possibilities were equally believable.

As for the houses around them, Lee could *feel* the staring eyes. "Lock your doors and mind your own business." That was all most people could do.

"Okay," Ferris said. "It looks clear . . . We'll cross the street with fifteen-foot intervals between each person. Worley . . . Take the lead. Collins . . . You're on drag. Let's go."

Lee was still in the five slot so she had time to watch Worley run. She figured the desk jockey was carrying at least twenty pounds of extra weight and loaded with thirty pounds of gear. So as Worley's legs pumped, it looked as if he were running in slow motion.

The police officer was halfway to the other side when a bullet struck his left arm, passed through his armpit, and penetrated his chest. He took a nose dive and skidded half a foot before coming to a stop.

The report was like an afterthought, and Lee caught a momentary glint of light from the corner of her eye. She brought the .223 Remington up and took a look through the scope. That was when she caught a hint of movement. "Ten o'clock," she said. "Shooter in the church tower."

"Can you get him?" Ferris inquired.

The Rem wasn't a sniper rifle as such. But the rest of the team members were carrying submachine guns and shotguns. Weapons which, while ideal for close-quarters combat, lacked the ability to reach out and touch someone a block away. "I'll give it a try," Lee replied. "I'll put his head down if nothing else."

"Right," Ferris said. "When Lee fires, three of us will go. Collins will stay back to provide security for Lee."

Lee knelt with her left elbow on her left knee and the Remington raised. She'd always been better with a pistol than a rifle. And that was fortunate, since cops rarely get the chance to break out a long gun. But she had the necessary training—and the ability to think her way through a problem. She couldn't see into the tower . . . But figured the sniper was directly inside the vertical opening, where he could spy on the police.

There was no crosswind to speak of, and since the target was no more than two hundred feet away, Lee saw no reason to aim high. But the need to pump a shell into the receiver after each shot could pull the rifle off target.

Lee put the crosshairs on the target area, took a deep breath, and let it out. Having never fired the weapon before, she was pleased to discover that the rifle had a crisp trigger pull. The report sounded in her ear as the rifle butt thumped her shoulder. Then it was time to pump a second cartridge into the chamber and fire again.

A rifle fell out of the tower and shattered on the pavement below. "You got him!" Collins exclaimed. "Let's haul ass!"

Lee got up and ran. A blood trail began in the middle of the street and led all the way over to the narrow space between two houses. That's where the surviving members of the team were gathered around the body. "Nice work," Ferris said.

Then his eyes surveyed the team. "Strip Worley," he said harshly. "We could need the stuff he's carrying. Spread it around. And get his ID."

Lee could see the pain in the other officer's eyes. Ferris had chosen Worley knowing the man couldn't run—and now the policeman was dead. She wanted to comfort him, to tell Ferris that Worley understood the risks, but she couldn't. Not in the middle of an operation.

The team heard an explosion, and all heads turned to the south. They could see the black smoke that was boiling up into the sky, and the sight of it made Lee feel sick to her stomach. Ferris was on the radio by then. "Ground Six to Skyrider-One. We heard an explosion and can see a column of smoke. What happened? Over."

The rest of them stared as Ferris nodded, and said, "Roger that." Then he looked from face to face. "Somebody got close enough to hit our bird with an RPG," he announced. "All of the crew were killed. The zoomies are going to hose the area down."

"And the mission?" Lee inquired.

"Our job is to extract the mayor," Ferris replied grimly. "And that's what we're going to do."

Lee could see a gunship off to the south. She heard the roar of the ship's minigun as the pilot fired on a target she couldn't see. Five people had died so far. Was the mayor worth it? Time would tell.

THREE

The sun was up, the power was off, and the air in the third-floor apartment was starting to get warm. It was a large space and open, with the exception of the bathroom. That, plus the high ceilings and good light made for the perfect studio, as well as a place to hold private meetings. A dozen large paintings had been hung on the walls, but none of them was especially good. A fact that was lost on Maxim Belikov—a young man who believed that he'd been Pablo Picasso in a previous life.

So why did Mayor Melissa Getty continue to give him money? Not to mention access to her upper-crust friends? Some of whom were stupid enough to buy his art? Because he was good in bed, that's why . . . And a welcome relief from the pressures associated with her job.

Did her husband know about the relationship? Maybe. But if he did Mark was smart enough to ignore the affair and do what he did best, which was to play golf with the people who funded her campaigns. But now, in the wake of a sneak attack by the Aztecs, the city of Los Angeles was struggling to survive while its mayor was trapped in Hawthorne. Getty had been up and pacing the floor for hours while her lover continued to sleep.

Now, for the umpteenth time, she made her way over to one of the large windows that fronted the apartment. The blinds were closed, but by lifting one of the slats, she could look out. Where were they? The people who were supposed to rescue her. Damn them! She should be in her office . . . On television . . . Leading the effort to put the city back together again.

But what if Chief Corso wanted to be seen as the person who saved the city? What if he *wanted* her to die? She wouldn't put it past the bastard. *No,* Getty told herself, *he's ambitious but not that ambitious. Get a grip. Help is on the way.*

Getty's thoughts were interrupted as a low-slung *especiale* came into view. Most of Pacifica's postplague industrial capacity was devoted to reconstruction and defense. That meant new cars were a rarity. The majority of vehicles had been rebuilt more than once, and some, like this car, were rolling works of art.

The *especiale* came to a stop. The doors opened, and four men emerged. All of them were armed. And, judging from the identical neon green mesh shirts they wore, they belonged to a gang. Getty held her breath. Did they know she was present? Had they been sent to get her? If so, Maxim would offer no protection whatsoever.

The answer came seconds later as they sauntered up to her car. The black roadster had been a fiftieth birthday present from Mark. Getty winced as one of the men used a crowbar to smash the driver's side window. The horn started to beep, but the car thieves knew there was nothing to worry about. The police had been neutralized.

A second man unlocked the door, knelt next to the car, and went to work. The horn stopped beeping thirty seconds later—and the engine started a minute after that. Then, with the roadster following along behind it, the *especiale* left. Getty heaved a sigh of relief. The car could be replaced.

The next half hour passed slowly as Maxim snored, and Getty stood watch at the window. The first hint of additional activity came when a soldier came into view. A rifle was hanging across his chest, and he was riding a bicycle equipped with a pink cargo basket, and matching handlebar tassels.

That was strange but so was the spiral-shaped horn protruding from his forehead. A mutant! That meant an Aztec army unit was in the area. Getty watched the man remove a radio from the pink basket and say something into it. He was a scout then . . . Giving other soldiers the all clear. Getty nearly jumped out of her skin as her cell phone rang. The professional tone was a matter of habit. "Getty here."

"My name's Ferris," a male voice told her. "Lieutenant Mick Ferris. I'm in charge of the extraction team that was sent to get you out. We're about a block away. What, if anything, is happening at your location? Have you seen any enemy activity?"

Getty's mind raced. What would happen if she told him the truth? Would he come anyway? Or would he pull back rather than risk a head-on collision with an Aztec army unit? Getty decided to play it safe. "No . . . Some gangbangers stole my car half an hour ago but they're gone now."

"Good," Ferris replied. "Tell me about the building you're in. What does it look like? And what floor are you on?"

Getty told him. "Got it," Ferris said. "Watch for us and be ready to unlock the front door." That was followed by a click.

Getty felt a surge of relief. The police were coming and, with any luck at all, she'd be at her desk later that day. And most of the city's citizens would assume she'd been on duty the whole time. Getty smiled. It was good to be her.

A pair of fighters left white tracks across the sky as they headed west. To seek out Aztec ships? There was no way to know as Lee followed Quigley up a paved alley. When Ferris turned right, the rest of them followed. That took them through a small parking lot and into the passageway separating the two buildings.

Lee smelled the mouthwatering odor of freshly baked bread and realized that she was passing the exhaust vent for a bakery. It seemed that at least one business owner was determined to open no matter what.

A bicycle with a pink basket was leaning against the right-hand wall. Ferris passed it before stopping to examine the area ahead. Collins was facing the other way, guarding the team's six, but the rest of them could see beyond Ferris. A car passed them, but there was no other traffic. "That's the building over there," Ferris said as he pointed across the street. "The white three-story. The mayor will open the front door for us. I'll go first. The rest of you will cross two at a time."

So saying, Ferris looked left and right before sprinting across the two-lane road. Bear and Quigley went next. Once they were safely on the other side it was time for Lee and Collins to follow. As they crossed the white line, a man with a horn protruding from his forehead stepped out of the bakery. He had a doughnut in one hand and a rifle in the other. He yelled, *"Alto!"* (stop) before cramming the rest of the doughnut into his mouth and bringing the weapon up to his shoulder.

Lee saw movement out of the corner of her eye and heard the steady bang, bang, bang of semiauto fire as projectiles buzzed past her. Having failed to lead his targets the way he should have, the soldier was swinging his weapon to the right when Ferris cut him down. Lee turned to look as she arrived in front of a hair salon. "Thanks."

"You're welcome," Ferris said. "Let's get the mayor and haul ass before that guy's friends arrive." The apartment house was only steps away—and the front door swung open as they approached. Getty was there to motion them into the lobby.

Lee had seen the politician hundreds of times on TV and been on the receiving end of her directives, but never met her in person. Getty had brown hair, cold blue eyes, and a long face. Rather than one of the mannish suits that she normally favored, Getty was dressed in a crisp white blouse, jeans, and expensive half boots. "I'm sorry about the mutant," she said. "I don't know where he came from."

"He was in the bakery," Lee answered factually.

Getty's eyes narrowed. "You look familiar . . . Have we met?"

"Perhaps you've seen her on television," Ferris interjected. "This is Detective Cassandra Lee."

"Of course!" Getty said. "I think Detective Lee is the only woman in LA who gets more press than I do."

It was said jokingly, but there was an edge to it. Lee was trying to formulate a response when Bear spoke. He was peering out through the vertical window located next to the door. "We've got company," he said. "They're checking the body."

Ferris swore and went to look. "There are nine of them," he said. "Hopefully they'll go away. But if they attempt to enter the building, we'll deal with them. Collins, warn the residents and tell them to shelter in place. Lee, get up on the roof and find a good spot. Bear, find the back door and get ready to defend it."

There wasn't any power, so Lee had to climb four flights of stairs to reach the door labeled, ROOF DECK. It wasn't locked, which allowed her to walk onto the flat surface. After a quick look around, Lee saw that one building was taller than the apartment house and was only half a block away. That meant a sniper could fire down on her. Something to remember.

On her way to the front of the building, Lee passed a hot tub, three conversation areas complete with sun-bleached deck furniture, and a pair of stainless-steel barbecues. She made her way past them to the front of the building, where she crawled up to the waist-high wall. It was pierced by regular gaps, one of which allowed Lee to look down into the street.

Even though the Aztecs knew that one of their friends had been shot—they were standing out in the middle of the road as if they had nothing to worry about. That was fine with Lee. Some of the 'tecs had visible deformities, like the guy with three arms, but Lee knew that most of their mutations would be less obvious.

One of the soldiers was wearing what looked like SCUBA tanks—and they drew her attention. Lee noticed that he was clutching a wand as well. It was similar to what an exterminator would use, only larger, and equipped with two grips. What the heck? Then it came to her . . . A flamethrower! The bastards were using flamethrowers to *what*? Fight Pacifica's troops? *And* start fires that would level entire neighborhoods? Yes.

As Lee watched, the soldier pulled the trigger, the igniter sparked, and a gout of flame shot out of the wand. At that point he began to waddle her way. It looked as though the 'tecs were going to flame the buildings adjacent to the spot where their buddy had been killed. Ferris spoke into her ear. "Cap that guy, Lee . . . The one with the flamethrower."

Lee shoved the Remington through the hole and put her eye to the scope. She could aim for the top of a tank or the man himself. She chose the tank. The crosshairs drifted onto the target and her finger tightened. There was a loud boom as a ball of flame engulfed the soldier and reduced him to a black stick figure. His helmet bounced and rolled away as the remains of his body crumbled.

Meanwhile, the rest of the team had been firing as well, and it wasn't long before all of the 'tecs were down. Ferris spoke again. "Lee, Bear, return to the lobby. We're out of here."

Lee was in the stairwell going down when a man appeared. He was young, unshaven, and half-dressed. His eyes widened when he saw the letters LAPD on her vest. "I heard an explosion and gunfire . . . What's going on? And where's Melissa?"

It took Lee a second to remember that the mayor's first name was Melissa. "Some Aztecs were going to set the building on fire, so we shot them. The mayor is on the ground floor. And you are?"

"My name is Maxim . . . I'm Melissa's, ah, friend."

Now Lee understood. Here, standing in front of her, was the reason why Getty was in Hawthorne. "Okay, Max, are you coming with us? If so, you have exactly five minutes to put the rest of your clothes on and report to the lobby. You can bring a knapsack, nothing more, and the five-minute limit is for real. The explosion you mentioned is likely to draw the wrong kind of attention." Maxim nodded, and she turned away.

The team was ready to leave when Lee arrived in the lobby. "Here's the plan," Ferris said. "We'll travel north for half a mile—then we'll follow West Rosecrans Avenue all the way to the beach. A boat will pick us up."

Getty was incredulous. "'Travel north'?" she interjected. "'Follow Rosecrans'? What the hell are you talking about? I was told that a helicopter would pick me up."

If looks could kill, the expression on Ferris's face would have been sufficient to drop the mayor in her tracks. "There *was* a helicopter," he said coldly. "But it was destroyed by an RPG. We lost two pilots as well as the officers who volunteered to serve as door gunners."

Getty looked from face to face as if to confirm what she'd heard. And as Getty's eyes made contact with Lee's, she nodded. "And that doesn't include Officer Worley," she said. "We lost him on the way over here."

Lee wanted to shock Getty, wanted to see the comprehension

in her eyes, but was doomed to disappointment. The only thing she saw on Getty's face was fear.

That was when Maxim arrived. He was dressed in a blue polo, white trousers, and a pair of two-hundred-nu sandals. A man purse was slung over one shoulder, and he looked like a magazine ad. "There you are," Maxim said as he went over to give Getty a hug. "Why didn't you tell me?"

Why indeed? Lee wondered. Because Getty hoped to hide her extramarital affair? Or were her motives even darker? Had she been hoping to leave Maxim behind? Or was that taking it too far? Whatever the reason, one thing was for sure: Her failure to mention Maxim hadn't been lost on Ferris. There was a wintry expression on his face. "I wasn't told there would be two people. That will make our journey more difficult."

"Why can't they send a *second* helicopter?" Getty wanted to know.

"I asked for one, and the answer was 'no,'" Ferris replied. "Everything is in short supply, *especially* helicopters. We'll have to hoof it. Okay, put masks on just to be safe. I'll take the point. Bear, you're next, followed by Quigley, the mayor, her friend, Lee, and Collins. And remember—don't bunch up." And with that, Ferris opened the front door.

There wasn't anything Getty could do except fall into line and follow Quigley. As Lee left the building she saw columns of smoke all around. Not a good sign.

The Aztec bodies lay in a wild sprawl surrounding the black spot where the explosion had occurred. Lee noticed the body of what appeared to be a teenaged boy. An open shopping bag lay next to him, and candy bars were scattered about. Was he a soldier? Or a human sacrifice? The answer seemed obvious.

Ferris began to jog. But it quickly became apparent that Getty wouldn't be able to keep up. So the best the group could do was a ground-eating walk. Rather than follow the arterial north, Ferris took them into the residential area located two blocks west of the business district. Both sides of the street were lined with shabby homes.

It was only a matter of minutes before they encountered a barricade. It consisted of old cars, a beat-up travel trailer, and piles of junk. Lee thought they were about to confront a gang until a middle-aged man stepped into the gap between a car and the trailer. He was armed with a rifle and a megaphone. "Stop right there," he told them. "If you can prove that you live in this neighborhood, then send one person forward to present that proof. Otherwise, turn around and go back to where you came from."

Ferris held up a hand. That brought the team to a halt. "I'll go forward and talk to them. Lee, you're in charge. Put out flankers and be ready to provide covering fire."

As Ferris made his way forward, Lee sent Bear and Collins out to watch their flanks. Getty took the opportunity to plop down on a set of concrete stairs. "I'm thirsty," she complained. Lee was thirsty, too, and suspected that the rest of them were as well. The original plan called for a short hike to and from the apartment, so none of them had canteens.

But much to Lee's amazement, Maxim pulled a bottle of springwater out of his man bag and offered it to Getty. "Here you go," he said kindly. "It's your favorite."

The mayor took two long swigs before screwing the top back on. Lee waited to see if Getty would pass the bottle around and wasn't surprised when she didn't.

Ferris had returned by then and produced a whistle that brought the flankers back onto the street. "They call themselves the Manzanita Militia," he said. "And they plan to keep both the gangs and the 'tecs at bay until the military arrives."

The locals chatted with the group and gave them paper cups filled with water as they trooped through the roadblock. Lee was impressed by how good their morale seemed to be and wondered if any of them recognized the mayor.

The team had to pass through a second checkpoint a few blocks later. The people assigned to that location were sitting beneath mismatched umbrellas. Some held shotguns across their laps, and one man was drinking beer from a can. Could they keep a gang like the Diablos at bay? That was unlikely. But Lee hoped the authorities would regain control of Hawthorne before it came to that.

Ferris was in the lead as the group walked the rest of the way to West Rosecrans Avenue. It was an east–west thoroughfare bordered on both sides by businesses that would be a magnet for Aztec troops *and* looters. But what made Rosecrans important was the fact that it would take the extraction team *under* the 405 Freeway, which most surface streets couldn't do. As the team left Manzanita and turned onto West Rosecrans, Lee saw that the street was four lanes wide and flat as a pancake. The Remington was ready, and Lee's senses were on high alert as she followed Quigley along the south side of the street.

When Lee looked west, all she could see was devastation. Dead bodies had been left to rot in the sun, tendrils of smoke drifted away from shot-up cars, and shards of glittering glass crunched under her boots. It looked as though a war had been fought on the street. And while Lee figured that a wide variety of people had been involved, she suspected that south side gangs were responsible for most of the devastation.

So where were they? Crows pecked at the bodies that lay sprawled on the pavement—while stray dogs fought for possession of an arm. But there were no people to be seen. None who could get up and walk around, anyway.

Maybe that was to be expected. After collecting lots of loot during the night, perhaps the gangs had gone home to rest and rearm. If so, that could work in the team's favor although stragglers could be picking through whatever remained. Had the group been larger, they would have cleared each building before proceeding farther. But they couldn't do that. So it was best to move quickly and avoid conflict.

Lee kept her head on a swivel as they came up on a bank. A yellow backhoe had been used to crash through the front door and was still buried in the building. Half a block farther on, they had to make their way across the sea of rejected shoes that were scattered in front of a store.

Then they passed a beauty salon that had been left untouched before coming up on a city bus. The wheels on the right side were up on the sidewalk—and the front end was in contact with a bent lamppost. Ferris raised a hand. "Take up defensive positions. Collins, try to start it. Lee, give him a hand."

She could see what Ferris had in mind. The bus was large

enough to hold everyone and push smaller obstacles out of the way. If the team could get the vehicle going, they'd be able to reach the ocean more quickly. And that would be a good thing.

As Lee followed Collins onto the bus, a foul stench invaded her nostrils, and she soon saw why. A woman was slumped sideways on a seat three rows back, and judging from the hole in the window next to her, had been shot from outside. Collins ignored the body as he went to inspect the dash. "The bus driver took the keys," he observed. "But I like a challenge."

Lee watched Collins remove a small tool kit from a cargo pocket and go to work. "So what are you?" she inquired. "A cop or a car thief?"

"I restore cars in my spare time," Collins explained. "So it was necessary to learn a thing or two about electrical systems. Now let's see if I'm as good as I claim to be."

Lee heard the engine start and knew the answer was "yes." They worked together to remove the female passenger from the bus and lay her body on the sidewalk. Collins closed the woman's eyes, murmured a prayer, and stood. It wasn't much of a funeral—but more than many were likely to receive. "Get on the bus," Ferris ordered, "and be ready to defend it. Okay, Collins . . . Take us to the beach. I'd like to work on my tan."

Before Collins could take them to the beach, he had to back the bus away from the light pole, put the transmission in drive, and turn onto the street. Lee was seated two rows back and felt a pair of thumps as the tires came down off the curb.

Then they began to move forward. But because of all the wrecked cars, Collins had to weave in and out between them. That limited the bus speed to three or four miles per hour. More than once, Lee saw a flock of crows take to the air ahead of the bus and knew what they'd been feeding on. Then the bus would lurch as it rolled over a corpse. There were seagulls, too, great wheeling flocks of them, all waiting for their portion of the feast.

Meanwhile, the mayor was back at work to the extent that the on-again off-again cell service would allow her to be. The problems stemmed from the excessive call volume—and Lee heard Getty unleash a string of swearwords as another call dropped out. It was impossible to hear everything the other woman said—but Lee got the impression that the mayor was trying to summon a military helicopter.

Ferris was standing in the aisle and bent over so he could see through the front windshield. "There it is!" he proclaimed. "The 405!"

Lee knew that the freeway was an important landmark because once they passed beneath it, they could leave West Rosecrans Avenue if they wanted to. As she peered through the dusty windshield, Lee could see the elevated freeway *and* the tractor-trailer rig that dangled over the side. If that was indicative of what 405 was like, then the north–south freeway was a total mess. That was when Collins shouted, "Incoming!" and Lee saw him dive sideways out of the driver's seat. The RPG had been fired from the freeway—and it went off with a loud boom as it struck the front of the bus. The impact dumped Ferris onto the floor.

Lee heard Quigley yell, "Out! Out through the back door!" And she was about to go forward when Ferris grabbed the back of her vest.

"Collins is dead," Ferris said as a burst of automatic fire shattered what remained of the front windshield. "There's nothing you can do."

Lee swore as she followed Ferris off the bus. The rest of the team took cover behind the big vehicle as the people on the overpass continued to fire down on them. "A gang might shoot up a bus just for the fun of it," Ferris observed, "but they wouldn't have an RPG. So I figure those bastards are Aztecs."

"Maybe," Bear allowed. "But they could have taken an RPG off a dead 'tec."

Ferris nodded. "Point taken. Lee, take a look. See if you can thin them out."

Killing the soldier with the flamethrower was one thing—but this was something else. The overpass was at least eight or nine hundred feet away, and she would be shooting into the sinking sun. Thanks to the fact that the bus was angled slightly relative to the freeway, Lee could slip along the side of it without exposing all of her body. But once the assholes on the bridge spotted the movement, bullets began to ping around her.

Having gone as far as she could, Lee raised the rifle and peered through the scope. It looked as if there were three shooters—all of whom were little more than fuzzy silhouettes. One glance was all she needed. There was no way in hell she could hit those targets at that distance with the rifle at hand. And someone had to if the group was going to pass under the freeway. She backed away. "So?" Ferris inquired, as she arrived. "What did you conclude?"

"There are three of them," Lee replied. "If I managed to hit one of them, it would be more luck than skill. How about Quigley here? I'll bet he could do it."

Getty was talking on her cell phone as the police officers looked at Quigley. His eyes slid away. "Lee's mistaken," he said. "People call her Deadeye, for God's sake."

"She's an expert with a handgun," Ferris allowed. "But you're an LAPD firearms instructor . . . And according to what I heard, you were a sniper before that."

"A sniper who missed," Quigley said bitterly. "And because I missed, a little girl is dead. Had I made the shot, she'd be all grown-up with children by now."

Suddenly, Lee remembered. The incident had occurred before her time but she'd heard about it. Two guys attempted to rob a bank. One of the tellers triggered an alarm. The cops arrived and as they threw a cordon around the building the perps came out. Both had hostages. A young mother and her five-year-old daughter.

Meanwhile, two snipers had been ordered to take up positions on an adjacent rooftop. And when the first bank robber shot the woman to show how serious he was, the incident commander ordered the sharpshooters to fire. The first sniper was dead-on. The murderer went down.

Peter Quigley was just a hair off. And because of that, his man had the fraction of a second necessary to kill the little girl before dying in a hail of bullets. There was an investigation, and Quigley was exonerated. A miss is a miss. It could happen to anyone. So Quigley was reassigned to the shooting range, where he earned his reputation as a strict taskmaster, and the nickname: "Shithead."

"That was then," Lee told him, as she offered the Remington. "This is now."

Quigley's eyes came up to meet hers. She could see the sorrow there—and the years of self-hatred. "You can do it," Lee said. "We need you."

Quigley took the rifle, examined the weapon as if he'd never seen one before, and turned away. Then he began the perilous journey up to the spot where Lee had been earlier. What seemed like a long time passed. The bad guys continued to fire—but intermittently. They knew people were hiding behind the bus and were waiting for them to emerge.

Ferris had started to fidget. And Lee could tell that he was about to give up on Quigley when three shots rang out. The reports came in quick succession, as if produced by a semiautomatic rifle instead of a pump gun. Then there was silence. And as Quigley came back to rejoin the group he made no attempt to conceal himself. That said it all.

Lee looked at Quigley's face, searching for some sign of redemption. There was none. But it did seem as if his back was straighter as he returned the rifle. "Here," Quigley said. "Don't forget to clean it."

Lee grinned. "You *are* a shithead."

Quigley offered a wry smile. "Yes," he said, "I guess I am."

Ferris was eager to capitalize on the victory. Bear was ordered to remove a variety of items from Collins's body, including the policeman's body armor, which was given to Getty.

Then Ferris led the group out into the open. Rather than walk, he chose to jog. That was hard on the mayor, but Maxim was there to assist her, and Lee was impressed by how patient the young man was. It felt good to enter the shade thrown by the overpass and emerge on the other side. The scene was no different from what Lee had seen on the east side of the freeway. Stalled cars, ravaged businesses, and the voracious crows.

Lee was tired by then, *very* tired, but determined to keep up. Perhaps Ferris was feeling it, too . . . Or maybe he was concerned about Getty. In any case, he slowed from a jog to a walk. The group approached a business complex ten minutes later. And that was when Lee heard a distant buzzing sound. She looked up and scanned the sky until she saw a tiny helicopter with a bubble-shaped canopy. It was coming straight at them, and she could hear the pop, pop, pop of rifle fire as people fired at it.

As the group watched, the chopper continued to lose altitude until it circled a nearly empty parking lot and prepared to land. That was when Getty broke company with the team and began to run. Maxim followed but stopped after a few paces. The helicopter was clearly too small for more than one passenger.

No one moved as the mayor climbed into the aircraft and sat down. She was fastening her seat belt as the chopper took off, gained altitude, and headed north. The sound of the helicopter's engine faded until the aircraft was little more than a dot. Then it disappeared. Bear was the first to speak. "Can you believe that shit?"

"Yes," Ferris said bleakly. "I can. All right . . . Here's the deal. The sun will set soon. And when it does, all sorts of whack jobs will come out to play. I suggest that we hole up and depart around 3:00 A.M. If you guys disagree, then speak up."

"I vote for staying the night," Lee put in. "I'm tired and hungry."

"That goes for me, too," Quigley said.

"I'm in," Bear added.

"How about you?" Ferris inquired, as he turned to look at Maxim.

"I don't know," Maxim replied doubtfully. "Maybe I should go home."

"That's bullshit," Lee said. "You won't make it."

"Then give me a gun," Maxim said fiercely. "I'll learn how to fight."

"Here's a pistol," Ferris said as he gave Maxim a Glock. "Quigley will teach you how to use it."

"Uh-oh," Bear said. "Hear *that*? It sounds like trouble is headed this way."

There was no mistaking the thunder of motorcycle engines, and that could only mean one thing: A gang was rolling their way. "Come on!" Ferris said. "Follow me." He took off running, and the group followed. The nearest hiding place was the boxy, four-story office building on the left. The glass from the shattered doors crunched under their feet as they hurried inside and took up defensive positions in the offices that flanked the lobby.

Lee eyed the street through a window as the first motorcyclist rolled past. A pole was attached to the bike's fork and a head with long blond hair was perched atop it. Golden locks fluttered as the other riders followed along behind. Perhaps a member of the gang squad would have been able to identify the beefy herd, but Lee couldn't. And it didn't matter. All of the outlaw clubs were interchangeable insofar as she was concerned.

But as a rider, she could admire the bikes if not the people on them. All of the machines were large and powerful like her Road King, but the similarity ended there. Each motorcycle was hand-built according to the preferences of its owner. So there was a wide variety of handlebars, gas tanks, and fender configurations to be seen.

Fortunately, none of the bikers showed the least bit of interest in the office building as they steered their brightly painted two wheelers through the maze of wrecks that partially blocked the road. "Okay," Ferris said, as the rolling thunder died away. "The break is over. Let's find a place to hole up."

Ferris led them out of the building, through the adjacent parking lot, and over a fence. The idea was to stay off Rosecrans to whatever extent possible. After passing a burned-out restaurant, they arrived next to a four-story hotel. Ferris raised a hand. "Bear . . . Lee . . . Go in and check it out. Give us a holler if you run into trouble."

Bear took the lead, and Lee entered, holding the Glock. The side entrance opened onto a hall, which led past a row of conference rooms to the main lobby. Not surprisingly the cash registers had been forced open—and all of the booze in the lounge had been stolen. But there was very little damage other than that. After quick visits to the upper floors, Bear opened his mike. "There won't be any room service—but the hotel is clear."

Once the rest of the team was inside, Ferris had to make a choice. Would it be best to go high, and run the risk of being trapped up there? Or stay low, where looters were likely to detect the group's presence? After consulting with the others, Ferris chose low on the theory that were someone else to enter the hotel, they might set the place on fire. And that would be lethal for people on the floors above. He sent Quigley and Maxim up to the roof, however, where they could act as lookouts, and the civilian could learn to handle a pistol.

With an overlook in place, it was up to the others to secure all five of the ground-level entrances and set up shop in the reception area. It was dark by then. But after shielding some of the hotel's emergency lanterns from the outside, they could see. And after making withdrawals from dozens of minibars, they had more water, soft drinks, and candy bars than they could consume. Lee's Diet Coke was warm, but wet, and it went with peanuts.

Then it was time for Lee to grab some sleep on one of the couches in the lounge. Going to sleep was like a fall into oblivion. And when Bear woke Lee, it was to find that a blanket had been thrown over her. "Time to rise and shine," Bear said. "We're on duty in fifteen minutes. Which would you prefer?" he inquired. "The overlook? Or roving patrol?"

"I'll take the overlook," Lee answered, as she swung her boots onto the floor.

"Works for me," Bear replied. "Take the blanket with you. It'll be cold up there."

By that time, a makeshift coffee bar had been established on top of the bar. It consisted of a gas-fueled food warmer that had been liberated from the hotel's kitchen, plus a pot of water and a basket of makings from one of the maid's closets.

Lee took the opportunity to make herself a gigundo cup of joe which, when combined with a large chocolate bar, was equivalent to a shot of adrenaline. Thus fortified, she climbed the stairs to the roof. Some of the smoke had cleared by then—and there was enough starlight to see by. Ferris lowered his binoculars and turned to look at her. "What's up?" Lee inquired. "Any problems?"

Ferris shook his head. "Not really . . . Groups of people have been traipsing back and forth all night—but none of them took an interest in the hotel."

"Good. I like it. How 'bout the big picture? Did you talk to Jenkins?"

"Yup. And you'll be glad to know that the mayor arrived safe and sound."

"Thank God for that," Lee said sarcastically.

"And the marines are pushing up from the south," Ferris added. "It sounds like they're kicking some 'tec ass."

Lee took a sip of coffee. "I'm glad to hear it."

"Yeah, me, too. The only problem is that the marines are pushing the mutants up into south LA . . . And that's where *we* are."

"That sucks, for us, and the people who live here."

"Exactly," Ferris agreed. "But we can't stop it, so it's important to pull out at 0300. Keep your eyes peeled—and holler if you see something."

Ferris left and, as Lee scanned the horizon, she saw that some lights were on to the north. A sure sign that repairs were under way.

But when she turned to the south, everything was dark except for the neighborhoods that were on fire. Then a series of explosions lit up the night. Were the marines shelling the 'tecs? If so, they were shelling the residents of LA, too. Each salvo sounded like thunder, and Lee thought about what Ferris had said. The beach was a mile or two away . . . And the sooner they arrived the better.

The coffee was gone by then, so Lee pulled the blanket in around her body and began to walk the roof's perimeter. Time passed, albeit slowly since there wasn't much action. But then, a little after 0100, she heard the rumble of engines. Was it the motorcycle gang? Going home for the night? No, as dozens of headlights appeared off to the west, Lee knew she was looking at some sort of convoy.

She raised the rifle and peered through the scope. It didn't help, so she lowered it again. Was she looking at a gang? A citizen militia? Or a sizeable force of 'tecs? It felt as if cold fingers were wrapped around her gut. She opened her mike. "Bear . . . Tell Ferris that at least a dozen vehicles are coming in from the west. I don't know if they will turn in here, but if they do, we'll be in some deep shit."

"Roger that," Bear replied.

As Lee watched the lights come closer, the engine noise grew louder. Now she could see that the convoy included a menagerie of delivery vans, pickup trucks, and cars. *Keep going*, she prayed. *Pass us by . . . Don't stop here.*

"What you got?" Ferris said as he appeared next to her. "*That*," Lee said as she pointed at the line of vehicles.

Ferris swore under his breath. "Just what we don't need . . . But why stop here? They'll pass us by."

But the convoy *didn't* pass them by. The first car slowed, turned into the mostly empty parking lot, and the next vehicle followed. Both maneuvered to put their headlights on the front of the building, and that's when the troops poured out of the vehicles behind them. The Aztecs had arrived.

FOUR

Lee felt her heart sink as soldiers poured out of their vehicles and a squad-sized detachment of 'tecs started toward the building. "We need to buy time," Ferris told her. "Kill as many of them as you can. That will slow the bastards down."

Ferris was yelling into his mike as he turned and ran. There was a tightness in Lee's gut as she crawled to the edge of the roof and peered down into the parking lot. Thanks to someone's stupidity, the squad was backlit by the headlights aimed at the building. Lee chose the first man in the column of soldiers and shot him in the head. And that was best because it was safe to assume that the 'tecs were wearing body armor.

Lee was already pumping another cartridge into the chamber and firing as the body fell. *Another* head snapped back, and *another* 'tec died. Then all hell broke loose. Orders were shouted in Spanish, whistles sounded, and the headlights were extinguished. That was followed by a ferocious hail of bullets that shattered the hotel's windows and dug divots out of the brick façade.

The fire wasn't aimed at any particular spot because the mutants had no idea where the shots had originated. Lee knew that wouldn't last and was determined to cash in on it. She chose a muzzle flash, aimed at a point just above it, and triggered three shots. It was too dark to confirm a kill, but that weapon fell silent.

But what goes around comes around as the old saying goes,

and the muzzle flash from the Remington quickly drew fire. That forced Lee to back away from the edge of the roof as bullets tore into the area where she'd been. *Maybe they'll pull out now,* she thought to herself. *After all, why fight for this hotel, when there are others?*

Unfortunately, it soon became apparent that the mutants *were* going to fight for the hotel. Maybe they were tired of being pushed around, maybe they thought they were in contact with a group of marines, or maybe anything. What was, was. And if they continued to attack, the bastards would win. Ferris spoke in her ear. "Good job, Lee. Come on down. I put in a call for air support and, if we get it, these people will be toast."

"And if we don't?"

"We'll take a lot of them with us."

Lee felt a lump in her throat but managed to swallow it. "Roger that . . . I'm on my way."

Lee took the stairs two at a time as she made her way down to the ground floor. "Here I am," Lee said as she entered the reception area. "Where do you want me?"

Ferris and Bear were positioned near the front door. There was a loud boom, the building shook, and dust rained down from the false ceiling. Ferris pointed. "Grab Worley's shotgun and head thataway . . . I think the hotel has a new door. Seal it off."

The twelve-gauge was sitting on a counter, along with a plastic bag filled with shells. Lee took both and hurried down the hall that ran east and west along the front of the building. Moments later, she came to the jagged hole that Ferris had referred to. It looked as though an RPG had been used to create a new entry. A tactic that would split the defenders in two. *They're getting smarter,* Lee thought to herself, as she took cover behind a pile of rubble. *And that isn't good.*

The Aztecs were still firing but without the previous intensity. That suggested they would attack soon. So Lee took the opportunity to ensure that the shotgun was loaded. It was.

Now she had a moment to feel thirsty and think about Kane. What was he doing, she wondered? Sleeping? Maybe so. Maybe . . . And that was when the attack began.

The 'tecs were using their heads this time. Rather than run

headlong into a wall of defensive fire, they sent two trucks forward to crash into the waist-high planter box that fronted the building. It was tempting to open fire, but Lee chose to wait rather than waste some of her precious ammo. A whistle blew, and a squad of mutants surged through the gap between the trucks.

Lee threw one of her two grenades at them. It took a bounce and exploded a foot off the ground. Shrapnel cut the legs out from under two mutants and dumped them screaming onto the ground. That was the good news. The bad news was that more of the bastards were on the way, and she didn't have enough time to pick targets.

Lee grabbed the shotgun and fired it into a big noncom with ruby red eyes and a snout instead of a nose. The force of the blast hurled him back and slowed those who were trying to drive forward.

Lee took advantage of the slight pause to fire seven additional shots. And since each shell was packed with the equivalent of eight .38 caliber bullets, they tore the next wave of attackers apart. A grenade landed in front of her and Lee was forced to throw herself sideways in an effort to escape the force of the explosion. There was a loud bang, and her ears were ringing as she sat up.

The twelve-gauge was empty, which gave her a choice of reloading or going for the Glock. But with hazy forms still charging through the gap, the choice was no choice at all. Lee drew the Glock and felt it jump in her hand. It was like an old friend who knew exactly where to point and when to fire. As it did, the pile of dead and dying bodies continued to grow. Then a shrill whistle blew, and the attack came to an end. *That's it!* Lee thought to herself as she hurried to reload both the Glock and the shotgun. *They've had enough. They're going to leave.*

"Uh-oh," Ferris said over the radio. "More troops are coming in off Rosecrans . . . And there are two light tanks with them."

Lee felt a sense of disappointment. To come so far, to fight so hard, and to die in a hotel . . . That sucked.

"Lee!" Ferris shouted into her ear. "Two air-force planes are coming our way! Get up on the roof and pop red smoke. This ain't over yet."

Lee felt a sudden surge of hope as she grabbed the long guns and made a mad dash down the hall. Bullets continued to ping the front of the building as mutant snipers tried to keep the defenders on edge. She saw the bodies piled up at the front door as she turned the corner and realized that Ferris and Bear had been up to their asses in 'tecs as well. And Bear had a piece of bloodstained curtain wrapped around his right bicep.

From there Lee ran down a hall and entered the stairwell. There were lots of stairs to climb. But Lee was so charged with adrenaline that she barely noticed, and as she burst out onto the roof, Lee saw what looked like pink frosting. The sun was rising in the east.

She hurried forward, pulled the pin on the grenade, and threw it toward the center of the roof. The canister rolled as it landed, and red smoke began to spiral out. An ocean breeze carried the red mist off to the east. Lee didn't know what the 'tecs would make of the smoke and didn't care.

As she waited for the planes, Lee crawled forward to the edge of the roof so she could watch what was going on. The tanks were positioned side by side. One of them fired, and Lee heard a loud boom as a shell hit the hotel. The whole building shook, and she was in the process of backing away from the edge when a female voice filled her ears. Someone had been able to patch the zoomies in. "This is Skyraider Three and Four. We have your smoke . . . Stand by . . . We're rolling in hot. Over."

No more than fifteen seconds passed before an air-force A-12 roared overhead. The twin-engine jet was a direct descendant of the famous A-10 and was intended for the sole purpose of attacking ground targets like tanks. The mutants fired at the plane as it flashed overhead and began to circle back. But they were wasting their time. The A-12 was firing flares intended to pull shoulder-launched missiles off target, and the plane was extremely sturdy.

Lee ducked as the *second* plane passed over the hotel and entered a sweeping turn. The first A-12 was making a run by then, and she saw rockets flash off its wings as the 30mm cannon mounted in the nose began to fire. The weapon made an ominous sound, and the effects were spectacular.

It was stupid to stand on the roof and watch, but Lee couldn't resist. So she had a front-row seat as the rockets struck one of the tanks—and the cannon shells turned the rest of the enemy convoy into a scattering of burning hulks. Then the pilot pulled back on her stick, and the Warthog entered a steep climb.

Now it was the second A-12's turn. It made its run in from the west with the same devastating results. And by the time it roared past, there was nothing left to attack. Lee heard Ferris thank the pilots, who promised to fly cover as the police officers made their way to the beach. Lee hurried down the stairs and made her way into the lobby. Ferris was there, along with Bear, and Quigley. But Maxim was nowhere to be seen. "Where is he?" Lee inquired. "Where's Max?"

"He didn't make it," Quigley answered. "The muties broke in through the back door. Max nailed the first guy, through . . . But he wasn't wearing armor. They shot him in the chest."

Lee didn't ask what happened to the 'tecs. The fact that Quigley was standing there said it all. "That sucks," she said sadly. "I liked him. He deserved better."

"Yeah," Ferris agreed. "I liked him, too. Come on . . . Those birds can't circle forever. Let's haul ass."

The ensuing journey had a surreal quality. First came the trip out into the hotel's parking lot, where bodies, and parts of bodies, lay scattered like pieces in a grisly puzzle. Meanwhile, vehicles continued to burn—and the smoke hung over the scene like a gray shroud. Lee could hear the cries of wounded soldiers and felt sorry for them. Suddenly a man lurched out of the haze with his hands raised. "Don't shoot! I'm a doctor."

"Then act like a doctor," Lee said harshly, "and cover your nose and mouth. And order the wounded to do so as well. Otherwise, the next group of norms who happens along will kill you."

The doctor had protuberant eyes and a lopsided face. He nodded. "I will. Thank you."

Then they were out on the street and jogging west. There were no people to be seen. And no wonder . . . People who had witnessed the devastating air attack weren't about to come out so long as the A-12s continued to fly lazy eights overhead. With the exception of some scavenging dogs, the team had West

Rosecrans to themselves as they ran single file.

Lee got her first glimpse of the glittering ocean twenty minutes later as they crossed Highland Drive. This was the area where a retro band called the Beach Boys had originated—and at least half of the restaurants, bars, and tee-shirt shops bore names related to their music.

Then the team crossed Ocean Drive and was soon jogging through soft sand. Two police officers could be seen guarding the RIB boat that awaited them.

Ferris thanked Skyraider Three and her wingman, and both planes waggled their wings as they banked toward the east. Then the team waded into the water to help launch the boat. Once the outboard was running, it was time to climb in and hang on as the inflatable bucked its way out through light surf. Lee took a soaking as the boat broke through a wave but didn't care. She was alive, and took a moment to savor that, as the RIB boat cleared the rollers and roared toward the fifty-foot police launch half a mile beyond.

Once aboard the larger boat, the team was fed coffee and enormous sandwiches as the patrol boat made the trip to Marina Del Rey. Upon arriving ashore, they discovered that two squad cars had been sent to ferry them back to the secured zone.

During the trip, Lee had an opportunity to see that a great deal of progress had been made in the last day or so. The traffic lights were working, the fires had been extinguished, and a lot of the city's businesses were open. Lee saw burned-out buildings, though . . . As well as a line of crude crosses in front of a crater— and the message that had been spray painted onto a wall: "Pray for the fallen . . ." And, "Kill the freaks." Lee figured that was just a hint of the hatred that was simmering in the city of angels.

There were a lot of soldiers, though. They were directing traffic, standing guard in front of key buildings, and patrolling the streets. And when Lee mentioned that fact, their driver nodded. "People have started to trickle back into the city," he said. "And while the army pushes the muties south, the marines are driving them north. Mayor Getty says we'll have the city back by sundown." Images blipped through Lee's mind. Quigley shooting the dog. Worley falling. Getty waiting at the door. Maxim in his boxer shorts. The flamethrower exploding. Marching west. And Getty running for the helicopter. The bitch.

Once inside the security zone, the police officers were taken to the Olmsby Hotel, which had been commandeered for use by city workers of every possible description. "Grab some sleep," Ferris told the team, as they entered the lobby. "And let's meet at the Street Services Garage at six. Oh, and one more thing . . . You people did one helluva job. Thank you."

After going through a perfunctory registration process, the group broke up and went their separate ways. The hotel was anything but posh. It was clean, though . . . And that was enough for Lee. Her room was on the third floor with an excellent view of a ventilation shaft. Lee dropped the vest in a corner, cleared the long guns, and laid them on the floor. Would Quigley clean his weapons before going to bed? It wouldn't surprise her.

Her clothes were filthy, but she wouldn't have access to her suitcase until later in the day. But Lee could take the hot shower that she'd been dreaming of, and it *was* heavenly. Then, with a cold Diet Coke at hand, she perched on the edge of the bed. Her cell was off, and she turned it on. She figured Kane would be at the hospital and wanted to hear his voice. But after four rings the call went to voice mail: "The voice-mail box associated with this number is full. Please try your call again later."

Lee felt a mild sense of alarm as she hurried to check her voice mail. Kane was more than a little OCD where things like checking voice mail, returning e-mails, and arriving on time were concerned. So much so that she teased him about it.

There were lots of messages, and Lee skipped through them until she found the one from Kane. His voice was strange, as if he was *trying* to sound casual, but under considerable pressure. "Hi, hon . . . It's me. Sorry to bother you, but I'm in jail. No, this isn't a joke. I was arrested for murder about an hour after you left for work. They're holding me at the MDC, and I need some help. Okay, I guess that's all. Love you." And that was followed by a click.

Lee could hardly believe her ears and listened to the message again before calling the MDC. She knew at least a dozen people there—and it didn't take long to hook up with a clerk who could confirm that yes, they did have a prisoner named Lawrence Kane, and yes, he was being held on a murder charge.

Lee's hand shook as she dialed Marvin Codicil's number. Codicil was her attorney and had been able to resolve a number of legal problems in the past. And, since he knew Kane, Codicil seemed like the right person to turn to. He answered on the second ring. "Hello, Cassandra . . . I wondered when you'd call."

"I was working," Lee replied. "It sounds like you already know about Lawrence."

"Yes," Codicil said. "He called me as soon as he could."

"So what the hell is going on?"

"I'm due in court five minutes from now," Codicil said, "so I can't go into a lot of detail. Suffice it to say that Lawrence had left his condo, and was on his way to St. John's, when he saw two men accost a young woman on the street. He stopped, got out of his car, and ordered them to stop. They turned, and one of the men fired a shot at Lawrence. He returned fire using the .45 that *you* gave him. The man with the gun fell dead.

"And even though cops were almost impossible to find in all of the chaos, a patrol car happened along seconds later. The surviving suspect took the dead man's pistol and ran. The police officers ordered Lawrence to surrender his weapon, and he did so. Then, when they asked him to explain the shooting, he realized that the young woman had disappeared. And when Lawrence asked the police if they'd seen her, they said 'no.' End of story."

Lee groaned. With no witness to support his account, and no gun other than the .45, Kane would look guilty as hell. "So you're on it? You took the case?"

"Of course I took the case," Codicil answered. "And I'll try to get him out on bail."

"I'll visit him as soon as I can," Lee said.

"No, you won't," Codicil replied. "Remember, you're living with him, and he killed the man with a weapon that *you* gave him. Your public profile is iffy already . . . Imagine the headline: 'Controversial Detective Visits Boyfriend in Jail.' How would Chief Corso like *that*?"

Lee sighed. Codicil was correct. Going to visit Kane could generate a lot of negative publicity and might be viewed as unethical. "Okay," she said. "Please tell Lawrence that I love him."

"I will," Codicil promised. "Gotta go. I'll keep you in the loop." And with that, the call came to an end.

Lee drew the curtains and crawled into bed. Kane's situation was disturbing to stay the least—but the weight of her exhaustion pulled her down. There were dreams, but they were filled with conflict, and when the alarm sounded, Lee was happy to escape them.

She turned the alarm off and swung her feet over onto the floor. It was 5:00 P.M., and she was supposed to be at the Street Services Garage by 6:00. Lee cleaned up to the extent that she could, hauled the arsenal down into the lobby, and was pleased to discover that a shuttle had been set up to ferry workers to and from city buildings. Bear was there, too . . . And they garnered some strange looks as they boarded the bus carrying a wild assortment of weaponry.

They got off at the Street Services Garage and were able to hand the artillery in before going to the meeting. It was held in what had been a supervisor's office. Ferris was waiting for them and passed out copies of the report he'd been working on while they slept. "Take a look," he instructed. "If you agree with what I said, please sign above your name and date it. If you take issue with something, let's step outside and talk about it."

Lee read the report and was struck by how professional it was. Even where Getty was concerned. "At that point," the text stated, "a two-person helicopter arrived to take Mayor Getty north." There was no mention of the fact that she hadn't informed Ferris about the chopper in advance—or her apparent lack of concern about what would become of the team after she left. None of that mattered. The purpose of the mission was to rescue Getty, and that had been accomplished. So what if she neglected to say, "Thank you?" She was the mayor and had things on her mind. So Lee signed the sheet of paper and handed it in. The rest of the team did likewise. "Thanks," Ferris said. "Deputy Chief Jenkins would like to speak with you . . . Then you can go home."

Ferris left the room and returned with Jenkins in tow. He still looked fresh, and Lee wondered how he did it. "Welcome back," Jenkins said soberly. "The team did a terrific job. I was sorry to hear about Worley. He'll be recognized along with eighteen other police officers who lost their lives during the last two days."

Jenkins had green eyes, and they swept the room. "I wish everyone could take a few days off at this point, but we were shorthanded to begin with, and the situation is even worse now. The army and the marine corps are cleaning up down south—but nearly a thousand prisoners escaped from jail during the attack. They're on the loose, and we're already seeing the effects of that. And the cases you were working *before* the attack are still open. So it's going to be necessary to put in some long hours in order to catch up."

Jenkins smiled. "But that's for tomorrow. Go home, see if it's still there, and take care of your families. I'll see you here at 9:30 A.M. tomorrow. At that point, it might be possible for most if not all of you to return to your normal duties."

The 9:30 A.M. roll call meant Lee would have two extra hours, and she was grateful. Would she be able to get a car? That problem was foremost in her mind as the meeting came to an end—and Quigley came over to speak with her. "Have you got a couple of minutes?"

Lee wanted to leave, she wanted to go home to see if Kane's condo was still there, but she forced a smile. "Sure. What's up?"

"It's about the way that Maxim died," Quigley said. "I didn't go into detail at the time, but it took a while. The 'tecs broke in, Maxim shot one of them, and took a bullet in the chest. I managed to kill the rest. Then, when I went over to help, I saw there was a lot of blood. Too much. I put a towel over the entry wound, but I could tell that it wasn't going to be enough."

Lee could see it in her mind's eye. The drift of gun smoke, the sprawl of bodies, and a pool of blood on the floor. The whole thing was sad—but why tell her about it? Unless Quigley felt a need to vent. She forced herself to listen. "Max knew he was dying," Quigley continued. "That's why he gave me *this*."

Quigley offered Lee a thumb drive. She took it. *"Why?"*

"Max told me to give it to Getty," Quigley replied. "He said it was a going-away present. And then he died."

"So why not send it to Getty?"

Quigley smiled, but there was no humor in it. "I'm a cop Cassandra . . . A has-been, but a cop nevertheless. I was curious. So I asked the hotel manager to let me use his computer. There are five video clips on the drive—and I think you should look at them."

Lee opened her mouth to speak, and Quigley raised a hand. "No, I want you to form your own opinion."

So Lee shrugged. "Okay, Peter, I'll check 'em out."

Quigley said, "Thanks," and turned away.

After seeking directions, Lee found her way to a desk labeled, MOTOR POOL. A middle-aged civilian was there to greet her. She was fortysomething, her hair was an improbable shade of red, and she had nails to match. "Hi, hon, what can I do for you?"

"My name is Cassandra Lee, and I need a car."

The woman turned to her computer, ran a bright red nail down a list, and nodded. "You have the necessary authorization—but we don't have a car to give you at this time. I suggest that you check back with me later tonight. Maybe something will come in."

Lee tried to imagine how she would get home and couldn't. "Are you sure?" she inquired plaintively. "I'll take anything."

"Well," the woman replied, "there is the paddy wagon."

"The what?"

"You know . . . The old-fashioned truck that the benevolent association uses in parades."

Lee had seen the old-timey vehicle loaded down with some of the LAPD's finest all dressed as early-twentieth-century Keystone Kops. A rowdy group that the city's citizens had come to love. "Really?" Lee said. "That's all you have?"

The woman smiled. "I'm afraid so."

"Okay," Lee said. "I'll take it."

The woman typed some information into a form, hit a key, and was there to receive the sheet of paper the moment that the printer produced it. "Give this to the guard."

Lee thanked her, went outside, and towed her suitcase over to the motor pool. And sure enough . . . The paddy wagon was parked in a corner right next to a badly mangled creeper.

A member of the police reserve unit was there to accept the form. He looked up into her face. "You must be joking . . . The paddy wagon?"

"Yup, I'm in the mood for something different."

The guard laughed. "Okay, the key is in the ignition. Be careful out there."

After putting the suitcase in back, Lee slid behind the wheel and turned the key. The engine started with a roar. So far so good. But, as she drove the truck out of the lot, Lee learned two things: The paddy wagon was top heavy and underpowered. That didn't matter in a parade, but it was going to be a problem out on the streets, and it wasn't long before Lee's vehicle attracted the ire of fellow motorists. Not all of them, though . . . One man smiled and waved.

Lee couldn't take the truck onto the freeway, so she was forced to use regular streets all the way to Santa Monica. She had no idea what to expect. Had the condo been leveled? The way other beachfront buildings had? Or looted? There was no way to know until she was half a block away and saw the lights. The condominium was still there! And untouched insofar as she could tell.

Lee's spirits began to rise as she pulled into the parking garage and into one of the two empty slots that belonged to Kane. Where was his sports car? Sitting in an impound lot somewhere racking up charges. She would need a power of attorney or something to get it out. Still another problem to take care of.

After riding the elevator up to the top floor, Lee towed her suitcase to the condo, unlocked the door, and made her way inside. Everything was just the way Kane had left it, which was to say immaculate. It was weird to be in a relationship with a man who put things away. The place felt empty without him, and that was something she would have to remedy.

Lee locked the door and went straight to the kitchen, looking for something to eat. But the power had been out for a long period of time, so when she went to open the refrigerator, most of the food inside was spoiled. The next twenty minutes were spent making trips to a Dumpster down on the parking level and cleaning the inside of the refrigerator.

Then it was time to open a can of tomato soup, heat it up, and add a handful of crushed soda crackers. Lee watched the news as she ate. It seemed that most of the 'tecs in and around LA had been captured or killed—but the city of San Diego was still in enemy hands. So Pacifica and the Republic of Texas had entered into a formal alliance and declared war on the Aztec Empire. That meant norms and mutants were fighting a common enemy. Would that lead to a better relationship in the future? Or was the alliance a short-term marriage of convenience and nothing more? Time would tell.

After dinner, Lee took a shower, did a load of laundry, and went to bed. It seemed as if less than a minute passed before the alarm went off, and it was time to get up. That had always been difficult, but Lee knew if she put her feet on the floor, the rest of her body would follow. It did.

Lee arrived at the Street Services Garage half an hour early . . . A first for her. Then she parked the paddy wagon and went inside to request a car. A different person was in charge of the motor-pool desk by then and promised to do the best he could.

After sitting through roll call, and all of the bullshit that went with it, Lee followed some other detectives out into a garage that had been converted into temporary office space. There were rows of mismatched desks, cables that snaked overhead, and the faint odor of exhaust fumes in the air. After some searching, Lee found the tent card with her name written on it. It was sitting on top of an old metal desk that had probably been in storage somewhere. The chair squealed like a stuck pig when she sat on it and made a rattling noise as it rolled.

But by means of some sort of technological wizardry, the geeks had been able to bring *her* computer over from the heavily damaged LAPD building and make it work! That gave Lee's spirits a welcome boost, and it was only a matter of minutes before Yanty arrived carrying two cups of coffee. "Welcome back," he said as he put a cup on the surface of her desk. "There you go . . . Complete with all the crap you like to put into it."

"Gee, thanks," Lee said as she took a sip. "You're so nice."

"That's what they tell me," Yanty deadpanned as he sat on the corner of her desk. "I hear you took a stroll through Hawthorne."

"Anything to get out of the office," Lee agreed.

Yanty nodded. "So, slacker, while you were sucking up to the mayor, I came up with a lead."

"On the face case?"

"Exactly."

"Way to go . . . What have you got?"

"During your interview with Dr. Kottery at the UCLA Medical center, she mentioned the need to perform a tissue match, prior to carrying out a face transplant."

"Right," Lee said. "It's called KLA typing—or something like that."

"It's HLA typing," Yanty replied, "and it turns out that only two labs can perform the procedure."

"In LA? Or the whole country?"

"In LA," Yanty responded. "I figured we could widen the search if necessary."

"Right . . . That makes sense."

"I approached both labs and asked to see a list of companies or individuals who had submitted requests for HLA typing during the last six months. The first lab gave me three names, and the second one sent five, four of which were well-known institutions like UCLA. One stood out however . . . And it is called ABCO Medical Technologies. None of the lab folks knew much about the organization, and when I tried to call ABCO, all of my calls went to voice mail. So I drove to the company's street address, and guess what?"

"It was a drop?"

"Exactly. The office belongs to a guy named Joe Pody. He sells insurance, provides payday loans, and stands ready to do your taxes."

"But you didn't tip him off."

A pained expression appeared on Yanty's face. "Give me a break."

"So we wait for ABCO to submit a test, follow the results to Pody's office, and wait to see who comes to get them."

Yanty smiled. "You're smarter than you look."

Lee laughed. "Nice work, Dick . . . I'll take your plan to

Jenkins. And, assuming that he approves it, we'll track these people down."

Lee's phone rang at that point, and Yanty waved good-bye. She lifted the receiver. "This is Detective Lee."

"I promised to keep you in the loop," Codicil told her. "And here I am."

"Thanks," Lee responded. "So give . . . Can we bail him out?"

"Not unless you have two million nu lying around," Codicil replied. "That's what the judge set bail at."

"But *why*?" Lee wanted to know. "Lawrence is a well-respected psychologist, for God's sake. A man with no criminal record."

"If only that were true," Codicil replied. "Unfortunately, Dr. Kane was accused of murder once before."

"Murder? What? Of who?"

"His wife," Codicil replied flatly. "So that gave the DA grounds to request a higher bail. And he got it."

Lee wanted to ask, *"What wife?"* but knew she wasn't ready to deal with the answer. So she thanked Codicil, promised to call him soon, and broke the connection.

It felt as if her entire world had come apart—and she didn't know how to put it together again.

FIVE

It was early morning, a thin scattering of stars was visible in spite of the city lights, and military helicopters were flying low as they searched LA for mutant soldiers. That meant the Bonebreaker had to stop work occasionally and take cover as engines roared and blobs of white light drifted over the graveyard. But the Bonebreaker was tired, so such breaks were welcome.

First, it had been necessary to drag each soldier through the ossuary's tunnels and up to the surface. Then the Bonebreaker had to dig a grave deep enough to accommodate *three* bodies. And making a difficult task even more arduous was the fact that the graveyard had been the site of a so-called recovery camp during the early days of the plague, so there was lots of debris mixed in with the dirt.

Of course, that made the graveyard hallowed ground insofar as the Bonebreaker was concerned—and the decision to bury the Aztecs there hadn't been made lightly. But after giving the matter a lot of thought, the Bonebreaker concluded that, like those interred all around him, the soldiers were victims, too . . . And as deserving of a hole in the ground as anyone else. Even if the digging was hard.

It was almost 4:00 A.M. before the Bonebreaker could pull the ladder up out of the hole and roll the bodies into their final resting places. Ruiz went first, followed by Lopez, and Alvarez.

He fell facedown, so when the Bonebreaker scattered loose soil into the grave, it landed on the soldier's back. "Forasmuch as it hath pleased Almighty God to take unto himself the souls of these mutants, I hereby commit their bodies to the ground. Earth to earth, ashes to ashes, and dust to dust."

Having completed the funeral service, the Bonebreaker went to work shoveling soil into the hole. At one point, his shovel turned up a toy truck, still yellow after thirty-plus years in the ground, and an object that could have been his.

Tears streamed down the Bonebreaker's cheeks as he finished the job and paused to look around. He was surrounded by row upon row of identical markers, all made of cheap metal, all covered with a patina of rust. The Bonebreaker could hear the familiar babble of voices in his head. They were asking for justice—pleading with him to make things right. "I hear you, my brothers and sisters," he told them. "God sent me to kill those who put you in the ground, and some are in hell already. More will follow."

And with that, the Bonebreaker carried his tools back to the carefully camouflaged door, the ramp that led down into the ossuary, and the bed that was waiting for him. Dreams were waiting—but none of them were sweet.

The sun was up, and after a long, mostly sleepless night, Lee was on her way to the MDC. Lee knew she was about to take a big risk and didn't give a shit. She felt angry, hurt, and confused all at once. *Kane had been married?* Okay, she could live with that. A lot of men had been married. But why hadn't he told her? And what about the murder charge? The whole thing was eating away at her—and that's why she had decided to ignore Codicil's advice and visit Kane.

Although Lee had entered the MDC on many occasions in the past, it had always been as a police officer rather than a friend and lover. That meant the process was new to her. First, it was necessary to show ID. Then Lee had to fill out a form and surrender her weapons. Then she was required to pass through a metal detector and submit to a health screening before entering the waiting room.

It was early in the day, so the space was half-empty. The walls were puke green, the plastic chairs were orange, and the floor consisted of polished concrete. As Lee looked around, she saw that most of the visitors were female. Women like herself who had hooked up with a lying, cheating, son of a bitch and were paying the price for it.

Really? Lee asked herself. *Lawrence doesn't get to explain? Suddenly he's a lying, cheating, son of a bitch?*

Okay, Lee agreed. The lie was a lie of omission. And being married isn't equivalent to cheating. As for his mother, she's dead, and it wasn't right to call her a bitch.

"Visitor eighteen can approach window seven," a disembodied voice said over the PA system.

Lee glanced at the slip of paper clutched in her hand, saw the number eighteen, and stood. A short walk took her over to the row of booths that divided the room in half. They were narrow and anything but private since the people to either side would be able to listen in if they chose to. Visitors were separated from the prisoners by a thick wall of Plexiglas—and in order to have a conversation, both parties were required to use a black handset. That meant all conversations could be monitored by the MDC's staff, and Lee made a note to remember that as she sat on a rickety chair and waited for Kane to appear.

About a minute passed before he was released from a holding area and allowed to come out. Lee was shocked by what she saw. Kane looked years older, and there were deep circles under his eyes. He managed a smile as he sat down opposite her. The phone made his voice sound hollow. "Hi, hon, I wish you hadn't come. Codicil told me that it would be a bad idea."

Lee shrugged. "I had to," she said honestly.

Kane made a face. "I'm in trouble, huh?"

"Yes, you are. It doesn't get any worse than murder."

"I meant with you," Kane replied.

Lee's eyes met his. *"Why?* Why didn't you tell me? You're a psychologist, for God's sake."

Kane looked down. "I'm a psychologist, but I'm human. I planned to tell you. And I started to tell you on two different occasions. But I didn't want to lose you. And I was afraid that I might."

"That was stupid. It isn't like my life is perfect . . . And you knew that."

Kane's eyes came back up. "I'm sorry."

"So tell me now. Tell me about your wife—and the first murder charge."

Kane shrugged. "We met in college. There was an explosion of pheromones. Sometimes we had sex three times a day. It seemed as if we were perfect together, and Monica was in a hurry to get married. So I agreed. Everything went well at first. But it wasn't long before I came to realize that Monica was bipolar. And when she was in the manic mode, we had a tendency to fight. That resulted in loud disturbances that caused the neighbors to complain. So when Monica failed to arrive at work, and was found dead in her car, the police took a close look at me."

"I would," Lee said.

Kane nodded. "And, since I'd gone camping by myself, I had no alibi. Making a bad situation worse was the fact that the local DA was up for reelection. My case looked like a slam dunk, so he filed charges against me. But the whole thing came apart a couple of days later when a meth freak named Matt Hickey was arrested for speeding. They found Monica's purse in his car. Subsequent analysis of a gun found in Hickey's apartment confirmed that it had been used in the murder."

"So the charges were dropped."

"Yes."

They were silent for a moment. "Okay," Lee said finally. "Tell me about *this* murder charge. You left the condo . . . Then what?"

Kane told her about the chaos on the streets, how he'd been caught up in a rolling traffic jam and noticed the girl. She was walking up the street with a knapsack on her back. There was a steady stream of such people. Then Kane saw two men step out of a doorway and block her path. The streetlights were still on at that time, and Kane saw the men grab her.

At that point, Kane half expected some of the other pedestrians to intervene. They didn't. The Aztec navy was shelling LA, and it was every man and woman for themselves. So Kane pulled over, got out of his car, and yelled at the men to stop. And when one of them fired a shot, Kane fired back. "It all happened so fast," Kane said. "I pulled the trigger, felt the recoil, and saw him fall. The fact that I hit him was more luck than skill. A patrol car arrived seconds later. That was when I realized that both the girl and the second man had fled. I told the cops that I'd fired in self-defense, but they couldn't find the dead guy's gun. So they placed me under arrest, and here I am."

"And Codicil hasn't been able to find the girl?"

"Not that I know of," Kane answered.

There was another moment of silence. "So," Lee said. "Is there anything I can get for you?"

Kane shook his head. "You're staying at the condo?"

"Yes."

"Good. Keep your eye peeled for bills. If you'll pay them, I'll pay you back."

"Sure," Lee replied.

"Are you mad at me?"

"Yes."

"Will you get over it?"

"Maybe."

"Thirty seconds," a third voice said over the phone.

"Thank you," Kane said. "Be careful out there."

"I will," Lee promised. "And you be careful in here." The visit was over.

Lee got up, turned, and crossed the room. Her thoughts were churning as she left the building and walked into a media ambush. As a police officer, she knew that some reporters had paid informants inside the MDC. And when Channel 7's Carla Zumin rushed over to shove a mike in her face Lee knew that she'd been sold out. "Detective Lee," Zumin said breathlessly. "Your boyfriend has been charged with murder . . . Are you working his case?"

"No," Lee said flatly as she continued to walk. "That would be unethical."

"Do you think Dr. Kane is innocent?" Zumin asked, hurrying to keep up.

Lee was interested to hear the certainty in her own voice.

"Yes, I believe he's innocent. And I have nothing else to say at this time." Lee figured the interview would make the twelve o' clock news. Codicil would be pissed.

Lee forced herself to put Kane and his situation on a back burner as she made her way to a nearby parking lot and the creeper that was parked there. After checking the vehicle for trackers, she got in, started the engine, and drove to the Street Services Garage. She was thinking about the face case as she cleared security and went to her desk.

But before Lee could talk to Yanty, she needed to check her voice mail. And that was when she heard Quigley's message. "Hi, Cassandra . . . This is Peter. What did you think of the stuff on Maxim's thumb drive? Please call me when you have time."

Lee felt a pang of guilt. The truth was that the memory stick hadn't even crossed her mind. So she opened her bag and looked inside. And there, in among some loose bullets, stray breath mints, and pennies was Maxim's thumb drive.

With other desks all around, there was no such thing as privacy in the new bull pen. So Lee inserted a pair of earbuds, slipped the drive into a port on her computer, and clicked play. There was a moment of black followed by some low-quality video. The camera was static and, judging from the angle, located fairly high. In Maxim's apartment? That seemed like a reasonable guess.

There were two people in the shot. One of them was Mayor Getty, and the other was a man who looked familiar but Lee couldn't place at first. Then a crawl appeared at the bottom of the frame. The date and time of day was followed by a title: "Mayor Melissa Getty meets with Mr. Sydney Silverman." Lee knew that Silverman was the controversial real-estate magnate who'd been buying up large chunks of postplague LA on the theory that land prices would rise.

At first, the conversation was focused on golf. But it wasn't long before the discussion turned serious. Silverman had a full head of white, shaggy hair, and craggy good looks. There was passion in his voice. "People are so focused on the present," he said, "that they can't see past it. Yes, it will take years to rebuild LA. But is that what we want? The *old* Los Angeles? Including all of the problems it's known for? I don't think so. We need to think *big*. The population is growing, Melissa . . . My experts project that 90 percent of the empty houses in LA will be occupied in ten years. And it won't end there. So where will people live? In the suburbs? Sure, some will. But what if we could provide them with an alternative? A floating city just offshore? Here . . . Take a look at this."

Silverman handed a binder to Getty at that point, and even though the camera couldn't see what was in it, Silverman's comments were sufficient to give Lee a pretty good idea of what the real-estate magnate had in mind. "We call it *Oceana*," he said. "It would be eight hundred feet wide, five thousand feet long, and twenty-five stories tall. In addition to housing fifty thousand people, *Oceana* would employ three thousand workers. That's a significant number of jobs, Melissa . . . And a lot of voters.

"As presently conceived, the complex would have its own heliport, hospital, and schools. An underwater high-speed train would carry people back and forth to town. Water, power, and government services would be supplied from shore. And that's where *you* come in . . . We need your help to share the vision, obtain the necessary permits, and coordinate the governmental aspects of the project."

"I don't know," Getty said doubtfully. "It's a bold idea. I'll give you that. But it would be a hard sell where most of my constituents are concerned. How much would a home in *Oceana* cost?"

Silverman shrugged. "About five million or so."

"I rest my case."

"I understand your caution," Silverman assured her. "I really do. But consider this . . . You have an election coming up in less than a year. *My* party, which is to say the Constitutional Party, can field a *very* strong candidate. You know who I'm talking about. But, if conditions were right, we could put forward a *weaker* candidate. Someone you could easily defeat. Think about it."

Based on Getty's expression, Lee knew she *was* thinking about it. "That's a very interesting idea, Sydney . . . Very interesting indeed. But it's the sort of proposal that will require some thought. How 'bout I get back to you in a week or so?"

Silverman agreed. And a new crawl appeared: "Three weeks later, in a joint press conference with Sydney Silverman, Mayor

WILLIAM C. DIETZ

Getty endorsed the floating-city concept. Subsequent to that, a private/government study group was announced and is currently working to complete a Silverman-funded feasibility study."

Lee clicked pause. Now she could see why Quigley was concerned. Although Getty hadn't agreed to the scheme on tape— the combination of the offer and the subsequent endorsement spoke volumes. And might cost Getty the next election if it were known. Could the video put her in jail? Maybe . . . Only the DA could say for sure.

But *why*? What motivated Maxim to set up the camera and make the recording? Lee figured that the tape was an insurance policy of sorts. A way for Getty's lover to force a financial settlement should that become necessary.

However, in the final moments of his life, it looked as though Maxim decided to give the thumb drive to Getty as, what he called, "a going-away present." It was an empty gesture perhaps, since he knew he wouldn't need the leverage, but it could have been more than that. Maybe Max felt something for Getty . . . Maybe he was in love with her.

The next hour was spent viewing the rest of the videos. Five in all. Included was a plot to green-light a zoning change in return for a donation to Getty's favorite charity, an agreement to tolerate a garbage strike if the Sanitation Workers Union would support the higher transit fares that Getty was seeking, and a deal with the Church of Human Purity to let LA's stringent antimutant ordinances stand in exchange for an energetic "Vote Getty" campaign. All of which led Lee to believe that she should take the matter up the chain of command.

She sent an e-mail to Quigley. "The material you gave me is very interesting. I'm going to pass it on to Deputy Chief Jenkins to see what he thinks. I suggest we keep the contents of the tapes to ourselves for the moment. More when I have it. Cassandra."

Lee reached for the thumb drive, and was just about to remove it from the computer when she thought better of it. The next minute was spent copying the contents to a password-protected "box" in the cloud. Why? Just in case, that's why. Then she took the memory stick out and placed it in a pocket.

A short walk through a busy corridor took her to Jenkins's

84

office. He was talking to a member of the vice squad. So Lee had to wait until the other detective left. He was dressed like a pimp and winked at her on his way out. Jenkins waved Lee in. There was a frown on his face. "Have a seat," he instructed. "There's something I want you to hear."

Lee sat on a guest chair as Jenkins turned the speakerphone on and entered a code. When the voice mail came on, Lee recognized Chief Corso's voice right away. "Lee's been at it again, Sean . . . It seems she went to the MDC for a visit with Doctor what's-his-name, and Channel 7 nailed her on the way out. I guess she's got every right to visit her boyfriend in jail, but not while she's on duty, which I believe she was." Click.

Lee winced. "Sorry, Chief . . . That was a mistake. It won't happen again."

"Good," Jenkins said. "I have enough problems without having Corso in my face. So, what's up?"

Lee stood and went over to close the door before returning to her seat. "Uh-oh," Jenkins said, "I don't like the looks of that."

Lee placed the thumb drive on the surface of his desk. Jenkins eyed the device but made no attempt to reach out and touch it. "What's on it?" he inquired warily.

"Videos of Mayor Getty cutting all sorts of political deals in return for various types of compensation," Lee said.

Jenkins's eyes widened. "You're joking."

"Nope," Lee said, "I'm serious."

"Where did you get it?"

Lee told him about Maxim, about his dying request, and about Quigley. "After looking at the videos, he decided that the Special Investigative Section should review them," she said. "So he gave the drive to me. And, having viewed the clips, I think you should eyeball them, too."

"Gee, thanks," Jenkins responded sourly. "I hope this is much ado about nothing. Our city has enough problems."

"But you'll take a look."

"Yes, I'll take a look. And Cassandra . . ."

"Yes?"

"Keep this to yourself for now."

"I will . . . And I told Quigley to do so as well."

"Good. Is there anything else? No? Then go out there and solve some crimes."

Lee left the office, took a right, and went looking for Yanty. He was eating lunch at his desk. It consisted of a P&J sandwich and a carton of milk—and that was as predictable as the sun's rising in the morning. "So, Dick," Lee began, as she plopped down next to him. "How's it going?"

Yanty wiped his mouth with a paper napkin. "My back hurts, my car broke down, and the Dodgers lost."

Lee smiled. "And the face case?"

"Try reading your e-mails."

"I'm a shithead."

"That's for sure," Yanty agreed expressionlessly.

"So?"

"So we're making progress. TransLab received a request from ABCO Medical Technologies yesterday morning. At 2:00 this afternoon, they're going to deliver the results to Joe Pody's storefront. And we'll be there to see who comes to pick it up."

"And we'll follow them."

"If you can fit it in."

Lee made a face. "I hate you."

"But you need me."

"True."

"I'll meet you in the parking lot," Yanty said.

Lee spent the next forty-five minutes plowing through e-mails and paperwork. Lunch consisted of a turkey sandwich and coffee purchased off the food truck out in the parking lot. Lee ate while Yanty drove. Thirty minutes later, they passed the strip mall where Pody's business was located.

His storefront was sandwiched between a beauty shop and a pizza joint near the intersection of Culver and Inglewood—a location that would be convenient to those who lived in or around the Vista Gardens Housing projects. The front window was hung with a variety of neon signs that read, OPEN 24 HOURS, PAYDAY LOANS, and PRIVATE MAILBOXES, all in bright primary colors. By parking in a lot on the other side of Culver, the detectives could watch the front of Pody's establishment without being noticed. But what about the back?

Lee had finished lunch by then and volunteered to take a look. She crossed the street at the nearest light, walked past the end of the strip mall, and entered the alley that ran behind it. Judging from appearances, that was where most of the local businesses got their deliveries. Pody's was the exception—and for good reason. Any place that offered payday loans would be a target for stickup artists, so Pody's back door was protected by a wrought-iron security gate, and there was a sign instructing customers to use the front entrance. This was a piece of good luck because it meant the detectives wouldn't have to monitor both entrances.

After completing her mission, Lee circled back to the car and Yanty. A vehicle wearing a TransLab logo arrived fifteen minutes later. "That's nice," Lee commented, as she peered through her binoculars. "Thanks to the logo, we know the delivery is being made."

"I requested that," Yanty said smugly. "And you're welcome."

Lee laughed. "Okay, but what about the ABCO courier? Chances are they won't arrive in a branded vehicle."

"Joe Pody's going to call me when they make the pickup," Yanty said confidently.

"Why would he do that? I thought we were going to leave him out of it."

"Because he's a good citizen," Yanty replied.

Lee looked at him. There was more to it than that . . . She could tell. Yanty had some sort of leverage where Pody was concerned but wasn't going to discuss it. Because cops weren't supposed to lean on people? Probably. Yanty might look like a CPA, but there was a hard-core detective behind the easygoing façade. She let the matter drop.

Five minutes elapsed before the courier came out, got in the minivan, and drove away. "Now comes the hard part," she predicted. "Who knows when ABCOM's messenger will arrive."

"True," Yanty replied. "But let's be optimistic. He or she might show up ten minutes from now."

But the courier *didn't* show up. Not in ten minutes, not in twenty, and not in forty. Time slowed. Yanty talked about the Dodgers, and Lee thought about Kane. Four o'clock rolled around. A mall cop told Yanty to move the car and apologized after getting a look at the detective's badge.

Lee went to get coffee and returned fifteen minutes later. Yanty shook his head as she got in. "You didn't miss anything."

"You're sure Pody will call?"

"I'm sure," Yanty replied as he took an experimental sip of coffee. "*What?* No doughnuts? We're cops. Haven't you been on a stakeout before?"

"I can't afford the calories, and neither can you."

"I'm in better shape than Prospo."

"True," Lee acknowledged. "But that isn't saying much."

That was when Yanty's phone burped. He thumbed it on. "Yanty."

Lee watched as Yanty listened. "Okay," he said. "The messenger is a Hispanic female, and she's leaving now. Well done . . . Thanks."

Lee raised her binoculars as Yanty started the car. "I have her . . . She's getting into a blue *especiale* with a rag top."

Yanty was pulling out of the parking lot and watching to see which way the courier would go. The answer was west on Culver Boulevard. Ideally, there would be a second unit to switch off with—but the department was too shorthanded to provide one. That forced Yanty to hang back farther than Lee liked and run the risk of losing the ABCO car at a light.

Fortunately, there was plenty of rush-hour traffic to hide in. Eventually, the suspect turned north onto Lincoln Boulevard. Then, after traveling a short distance, she turned west onto Mindanaoway. "What the hell?" Yanty exclaimed. "We're going to run out of land pretty soon."

And Lee knew that was true. They were on a finger of land that pointed out into the collection of highly commercialized basins known as Marina Del Rey. And why would anyone in their right mind choose to put an illegal medical clinic there?

Then, as the blue convertible turned into the Santa Monica Yacht Club's parking lot, alarm bells began to go off in Lee's head. A boat! The messenger was headed for a boat!

The LAPD had boats of its own, of course . . . Like the one that took the team off the beach at Hawthorne. But could she get one in time? And if she did, how could they follow without being noticed?

Yanty pulled into a slot about a hundred feet away from the blue *especiale*, and both of them bailed out. Rather than stick together, they split up to be less noticeable. The suspect was out of her car as well—and carrying a thin briefcase as she made her way out onto a dock. She looked over her shoulder once but didn't look concerned, and the reason for that soon became apparent.

Short of arresting the woman, and running the risk that she wouldn't talk, all Lee could do was stand and watch the courier board a sleek-looking launch. A crewman was there to cast off, and based on how quickly the bow came up, Lee figured the boat was equipped with two inboard engines. Yanty arrived at her side as the launch arrowed away. "Shit, shit, shit."

"That's a good summary," Lee said. "At least we have the car. We'll have it impounded."

"Good idea," Yanty replied, as he eyed his watch. "Then, if you have no objection, I'll buy you a beer."

"Are you going to talk about the Dodgers?"

"No."

"I'm in."

It was Saturday morning and the beginning of what promised to be another beautiful day. So that as Lee rolled out of bed and padded into the condo's living room, the vast sweep of the Pacific Ocean was laid out before her. Under normal circumstances, Kane would be up and preparing breakfast in the kitchen. Then, with steaming plates in hand, they would take them out onto the deck to eat. It would still be in the shade and a bit chilly. But with a jacket on and a hot cup of coffee at hand, Lee would enjoy the view, the food, and the man sitting next to her.

But none of that was going to take place. Kane was still in jail, and likely to remain there, until such time as Codicil could free him. And that was why Lee was scheduled to meet with the lawyer for brunch.

But first there were bills to pay, a load of laundry to do, and some housecleaning if she could manage to cram it in. So Lee prepared a light breakfast and sat down to watch the news. Thanks to the combined efforts of Pacifica and the Republic of Texas, the 'tec army had been pushed out of San Diego and into what had previously been known as Mexico.

That was good. What wasn't so good, not in Lee's opinion, anyway, was the hard line that some of the alliance's politicians were taking. They wanted to punish the Aztecs. To, in the words of one hawk, ". . . push the misbegotten bastards all the way down to the far side of the Panama Canal."

Fortunately, there were others who opposed that agenda. But some of those folks were pushing for a strong alliance between Pacifica and the Republic of Texas. Even going so far as to advocate a merger of some sort. That *sounded* nice, but having spent time in the RZ, Lee knew it was a shit hole, and she couldn't imagine full integration anytime soon.

After breakfast, Lee managed to get in almost two hours' worth of work before changing clothes and heading down to the parking garage. She had a police car at her disposal but wasn't supposed to use it for anything other than official business. And Kane's car was sitting in an impound lot. So Lee had every reason to ride her motorcycle—and was looking forward to it. She threw a leg over the monster and turned the key. The engine roared to life and produced the throaty rumble that she loved to hear.

Lee pulled out of the garage, took a left, and rode north. The Cliff Side Restaurant was located on the far side of Palisades Park just off the Pacific Coast Highway. Traffic was flowing smoothly, and Lee gloried in the feel of it. Maybe she could convince Kane to buy a bike . . . Then they could take a road trip up north and lose themselves among the trees. *You'll have to get him out of the slammer first,* the other her put in.

Even though he lied to me?

He didn't lie to you . . . Not really. But put that aside for a moment. You lied to him. Remember?

Yes, but that was different. I wanted to see my mother, and . . .

And you lied to him about it. So come down off your high horse and find a way to help him. Like he helped you.

You're a pain in the ass.

Look who's talking.

The internal bickering came to an end when Lee spotted a sign, made a right-hand turn, and rode up a steeply sloping driveway into a half-filled parking lot. Once the kickstand was down, Lee placed her helmet on the seat and followed an older couple into the restaurant. It was supposed to look like a home that had been converted into a restaurant, and it did. The interior had a vintage feel even though Lee suspected that the furnishings were fairly new. "A table for one?" the hostess inquired.

"No," Lee replied. "Has Mr. Codicil arrived?"

The hostess eyed her computer screen. "Yes, he has . . . Cindy will take you to his table."

Cindy was a bright-looking teenager with braces and a ponytail. Lee followed her to one of the tables along the west side of the restaurant. It looked down onto the highway and the ocean beyond. Codicil stood until she was seated. The attorney was bald on top, with white hair that was combed back along both sides of his head. His cheeks were hollow which made his face look gaunt. A pair of glasses, a pencil-thin mustache, and a neat goatee completed the look. He was dressed in a blue polo shirt and khaki pants. "Good morning," Codicil said. "It's good to see you."

"You, too," Lee said. "This seems like a nice restaurant. I've never been here before."

"I'm glad you like it," Codicil replied. "They have a good buffet if you're interested."

Lee wasn't much of a buffet fan, so she eyed the menu, and spotted a dish called *Huevos a la Mexicana*. Or Mexican scrambled eggs. And that's what she ordered.

"So," Codicil said as he sipped his coffee. "Lawrence sends his regards. I think he wanted to say more, a *lot* more, but couldn't imagine the words passing through my lips."

Both of them laughed. "How's he doing?" Lee inquired.

"He's a good listener," Codicil replied. "So other inmates are lining up to tell Lawrence their troubles."

"That's good," Lee commented. "He could use a protector or two. I feel badly about this . . . It's my fault."

Codicil's eyebrows rose. "*Your* fault? How so?"

"I gave him the gun. That's what got him arrested."

"*Au contraire, ma cher,*" Codicil countered. "Two men attacked a girl. *That's* what led to his arrest. Lawrence saw what they were up to and tried to help. Do you really believe that he would have remained in his car if he'd been unarmed?"

"No," Lee admitted.

"So," Codicil said, as if addressing a jury, "had it not been for the weapon he was carrying that night, Lawrence might very well be dead."

Lee knew that was true and allowed herself to take some comfort from Codicil's words. She smiled. "Okay, point taken. So how are we doing?"

Codicil frowned. "Not very well I'm afraid. The fact that we don't have any witnesses to support Lawrence's version of what took place puts us in a tough spot. All I can do is stall, push the trial date out as far as I can, and hope that something breaks our way."

Both were silent for a moment. "The woman is out there somewhere," Lee said. "And so is the other man."

"True," Codicil agreed. "But trying to find them is like looking for a needle in a haystack. I hired a private investigator to canvass the neighborhood where the shooting took place, but he came up empty."

"I can't work on it," Lee said. "Not directly. But I'm going to talk to a friend of mine. He might be able to help. So if a guy named Keyes calls you, please put him on the payroll."

"That's all? You won't tell me how Mr. Keyes might be of assistance?"

"Not yet," Lee said, "because I'm not sure myself."

The food arrived at that point, and the conversation resumed once the waiter left. "I have some papers for you to sign," Codicil said as he tackled an order of French toast. "Lawrence wants you to have a *full* power of attorney, so you can manage his affairs. I told him that wasn't necessary, and that a limited POA would be adequate, but he insisted. 'I trust Cassandra,' he said. 'She'll do all the right things.'"

Lee saw the expression on Codicil's face and knew he was

sending her a message. The unlimited POA was more than a legal document—it was Kane's way of telling her how he felt. She wanted to cry but didn't. "Okay, if that's what he wants. Tell him I'll use it to get his car out of hock."

"That will make him happy," Codicil predicted. "I think he likes that car almost as much as he likes you."

There was more, but nothing of consequence, and Lee enjoyed the meal. Once the dishes were cleared, Codicil summoned two restaurant employees to serve as witnesses, had Lee sign three copies of the document, and affixed his own signature as well.

After they said their good-byes, and parted company at the front door, Lee went to her bike. Her copy of the POA went into one of the motorcycle's panniers. Then she made a call. Keyes answered on the second ring. "Yeah?"

"This is Cassandra. Are you home? And, if you are, can I come by?"

"Sure," Keyes answered. "I'll be here . . . How about bringing me a pizza? Make it a large, so I can get two meals out of it."

"How about a medium and a salad?" Lee countered. "And you can still get two meals out of it."

"Thanks, Mom," Keyes replied. "Thin crust please." Then he hung up.

It took Lee more than an hour to make the trip to Chinatown, purchase the food, and take it to Keyes's walk-up. Lee suspected that the pizza was a bit lopsided after being transported on its side in one of the motorcycle's panniers but didn't think her friend would mind. And if the salad hadn't been tossed prior to the ride, it was by the time she arrived at Keyes's door.

Lee pressed the intercom button, heard the camera whir as Keyes confirmed her identity, and waited for the ensuing click. Once the lock was released, she entered the vestibule and began the long climb up to the second-floor apartment. The door was open, and, once inside, Lee saw that everything looked the same. Which was to say, piled high with junk.

Lee followed the winding path toward the front of the apartment, where Keyes was sitting in his wheelchair watching a soccer game. He made use of a remote to turn the sound down. "The pizza lady! Thank you."

"*De nada*," Lee said, as she placed the food on a cluttered table. "How's it going?"

Keyes shrugged. "Business is a little slow right now . . . People are still trying to recover from the attack."

"I might have some work for you," Lee said, "if you think the project is feasible."

The next fifteen minutes were spent filling Keyes in on Kane, the shooting, and the uphill battle to free him. "I'm sorry to hear that," Keyes said, once she was finished. "But where do I fit in?"

"I want you to use your computer savvy to find the missing girl," Lee answered. "As well as the other man."

Keyes frowned. "Can you give me some direction here? Some idea of what you have in mind?"

"Sure," Lee replied. "Use social media . . . Search the Internet. Here's the dead man's name," Lee added, as she gave him a slip of paper. "Did someone post something about his death? If so, who? And what did he or she say? And did someone 'like' the posting? And if they did, can you identify them?

"And what about videos related to the attack?" Lee added. "We know that Codicil's PI checked to see if local security cameras caught the shootout. And chances are that the detective in charge of the case did so as well. But just because they came up empty doesn't mean the footage doesn't exist. How about the people stuck in the traffic jam? Maybe one of them shot the incident with their cell phone. There are a lot of possibilities, and if you accept the assignment, I expect you to examine every one of them."

Keyes's expression had brightened by then. "Yeah . . . I see where you're headed. I'm in."

"Excellent. Mr. Codicil's name and number are on the piece of paper I gave you. You'll be working for him, not for me, and he's expecting your call. So get in touch and provide him with regular reports."

"Right . . . Got it."

Lee looked into Keyes's eyes. "This means a lot to me Ebert."

He nodded. "Don't worry . . . I'm on it."

The crowd roared as Portland scored a goal on San Francisco. Lee got up to go as Keyes turned his attention to the game. Keyes was reaching for the pizza as she left. The salad was untouched.

SIX

t was raining. That was good for lawns, for the farms east of LA, and for the area's water-starved reservoirs. But driving was dangerous because the city's drivers seemed to have forgotten how to navigate slick streets—and Lee could hear a continual stream of accident reports coming in over the radio. With that in mind, she was careful to maintain a generous space cushion between her car and the one in front of her.

After the meetings with Codicil and Keyes on Saturday, half of Sunday had been spent rescuing Kane's sports car from the impound lot, a laborious process made even worse by the fact that the cretin on duty didn't know what a POA was.

But after an hour-long struggle, she'd been allowed to drive the *especiale* off the lot. Then, knowing how Kane felt about the vehicle, she had the interior cleaned and vacuumed before taking it home. Would Kane be allowed to drive it soon? Lee hoped so but knew it was too early to expect any news from Codicil.

The sedan's windshield wipers squeaked rhythmically as Lee turned onto the road that led to the Street Services Garage. Then she had to wait for the vehicle in front of her to clear security before showing her ID. After passing through the checkpoint, Lee went looking for a place to park. Predictably enough, the slots closest to the building's entrance were full—so Lee had no choice but to get out and make a run for it. Her clothes were damp by the time she got inside and was asked to show her ID again.

From there it was a straight shot down the central corridor to her desk. Yanty was waiting for her, as was a hot cup of coffee. "Thanks," Lee said, as she put her bag down. "How did you know I was here?"

"I'm a detective," Yanty said mysteriously. "And I wanted to catch you before roll call."

"Yeah? What's up?"

"ABCO sent another request to TransLab, and they notified me. The test results will arrive at Joe Pody's storefront later today."

"Sweet!" Lee said. "So we're going to get another chance."

"Correct," Yanty replied. "And we're going to need a shitload of resources."

"Which is why you wanted to see me prior to roll call," Lee said as she took a tentative sip of coffee.

"Exactamundo."

"How about the ABCO car? The one the courier left at Marina Del Rey? Any luck with that?"

Yanty made a face. "It was stolen."

"Prints?"

"Nope. Judging from the powder residue left on the steering wheel, *la chica* was wearing surgical gloves. But never fear . . . This time we'll have an edge."

"Which is?"

"TransLabs agreed to put a tracker in the envelope along with the lab report."

Lee laughed out loud. "You're a genius! Nice work."

"If I were a genius, I would have thought of it before," Yanty said disgustedly.

"Bullshit. There was no apparent need. We thought she'd lead us to a building rather than a boat. So how should we play it? Do we follow her to the face place and crash the party? Or should we follow her to ABCO HQ and come back later?"

"I like plan two," Yanty responded. "That way we can scout the building first. Then, once we know what we're up against, we take 'em down."

"Makes sense," Lee agreed. "That's what I'll pitch to Wolfe. Is Prospo on board?"

"Yup . . . He's up to speed."

"Super. Let's do this thing."

Acting Assistant Chief Briana Wolfe was in charge of roll call—and looked like a police recruiting poster complete with a blond crew cut, high cheekbones, and a perfectly tailored suit. "Listen up, people," she said. "Those of you who forgot to qualify at the range need to transport your butts over there . . . And get your flu shots. Don't make Sergeant Thobo hunt you down. You'll be sorry if you do. Then there's the matter of performance reviews, which are due on the fifth. I'm looking at *you*, Detective Lee . . ."

Once the routine stuff was out of the way, Wolfe went around the room so that each lead detective could give his or her report on their team's current activities. When it was Lee's turn, she brought the group up to date on the face case, being careful to credit Yanty and Prospo as she did so. "So," she said, "we're going to get a second chance to follow the courier later today. But in order to track her, we'll need an unmarked boat with a drone on active standby."

"What?" Wolfe demanded. "No submarine?"

That got some laughs, and Lee smiled. "No, ma'am. But thanks for the offer."

Wolfe nodded. "See me after roll call . . . I'll help with the logistics."

At that point, Lee was prepared to sit back and let her mind wander. But the report from Detective Sanders piqued her interest. It seemed that Sanders and his team had been working on Operation Roundup. That was the name given to the effort to find Aztec soldiers who had been separated from their units and were hiding in south LA.

"This guy's name is Camacho," Sanders said. "We found him hiding in the attic of an abandoned house. He'd been wounded, an infection had set in, and the poor bastard was dying. It was difficult to get a statement because he kept drifting in and out of consciousness. And when Camacho did speak, he rambled on about underground tunnels, a room filled with bones, and a normale who wasn't normal. But the so-what of this is that three soldiers were with him. And, since they aren't in custody, it seems safe to assume that they're still on the loose. So please ask your people to keep an eye out for them. The patrol divisions have been notified."

Lee raised a hand. Wolfe nodded. "Yes?"

"A question . . . Did this guy survive? And if so, where is he? I'd like to speak with him . . . Or try to."

"We sent him off to the hospital," Sanders said. "And he pulled through. I lost track of him after that. Why?"

"I was wondering if he was one of the 'tecs we fought down in Hawthorne," Lee replied.

It was a lame story but enough to get by with since none of her peers cared. And that was fortunate since Lee didn't want them to know that she was thinking about the Bonebreaker. The possibility was so tenuous as to be laughable. But later, as soon as she could find the time, Lee planned to find Camacho and hear what he had to say.

Voices droned, and Lee allowed her thoughts to drift. Two motorcycles and a road that led north. That would make her happy.

Jenkins was seated in Chief Corso's interim office which, unlike the one at LAPD headquarters, was small and plain. Jenkins had viewed the material on the Getty drive twice since Lee had given it to him. But Chief Corso was viewing the tapes for the first time—and all the deputy chief could do was sit and wait.

Finally, after watching the final segment, Corso clicked pause and leaned back in his chair. "That," he said, "is fucking unbelievable. No, wait . . . I take that back. Actually, it's quite believable in that it explains some of the mayor's most surprising victories. Take the transit deal for example . . . That was slick."

Jenkins nodded. "Yeah, that's what I thought. So what should we do about it?"

Corso's eyes narrowed. "We have to take action. No doubt about it . . . Imagine what the press would say if they found out that we had this stuff and had been sitting on it."

Jenkins wasn't surprised. Launching an investigation was not only the right thing to do, it was the *smart* thing to do, especially if Corso wanted to run for mayor himself. And everyone knew he did. "Okay," Jenkins replied. "What do you have in mind?"

"I'll take it to the DA," Corso promised, "but he'll want corroborating testimony from at least some of the people on those tapes."

"They won't want to provide it," Jenkins predicted.

"Of course they won't," Corso agreed, "but maybe Lee can find some people who'd be willing to sacrifice Getty in order to save themselves."

"*Lee?* Why Lee?"

"Lee's already in the loop, and she has an enormous set of balls," Corso replied.

Jenkins was pretty sure that Corso's comment was in violation of the department's HR guidelines but wasn't about to tell the chief that. "Yes, sir . . . I'll let her know."

The rain had stopped, the sun was out, and the air inside the creeper was humid. True to her word, Wolfe helped Lee arrange for the necessary logistics. So the tech heads were ready to provide real-time tracking support, a remotely piloted drone from the Air Services Division was sitting on the runway, and an unmarked boat provided by the Harbor Patrol was waiting at Marina Del Rey. And by pulling Prospo off the Bonebreaker case for the day, Lee could field *two* chase cars instead of one.

So when two o'clock rolled around, and the TransLab messenger dropped the test results off at Joe Pody's storefront, they were ready. Lee and Yanty were positioned on the opposite side of the street as they had been before—and Prospo was half a block away in a supermarket parking lot. There were still reasons for worry, however. What if the ABCO courier changed her MO? What if she made, or appeared to make, a handoff, forcing Lee to stay on the first suspect or divide her forces between two targets? There were all sorts of possibilities. But all Lee could do was hope for the best as time passed, and she continued to sweat.

Lee was busy worrying and watching when Yanty's phone rang. "Yanty."

Lee looked at the other detective and saw him nod. "A white male with a shaved head. Got it. Thanks."

Lee raised the binoculars in time to see the suspect emerge from the store and enter an old pickup truck. The front plate was visible so she called it in. "This is 1-William-3 looking for wants or warrants on California plate Boy-Boy-Mary-two-nine-one."

Yanty started the engine as Lee made use of a handheld radio to alert Prospo. "The suspect entered a gray pickup with California plates Boy-Boy-Mary-two-nine-one. He pulled out of the lot and is turning onto Culver Boulevard westbound. We're on his six, two cars back. Be ready to pull up and take over."

"Got it," Prospo replied. "I'm coming up behind you."

There was a squawk of static as the police dispatcher spoke. "That is a stolen vehicle 1-William-3."

"Thanks," Lee replied, and dropped the mike into her lap. Although the courier was new, ABCO was using the same routine. Lee hurried to update Air Services and the Harbor Patrol before turning her attention back to the chase.

The new guy was either a more aggressive driver than his predecessor had been, or was a lot more skittish and determined to lose a tail if there was one. He had a tendency to switch lanes without signaling and put the hammer down in order to slide through yellow lights.

That forced Yanty to close the gap—and gave Lee reason to contact Prospo. "The suspect is kind of jittery," she said. "Let's switch off." Prospo clicked his mike by way of an acknowledgment and passed the first car a few seconds later.

Lee had a decision to make. The suspect was headed toward the coast, so maybe he was going to dump the truck and jump on a boat the way the previous messenger had. If so, it would be necessary to get the drone up early enough to take station over Marina Del Rey. But if Lee was wrong, and sent the RPV up too early, it could run low on fuel later on. All she could do was guess. The confirmation came back right away. "Roger that, 1-William-3. Your sky eye is taking off and will be on station sixteen from now. Over."

Like the first courier, the second one turned onto the Pacific Coast Highway and headed north. But, rather than exit onto Mindanao, *this* suspect took the next left and followed Bali Way out toward the water. Lee figured he was committed at that point and hurried to let the Harbor Patrol know.

Sergeant Hal Dexter was ready and acknowledged her request right away. "Bali Way . . . Got it. We're headed for the marina now. We'll tie up to the guest dock. Our boat is blue over white with a Bimini top and two outboards. Don't forget your sunscreen."

Lee couldn't help but smile. "Roger that."

"The suspect pulled into the marina's parking lot," Prospo announced. "Now he's getting out. He's holding a folder in his hand and he's headed for the basin on the north side of Bali."

"Tail him," Lee instructed. "And give us a description of the boat he gets into. We'll go straight to the visitor's dock. After we leave, secure the pickup truck and have it dusted for prints." Prospo clicked his mike twice.

Lee and Yanty got out of the sedan, locked it, and made for the water. It was a short walk, and Lee resisted the temptation to hurry. She could see Prospo up ahead and the suspect in the distance. It looked as though *all* of them were headed for the visitor's dock. Well, there was nothing wrong with that since boats were coming and going.

As the suspect walked down a metal ramp, Lee spotted the same launch ABCO's courier had used before. It was tied to the floating dock, and she could hear the burbling sound that its engines made. Meanwhile, off to the right, the unmarked police boat was visible. A man wearing a ball cap, tee shirt, and board shorts was busy fiddling with a mooring line. An act that put him on the dock where he could cast off quickly.

A young woman was standing in the boat's stern. She had black hair, a trim body, and was dressed in a modest two-piece bathing suit. Lee, on the other hand, was wearing a tee, jacket, and jeans. None of which were a fit with the situation. She waved and the woman waved back.

As Lee stepped onto the dock, she felt it heave as the wake from a cabin cruiser hit it. The man straightened and turned to greet them. He had blue eyes, even features, and a deep tan. There were crinkle lines around his eyes. "Cassandra! Dick! It's good to see you! Are you ready for a spin?"

Lee said that she was and allowed herself to be shown aboard the speedboat. "This is officer Carrie Soko," Dexter said. "She's ex–coast guard and a sharp cookie. Soko, meet Detectives Lee and Yanty."

Soko had Eurasian features and a no-nonsense demeanor. "It's a pleasure," she said. "Can both of you swim?"

Both detectives indicated that they could. "Good," Soko said. "The life jackets are located in the bins on both sides of the boat. The seat that runs across the stern is an arms locker. Should the shit hit the fan, lift the lid in order to access four assault rifles and two shotguns. All of them are loaded and ready for use. Do you have any questions?"

The detectives shook their heads. Dexter grinned. "Welcome aboard."

Lee's radio crackled. "You saw the launch?"

"I did."

"Excellent. It's pulling away. Good hunting."

"You heard the man," Lee said. "Let's follow them . . . But hang back. Do you have video from the drone?"

"That's affirmative," Soko said, as she took her place behind the wheel and pointed to a screen.

"Good," Lee replied. "Get Air Services on the horn, tell them which boat to follow, and let the bird lead the way."

Dexter had freed the boat by then and had just stepped aboard when Soko applied power and put the wheel over. Lee felt the bow come up a few seconds later and saw waves roll away from the hull as the boat cut through the water. Now, with Soko handling communications, Lee had time to appreciate the view.

The water was blue and sparkled with reflected sunlight. Boats of every possible description were crisscrossing the harbor. Some, like the police boat, were pounding through the waves. Not the sailboats though . . . They seemed to glide through the water as if speed was unimportant and the process was paramount.

Beyond the boats, high-rise towers stood by themselves or in clusters. Most were intact, but some had been damaged during the shelling. Lee was reminded of the building that *she* lived in, and of Kane, who would enjoy being on the water. Dexter forced her thoughts back to the problem at hand. "It looks like we're headed out to sea," he observed.

Lee frowned. "Out to sea? That's strange."

"Maybe the launch is going to meet up with a larger boat," Dexter suggested.

But that didn't happen. Instead, the launch made a gradual turn to the south. And as the trip wore on, they passed El Segundo on the left, followed by a string of beach towns, and the Palos Verdes Peninsula. Consistent with her orders, Soko was staying well back—and using the drone to maintain visual contact with ABCO's launch. Could the suspects see the RPV? Maybe . . . But that was unlikely since it was only three feet long and would look like a dot from below.

Lee was sitting on top of the arms locker when Dexter came back to join her. "We're entering the Long Beach Police Department's turf now . . . I need to let them know that we're in the hood."

"Okay," Lee said. "But don't provide any more information than you have to. A leak could blow the whole operation."

"I'll do my best," Dexter promised. "But we've got to cover our butts. If we don't, and the LBPD's chief places a call to Corso, the shit will begin to flow. And you know who lives at the bottom of the hill."

Lee laughed. "Roger that . . . Do what you gotta do."

Yanty had been on his cell phone. "This just in," he said. "Prospo talked the folks in the Latent Prints Unit into giving him a preliminary on the pickup. There aren't any prints on the handles, the wheel, and the dash."

"It figures," Lee replied. "These people are consistent if nothing else."

They were passing Terminal Island as Dexter came back to the stern. "The LBPD gave us the green light—and I think I know where the launch is headed."

"Where?"

"The THUMS islands. They're straight ahead."

"THUMS islands? I've never heard of them."

"They're artificial islands that were constructed back in 1965," Dexter explained. "The name stems from a group of oil companies that came together to exploit the East Wilmington Oil

Field. The consortium consisted of Texaco, Humble Oil, Union Oil, Mobile Oil, and Shell Oil. That's where the THUMS name came from. But pumping operations were suspended when the wells ceased to be profitable."

"So the islands are deserted?"

"Yes, and no," Dexter replied. "A millionaire converted one into a private retreat, a research facility is located on the second, a caretaker lives on the third, and there are lots of seagulls on the fourth."

Lee felt a rising sense of excitement. An island, especially one so close to the mainland, would offer ABCO plenty of privacy plus access to organizations like TransLabs. And there was another factor as well. A fast boat could leave the Costa de Playas south of San Diego and arrive off Long Beach in what? Two hours? Something like that.

Yes, the launch would have to evade the coast guard, but drug dealers did it . . . So others could as well. And if authorities stopped the boat, what would they find? No illicit cargo . . . Just a crew of mutants who claimed to be lost. That gave ABCO a good way to get patients in and out of the country.

But why dump a body behind St. Patrick's Church when they could drop it into the bay with a cinder block wired to its ankles? Because the doctor was Catholic, that's why . . . And wanted the body to be buried in the sacred ground of a Catholic cemetery.

That suggested an organization that was something more than a purely criminal enterprise. Or a criminal enterprise which, due to one or more of the personalities who ran it, was a bit quirky. "I think you're onto something," Lee said, as the boat broke through a roller and sent spray flying sideways. "We'll know shortly."

Lee's words proved to be prophetic. Soko delivered the news ten minutes later. She had to shout to be heard. "They're headed straight for the dock on White Island!"

Lee went forward to look at the screen. The drone was high, so the launch looked small but recognizable nevertheless. Yanty joined her as the boat slowed and came alongside the dock. Some nondescript buildings and a cluster of old storage tanks could be seen, along with a scattering of mature palm trees. In order to see more details, the drone would have to lose altitude, which would make the RPV easier to spot.

"Okay," Lee said. "Mission accomplished. We'll work with the LBPD to set up a raid. In the meantime, tell Air Services that they can have their bird back—and to preserve the video for use in court."

"Will do," Soko said as she reached for the mike. "Are we headed home?"

"Yes," Lee told her, and had to hang onto a support as Soko put the wheel over. Unfortunately, home was just a place to sleep until Kane was released. And there wasn't a damned thing she could do about it.

Desperate times call for desperate measures. That's what the Bonebreaker told himself as he stopped in front of the old bungalow. It was one of many older homes in the West Adams section of Los Angeles. It was around 10:00 P.M., and a partial blackout was still in place even though it seemed likely that the Aztecs already knew where all of the juicy targets were. But the citizens of Los Angeles weren't required to cover their windows— and the flickering light of a television set could be seen through the home's curtains.

The purpose of the visit was to murder retired Criminologist Alan Penn as an interim step to killing Cassandra Lee. And as the Bonebreaker climbed the cracked concrete stairs that led up to Penn's porch, he was carrying a suitcase with his left hand and holding a long-barreled .22 pistol down along his right leg.

Once on the porch, the Bonebreaker rang the bell and was rewarded with the sound of a distant chime. He could also hear the rumble of what he presumed to be Dr. Penn's television set. Sixty seconds passed without any response. Was Penn hard of hearing? He was eighty-six years old after all. Rather than press the button again, the Bonebreaker tried the door. It was unlocked! A practice that was practically unheard of in LA and a surprise given the nature of Penn's profession. But maybe the criminologist had grown a bit forgetful . . . Or maybe it was God's will. A sign that the Bonebreaker was on the right track. *Yes,* the Bonebreaker thought to himself as he entered the foyer, *wondrous are the ways of the Lord.*

The Bonebreaker put the suitcase down prior to entering a shabby living room. All of the furnishings were at least thirty years old, there were too many of them, and there was a lot of clutter. That wasn't surprising given Penn's age and the fact that his wife had been in poor health prior to her death a month earlier. All of which had been learned by combing online obituaries searching for a man with the right sort of background.

And there, sitting on a recliner, was Professor Penn. He was dressed in a plaid robe and pajamas. His eyes were closed, and had it not been for the regular rise and fall of his chest, the Bonebreaker would have believed him to be dead.

So it was easy to walk around the chair, turn his back to the flat-screen TV above the fireplace, and raise the pistol. Instead of a head shot, which might splatter brain matter onto the chair, the Bonebreaker elected to shoot Penn in the heart. The theory was that since the .22 caliber bullets weren't that powerful, there was a reasonable chance they wouldn't go all the way through.

Thanks to the suppressor attached to the pistol's barrel, the weapon made very little noise. There were two pops, neither of which could be heard over the sound produced by the TV set. Penn jerked slightly as the bullets struck him but remained as he was. "Go to the Lord and join your wife in heaven," the Bonebreaker said kindly. "Your work is done."

But *his* work was just beginning. The Bonebreaker took a quick tour of the home to make sure that Penn didn't have any houseguests before returning to the foyer to retrieve the suitcase. He carried it into the living room and opened the lid. All sorts of things were stored inside, one of which was a camera.

There was a series of flashes as the Bonebreaker took pictures of Penn's face from a variety of angles. By doing so quickly, within minutes of Penn's death, he hoped to capture the most current likeness possible. Images that could be used to perfect the Penn-like countenance that he was wearing. Based on the articles the Bonebreaker had read, he knew that Dr. and Mrs. Penn had been childless. So assuming that everything went according to plan, he wouldn't have to fool anyone other than the neighbors and Cassandra Lee. And there was no reason to believe that she knew the man.

Once the photo shoot was over, the Bonebreaker faced the difficult task of dragging the body down a short flight of stairs to the door that opened onto a one-car garage. It was full of junk— but a path led to the front of the house and the garage door. The Bonebreaker had Penn by the ankles, and as he backed away from the door, the old man's head bounced over the threshold.

Once the corpse was positioned just inside the garage door, it was time to locate Penn's car keys. The Bonebreaker found them in the pocket of a jacket that was hanging on a hook in the upstairs hall. The Bonebreaker felt confident that he would look like Penn from a distance as he got into the car and drove away. It was the perfect opportunity to pick up some food at a nearby grocery store—and the brown sack would explain his errand should any of Penn's neighbors see him return to the house. Would they take note of the fact that he *backed* in? No, if they noticed anything, it was likely to be the fact that Dr. Penn was out and about late at night. And that was a risk that the Bonebreaker would have to take.

After carrying the groceries into the house, the Bonebreaker returned to the garage, where he was careful to leave the light off as he opened the door to the deeply shadowed driveway. Then it was a simple matter to open the car's trunk and heave the body inside. There was a soft thump as he closed the lid.

With that accomplished, the Bonebreaker reentered the garage and made his way upstairs. It would definitely look suspicious if a snoopy neighbor saw Penn head out a *second* time, and even later at night, but there was no need. Not yet. So the Bonebreaker had time to kill.

The kitchen sink was full of dirty dishes, so he washed them before heating up a can of chicken noodle soup on the range. Then, having placed a bowl, spoon, and some melba toast on a tray, he carried it into the living room, where the TV was still going full blast. Once the recliner was in the "up" position, it made a good place to sit and have dinner while watching a program about fishing. He'd never been fishing but thought he would enjoy the sport if given the opportunity.

Time passed and it was well past two in the morning when

the Bonebreaker left the house, locked the door behind him, and got in the car. A quick check confirmed that the gas tank was half-full. The Bonebreaker figured that the biggest threat was one of the random roadblocks intended to intercept Aztec saboteurs. But with his disguise in place, and Dr. Penn's wallet in his pocket, the Bonebreaker was confident that he could con the average traffic cop.

The car had a nav system, which the Bonebreaker used to get onto Interstate 10 to Interstate 5 bound for Fullerton. The city was much darker than usual because of the partial blackout, but that didn't prevent the enemy from launching missiles into the area, and the Bonebreaker saw the flash of an explosion in the distance as he drove along. That was followed by what sounded like thunder. The whole business of disposing of bodies was an important topic—and one that the Bonebreaker felt Dr. Penn would find interesting even if the corpse was his.

In most cases, the Bonebreaker wanted his victims to be found as part of the war he was waging on certain members of the LAPD. There had been other murders, of course . . . The mailman in Compton came to mind. But those killings were incidental, and up until now, the corpses had been left wherever they happened to fall.

But Penn was different in that the Bonebreaker planned to *become* the criminologist for an extended period of time. And in order to do that, it would be necessary to get rid of the body in such a way that nobody would find it, or failing that, be able to identify it.

So to make sure that would happen, the Bonebreaker had dedicated a great deal of time to figuring out how to make the body disappear. The plan was to put Dr. Penn's corpse on a freight train headed east into the red zone. If things went the way he hoped they would, the body would remain undiscovered. However, even if someone in the RZ found the body, the Bonebreaker felt sure that the lack of coordination between law enforcement in the Republic of Texas and Pacifica meant that weeks if not months would pass before the dead man was identified.

But how to get the body onto an eastbound train? And not

just *any* train, but a train that included open ore cars, into which the body could be dumped. Figuring that out required the Bonebreaker to research schedules, routes, and deserted drop points. A time-consuming process.

But as the Bonebreaker arrived in Fullerton and followed a mostly deserted street into the city's industrial area, he felt that the effort had been worthwhile. Timing was everything now . . . Timing and luck. Because in spite of his careful preparations, the train could be late, a cop car could be sitting on the overpass for some reason, or any of a dozen other things could go wrong.

So the Bonebreaker's heart had started to pound, and his palms were sweaty as he took the necessary turn and drove out onto the overpass, where he stopped and switched on the emergency flashers. They would help to explain his presence and prevent the possibility of an accident. A quick check of his watch confirmed that he was on time.

The next step was to raise the car's hood. Then, should someone stop to help him, the Bonebreaker would claim to have fixed the problem and prove it by starting the engine. Hopefully, that wouldn't happen.

With that accomplished, it was time to carry out the most difficult part of the plan. And that was to open the trunk and remove the body. There had been no traffic thus far—and the Bonebreaker was running on time. But what about the train? The Bonebreaker felt a sudden surge of adrenaline as he heard the mournful sound of the locomotive's horn—and saw two vertically stacked headlights appear in the distance. So far so good.

After a final look around, the Bonebreaker stooped to lift the body. The easiest way to accomplish that was to cradle it with one arm under Penn's thighs and the other supporting the dead man's back. Then it was time to carry the criminologist over to the concrete railing. It seemed natural to swing Penn's feet out over the edge and seat him facing the oncoming train.

So far so good . . . But pushing the body off at the right moment would be critical. Because if the Bonebreaker missed, and the corpse wound up on the tracks, he'd have to abort the plan and return to the ossuary.

Then the critical moment was upon him as the locomotive

roared at him and disappeared. Box cars flashed by below forcing the Bonebreaker to wait for the ore cars. They were supposed to be there. *Had* to be there—or he was screwed. The light level was low due to the blackout, which was why the Bonebreaker failed to realize that the target cars were there until the first one rattled under him.

That was when the Bonebreaker realized how stupid he'd been and how difficult the task actually was. He had to try though and knew timing was the key. So he waited for the moment when an empty car was just starting to disappear under his feet and gave Dr. Penn a hearty push.

The body tilted forward as it fell, hit the leading edge of the *next* car, and performed a somersault in the air. The Bonebreaker watched in horror as the corpse seemed to defy gravity. Then the moment ended as the body disappeared into the ore car's open maw. *Or had it?* As the car disappeared under him the Bonebreaker strained his eyes in a futile effort to see if a body lay on either side of the tracks. But that was impossible with the train in the way.

All the Bonebreaker could do was wait for five agonizing minutes as the rest of the train rattled east. Then, by aiming a powerful flashlight at the tracks, the Bonebreaker was able to confirm that the corpse wasn't there. A truck passed him at that point but didn't slow down.

The Bonebreaker felt a sense of satisfaction. The train would arrive in the RZ in what? Twelve hours or so? Maybe, if he was lucky, the muties would dump a load of ore on top of the body. But it didn't really matter. He was going to get the time that he needed . . . And Cassandra Lee was going to die.

SEVEN

Cassandra Lee's day was off to a bad start. For the first time in weeks, she had overslept. As a result, she arrived at Maria's late, was forced to eat her breakfast burrito at work, and missed roll call. The shit show continued with a snarky e-mail from Assistant Chief Wolfe, who offered to buy her a new alarm clock.

So there she was, sitting at her desk and shoveling a bite of lukewarm burrito into her mouth, when Jenkins materialized next to her. "There you are," he said. "Do you ever check voice mail? You were due in my office ten minutes ago. Come with me, and yes, you can bring that disgusting mess with you."

Lee trailed along behind Jenkins as he led her to his office, waved her inside, and paused to close the door. "Uh-oh," Lee said as she watched him circle the desk. "Have I been suspended again?"

"You sound like someone with a guilty conscience," Jenkins observed. "So stop doing whatever it is that I wouldn't approve of. And no, you haven't been suspended. You have a new case, though . . . A very important case that Chief Corso selected you to work on."

"Like what? Did his dog run away or something?"

Jenkins shook his head sorrowfully. "You need an attitude adjustment, Lee . . . But that would take years. Remember the thumb drive? The one you gave me?"

Lee put the styrofoam container aside. "You must be kidding . . . Corso's going after Getty?"

"Of course he's going after Getty," Jenkins replied matter-of-factly. "It's the right thing to do. He took the thumb drive to the DA, who wants to file charges."

"He's going to convene a grand jury?"

"Nope. First the DA wants to churn things up. Maybe one of the principals will roll over. That would make the DA's job easier. And that's where *you* come in. Go out there, shake the trees, and wait for someone to fall out."

"That's a suicide mission," Lee objected. "The first person I talk to will notify the mayor, she'll go ape shit, and order Corso to fire me. Then somebody will leak information to the press, and they'll be on me like white on rice."

The chair squeaked as Jenkins leaned back in it. There was a big, shit-eating smile on his face. "So? What's your point?"

All sorts of things blipped through Lee's mind. Then she had it. Corso wanted to run for mayor! Everybody knew that. And here, like manna from heaven, was the perfect opportunity to neutralize Getty *and* do the right thing! As for Jenkins, maybe he'd have a shot at the top cop job. "So I'm going to be used as a tool."

"All of us are tools to one extent or another," Jenkins replied philosophically. "But you should feel good about this. This sucker is going to take a lot of skill, not to mention chutzpah, and you were handpicked for the job."

Lee stared at him. "I need to wrap the face case . . . And the Bonebreaker's still on the loose."

"Raid the island," Jenkins said. "And then you can put Yanty and Prospo back on the Bonebreaker full-time. Are you satisfied?"

"Do I have a choice?"

"No."

"Okay," Lee said. "Then I'm satisfied." The meeting was over.

After leaving Jenkins's office, Lee threw the rest of her breakfast into a trash can and went to see Yanty. He was on the phone when Lee arrived, so she sat down. "Okay," Yanty said, "I appreciate your cooperation, and I'll see you at 0400."

Then, as he put the receiver down, Yanty said, "Asshole."

Lee laughed. "Who was that?"

"Lieutenant Iffy in Long Beach. He wanted to launch the raid at 0500, so the press wouldn't have to get up earlier."

Lee frowned. "The press?"

"Yeah," Yanty replied. "The LBPD plans to take major credit for the bust. Fortunately, they're willing to let us come along as observers."

"You're joking."

"No, ma'am, I'm not."

Lee sighed. "Okay . . . The main thing is nail the perps. I heard you say four in the morning. Are we talking about *tomorrow* morning?"

"Yes we are," Yanty said with a smirk. "Try to be on time."

"You're a dick, Dick."

Yanty grinned happily. "Deal with it."

Marvin Codicil had a secret. Something he couldn't tell anyone, not if he wanted to live in Pacifica, and that was the fact that he was a mutant. But a lucky mutant if such a thing existed—since his mutation was hidden *inside* his body.

Fortunately for Codicil, the doctor who discovered the anomaly was a very nice man. "You aren't a carrier," the doctor assured him. "But you are a mutant. A third kidney is growing between the other two. That shouldn't cause you any distress, and odds are that you'll die of something else. But the mutation could be a harbinger of things to come. So examine yourself on a frequent basis and seek help if you see unusual changes. In the meantime, I recommend that you keep this condition to yourself."

And Codicil *had* kept the condition to himself. But it was a constant source of concern. So he had taken to scrutinizing his body with a battery of highly specialized mirrors, scanning for any sign of an incipient horn, the beginnings of a tail, or a sudden manifestation of scales. There hadn't been any, thank God, but Codicil awoke each morning frightened of what he might discover.

After completing his daily inspection, Codicil got dressed,

ate a light breakfast, and went to work. Not to his office—that would come later. No, Codicil had an appointment to meet with Ebert Keyes at that individual's place of business. Or was it his residence?

That wasn't entirely necessary, of course, since whatever information Keyes had could be conveyed electronically. But Codicil was curious. What sort of person would he be dealing with? And were Cassandra Lee's expectations of the man realistic? Codicil hoped so because, in spite of his best efforts to free Kane, the psychologist was still behind bars.

So Codicil drove to Chinatown, left his car in a lot, and completed the journey on foot. The area was anything but prosperous. And when Codicil arrived, it was to find that the entrance to Keyes's apartment was located between the Sue Yong nail salon, and an empty store with a for rent sign in the window.

Codicil pressed the intercom button and spoke his name into the grill. The camera mounted above his head whirred, moved fractionally, and stopped. Codicil heard a click and pulled the door open. A narrow flight of stairs led up to the second floor, where another door stood slightly ajar. It was equipped with a waist-high gun port. Codicil pushed the door open and was shocked to see the head-high piles of junk that filled most of the room. It appeared that Keyes was a hoarder, and that didn't bode well. The lawyer's spirits fell accordingly. "Mr. Keyes?" he called out. "Can I come in?"

"I'm up front," a voice replied. "Follow the trail."

Codicil did as he was told and soon found himself face-to-face with Ebert Keyes. The computer expert had a head of untamed hair, a bushy beard, and was seated in a powered wheelchair. "Please excuse me if I don't get up," Keyes said, and as Codicil went forward to shake hands, he sensed that the line had been used thousands of times before. It was an icebreaker of sorts . . . A way for Keyes to acknowledge his missing legs and put strangers at ease.

"Sorry about the mess," Keyes said, as they shook hands. "My maid took the day off. There's a chair under that pizza box . . . Take a load off."

Codicil put the empty box aside and sat down. "It's a

pleasure," he lied. "Cassandra thinks highly of you."

"And I think highly of her," Keyes replied.

Codicil thought he detected a subtle change in Keyes's expression at that point. A softening, a wistfulness perhaps, and that led to a flash of intuition. Keyes had a crush on Lee! The kind of hopeless love described in romance novels. *And that, Codicil decided, is why Keyes agreed to work on this project. For the money, yes, but to please Lee as well. Even if that means giving her to someone else.*

"So," Codicil said, "you have a lead for me? That would be wonderful."

"Yes," Keyes replied. "I do. Come over and take a look at this."

Codicil stood and went over to look at a large computer screen. "As you know, the dead guy's name is Deon Eddy," Keyes said. "Or D-Eddy to his homies. And within twenty-four hours of his death, a memorial page appeared on the *Todos Nosotros* (All of Us) social-media site."

Codicil watched a photo of a young man appear. The subject was posed with his head back, staring down his nose at the camera, and holding a pistol. Could it be *the* pistol? The one Eddy had used to fire at Kane? And was subsequently removed from the crime scene? Yes, it could . . . And even if it *wasn't,* Codicil could use the picture to prove that D-Eddy was the kind of person who liked guns and might carry one. Did he have a permit? Codicil would check but figured the answer would be no. "This is a very important find," Codicil said. "Well done."

"Checking for a memorial page was Cassandra's idea," Keyes replied modestly. "But there's more. Look at the list of people who 'liked' the page and/or posted a comment on it. There are twenty-six altogether—and how much you wanna bet that one of them was with D-Eddy on the street that night?"

"But most of the people who posted are using handles," Codicil objected. "Is there some way to figure out who they are?"

"Been there, done that," Keyes said proudly. "I ran a search on each handle and that turned up thousands of messages, postings, and mentions. As a result, I collected bits and pieces of information on all but seven of the people on the list.

"Take Tufenuf for example . . . I found a posting in which he mentioned a certain high school. Then I used facial-recognition software to scan that school's online yearbooks and came up with a photo that was a 92.2 percent match with Tufenuf's profile picture on *Todos Nosotros*. Once I had his *real* name, it was relatively easy to dig up more stuff, including his mother's address."

"That's terrific!" Codicil said enthusiastically. "Well done! How 'bout the missing girl? Have you had any luck there?"

"Not so far," Keyes admitted. "But I'm working on it."

"Good," Codicil said, as he accepted a thumb drive with all of the data on it. "Please stay in touch."

Keyes nodded. "Tell Cassandra that I said, 'Hi.'"

"I will," Codicil promised. "And, Ebert . . ."

"Yeah?"

"You the man."

The raid was scheduled to begin at 4:00 A.M. But the participants were supposed to attend a briefing at 3:00 A.M. And, since it would take Lee forty-five minutes to get there, she had to get up at 1:15! A horrible prospect—and a personal challenge.

But having been late to work the day before, Lee was determined to arrive on time. Especially since another police department was involved. So she set two alarms. One located next to her bed and another on the far side of the room. They conspired to create a cacophony of noise, and it was necessary to roll out of bed to silence the clock on top of Kane's dresser. With that accomplished she shuffled off to the bathroom.

Forty-five minutes later, Lee had her body armor on and was dressed for what would almost certainly be a cold boat ride. Three magazines for the Glock and two speed loaders for the Smith & Wesson went into her pockets, along with a tube of chapstick and a candy bar.

Then, with a fresh mug of coffee in hand, Lee made her way downstairs to where the creeper was parked. After performing a 360 on the car, she got in and checked her watch. She couldn't go to Maria's since that would be out of her way. But she could stop at a fast-food place before getting on 110 southbound. Intermittent flashes of light were visible off to the south. Was that lightning? Or a barrage of missiles aimed at Camp Pendleton? It was impossible to tell. It seemed that what Yanty referred to as "a three-way pissing match" was at a stalemate for the moment. Negotiations were ongoing, but so-called incidents were taking a steady toll of lives.

There wasn't much traffic, and Lee made such good time that she arrived fifteen minutes early. A personal best. The LBPD's Harbor Patrol unit was housed in a nondescript one-story building adjacent to the terminal's southwest basin. Lee followed the signs into a small lot and parked the sedan in a slot marked visitors. Then, with her ID hanging around her neck, she went inside.

A reception counter sat opposite the door, and Lee could see two desks beyond it. Yanty was sitting in the tiny lobby and rose to greet her. He was dressed for the cold, and it was the first time she'd seen him in something other than a plaid sports coat. "Good morning," he said. "How was the drive?"

"It was fine," Lee replied. "The traffic was light."

Yanty nodded, and Lee could tell that something was bothering him. But what? Before Lee could figure out a way to have a private conversation with him, a man with sandy-colored hair entered the room. He had a round face, the freshly scrubbed look of a scoutmaster, and his tac vest was one size too large. "Right on time!" he said cheerfully. "I like that . . . I'm Lieutenant Iffy. Come on back. We'll brief this thing, run out to the island, and wrap it up."

The officer behind the reception desk lifted a section of counter up and out of the way so that Lee and Yanty could enter the office beyond. From there they followed Iffy into a small meeting room. Four LBPD officers, all dressed in tac gear, were seated around a table. "This is Detective Lee," Iffy told them, "and Detective Yanty. They're going to accompany us as observers."

"Detective Lee, Detective Yanty, please allow me to introduce my team." Iffy pointed a stubby finger at each person as he named them. "That's Toomey, that's Beck, that's Garcia, and that's Perkins."

Lee plastered a smile on her face. "It's a pleasure to meet you guys!" Then, to Iffy, "Is this the entire team?"

"Of course it is," Iffy replied confidently. "How many people will we need to arrest some doctors and nurses? This isn't Los Angeles, you know . . . We don't turn every bust into a movie. Besides," he continued, "we've had the island under surveillance, and the place is practically deserted."

By then Lee knew why Yanty looked concerned. Maybe the raid would be as easy as Iffy said it would be. But what if it wasn't? His little team would be in deep shit, that's what. Lee scanned their faces in an attempt to pick up on what the LBPD officers were thinking. But they had their game faces on and she couldn't tell if they agreed with Iffy or not.

Lee and Yanty were invited to sit down and watch the briefing. It included aerial shots of the island and a look at the way the structures had been laid out before the pumps stopped. The plan was simple: Land and clear what Iffy considered to be the tertiary and secondary structures before tackling the administrative buildings. "That's where the surgical suite will be located," Iffy predicted, "and that's where we'll find most of the evidence.

"Once the island has been secured," he continued, "I'll call for the Scientific Investigation Division to come out and process the place. The press conference is scheduled for 3:00 P.M. in front of the admin building. That will give the TV crews plenty of time to make the five o'clock news."

"TV crews?" Yanty inquired. "Isn't that a bit premature? What if we come up empty?"

"Don't be silly," Iffy responded. "We know the bad guys are there because Detective Lee says they are." The comment was delivered with a shit-eating grin.

So there you have it, Lee told herself. *If the raid is a success, the LBPD looks brilliant . . . And if it fails, the LAPD looks stupid. Lovely.*

"I thought you weren't into movies," she said out loud.

Iffy's face clouded over. He wasn't used to negative feedback, and it showed. "Just do what you're told, Detective Lee . . . And everything will be fine."

"Good luck with that," Yanty said under his breath, but Iffy didn't hear him. He was busy lecturing the LBPD team on the importance of good communications.

After a quick break the team left the building through a back entrance. The air was cold, damp, and heavy with sea scent. The airborne moisture created halos around the streetlights as Iffy split the team in two and sent them into the RIB boats that were waiting at the dock.

Lee followed Toomey down a steep ramp to the floating platform, where she was ordered to board the first inflatable and don a life jacket. That plus three layers of clothes and her body armor made it difficult to move. Yanty waved as he stepped into boat two.

Given how large the boats were, the entire team could have ridden in one of them. But it made sense to take two so that one boat could assist the other if that was necessary.

Once the passengers were seated, an order was given, lines were cast off, and the officer positioned behind the RIB boat's stand-up control station applied power. The twin outboards roared enthusiastically, and it wasn't long before both inflatables were flying over the surface of the water, throwing sheets of spray to port and starboard. Once they left the basin for the rougher waters of the bay, the hulls began to bounce as they hit a steady succession of incoming waves.

Much to Lee's surprise, she discovered that she was having a good time. The combination of speed, adrenaline, and the cold air made for a heady mix as the two boats raced through the early-morning darkness. Off to the port, she could see the glittering lights of Long Beach. They looked like multicolored jewels scattered across black velvet. Thousands of people were still asleep and unaware of the drama about to unfold nearby.

Just the slightest hint of dawn could be seen off to the east as the island's low-lying bulk appeared up ahead. A flashing light marked the top of the highest tank on the island, and as the boat drew closer, Lee could make out what might have been some illuminated windows.

But there were no signs of activity, and it looked as though the bad guys were still in bed. Assuming there were some. What if she was wrong? What if the island was deserted? *No*, Lee told herself, *you watched the courier go there with your own eyes. Don't be silly.*

Both boats slowed as they neared land and wallowed as waves slapped their sides from the west. Lieutenant Iffy stood with his rifle at the ready as Lee's boat crept in next to a floating dock. There weren't any sentries.

Lee had been told to wait until the team was ashore before leaving the boat. So once they were gone, she stepped up and onto the dock where Yanty stood waiting for her. They took off after the team, which had already cleared the boathouse and was following an access road toward the center of the island.

Gravel crunched under Lee's boots, and she could hear the sound of Yanty's labored breathing as the team entered a pool of light. That was when the crack of a rifle shot was heard. Another followed, and two officers fell.

Lee swore as she ran faster. A sniper! Or *two* snipers . . . And as two members of the team fired blindly, the others were trying to tow the casualties out of the killing zone.

Lee heard *another* shot but ignored it as she and Yanty arrived to help with the evacuation. "Over there!" Lee shouted, as she pointed to a small building. "Behind the shed!"

After securing a grip on a victim's tac vest, and with assistance from Perkins, Lee dragged a casualty in behind the shack. Then she dropped to one knee, ready to apply first aid. That was when she saw who the officer was. A large chunk of Iffy's skull was missing, and he was dead.

Lee said, "Shit, shit, shit," as she took Iffy's radio and keyed the mike. "This is Detective Lee with Team White. We have two, repeat *two* officers down, and are taking fire from an unknown number of suspects. Officer requires assistance. Get some reinforcements out here as quickly as you can."

Lee paused as the dispatcher acknowledged the call. She looked at Toomey, who was crouched a few feet away. "How's the other casualty?"

"Beck got hit in the leg," Toomey replied. "But he'll make it."

"Stop the bleeding, and take charge of communications," Lee ordered. "Yanty, take Perkins. Garcia, you're with me."

One or more of the LBPD officers could have objected to her

instructions but none did. Garcia stared at her. "What are we going to do?"

"We'll circle right," Lee replied, "and flank the shooter. Yanty, open fire on that son of a bitch . . . Keep him busy."

Yanty had taken possession of Beck's shotgun by then and stepped out from behind the shed to fire a blast in the general direction of where the rifle fire had originated. The twelve-gauge was the wrong weapon for the purpose, but that didn't matter. The goal was to engage the sniper, and it worked. Yanty barely had time to reach cover before a quick flurry of shots smacked into the east side of the shack.

Confident that Yanty and Perkins would do their part, Lee took off running. Thanks to the maze of oil tanks, pumping stations, and clusters of pipe, there were plenty of places to take cover. Garcia stayed on her six while Lee pursued a zigzag course to the point where the sniper should be. And that was a huge oil tank.

More light was available by then, and Lee could see that the tank was crowned with a circular walkway. And sure enough . . . As Yanty and Perkins drew fire, Lee spotted a muzzle flash high above her. "I've got it," Garcia said. "Give me a moment to set the shot."

That was when Lee noticed that the LBPD officer was carrying a bolt-action sniper's rifle—and realized that he was probably the best shot on the team. "Go for it," Lee said. "I'll provide security."

And that was a necessity. There were bound to be more perps who, thanks to the sniper, had been given time to respond. And as Lee examined her surroundings, she spotted movement off to the right! It looked as if two or three men were trying to work their way over to the shed.

Lee had Iffy's scope-mounted assault rifle and brought it up. If her calculations were correct, the men would have to pass through the open area between the point where a thick pipe disappeared into the ground. If so, she'd be ready. Seconds ticked by, a figure stepped into the gap, and her finger tightened. The rifle butt kicked her shoulder three times, and the perp went down.

The next rifle shot was like an afterthought, and Lee heard Garcia say, "Got him."

"Good work," Lee responded, as she spoke into Iffy's radio. "Hey, Perkins . . . Alvarez nailed the sniper—but keep your head on a swivel. Some bozos are trying to flank you. I shot one of them, but more could be headed your way."

Perkins said, "Roger that. We'll work our way forward."

"What now?" Garcia wanted to know. Having smoked the sniper, he was raring to go.

"Do you have any flash bangs?"

"Affirmative. Two."

"Okay. Give me one of them. On the count of three we'll throw, close our eyes, and go after the guys on the right."

Alvarez gave her a grenade and prepped one of his own. Meanwhile, over to the left, a firefight was under way. A sure sign that Yanty and Perkins were duking it out with someone.

Lee said, "One, two, three," and both flash bangs flew through the air. They landed, bounced, and went off with what sounded like a single bang. The successive flashes were so bright that Lee could see light through her eyelids. Then the team was off and running full speed for the spot where the body was. But when they arrived, there was no one to shoot at. And the man who'd been shot was not only alive but crawling away.

Garcia went forward to secure him, and administer some crude first aid, as a helicopter swept in over the island. There was plenty of light by then, and Lee watched as the LBPD SWAT team slid down a rope like beads on a string. The cavalry had arrived—and they were just west of the administration building. Lee figured that more law-enforcement people would show up shortly because everyone with a badge comes a-running when they hear the words "shots fired" or "officer down" on their radio.

Lee brought Iffy's radio up to her lips. "This is LAPD Detective Lee . . . Can anyone on the LBPD SWAT team read me? Over."

"This is Lieutenant Newsome," a male voice answered. "I read you five-by-five. Can you give me a sitrep? Over."

"Yes. Lieutenant Iffy was killed, and one officer was wounded, but is in stable condition. We killed one perp and wounded another. There are an unknown number of armed suspects in the area around your position. Over."

"Roger that," Newsome began, but never got to say more

as someone opened up on the SWAT team with an automatic weapon. They fired back. "Come on!" Lee yelled. "Let's give those guys a hand."

Yanty and Perkins had joined her by then, and the group began to advance. "There are four of us," Lee said into the radio, "and we're coming up on your position from the south. Don't shoot us."

A full-fledged gun battle was under way at that point. The bang, bang, bang of small-arms fire could be heard over the intermittent chatter of automatic weapons and the occasional boom of a twelve-gauge shotgun. As they got closer Lee could see that the SWAT team was pinned down in and among some large pipes. People were firing on them from inside the structure, and there was a loud explosion as a grenade went off. "Alvarez, find a good position and put some fire on those windows. Perkins, your job is to provide Alvarez with security. Go."

They went. Lee turned to Yanty. "Come on . . . We'll circle east and look for a way in."

"Oh goody," Yanty said. "Bring Prospo next time. I only have six years to go until retirement."

Lee took off running. Yanty did the best he could to stay with her. There was plenty of cover, and it seemed as though the people in the building were so focused on the SWAT team that they were unaware of the flanking effort. So Lee and Yanty were about halfway to their goal when a group of people rounded the corner of the building.

The man in the lead was armed with a submachine gun. He tried to bring the weapon to bear, but Yanty shot him before he could do so. "Los Angeles Police!" Lee yelled. "Stop right there! Drop your weapons and raise your hands!"

Two men were carrying a large trunk. The kind that photographers and bands use. They put it down, raised their hands, and made no attempt to go for the rifles slung across their backs. The fourth man fired a pistol at Lee and took off.

Lee ran after him, managed to jump onto his back, and rode him to the ground. Then she scrambled to her feet and kicked his pistol away. Having dropped the rifle earlier she pulled the Glock. "You're under arrest, asshole . . . I'll read your rights later.

Now put your hands behind your back."

Lee was putting a pair of handcuffs on the suspect when a police officer dressed in tac gear appeared. He grinned. "Detective Lee I presume?"

Lee noticed that the shooting had stopped. "Are you Newsome?"

"Yup . . . Thanks for the assist. It looks like the people in the building were shooting at us so these yahoos could escape."

"That makes sense," Lee agreed, as she stood. "I don't know who this guy is . . . But he might be a leader of some sort."

"Look at this!" Yanty said, from a few feet away. "The chest is full of money!"

Lee turned to see that the other prisoners had been disarmed by members of the SWAT team and were facedown on the ground. And when she went over to look, Lee saw that Yanty was correct. The trunk was packed with bundles of shrink-wrapped currency. Each "brick" was labeled, 50,000 nu. That seemed like a lot more money than an illegal medical facility was likely to generate . . . But there it was. "Come on," Newsome said. "Let's see what was going on inside that building."

Garcia and Perkins were told to guard the prisoners while Newsome, his men, and the LAPD detectives approached the building with weapons ready. After all the noise, the scene was eerily quiet. Newsome led the group around to the east side of the building, where he motioned for Lee and Yanty to stay back. Then an officer with a shotgun went up three steps to a closed door. Newsome and the rest of the team were right behind him.

The shotgun was loaded with breaching rounds. The officer fired twice. One shot for each hinge. When the door sagged, Newsome threw a flash bang through the gap. As soon as the grenade went off, the man with the shotgun shouldered the door out of the way and the rest of the team poured in. Lee expected to hear gunfire but didn't. So she followed the last LBPD officer into the building. Yanty brought up the rear, and to his credit, was watching to ensure that no one could sneak up on the team from behind.

There was a whole lot of chatter on Iffy's radio by then. A coast guard interdiction team had arrived, a boatload of ICE agents were coming ashore, and a medevac helicopter was two minutes out. Newsome handled all of the various inquiries with aplomb even as his people checked each room on the first floor.

The building had clearly been used for administrative purposes originally. Since then, some of the offices had been converted into bedrooms, a conference room was being used as a lounge, and the walls were covered with layers of graffiti— much of which was in Spanish. Appearances aside, the place smelled to high heaven. The air was thick with the combined odors of cooking, stale ganja smoke, and urine.

But as Lee followed the SWAT team up a wide flight of stairs, things began to change. The graffiti disappeared, and the other smells were replaced by the harsh odors of disinfectants.

Then Lee heard some shouting and arrived on the second floor to find that six people, all dressed in green scrubs, were lined up against a wall with their hands on their heads. An LBPD officer was patting them down. All of the suspects were wearing masks, which suggested that they were mutants or norms who were working with mutants.

The SWAT team always wore masks when they went into action—but it was necessary for Lee and Yanty to pull theirs out and put them on. "Detective Lee," Newsome said over the radio. "I'm in the west wing. Please join me."

Lee took a left and followed a corridor to a pair of swinging doors. A neatly printed sign read: ICU, AUTHORIZED PERSONNEL ONLY.

She pushed her way through and entered another section of hallway. The lighting was good, the paint on the walls appeared to be fresh, and buff marks could be seen on the scrupulously clean floor. A couple of gurneys were parked next to the right-hand wall—and were covered with crisp white sheets.

Then came an alcove and the nurses' station. Beyond that, four hospital beds could be seen, two on each side of the central corridor. Only one was occupied. The patient was sitting up, wearing a hospital gown, and his or her head was swathed with bandages.

And there, seated next to the bed, was a striking figure. He appeared to be well over six feet tall and had a mane of shoulder-length gray hair. A bulging forehead and a beaklike nose identified him as a mutant, and judging from the clerical collar around his neck, he was a priest. A surgical mask dangled from his neck, and a silver crucifix hung below that. Newsome was present but made no attempt to interfere as the man in black recited a prayer.

"Lord, you are holy above all others, and all of the strength that I need is in your hands.

I am not asking, Lord, that you take this trial away. Instead, I simply ask that your will be done in my life. Whatever that means, that is what I want. But I admit that it's hard, Lord.

"Sometimes I feel like I can't go on. The pain and the fear are too much for me, and I know that I don't have the strength on my own to get through this.

"I know that I can come to you, Jesus, and that you will hear my prayer. I know that it is not your intent to bring me to this point just to leave me in the wilderness alone.

"Please, Lord, give me the strength that I need to face today. I don't have to worry about tomorrow. If you just give me the strength that I need today, that is all I need.

"Keep me from sinning during this trial. Instead, help me to keep my eyes on you. You are the Holy Lord, and all of my hope rests in you.

"Thank you for hearing my prayer.

"In Jesus' name. Amen."

Once the prayer was complete, the priest made the sign of the cross and leaned in to speak with the patient. "The police are here, my dear . . . I suspect that the authorities will move you to a conventional hospital, and that will involve some discomfort, but nothing like the pain you've endured since birth. I will pray for you, my child—and God will watch over you."

And with that, he stood and offered his wrists to Newsome. "Thank you for allowing me to finish . . . That was kind of you."

Newsome placed the cuffs on the priest's wrists and closed them. "And you are?"

"Dr. Antonio Haviclar . . . Or Father Haviclar. Whichever you prefer."

Newsome stepped back. "Are you in charge of this operation?"

"The second floor, yes. A drug runner named Mackey ran the

lower floor. I made the mistake of hiring him to transport my patients to and from the Aztec Empire. Then he started to store drugs and money here. There was nothing I could do."

That could be a lie, of course . . . Which was to say one criminal's effort to blame another. But Lee had heard a lot of lies during her career, and she believed Haviclar. It was the kind of mistake that someone with his background might make. "How many face transplants did you do here?"

Haviclar turned to look at her. Lee could see the surprise on his face. "Transplants? How did you know?"

"Your people dumped a body behind St. Patrick's Church in LA. We followed the trail here."

Haviclar produced a lopsided smile. "Mackey was against it. He wanted to bury the body at sea. But I insisted that Senor Pascal receive a proper burial."

"Then why did Mackey go along with your request?" Newsome wanted to know.

"Mackey was raised as a Catholic," Haviclar replied. "And even though he claims to be an atheist, he's a careful man. It always makes sense to hedge your bets."

Lee thought about the trunk of money and the man with the pistol. Mackey? Probably. "Put your mask on, Doctor," she said. "There's been enough suffering." A case had been solved.

EIGHT

The room was messy. Paper, ink, scissors, glue, photos, clippings, and other paraphernalia lay everywhere. All of which were part of the Bonebreaker's plan to create an irresistible piece of bait. Something that would claim Cassandra Lee's attention and suck her in.

That's why Dr. Penn's kitchen had been transformed into a laboratory of sorts. A place where the Bonebreaker could experiment with paper, ink, and other materials to create a journal. Or what *appeared* to be a journal that, if the ruse worked, Lee would attribute to him. A younger him, who had decided to document his first three murders and explain them.

The irony was that the contents of the fake journal would be *real*. And why not? The Bonebreaker knew that there was nothing more powerful than God's own truth. And after battling Lee for so long, the Bonebreaker wanted her to understand why she deserved to die.

The first step was to write a draft of what he wanted to say. No, *had* to say. That took two days. The process of writing it down, scratching things out, and rewriting was cathartic. But it was painful as well. And there were moments when tears trickled down the Bonebreaker's cheeks.

Once the narrative was complete, the second stage of production kicked in. And that was to make the journal look like the real thing. In order to accomplish that, the Bonebreaker had to comb yard sales and dusty bookstores looking for a faded three-ring binder, a ream of slightly yellowed paper, and newspapers old enough to include articles about the plague.

He'd been a child back then and lived life the way children do, without understanding what's happening around them.

Once he got the materials home, if Penn's house could properly be referred to as such, he sat down to read some of the articles for the first time. That, too, was an emotional experience and one that caused more pain. So much pain that he was forced to take a day off to recover.

Then the Bonebreaker went to work. As a servant of God, he knew that the devil was everywhere, especially in the details. That made it necessary to create a mock-up prior to starting work on the real thing. A dozen different pens were used to make it seem that the journal had been written using whatever instrument was at hand. Clippings had to be fitted to each page while loose photos were inserted here and there. And the Bonebreaker made sure that there were gaps as well. Days, weeks, even months that elapsed without comment so as to suggest periods of quiescence and frantic activity.

But that wasn't all. Once the journal was complete, there was more work to do. The Bonebreaker went through the binder page by page, adding coffee stains, creases, and marginal comments. Then he chose a page at random and ripped it out. And it was painful because all of the things written on it were true . . . But the sacrifice was necessary in order to make the overall document feel authentic. So he burned the sacrifice in a frying pan and cried while he did it. The final result was bait. But more than that, it was a confession and a work of art. Would his plan be successful? Time would tell.

Two days had passed since the raid on White Island. And, consistent with Yanty's prediction, the Long Beach Police Department got most of the credit. Of course, they took most of the flak, too, since it was apparent to all concerned that the initial landing had been bungled. A fact that put their police chief in an awkward position. What should she do? Place the blame where it belonged, which was on a dead officer, or shoulder it herself? Not a pleasant choice.

Fortunately for Lee, she was well clear of the disaster zone and free to focus her energies on other things. And that included the Getty investigation, the Bonebreaker case, and Lawrence Kane. Lee couldn't visit Kane without running the risk of a TV news ambush. But she could speak with him on the phone and was scheduled to do so at seven that evening, something she was looking forward to. But first, it was necessary to get through the day.

Immediately after roll call, she and a two-man team consisting of Yanty and Prospo entered a well-secured conference room. In order to keep what they were working on under wraps, the investigation was code-named: "Operation Grab Bag."

Thanks to Prospo's efforts, photos and short bios for each player were taped to one of the walls. The principals included Sydney Silverman, the real-estate developer/visionary who had been able to secure Getty's support for the *Oceana* project through a political deal; business tycoon Carolina Moss, who had donated a large sum of money to Getty's favorite charity immediately before receiving a zoning change her company needed; and Jack Stryker, who, as president of the Sanitation Workers Union, voiced his support for the higher transit rates that Getty was after in exchange for her willingness to tolerate a brief strike.

Then there was the Church of Human Purity's Bishop Herman Jones, who agreed to lead an enthusiastic "Vote Getty" campaign in exchange for the mayor's commitment to leave LA's stringent antimutant ordinances in place. And last, but not least, there was Western Waves Casino owner George Ma, who agreed to buy five hundred thousand dollars' worth of pro-Getty advertising so that she wouldn't get in the way of his proposal to place slot machines in convenience stores. A sweet deal indeed.

"Okay," Lee said, once all three of them were seated. "Who should we tackle first?"

"What sticks out to me is the fact that some of these deals are more egregious than others," Yanty said.

"*'Egregious'?*" Prospo demanded. "Did he say 'egregious'?"

"I believe he did," Lee replied. "Could we stay on topic, please? Dick makes a good point. We should tackle the most prosecutable cases first. Those having a clear *quid pro quo*."

"The zoning thing is weak," Prospo observed. "Especially since Carolina Moss has been making donations to that charity for years. Getty's attorneys would call her gift a coincidence—and it might be very difficult to prove otherwise."

"Good point," Lee said. "In fact, looking at all of them, I'd put Moss in the five slot."

"Agreed," Yanty said. "I think Mr. Ma looks good for number one. After he put half a mil into Getty's campaign, she put up little more than token resistance to the slot-machine proposal. And that was after she gave speeches condemning the measure six months earlier."

"He's a strong candidate," Lee admitted. "But how 'bout Silverman? He's a huge donor to the Constitutional party—and they put forward a candidate so weak that Getty won 67 percent of the vote. And that was when she came out in favor of Silverman's *Oceana* project."

There was a moment of silence while the detectives considered their options. Prospo was the first to speak. "I vote for Silverman first and Ma second."

"What a suck-up," Yanty said disgustedly.

Lee laughed. "Now that we have a starting point, let's set some ground rules. Not only can we see the light at the other end of the tunnel, we know we're looking at a train! Once we start to turn rocks over, someone will tell Getty, the media will get wind of it, and all hell will break loose. When that occurs, the spotlight will swivel onto us as Getty and her supporters try to discredit the investigation. With that in mind, please tape everything that can be taped and be very careful regarding what you put into e-mails related to the case."

Yanty looked at Prospo. "Am I dreaming? Or did loose-cannon Lee tell *us* to behave?"

"Nope," Prospo said solemnly. "You weren't dreaming. This shit is for real."

"Damn," Yanty said. "Wonders will never cease."

"Okay," Lee said, "I'm out of here. I can get abuse anywhere."

Both men laughed as she left the room.

The rest of the day was spent filling out reports and making phone calls, the most important of which was to Silverman's office. Lee had to battle her way through two layers of secretaries in order to speak with Silverman's personal assistant. "This is Veronica Facey . . . How can I help you?"

"This is Detective Cassandra Lee with the Los Angeles Police Department. I would like to interview Mr. Silverman in connection with an active investigation."

"I see," Facey said gravely. "May I inquire as to the nature of your investigation?"

"No, you can't."

A moment of silence followed. Lee had a feeling that Facey didn't hear the word "no" very often. "Okay," Facey said finally, "I can fit you in next Wednesday. Mr. Silverman has an opening at two o'clock."

"That isn't acceptable," Lee replied coolly. "I want to see him tomorrow. Please take another look at his schedule."

Although Lee had been careful to stop short of issuing anything that would sound like a threat, Facey said, "Just a moment," and went off-line. Or pretended to. Then she was back. "Could you meet with Mr. Silverman at noon? During his lunch hour?"

"That would be fine," Lee replied. "Where will he be?"

Facey supplied an address, and the call came to an end. Would Silverman be worried? No, not yet. Curious, maybe, but not concerned. And that was fine.

Lee ran some errands after work, went home to the condo, and changed her clothes. Then it was time to put a three-hundred-calorie chicken and rice dinner in the microwave. The meal was a far cry from the dinners Kane prepared—and a reminder of how much she missed him.

She ate on the deck, and time seemed to drag during the lead-up to seven o'clock, when the phone finally rang. Lee brought it up to her ear. "Hello?"

"It's me," Kane said. "How's it going?"

Lee could tell that he was trying to keep it light—but she knew the situation was bringing him down. "It's going well," she answered. "Now that the face case is closed, I'm spending most of my time on my nails. Which do you like better? Green? Or Blue?"

Kane laughed. "Green. And I want to see them."

"Enough about me," Lee said. "I'm sure Codicil told you about the guy that Keyes turned up."

"Yeah, that sounds promising. Do you have any news?"

"A little," Lee answered. "Tufenuf's *real* name is Elias Jarvis. A couple of patrol officers nabbed him yesterday, and he's sitting in the LA County Jail."

"Too bad," Kane said. "I'd like to chat with him."

"I'll bet you would," Lee said dryly. "And that's why he's being held somewhere else."

"Okay, so what does Mr. Jarvis have to say for himself?"

"Nothing so far," Lee replied. "He lawyered up. But he'll want to cut a deal at some point."

"Really?" Kane inquired hopefully. "You think so?"

"Yes, I do. Hang in there. We'll get through this."

"I'm sorry," Kane said. "You have enough on your plate already."

"Don't worry about it," Lee said. "I miss you."

"And *I* miss you," he said. "I love you, babe. Be careful out there."

"I love you, too," she assured him. "And be careful in there."

"I'll call you at the same time tomorrow."

"I'm looking forward to it."

"Bye."

"Bye, bye, hon," Lee said, and heard a click. There was a lump in her throat, and she wanted to cry. But she didn't. *It isn't that bad,* Lee told herself. *We're making progress.*

It was well past midnight, and southbound traffic was relatively light. The motorcade consisted of an armored limo, the bus-sized RV carrying George Ma, and an SUV loaded with bodyguards. All of the vehicles wore the same shade of gunmetal gray paint and had tinted windows. The interior of the bus was equipped with every possible convenience, including a lounge, a bath, and a private bedroom in back. That meant the relatively short trip from Los Angeles to San Diego should be pleasant.

But, owing to the nature of the journey, Ma had reason to worry. As one should worry if they're about to do a deal with the devil, or if not the devil himself, then one of his close associates. And based on what Ma had heard about Senora Anna Avilar, she was a very formidable person. An ambassador who could cut deals on behalf of the Aztec Empire and literally knew where at least some of the bodies were buried.

"Can I get you a whiskey, Mr. Ma?" Lora had been employed as a cocktail waitress at the Silver Spur Casino in Sacramento until Ma spotted her. Now she was his personal assistant and an attractive one, too. She had bleached blond hair, sloe-shaped eyes, and Slavic good looks. And rather than one of the skimpy outfits that Ma required his cocktail waitresses to wear, Lora was dressed in a nicely tailored suit.

"No, Lora . . . Thank you. I'll need to have my wits about me for this meeting. But I would like a glass of orange juice and half a sandwich."

Lora didn't need to ask what kind of sandwich since she already knew. Ma's favorite consisted of sliced cucumber on French bread with light mayo and a sprinkle of pepper. As she left for the galley, Ma's thoughts returned to the upcoming meeting.

The initial contact had been made through a paid intermediary. Now he had to cut a deal. The sort of deal that would protect him and his holdings should the Aztecs overrun the state of California. It was insurance. But how much would that insurance cost him? Avilar was said to be a tough negotiator.

After eating his snack, Ma retired to his bedroom for a nap. The intercom woke him up. "I'm sorry to disturb you, sir," the driver said. "But we are going to arrive at Mission Basilica San Diego de Alcalá in fifteen minutes."

Ma pushed a button, said, "Thank you," and sat up. He understood the need to meet in San Diego. Odds were that Avilar had some way to sneak across the border from what had once been Mexico. But the mission? The point of that escaped him.

The businessman slipped into his bathroom to freshen up and was ready by the time the motorcade left the freeway—and took a series of turns that led to San Diego Mission Road. A left took the convoy up to the mission.

Ma was up front by then, waiting for the "all clear" from Luis Ontero, his chief bodyguard. A full five minutes elapsed before it came. The radio in Lora's hand burped static as Ontero spoke. "Everything looks good, boss . . . There are some guards outside, but most of the 'tecs are in the mission. Our guys are in position."

"Thanks, Luis," Lora replied. "Mr. Ma is on his way."

Cool air surged into the bus's interior as the door hissed open, and Ma descended to the ground. The Spanish mission was about a hundred feet in front of him. Floods threw fans of light up the white walls to highlight the bell tower and the beautifully scalloped roofline. There were armed guards to each side of the arched entryway, the wooden door was open, and Ma could see the soft glow within.

"Your mask," Lora said, as she handed it to him. It was a so-called doppelganger. Meaning a mask made to look like *him* and was sufficiently flexible to replicate a frown or a smile. Ma looked through the eyeholes as he brought the self-adhesive mask up against his face and pressed it into place. The membrane that covered his mouth was designed to intercept and block all airborne pathogens including *B. nosilla*.

Lora, Ontero, and one of Ma's bodyguards followed him as he approached the mission and went inside. The long, narrow chapel had a high ceiling that was supported by exposed beams. A beautiful altar flanked by two side niches could be seen against the far wall. An ambo sat in front of that. And farther back, divided by a central aisle, were rows of wooden pews. Only one other person was present—and she was seated halfway back.

The sound of Ma's footsteps echoed between the whitewashed walls as he made his way forward. Once he arrived at the pew where the woman was seated, the businessman slid in beside her. Her eyes were closed, and she was speaking Spanish. A prayer? Ma assumed that to be the case as she crossed herself.

When Avilar turned to look at him, Ma saw that she had carefully coiffed black hair which was partially covered with a lace-edged scarf. Her eyes were dark, her eyebrows were perfect, and her lipstick was red. "Good evening, Mr. Ma," she said. "I am

Anna Avilar. It's a pleasure to meet you."

"Thank you," Ma said carefully. "It's an honor to meet you."

Avilar smiled as if to acknowledge the compliment. "I asked you to meet me here for a couple of reasons," she said. "First, the mission is convenient to the border. And second, it's symbolic of what my people are fighting for. Simply put, we were the first to rule this land.

"The Mission Basilica San Diego de Acalá was the first Franciscan mission in the Las Californias Province of New Spain. It was founded in 1769 by Friar Junipero Serra. Think about that, Mr. Ma . . . He came here seven years before the United States of America proclaimed its independence from Great Britain!

"The mission was named for Saint Didacus . . . A Spaniard commonly known as San Diego. And the rest, as they say, 'is history.' Come, let's take our conversation outside. It would be unseemly to discuss earthly affairs here."

Ma stood and made his way out to the aisle, where he waited for Avilar. She paused to genuflect and cross herself for before leading Ma through a side door and out into a beautifully kept garden. It was well lit and private. "So," Avilar said as she turned to face him, "I understand that you are interested in helping the Aztec Empire reconquer the lands that rightfully belong to it."

That wasn't Ma's motivation. He hoped the 'tecs would fail. But he couldn't say that and didn't. "Yes," he said awkwardly, "that's correct."

"Good. We need allies . . . Especially ones who, like yourself, can bring certain assets to bear when called upon to do so."

Ma cleared his throat. "Yes, of course. May I ask what resources you have in mind?"

"Money for one," Avilar replied easily, "but other things as well. We have agents located throughout the state of California, and they need help from time to time. The sort of help that a man with your assets can provide."

Ma started to speak, but Avilar raised a hand that had only two digits. A reminder of the fact that Avilar was a mutant. "Have no fear, Mr. Ma . . . We won't drain you dry. That would be foolish. But if you have fears in that regard, I suggest that you mention my name to Mr. George Nickels."

Ma had never met Nickels but knew the mutant owned a casino in the red zone, and had done some deals with him. So the fact that Nickels was working with the 'tecs was reassuring indeed. "Yes, Mr. Nickels and I trade favors occasionally."

"Exactly," Avilar said, as if she knew all about the relationship between the two. "And when the reoccupation day comes, I promise that both of you will continue to flourish."

The meeting came to an amicable conclusion shortly after that, and the two parties went their separate ways. As the bus carried Ma north, he felt a sense of peace. *I will succeed come what may,* Ma thought to himself, as Lora handed him a whiskey. It slid down the back of his throat and produced an explosion of warmth in his belly. Success felt good.

Lee rose the next morning to discover that the ocean beyond the big picture windows was partially obscured by rain—and a stiff breeze was pushing an endless succession of waves in to break just short of the beach. She knew the storm would be a blessing for farmers but a curse for everyone else, especially those who were flooded. Not to mention the fact that the slick roads would contribute to a lot of accidents. It was going to be a tough day for the department's patrol officers. The combination of the rain and slow traffic made Lee late to work. But so were lots of other people, so she got off easy.

The morning was spent reading all of the background stuff Prospo had dug up on Getty. Even though the woman was well into her first term as mayor, Lee had never thought about her as a person until she'd been forced to do so during the rescue mission.

Now, as Lee read Getty's bio, she discovered that the politician had been born in Berkeley, was the only child of a single mother, and put herself through UCLA by working as a janitor. A story she liked to tell at political rallies in order to connect with blue-collar voters.

Then, thanks to a degree in political science and what one observer later called an "air of cool invincibility," Getty had taken a low-level job working for Senator Calvin Dealy, president pro tempore, and a very powerful man. He came to see Getty as a protégé and taught her how to handle herself. It was according to one journalist ". . . an education in how to do deals, twist arms, and game the system." All skills that were very much in evidence when Getty moved to LA and ran for the city council four years later. She lost the first time around but won the second, and subsequently rose to the position of president.

During Getty's tenure, some of her opponents accused her of making unseemly deals. But none of their claims were substantiated—and most people wrote the criticisms off as being politically motivated.

Then, at the age of forty-one, Getty met Dr. Mark Holby, grandson to Hollister Holby, the founder of Holby Computing. Though trained as a dentist, it seemed as if Holby spent most of his time playing golf and hobnobbing with the city's movers and shakers. And according to a *Times* article written two years earlier, Holby's social activities put him in a position to make friends and solicit campaign donations. All of which had proven to be helpful to his wife.

But unknown to Holby was the fact that his wife had a boyfriend on the side. A man who seemed to be in love with Getty—but knew her well enough to have an insurance policy just the same. In this case a series of videos that could bring her down.

There was more reading to do, but Lee had to quit at that point in order to keep her appointment with Silverman. His offices were located in the Pacifica Bank Tower at 633 West Fifth Street. That put the seventy-three-story building within walking distance on a nice day. But since it was raining, Lee decided to drive.

Unfortunately, the need to go outside and dash across the partially flooded parking lot meant that she was damp by the time she reached the car. A short drive through rain-slicked streets took her to the tower. It was so tall that the top was lost in the mist—and Lee liked the vaguely art deco look that the structure had.

Lee's badge got her through security and into the underground parking garage where, as a visitor, she was relegated to what seemed like the bowels of the Earth. After parking the creeper, and writing the stall number down, Lee followed the signs to the elevators. There were two. A high-rise and a low-rise. And, since Silverman's office was in Room 7103, Lee had to wait for a high-rise elevator before stepping aboard.

The elevator stopped on the first floor. But after that it was a straight shot up to thirty-five, where the low-rise lift topped out. Then, after pausing occasionally, the ride came to an end. Lee found herself in a nicely furnished lobby as she got off. A mahogany reception desk was located directly in front of her—and a pair of security guards was stationed behind it. Both wore blue blazers emblazoned with gold logos. One, a stern-looking woman with her hair in a bun, nodded politely. "Good morning, ma'am. Welcome to Silverman Enterprises. How can we help you?"

"I'm Detective Lee. I'm here to see Mr. Silverman."

The woman glanced at a screen. "Right . . . Could I see some identification please?"

Lee produced her ID case and flipped it open. The rent-a-cop eyed the picture and made a production out of comparing it to Lee's face. "Thank you, ma'am. Please have a seat. Miss Facey will come out to get you as soon as Mr. Silverman is available."

Lee had no choice but to do what she was told—and took a seat next to a nattily dressed businessman. He looked up from his tablet to smile at her before looking down again. She saw that three other people were on hold and wondered how long they'd been waiting.

Time crawled by. And when twelve thirty rolled around, Lee wondered if she was being punished for being pushy. She was about to get up and leave when a door opened and a woman entered the lobby. She had long black hair, steely gray eyes, and slightly mannish features. But the combination of high cheekbones and the way she carried herself made her attractive. And what Lee estimated to be five or six thou worth of high-fashion clothing didn't hurt either.

Was Lee looking at Facey? Yes, she thought so, and that impression was confirmed as the woman came straight over to greet her. It was as if Facey knew what Lee looked like.

"Detective Lee? Please accept our apologies. Mr. Silverman's eleven o'clock teleconference ran long. Please follow me."

Facey's high heels produced a clicking sound as she led Lee through the door and into the sprawling offices beyond. Dozens of workers could be seen—all sitting in semitransparent U-shaped enclosures. The atmosphere was hushed, like the interior of a library, and the scent of freshly washed linen floated in the air. It was a far cry from the atmosphere in the bull pen where Lee worked.

No one turned to look as Facey led Lee down the central corridor toward a pair of frosted-glass doors. They parted as if afraid to slow Facey down. As Lee entered, she saw that there was a minikitchen off to the left and a bar on the right. A glass-topped conference table claimed the center of the room, and an executive-style desk could be seen beyond that, along with the enormous window that framed it. "Please," Facey said, as they arrived at the conference table. "Have a seat. Mr. Silverman will be with you in a moment. He's having a crab salad for lunch. May I order one for you as well?"

Lee hadn't had lunch yet but wasn't about to accept a gift or hospitality from a suspect. "No, thank you."

"As you wish," Facey said, and turned away. Her heels made a clacking sound as she left the room.

Lee took the opportunity to remove a small recorder from her bag and place it on the table. That was when she noticed the folder with her name on it. She flipped it open to see a picture of herself and a thick sheaf of newspaper clippings. Someone, Facey seemed like the best bet, had been doing some homework. Had the folder been left there by accident? Or was it part of an effort to intimidate her? The answer was obvious.

"You have quite a record," a male voice said, and Lee turned to find that Silverman was standing behind her. It seemed that he could move very quietly. Silverman had a high forehead, wispy blond hair, and a sailor's ruddy complexion.

Rather than a business suit, he was dressed in a polo shirt, khaki pants, and rubber-soled deck shoes. He extended a hand. "My friends call me Syd. What do you go by? Cassandra? Or Cassie?"

Lee could feel the man's strength as they shook hands. "I

go by Detective Lee," she said. "Thanks for agreeing to see me during your lunch hour."

Silverman laughed as he circled the table and sat down. A woman in a gray uniform had appeared and was serving his salad. "A no-nonsense straight-shooting cop. I like it. So *Detective* Lee, what can I do for you?"

Lee turned the recorder on. "Please be aware that I am recording our conversation and whatever you say could be used against you in a court of law. I am the lead detective on a team that's looking into what may be an illegal agreement between Mayor Getty and you."

Silverman looked surprised. "*Me?* You must be joking."

"No," Lee said levelly. "I am not joking. It's a known fact that you are one of the Constitution Party's largest contributors. And we have evidence that you made use of your influence to get Mayor Getty elected even though she was running against your party's candidate."

Silverman had yet to touch his salad. His face was flushed, and there was anger in his eyes. "There's nothing illegal about backing a candidate I believe in regardless of my party affiliation."

"True," Lee agreed. "But if you and your party agreed to put forward a weak candidate in return for a political favor, like support for the *Oceana* project, *that* would be illegal."

Lee saw what might have been the first signs of concern in Silverman's eyes. And as Facey materialized at Silverman's side, Lee knew that the woman had been summoned somehow. "Excuse me," Facey said. "But as Mr. Silverman's attorney I would like to take part in this conversation."

So Facey was more than Silverman's assistant. Lee nodded. "Suit yourself."

Facey turned to look at Silverman. He shrugged. "Detective Lee claims that my support for Mayor Getty was part of a deal to obtain support for the *Oceana* project."

"I see," Facey said as she switched her gaze to Lee. "And you have what you consider to be evidence that will support such a charge?"

"Yes."

"And what is that evidence?"

"I can't comment on that at this time," Lee replied.

"Do you intend to arrest Mr. Silverman?"

"Not today, no."

"Then what is the purpose of your visit?"

The purpose of her visit was to scare the shit out of Silverman, start what might turn into a rat stampede, and wait to see what would happen. Hopefully, someone would come forward and agree to testify as to the veracity of Maxim's tapes. But Lee couldn't say that. "It was my hope that Mr. Silverman would confess," Lee said expressionlessly.

Silverman produced an explosive laugh. "You are an idiot! I'll have you fired."

"You can try," Lee said calmly. "And if you succeed, that will prove the extent of your influence over the mayor."

"This has gone far enough," Facey said sternly. "Turn the recorder off and leave."

"Yes, ma'am," Lee said as she removed the device from the tabletop. "Have a nice day."

And with that, she stood, turned, and left the office. Her heart was racing, her hands were sweaty, and she felt light-headed. The shit was in the air and about to hit the fan.

Keyes was sitting in his apartment, staring at a clip on Flitvid and eating a slice of lukewarm pizza when he saw the woman. He'd been forced to wade through sixty-two videos across three different platforms so far . . . And all of them had been made within minutes of the shooting and within a block of the spot where the incident had taken place. But this was the first upload that had been captured by a sparrow-sized fly cam—and the first that included a shot of the woman.

The fly cam's pilot was male and, judging from the voice-over, had been trapped in the same traffic jam Kane was in. "We took the RV because we can live in it if we have to," the man said. "But it's hard to maneuver in the city. I told Doris to kill the engine. It's stupid to waste fuel, especially when it could be difficult to get more.

"Anyway, I launched the fly cam in order to see what's up

ahead, and the answer is more traffic. Pedestrians are moving faster than we are. Uh-oh! This looks like trouble . . . Two yahoos grabbed a girl. Wait a minute . . . Here comes a guy to help. I don't know if I can get through, but I'll call the . . ."

At that point, the video dumped to black. Had the operator flown the cam into the side of the building? Or? There was no way to know.

But Keyes didn't care. The pizza was forgotten as he went back to still-frame the girl. Then he opened an editing app, which he used to make the image larger. There was a limit to how far he could go, and once it went fuzzy, Keyes had to back off.

The result was a photo of a young woman with shoulder-length hair and a frown on her face. That was interesting since most people would look frightened. Keyes caused the virtual camera to zoom out. Elias Jarvis, AKA Tufenuf, was clearly visible and standing immediately behind the woman with an arm around her throat. Codicil would love that . . . And might be able to use it for leverage. And the dead man was there, too, with his profile to the camera.

All of which was good but not good enough. He had a picture of the woman's face but no name. How to get one? Keyes leaned back in his chair and reached for the pizza. The slice was cold, but Keyes didn't notice. He was chewing when the answer occurred to him. What he needed was help from someone with a humungous computer. But could he secure it? Keyes dialed a number.

After meeting with Silverman, Lee returned to work and went to visit Jenkins. He listened to the recording with obvious interest and shook his head when it ended. "Damn, girl, you know how to light a fire! My phone will start to ring soon."

Lee nodded. "Buy some fireproof boxers, boss . . . You're gonna need 'em."

After that, Lee turned her attention to something she'd been wanting to do for days—namely to talk with the Aztec soldier named Roberto Camacho. The man who, along with members of his squad, had strayed into some sort of underground complex down in south LA and run into what sounded like a lunatic. After making some calls, Lee learned that Camacho had been released from the hospital and transferred to a holding facility at Camp Pendleton. Two additional calls were necessary to set up an interview for later that afternoon.

Prospo was available, so Lee invited him to come. Together, they drove south through Fullerton, Anaheim, and Mission Viejo to Oceanside and the entrance to the Marine Corps base. It was about four o'clock by the time they arrived, the cloud cover had broken, and the air was humid. Evidence of the recent missile attacks could be seen in the area along with early efforts to make repairs. Lee saw lots of shell craters, burned-out buildings, and clusters of white crosses marking the spots where civilians had been killed.

Thanks to the arrangements made earlier, the marines on the gate were expecting the detectives. After examining both sets of ID, a corporal sent them east on Wire Mountain Road with instructions to turn left on Ash Road, and to watch for the POW holding facility on the right.

As Lee turned onto Ash, a column of combat-ready marines jogged past, headed in the opposite direction. A noncom was running backward next to them, shouting words she couldn't make out, but could guess at. Quigley came to mind for some reason.

There were all sorts of neatly kept buildings on the right and left, but they began to thin out after a while. Then, after a mile or so, Lee spotted the camp. It was on the right behind a tall cyclone fence topped with razor wire. And it wasn't a building so much as a two-story-tall metal framework with guard towers at each corner.

Lee was forced to pause and show ID at a gate. "Thank you, ma'am," a sergeant said as he handed the case back. "Don't forget to wear masks inside the wire. All of the prisoners are BN positive."

Lee thanked him, followed the signs to the visitors' parking lot, and put a mask on. Prospo did likewise. A lieutenant in crisp camos was waiting for them in front of the inner gate. Her face was invisible behind one of the leering skeleton masks that the marines favored. "Detective Lee? And Detective Prospo? My name is Lieutenant Anders—and I will accompany you during your visit. Are you armed?"

"Yes," Lee replied.

"Right," Anders said. "Please give your weapons to Private Murphy. He'll return them when you leave."

Murphy was stationed at a small kiosk just inside the gate. His eyes widened as Lee gave him *two* pistols. "She usually carries three," Prospo told the soldier, as he surrendered his Glock. "But she's traveling light today." Murphy nodded as if that made perfect sense.

Anders led them up a flight of stairs. And that was when Lee got a look at how the temporary prison had been thrown together. It consisted of a muddy pit where hundreds of mutants were standing around, sitting at concrete tables, or trying to sleep in tiers of tarp-draped bunks. Judging from the huge inlet pipes, the pit could be flooded if necessary, thereby forcing the prisoners to swim. It would be very difficult to riot and swim at the same time. And if some of the 'tecs didn't know how to swim? Too bad.

Twenty feet above the basin, a latticework of catwalks allowed the guards to patrol back and forth while looking down at the POWs twenty-four hours a day. Metal clanked as Anders led the detectives out to a platform at the center of the matrix. Lee heard wolf whistles from below and realized that the prisoners could see Anders and her for that matter. There were lots of obscene requests—but Lee had heard all of it before.

Once they arrived on the center platform, Lee saw that a light-duty crane was located above an open hole so that a cable could be dropped into the pit below. "Once we call a prisoner's name over the PA system," Anders explained, "they come over to the lift on the double. Then we pull them up."

Lee's eyebrows rose. "And if they refuse to obey?"

"Then we activate the bracelet that each prisoner wears," Anders replied matter-of-factly. "The pain is quite intense, and most of them change their minds in a hurry."

Lee was still thinking about that as a motor whirred, and Roberto Camacho was hoisted up from below. He was wearing a mask that had a big smile printed on it and was sitting on what looked like a swing seat. His clothes appeared to be damp, and there was mud on his boots. A guard pulled the mutant over away from the hole, and when Camacho stood, Lee could tell that most of his weight was on his left leg. After a pat down, one of the marines gave Camacho an unnecessary shove. The mutant stumbled, found his balance, and stood at something like attention. "I'll take it from here," Lee said to the guard. Then she turned to the prisoner. *"Hablas Ingles?"*

There was a nictitating membrane over Camacho's eyes. It opened and closed. "No."

"Okay," Lee said. *"Hablaremos Español."* (We'll speak Spanish.) "My name is Detective Lee—and this is Detective Prospo. Let me begin by saying that I'm going to record this conversation. You aren't in trouble, and nothing you say will be held against you. We are looking for a murderer, a *normale*, and based on what you told police earlier, there's a possibility that you can help us. Do you understand?"

Camacho nodded. *"Si."*

Lee gestured to a plastic chair. "Please, have a seat. Would you like something to drink?"

After Camacho sat down, he stuck the injured leg straight out in front of him. "A soft drink . . . A *cold* soft drink. *Por favor.*"

Lee turned to Anders and switched to English. "Could you send for a cold soft drink, please?" Anders said she could and turned away.

"The drink is coming," Lee told Camacho. "While we're waiting, please tell Detective Prospo and me about the invasion. How did you arrive? By boat?"

No, Camacho told them. He and the rest of his squad were members of the elite *Battalon de Aguilas* (Battalion of Eagles), which had been brought in on transport planes shortly after the naval attack. He and his *companeros* had jumped when they were ordered to do so. Unfortunately, half the squad landed in a cemetery. At that point, Sergeant Alvarez attempted to lead them out. But they hadn't gone far when the ground gave way under Ruiz's weight and dumped him into a tunnel. The paratroopers assumed they had stumbled into a hidden military installation—and Sergeant Alvarez ordered them to explore it.

Camacho paused to accept an ice-cold can of 7-UP—and drank

at least half of it in a series of gulps. The narrative continued after a prodigious belch.

Once inside the tunnel complex, it quickly became apparent that it was home to a maniac rather than soldiers. After Ruiz and Lopez were killed, Camacho ran back to the cave-in and managed to climb out. He looked down at his boots at that point and his voice dropped an octave. *"Dejé el sargento detrás y me arrepiento de eso."* (I left the sergeant behind and I regret that.)

"You did what you had to," Lee lied. "What happened next?"

After climbing up onto solid ground, Camacho went south, hoping to connect with other Aztec soldiers. But, while passing through a backyard, someone shot him from a window. The bullet hit his leg, and he collapsed. Though still under fire, Camacho dragged himself out into an alley, applied compresses to both wounds, and struggled to his feet. Then he went looking for a place to hide. The gringos found him two days later.

Once the narrative was complete, Lee and Prospo took turns asking follow-up questions. How many people lived in the tunnels? Did he see the maniac? Had he been exaggerating about a room with bones in it? Unfortunately, when the interview was over, Lee didn't know much more than she had to begin with. And that was that some sort of weirdo was living under a graveyard in Compton.

Still, that was important, and what *if*? What if the weirdo was the Bonebreaker? That would be a big deal. There were no guarantees, of course . . . But Lee was more hopeful than she had been in years. She thanked Camacho and told him that according to what she'd heard, prisoner exchanges were going to take place soon. With any luck, he'd be going home soon.

Anders led the detectives back to the gate, where Murphy returned their weapons. Then it was back to the car and the trip home. "Well?" Prospo said, as Lee pulled onto the freeway. "What do you think?"

"I think we're onto something," Lee replied. "And it's about time."

NINE

It was early Saturday morning, and the air was still cold, which meant that very few golfers were on the course. The Riviera Country Club dated back to 1927—and had always been a favorite among LA's elite. That included the foursome made up of real-estate mogul Syd Silverman, his attorney Veronica Facey, Mayor Melissa Getty, and her husband, Dr. Mark Holby. They had just finished playing the first hole, and were about to tackle the second. The notoriously difficult par four was subject to sudden breezes. And players were required to make a straight tee shot to a fairway that was flanked by trees and a driving range.

Although such things were of great importance to Getty's husband, the mayor didn't care. She was there to talk with Silverman. Something that would be dangerous to do on the phone—and was sure to be noticed if they met downtown. In order to facilitate communication, Getty was riding with Silverman and Holby with Facey. "All right, Syd," Getty said, as the cart came to a stop. "Why am I wasting a perfectly good morning playing golf?"

"The fresh air will do you good," Silverman replied. "And golf is never a waste of time! But yes, there is something we need to discuss. A detective named Cassandra Lee came to see me yesterday."

Even though Getty didn't *like* to play golf, she knew how, and took an iron out of the two-thousand-nu golf bag that Holby had given her for Christmas. "Lee came to see *you*? Whatever for?"

"So you know her," Silverman said, as they walked toward the green.

"Of course I know her," Getty replied. "Her name is probably more recognizable to the public than mine is . . . She's a loose cannon—but good at what she does."

What Getty didn't say was that she owed her life to Lee— and the policemen who had gone into Hawthorne to rescue her. Fortunately, the press had been so busy reporting on the Aztec invasion that the rescue mission had gone largely unnoticed. And no mention had been made of Maxim, thank God. "So Lee's competent," Silverman said as he placed his ball on a tee. "I'm sorry to hear that since she's trying to send us to jail."

Getty frowned. "*Jail?* What are you talking about?"

"Lee claims that I used my influence with the Constitution party to put a weak candidate forward," Silverman replied. "A man you could beat without breaking a sweat. Then, according to Lee, you repaid the favor by supporting the *Oceana* project."

Getty was momentarily speechless. Both of them knew the allegation was true. But how did Lee know? And who was behind the investigation? Lee couldn't launch such an effort by herself. Corso! It had to be Corso. The bastard had something . . . Evidence of some sort. Either that, or he was trolling for evidence. And he was planning to run!

All of that flashed through Getty's mind in an instant. Her heart was beating faster, and she felt slightly light-headed. But she'd learned any number of things from Senator Dealy, and one of his favorite sayings came to mind: "Never let them see you sweat."

"I see," Getty said calmly, as Silverman took a practice swing. "And how did you respond?"

"I told her the allegation was absurd," Silverman replied, as the swing completed itself. "And Veronica told Lee to take a hike."

"This feels like the opening move in a game of political chess," Getty said. "I'll bet Corso is behind it."

"Maybe," Silverman allowed. "But maybe not. If Corso had something solid, he'd send cops to arrest us and issue a press release ten minutes later."

Getty knew there was some truth in that. But she also knew that such things can be complicated. Perhaps Corso knew something, or thought he knew something, but the DA was hesitant. If so, the police chief might be trying to spook Silverman and her as well.

Silverman's club made a whirring sound as it cut through the air. That was followed by a loud thwack as the driver came into contact with the ball and sent it sailing down the course. It looked like a good shot at first. Then a sea breeze hit the ball, and everything changed. Silverman swore as the white dot vanished into the trees. Was that a bad omen? Getty feared it was.

After returning to LA from Camp Pendleton, Lee had gone to see Jenkins, played the Camacho tape for him, and requested permission for a raid. Following a talk with Corso, Jenkins said, "Yes," and Operation Mole Hole was born. That was about 8:00 P.M. The next five hours had been spent creating a plan and going over logistics. Then Lee went home to grab four hours of sleep before returning to the office at seven o'clock.

So despite the fact that it was Saturday, more than half of the S.I.S. detectives were in the office. And for good reason. Maybe the whack job living under the cemetery in Compton was the Bonebreaker, and maybe he wasn't. But the possibility was enough to justify a maximum effort. And as the lead detective on the case, Lee was scheduled to give the other participants a briefing at nine.

That was pressure enough . . . But Lee was dealing with feelings of guilt as well. Because when she checked voice mail the night before there had been a message from Kane. "Hi, hon . . . Sorry I missed you. Take care out there. Click." It was all very casual, intentionally so, and made her feel terrible. But she couldn't provide the moral support Kane needed until the raid was over. Would he understand?

The question went unanswered as Lee gathered her presentation materials and made her way down the central corridor to the largest conference room the Street Services Garage had. It was already half-full, and more people continued to arrive as she prepared to speak. The crowd included patrol officers from the Compton area, the SWAT team, and a delegation from Technical Services.

Chief Corso, Deputy Chief Jenkins, and Lieutenant Wolfe were among the last people to take their seats. A sure sign that they'd been in a meeting of their own minutes earlier. About *what*? *About whether this is the real deal*, Lee thought to herself. *And how to harvest the credit if there is any—and how to avoid being blamed if something goes wrong. Was that fair? No, probably not. And what difference did it make? None, insofar as she was concerned. Nailing the Bonebreaker would be its own reward.*

Jenkins stood and turned to look at the audience. "Okay, people . . . You know why we're here. Detective Lee is going to brief you on what we know, what we *don't* know, and the way this raid will go down. So listen up. And remember," Jenkins added, "Operation Mole Hole is top secret. This suspect may or may not be the Bonebreaker. But, if he is, we know he monitors the news . . . That means the slightest leak could be disastrous." Jenkins turned back to Lee. "Okay, Cassandra . . . Take it away."

Lee nodded. "Like the chief said . . . You know why we're here—and you've heard the Camacho tape. So I'm going to get into the operational stuff right off the top.

"Rather than go after this guy during the day, we're going to hit him just after dark. And, rather than drop the whole department on his ass, we're going to enter the cemetery quietly. So quietly that people in the surrounding homes won't be aware of us.

"There are a number of reasons for choosing this approach, the first of which is that if the bastard realizes that we're in the area, he might be able to escape via a system of tunnels that the 'tec troopers fell into."

Lee eyed the faces in the front row and saw Prospo wink at her. "Additionally," Lee said, "the LAPD isn't that popular in Compton and never has been. So a full-on invasion could trigger civilian unrest and produce all sorts of unintended consequences. That makes stealth all the more important.

"Last, but not least, it would be next to impossible to launch a high-profile raid without the media's getting wind of it. And that takes us back to my first point. If the perp knows we're coming, he'll run. Any questions or comments so far?" There weren't any.

"Okay," Lee said as she pointed a remote at the wall screen, and an aerial shot of the graveyard appeared. "Here's the plan. What you're looking at is a mutant-only graveyard, which is bordered by South Central Avenue to the west, the Glenn Anderson Freeway to the north, and South Wilmington to the east. It ends down here." At that point, Lee's laser pointer drew a line under the Imperial Highway.

"Now here's how the cemetery came into being. Shortly after the plague was released, this area of Compton was taken over by the city, condemned, and bulldozed to make way for a quarantine camp. Why *this* area, you ask? Because the people who lived here were poor, a lot of them were too sick to fight back, and city officials were scared shitless. So scared they were willing to do just about anything." Lee looked around to see if any members of the audience would challenge her. None did.

Lee picked up where she'd left off. "As conditions grew worse, the authorities began to call it a 'holding area.' Then it became a 'relocation center.' And finally, as hundreds of people died, it became a cemetery."

Lee could see the sadness in the faces arrayed in front of her. Every single one of them had lost relatives to the plague, and the graveyard was a reminder of that. "I couldn't find any records covering *how* the area was razed," she told them. "But here's my theory: City officials were in a hurry, as were the people operating the bulldozers and hauling the rubble away. The result was a sloppy job. As buildings were leveled, some of the basements were filled in, and some weren't. That meant there are cavities in the rubble—and large storm drains that were left in place. If my hypothesis is correct, the perp discovered one or more of those spaces, moved in, and made a lot of improvements. That would account for what Camacho saw underground."

"It would also account for the room full of bones," Detective Dooly volunteered. "Maybe they belong to skeletons he came across while digging."

"That's possible," Lee agreed. "Because even though the

Bonebreaker murdered nine cops, that isn't enough people to fill a room with bones, especially given his propensity to dump some of the remains next to the Hollywood Freeway. Assuming the suspect *is* the Bonebreaker, which may or may not be the case." All of them knew that some of her father's body parts had been disposed of in that manner, and some of them looked down.

"Based on what Camacho told us," Lee continued, "we figure that Ruiz fell into a tunnel right about *here*." As she pointed, the red dot wobbled over a single point on the map. "So we are going to enter from over *here*, using an old RV for transportation, and a stepladder to get over the fence quickly. Once the team is inside, the RV will depart.

"From there it will be a short trip to the entry point, where a two-man pick-and-shovel team will go to work while Lieutenant Ferris and three members of the SWAT team provide security. Once the tunnel is breached, the SWAT team will drop in, followed by Detective Prospo and me. At that point, the pick-and-shovel team will switch to a security role. Milo, tell them what you came up with."

"We know this guy has power," Prospo said, as he came to his feet. "Because the tunnels were lit when Camacho was down there. Plus, if this *is* the Bonebreaker's hideout, we know he watches TV. So I told the power company to look for a tap, and they found one. They'll cut it when Lee gives the order."

Lee nodded as Prospo sat down. "And, since we'll be using night-vision gear, we'll be able to see. That could give us an edge."

"But what if the perp detects the break-in," a detective wanted to know. "He could pop up anywhere."

"That's a good point," Lee replied. "The plan is to throw a cordon of unmarked cars and vans all around the cemetery while an infrared-equipped drone circles overhead. If the bastard surfaces, there's a good chance that you folks will be able to nab him. And remember . . . Even if the perp isn't the Bonebreaker, he's a killer. So be careful."

There was more, much more, including the need to brief the team regarding communications, emergency medical, and the possibility that the tunnels would be booby-trapped. A member of the bomb squad handled that part of the presentation for her.

Lee was exhausted by the time the briefing came to an end and went looking for a place to take a nap. Thanks to the fact that it was Saturday, a few offices were temporarily vacant, and that included the one belonging to the head of HR. Lee entered the woman's office, killed the lights, and went to sleep on the floor.

Three hours had passed by the time she woke up, feeling stiff and groggy. After a trip to the ladies' room, it was time to buy a couple of tacos off the food truck parked outside, and return to work. She had lots of e-mails waiting, including one from Keyes marked "Urgent." It took all of Lee's willpower to ignore it, and by doing so, to ignore Kane's predicament as well. But that's what Lee had to do to focus in on all of the mission-related inquiries awaiting her attention. The clock was ticking down toward 8:00 P.M. and the time when the various teams would depart for Compton.

So Lee put her head down and went to work. And it seemed like no more than fifteen minutes had passed when Prospo appeared at her desk. She had never seen him dressed in tactical gear before and couldn't help but grin. The helmet, heavily loaded vest, and submachine gun made the portly detective look like a parody of an LAPD SWAT officer. "That's a scary outfit, Milo . . . The Bonebreaker will shit his pants if he sees you."

"Very funny," Prospo responded sourly. "Grab your stuff and let's go. The SWAT team is in the RV, and Ferris is getting antsy."

Lee glanced at her watch. It was 7:45. There were plenty of things Lee wanted to check on one more time—but that wasn't going to happen. So she put the vest on, hung her ID around her neck, and checked to make sure that both pistols were loaded. Not that she expected to need them given all of the firepower the SWAT team was bringing along. Then, with the helmet tucked under one arm, she followed Prospo outside.

Jenkins was waiting next to the old RV. He was smiling, but Lee could see the concern in his eyes. "Good hunting, Cassandra . . . Give me a holler when it's over."

"Will do," Lee answered. "Let's hope that it's who we think it is." And with that, she boarded the RV. The interior lights were on as the vehicle got under way, but all the curtains were closed.

That meant people couldn't see in—but it also meant that Lee couldn't look out.

Conversation, such as it was, consisted of a competition to see which SWAT team member could produce the most impressive belch. Lee knew it was a way to manage stress, and when she made eye contact with Ferris, he winked as if to say that some things are best ignored.

Lee took the opportunity to put her helmet on and let her head rest against the plastic paneling. She could hear occasional bursts of conversation over her radio as various units began to converge on the cemetery. Thanks to Lee's visor, no one could see her face, and she was glad. The e-mail from Keyes was very much on her mind. Urgent good, or urgent bad?

Forget that, Lee told herself. *You have a job to do. Concentrate on that.*

Sure, the other part of her said. *That's what Dad did. And how did that work out?*

Ferris interrupted her chain of thought. "Okay everybody, cut the bullshit . . . We're almost there. Remember, speed is everything. Get over the fence, take cover, and wait for orders. Sound off."

Lee listened as each member of the team said his name, thereby confirming that the com network was still intact. Once the SWAT team was finished, and the "diggers" were accounted for, Lee spoke up. Prospo went last, and Ferris turned the lights off.

Lee felt the RV come to a stop. At that point, the driver was supposed to get out and circle the vehicle while pretending to check the tires. Then, assuming the area was clear, he would remove the stepladder stored under the RV and put it in place against the fence.

Meanwhile, the drone was circling above, and if a threat was detected, the vehicle's operator would notify the team. But there weren't any alerts. And the driver was able to place the ladder without spotting any witnesses. Once he opened the door, Ferris and his team went outside and crossed the fence seconds later.

The pick-and-shovel men went next, followed by the detectives. Even though the ladder made it easy to climb up, it was necessary to jump down. Prospo hit hard and fell. He swore but was back on his feet seconds later.

As soon as Lee crossed the fence, the driver snatched the ladder away and returned to the RV. The boxy vehicle was in motion sixty seconds later. Lee checked her watch and saw that the whole sequence had taken just under the five minutes. Not bad. She opened her mike, knowing that everyone including Jenkins could hear her. "This is One-Eight . . . We're on-site. Over."

Their com-net transmissions were scrambled, but anything that can be scrambled can be unscrambled, so every member of the team had been given a unique mission-only call sign along with orders to avoid using names. "This is One-One," Ferris said. "Follow me."

With the rest of the team in tow, Ferris led them through a maze of markers to the spot where the Aztec soldiers had fallen into the tunnel. Then, as the diggers went to work, the SWAT team set up a security perimeter to protect them.

Lee looked up but couldn't see the drone against the black sky. So she focused her attention on the diggers and hoped they were in the right spot. What if they weren't? What if they dug four or five holes without success? *You'll look stupid,* Lee thought to herself. *But what's worse is that the perp might get away.*

Lee bit her lower lip as dirt flew. Then a thud was heard. A coffin perhaps? Or the roof of the tunnel? Which, in the wake of the cave-in, had probably been repaired.

Lee couldn't see into the hole, but she heard the whine of a battery-powered drill as the diggers began to bore holes through a section of wood. That was followed by a buzzing sound as a power saw connected the holes. Lee feared that the entire city of Los Angeles could hear the noise but knew that was silly. Then the saw stopped, and she watched as a piece of plywood was removed. "This is One-One," Ferris announced, "phase one is complete. We're starting phase two."

Lee felt a profound sense of relief. The tunnel was there! But that emotion was followed by a stab of fear. What if the complex was booby-trapped? Or what if the perp shot the first person in? A demolitions expert lowered himself into the hole with extreme care. Lee's heart thumped in her chest as seconds turned into minutes without receiving any report. Finally, after what seemed like an eternity, One-Four's voice was heard. "Four here . . . The lights are on, there's no sign of the perp so far, and this area is clear of traps. Over."

Lee didn't realize she was holding her breath until she let it go. A clean entry . . . Or that's the way it seemed, anyway. Maybe the suspect was snug in his bed. That would be perfect. Now it was her turn to speak. "This is One-Eight . . . Members of team one will activate their night-vision gear. Members of team three will cut the power. Over."

"This is One-Four . . . The power is out."

"Roger that," Lee replied. "Thanks, team three. One-One, over to you."

"This is One-One," Ferris said. "We're going in." The demolitions expert had gone in first, so Ferris was the second person to drop through the hole. The rest of his team followed. If the perp was up, and watching TV or something, he would notice the outage. Would that spook him? Maybe, and maybe not. How reliable could an illegal tap be? Maybe he was used to outages; if so, he might assume everything was okay. Or maybe he was a paranoid son of a bitch . . . In that case, they'd be up against a man who was armed, dangerous, and prowling tunnels he knew by heart. Not a pleasant prospect, even with their night-vision gear to rely on.

Lee watched Prospo's ghostly green image drop out of sight, gave him a moment to get clear, and followed. The earth swallowed her up.

The living-room lights were turned down, and the Bonebreaker was seated in Dr. Penn's favorite chair, watching a documentary about serial killers. California boasted forty-six in all. But it soon became apparent that the show's producers were determined to focus on those having the highest body counts.

That meant they spent lots of time on people like Lonnie "The Grim Sleeper" Franklin, who had thirteen confirmed kills; Charles Hatcher, who had sixteen to his credit; and "Score-Card Killer" Randy Craft, who claimed sixteen victims by 1983.

Then there was Richard "The Night Stalker" Ramirez, who was "credited" with capping fourteen citizens before being arrested in 1985, and the underappreciated Tommy Lynn Sells, "the Coast to Coast Killer." The authorities had reason to believe that the drifter had been responsible for up to fifty murders, but they'd only been able to confirm thirteen of them prior to his execution in 2014.

But in spite of the fact that the Bonebreaker only had nine kills, soon to be ten, he'd been included in the documentary. More than that, it looked as if they were going to end the program on him! A signal honor in the Bonebreaker's opinion, and one that stemmed from the fact that while his competitors had higher body counts, he was the only killer who specialized in killing cops. And who remained on the loose.

So the Bonebreaker was paying close attention as the narrator began to talk about the McGinty murder when his phone beeped. The Bonebreaker didn't have any friends or acquaintances. But he did have an automated system that was set up to notify him if a malfunction occurred inside the ossuary. The text message read: "The power is out. Check and repair."

The Bonebreaker wasn't alarmed. It was possible that one of the power company's techs had stumbled across the tap and cut it off. That happened from time to time. Or maybe a rat had gnawed through the insulation and fried itself. He could cope with either one.

Assumptions could be dangerous, however, so the Bonebreaker opened a remote security app and selected one of three battery-powered cameras located in the ossuary. What the Bonebreaker saw was so unexpected that he thought it was some sort of anomaly. But it soon became apparent that the image was real. At least half a dozen cops were inside his home! Suddenly, the Bonebreaker felt as if liquid lead had pooled in the pit of his stomach. *How?* How, after all those years? And what else did they know?

The Bonebreaker struggled to fight the rising tide of panic. *Calm down,* he told himself. *They don't know where you are. Only God knows that—and thanks to his protection, you're safe. Were it otherwise, they would be inside the house by now. Plus you foresaw this possibility and have a place to go.*

That was when one of the invaders spoke and, thanks to a hidden mike, the Bonebreaker could hear. "This looks like his bedroom," Cassandra Lee said, "but he isn't here." The Bonebreaker uttered a primal scream and threw the phone across the room. It hit the wall and clattered to the floor.

"This is One-One," Ferris said. "The tunnel complex appears to be clear. But there could be a hiding place somewhere, so keep your heads on a swivel. Over."

Lee had been concerned about the team's radios—and how well they would work underground. But so far so good. She keyed her mike. "This is One-Eight to Three-One. Restore power. Over."

A lightbulb was dangling from the ceiling, and it came on as Lee turned the night-vision device off. All sorts of emotions battled each other for dominance. She felt a sense of joy because here, after years of trying, was a victory of sorts. The theory would have to be confirmed, of course—but Lee felt certain that she was standing in the Bonebreaker's lair. And that meant there would be evidence to process, lots of it, all of which would be valuable.

But Lee felt a profound sense of disappointment, too. The man who was responsible for so much death and misery was still on the loose—and her hopes for a final resolution to nine murders had been dashed. That's what Lee was thinking about when she noticed the tiny camera up in a corner of the room. She keyed her mike. "One-Eight to One-One . . . There is a security cam in the bedroom. How much you want to bet there are more? The bastard could be watching us right now. Over."

"Roger that, Eight-One," came the response. "I'll have One-Five take them down. Over."

Lee clicked her mike on and off by way of a response. That was when Prospo entered the room. His helmet was tucked under his left arm. "What have we here?" the detective inquired.

"It looks like his bedroom," Lee replied. "Notice the metal door. He liked to lock himself in. Creepy, huh?"

Prospo nodded but failed to smile. "Listen Cassandra . . .

I think it would be a good idea if you went topside. Jenkins is waiting for a report. Plus some decisions need to be made. Should the department hold a press conference or not? That kind of stuff."

Lee looked at him. Prospo had never been one to worry about press conferences. So why now? Because he was trying to get rid of her, that's why. "Don't bullshit me, Milo . . . What are you trying to hide?"

Prospo made a face. "There's a room, Cassandra . . . A room with some sort of contraption in it. I think you should go topside."

Horrible images blipped through Lee's mind. She had seen a replica *and* a video featuring the real thing. "Thank you, Milo . . . But I have to go in there. I have to see it."

Prospo opened his mouth as if to object but closed it again. He knew Lee . . . And knew she would make herself look no matter how stupid that was. So he turned and went out into the tunnel beyond. As Prospo led Lee deeper into the complex, she saw a room filled with bones, and caught a glimpse of a freestanding toilet, before entering the *what*? Lab? Kitchen? Execution chamber? It seemed to incorporate elements of all three.

But it was the structure in which her father and so many others had screamed out the last seconds of their lives that claimed Lee's attention. Once in the contraption, there was no getting out when the Bonebreaker came to butcher them.

Lee struggled to hold the tears back but couldn't. The sobs came from somewhere deep inside and racked her body. All strength seemed to leave Lee's limbs, but Prospo was there to hold her up. "That's enough," he said kindly. "You did everything you could. Your father would be proud. It's time to put this room behind you." And with that, he led her away.

It was well after midnight, and the man had been sitting inside the car for more than seven hours by then, trying to ignore the stench of stale cigarette smoke. Once darkness fell, he'd been able to get out and pee thanks to the partial blackout that was in force in the city. He hadn't had the foresight to bring food with him however—since he expected his prey to leave the Street Services Garage around six or six thirty. That was a mistake he wouldn't make twice.

Each time the door opened, a shaft of light shot out into the darkened parking lot. Sometimes people went in, but given the late hour, most of them went out, presumably headed home. The volume of the comings and goings was a surprise to the man—but the flow might be normal for all he knew.

Regardless of that, he knew he wasn't likely to identify Chief of Police Corso as he left the building. There wasn't enough light. But that didn't matter because he could see Corso's bright red sports car—a photo of which had been part of a glossy magazine spread two months earlier. The title of the article was "LA's Most Eligible Bachelor," and it was primarily focused on the chief's famously long string of love affairs. None of which held any interest for the man. What *did* interest him was where Corso lived and was likely to be most vulnerable.

The man sat up straight as the door opened, and light splashed the pavement. Was this the one? *Yes!* He watched the person who had left the building make his way over to the red *especiale* and slide inside. That was his cue to start his engine and get ready. Fortunately, it *did* start, something that was by no means certain since he'd been forced to buy the vehicle *sin papeles* so the police couldn't connect it to him.

So as Corso drove out of the lot and turned onto the street, the man was on his tail. The trick was to get through the same traffic lights that his quarry did—but hang back far enough so as to avoid attracting attention. He felt a fluttery sensation in his stomach and recognized it as the sense of excitement that always preceded a kill.

Even with roughly half the streetlights on, there was less light to see by as Corso left the parking lot and headed home. He was in a good mood, and why not? An arrest would have been even better. But assuming that the preliminary reports were correct, the Bonebreaker had been living in an underground complex down in Compton. The plan was to keep a lid on the news long enough to throw a cordon around the cemetery and confirm the connection.

So long as everything went smoothly, he would call a press conference at 3:00 P.M. That would allow the local TV stations to lead the five o'clock newscasts with what promised to be a sensational story. He could image the headline: "Serial Killer Living Under Cemetery!" It was such a good story that Corso felt sure that the national media would cover it, too.

He glanced in the rearview mirror and saw a pair of headlights. But that's what he expected to see, and his thoughts turned to the mayoral race. It had long been his intention to run. But, before watching what he thought of as the Getty tape, Corso had assumed that he'd have to wait for the mayor's second term to end before announcing his intentions. Now there was the very real possibility that Getty would have to step down. And as the police chief who threw the crooks out, Corso would be in a strong position to replace her. He smiled as the next traffic light turned green.

The Triumph Tower had been built *after* the release of the plague, hence the name. It was fifty stories tall, and home to luxury condos on the top ten floors, with hotel rooms below. Corso's two-bedroom condo was located on the forty-sixth floor. But the man had no intention of going up there, so it didn't matter.

He watched Corso's taillights turn left and disappear into the parking garage located under the high-rise. The man had done his homework and knew that although residents had assigned parking slots, they had to share the facility with the hotel's guests. And that meant he could enter, take a ticket from the automated kiosk, and follow Corso down.

The pause took longer than he expected, and by the time the white arm lifted up and out of the way, the man was beginning to worry. Rubber squealed as he gunned the engine and hurried to catch up. Thanks to the late hour, none of the parked cars backed out to block him—and only a few seconds passed before Corso's taillights appeared.

Then, as the police chief pulled into a slot marked reserved, the man stopped behind him, which made it impossible for

Corso to back up. After putting his vehicle in park, the man got out, slid a hand inside his jacket, and removed the single shot Contender pistol from the hand-tooled cowhide holster under his arm. The weapon looked like something from the nineteenth century but was engineered to accept a wide variety of barrels including the .45 caliber tube presently in place.

Corso was out of his car by then and turned to look at the man who had just rounded the front of the old car. He was wearing a cowboy hat, a spit mask, and a duster. That was unusual in Los Angeles, but it was the antique pistol that caused a stab of fear.

All sorts of thoughts ran through his mind as the weapon came up. The Glock that was sitting on his dresser, the headlights in the rearview mirror, and how stupid he'd been. Then Corso saw sparks fly, felt a sledgehammer hit his chest, and was thrown backwards.

An empty casing popped out as the man broke the Contender open. He caught it with his right hand, dropped it into the side pocket on his duster, and felt for a fresh round. After selecting one, he slid it into the open chamber and closed the receiver. Then he fired again. The gunshot was extremely loud and echoed between concrete walls. Corso's head jerked, and red blood splattered the red car. One bullet in the chest and one in the head.

Satisfied that his mission had been accomplished, the man got into his car, drove around to the up ramp, and hit the gas. There were lots of security cameras in the garage, so he had to assume that the tower's security people had dialed 911 by then. Tires screeched as he rounded a curve. That was when he saw the drop arm fall up ahead.

Rather than brake, the man put his foot down. There was a loud crash as the front end of the car broke through the yellow barrier, and splinters of wood flew every which way. Then he was through and on the final approach to the street. Sirens could be heard off in the distance as he made the turn and drove away.

TEN

Specialists from the Criminalistics Lab were entering the cemetery as Prospo found a patrol officer and instructed her to take Lee back to the office. And Lee was grateful. Because even though she'd known what to expect, visiting the place where her father had been killed had left her shaken.

Once Lee arrived, she went looking for Jenkins in order to give him a quick update. But the deputy chief was nowhere to be found—and a secretary had seen him rush out of the building. So Lee drove home. There was a lot of radio traffic—and Lee got the impression that half the department had responded to a 187 downtown. But the transmissions were so guarded that she couldn't discern any details.

After entering the condo, Lee took a hot shower and placed a call to Ebert Keyes, but the computer expert didn't answer. So Lee went to bed, where she expected to fall asleep quickly. But that didn't happen, not with the images of the Bonebreaker's underground lair so fresh in her mind, so the phone call came as a relief. "This is Cassandra Lee."

"Sorry to bother you," Jenkins said. "But I've got some bad news to share."

Lee's heart skipped a beat. Was Jenkins talking about Kane? All sorts of bad things could happen to a person in the MDC. Her voice sounded strange even to her ears. "What's up?"

"Someone shot Chief Corso," Jenkins said matter-of-factly.

"Once in the torso and once in the head. He was wearing a vest, thank God—but the impact broke some ribs. The head wound is classified as serious. He's in surgery."

"That's terrible," Lee said, and felt a sense of relief. Kane was safe. Then came a surge of guilt. What was wrong with her anyway? True, the chief was the sort of police officer she didn't like in many ways, meaning a man more focused on getting ahead than on fighting crime. But, when push came to shove, he'd been there for her.

"Yes, it is," Jenkins said soberly. "And we have a serious problem. Even if Corso makes a full recovery, the doctors predict that it will take months. That means Getty will get to pick a person to replace him."

It took a moment for Lee to grasp the full import of what Jenkins had said. Immediately after Corso authorized an investigation of Getty's political operations he'd been shot! By an old enemy? By a lunatic? Or by one of the mayor's coconspirators? Lee was tempted to go with theory three even though there wasn't any proof. And if Getty or one of her coconspirators was responsible for the shooting, the mayor could appoint a chief who was willing to hinder the investigation. Would the DA allow it? That remained to be seen. But even if he didn't, Getty could use the situation to stall. "Holy shit, boss," Lee said. "If the shooting has something to do with Getty, that would be a disaster."

"You got that right," Jenkins replied. "So here's the deal. You and your team need to figure out if the shooter is a person with a grudge, a nutcase, or one of the coconspirators. Then, if it's one of Getty's buddies, you need to sort out which one and do so *quickly*. Because if you don't, she might slam the door on you."

"That makes sense," Lee agreed. "But what about the Bonebreaker? Now we have a lot of evidence to sift through . . . And it's the kind of stuff that could lead to an arrest."

"I understand that," Jenkins assured her. "But you can work the Getty case while the forensics people process the site."

Lee sighed. "Okay . . . What about the press conference?"

"It's still on," Jenkins replied. "But it will focus on Corso at this point. So get some sleep but come in as early as you can. No later than ten."

"Got it," Lee answered. "I'll be there."

After Jenkins broke the connection, Lee leaned back against her pillows. The chief was right . . . They needed to crack the Getty case ASAP. But there was *another* case that required her attention as well. Lee dialed Keyes's number and listened to the phone ring. Finally, just when she thought the call would go to voice mail, he answered, "Yeah?"

"This is Lee . . . Did I wake you?"

"No, I was playing a video game online—and some twelve-year-old was kicking my ass."

"So I saved you."

"Yeah. Did you get my e-mail?"

"I did. What's up?"

"I have her . . . The missing woman, that is. But I'm going to need your help."

"*My* help?" Lee inquired. "To do what?"

"I don't want to discuss it on the phone. Come see me and bring a breakfast pizza with you."

"*A breakfast pizza?* There is such a thing?"

"Of course there is . . . Bacon, eggs, and cheese. You can get one at Chet's down the street from my apartment."

"A steady diet of pizzas isn't good for you. How about I bring you something healthy instead?"

"Nope, the pizza is what I want."

"Okay," Lee replied. "I'll be there at eight thirty."

"Cool . . . See you then."

Lee looked at her watch. It was 2:53. That meant she might be able to get four hours of rest. Lee set her alarm and scooted down in bed. And, this time, sleep was there to embrace her. When the alarm went off, Lee not only felt better but had no difficulty getting up. That was unusual and partly because she was eager to visit Keyes.

After a shower, Lee got dressed and went into the kitchen for a bowl of cereal. Predictably enough, the attack on Corso was front and center on the TV news. And later, as Lee drove across town, she heard more on the car's AM radio. Both the hospital and the LAPD were being characteristically tight-lipped. And while the reporters didn't like that, they were hoping to learn more at the presser scheduled for later that day.

Frustrations aside, one of the Triumph Tower's security guards had seen the hotel's security footage and was busy running her mouth. According to her account the police chief had entered the garage around 1:15 A.M., with another car right behind him. Corso had parked and was exiting his vehicle, when a clunker pulled in behind him. At that point a man dressed in Western-style clothing got out and circled his car. One shot was fired, followed by another, and Corso went down.

After returning to his vehicle, the shooter fled the scene, breaking through a barrier on his way out of the garage. Fortunately, a second guard had seen the whole thing go down and called 911 moments after the second shot was fired. That meant that the medics arrived quickly. It was a pretty coherent account and one that would probably cost the woman her job since she wasn't authorized to speak for the hotel.

Lee killed the radio as she entered Chinatown and went looking for Chet's Pizzeria. Much to her amazement, it was open, and Keyes was correct. There *was* such a thing as a breakfast pizza. After waiting for the pizza, Lee reparked her car in a tow-away zone, confident that the local traffic officers wouldn't have the creeper towed.

Then it was time to buzz in and make the long climb up to the second floor. The door to Keyes's apartment was ajar, so Lee went inside, and followed the winding path to the open area up front. Some early-morning light was leaking in through the filthy windows. "That smells wonderful," Keyes said, as Lee placed the cardboard box on the table in front of him. He was reaching for it when she snatched the pizza back. "Not so fast . . . Tell me about the woman. *Then* you can abuse your body."

"Okay," Keyes replied, "come over here."

Lee circled the table to look over his shoulder. Keyes preferred a keyboard to voice commands, and his blunt fingers seemed to dance across the keyboard. A photo appeared. "Here's the mystery woman," he said, as a picture of a young woman with shoulder-length hair popped onto the screen.

Lee had heard about the photo from Codicil but hadn't seen it and was struck by the look on the woman's face. What was that anyway? Not fear . . . No, it was more like anger. Or so it seemed to Lee. "I gave this image to a friend of mine. He has access to an ACURON3000 supercomputer."

"Define 'access.'"

"He mops the floor in the climate-controlled room where the 3000 is located."

"He's a hacker."

"Of course he's a hacker . . . Why else would a guy with a masters in computer science spend his time mopping floors? But he doesn't have access to any secret stuff. Nor does he want to. He uses the 3000 to work on a personal project that no one's been willing to fund. That means everything you're about to see is out on the net where anyone can access it if they know where to look. But that's the problem . . . Without the 3000, and the correct software, you could search for years without finding these images. And even then, my friend only got three hits. Here's the first one. Her name is Janice Olin."

Lee watched as the face of a teenaged girl appeared. "That's what she looked like during her junior year of high school," Keyes said. "And here's a photo that was taken five years later."

The first image was replaced by another. Rather than one person, there were *five*. "The man in the middle is Rafael Corbon," Keyes said. "He's a Mexican, excuse me, *Aztec* drug dealer. And the others are or were members of his gang. It's impossible to know *who* took the photo, but it wound up on the Internet. Look at the woman in the far right . . . The one with the submachine gun."

Lee watched as the woman's face grew to fill the screen. Olin was wearing sunglasses but still recognizable. "You're kidding . . . She's a drug dealer?"

"No, I don't think so," Keyes replied. "I think she's an undercover cop . . . A fed who worked her way into Corbon's gang."

When Keyes said "fed," Lee knew he meant an agent who worked for *Pacifica's* federal government, since the United States government no longer existed. "And what do you base that theory on?" Lee wanted to know.

"Based on *this*," Keyes answered. "I told you there were three images. Which, by the way, is not very many. If you searched my name, you would come up with hundreds of images, and I'm a virtual recluse. That suggests that Olin is *trying* to maintain a low profile . . . Or someone is hard at work doing it for her. Here's the money shot."

Another picture appeared on the screen. This time Lee found herself looking at two women with a male prisoner sandwiched in between them. Not Corbon but someone else. The caption under the photo read, "CID agents with alleged spy." According to the date printed at the bottom, the picture had been taken thirteen months earlier. "Olin is on the left," Lee observed.

"Bingo," Keyes replied, as he turned to reach for the pizza box. "And how much you wanna bet she was undercover the night that Kane shot D-Eddy?"

"Which would explain why she didn't come forward."

"Correct," Keyes said, as he pulled a triangle of pizza off the pie. "And if she knows about Kane's predicament, she doesn't give a shit."

"Damn!" Lee exclaimed. "I've got to find her."

"Right," Keyes replied through a mouthful of food. "You could call up the CID and ask."

"And they would tell me to screw off."

"Exactly. And that's why you'll have to run her name through the LAPD's databases. I'll be surprised if you find Olin, but odds are that you'll locate members of her family, and you can turn the screws down on them."

Lee frowned. "That would be illegal."

Keyes nodded. "Gotcha. So let your boyfriend rot."

Lee was facing him by then. "You're a jerk. A talented jerk . . . But a jerk nonetheless."

Keyes smiled. "You'll get my bill. Don't let the door hit you in the ass on the way out."

Keyes watched Lee leave. Even though Kane was rotting in the MDC, Keyes would have given anything to switch places with him. The lucky bastard.

All sorts of things were flitting through Lee's mind as she drove to work. The fact that Keyes had been able to come up with the mystery woman's identity was a major victory, so she should feel happy. Unfortunately, Lee was in a trap of her own making. Working on the Kane case was unethical, not to mention a clear violation of departmental policies. And using her powers as a police officer to troll police records would make the situation even worse.

But what option did she have? The detective in charge of the case was a well-known plodder named Harmon Sloan. Could she talk to Sloan? And work through him somehow? Maybe, if forced to . . . But she barely knew the man. And once Lee approached him, there was a very real possibility that Sloan would turn her into Internal Affairs.

That's what Lee was thinking about as she paused to show her ID prior to parking in the lot outside the Street Services Garage. What with the Corso shooting, and the aftermath of Operation Mole Hole, police headquarters was even busier than usual. A number of people, including a patrol sergeant, congratulated Lee on the raid as she made her way down the main corridor. "Thanks," Lee said. "How's the chief? Have you heard anything?"

"He's out of surgery," the sergeant told her. "And they say he's stable."

"I'm glad to hear it," Lee said, and went from there to Yanty's desk. He was on the phone and held up a finger. "Okay, that sounds good," Yanty said. "We'll see you at eleven."

"That was Mary Solby with Criminalistics," Yanty told Lee as he put the receiver down. "We're meeting with her folks at eleven in Conference Room B. They're going to brief us on the early findings from the cemetery *and* the Corso shooting."

"Good. Where's Prospo?"

Yanty grinned. "He heard about the chocolate-covered doughnuts in the break room. But when he isn't eating, he's working on a rough draft of the Mole Hole report."

"Bless his heart," Lee said sincerely. "I'm way behind, and Jenkins wants us to focus on the Getty case. And that includes the Corso shooting."

Yanty nodded. "It's been a long time since Corso arrested anyone . . . But I'm checking to see if one of the people he busted just got out of prison or something like that. Speaking of which, George Ma was charged with assault and battery six years ago . . . And it's common knowledge that his organization plays for keeps. So he seems like a good place to start. In the meantime, the tech heads are scanning the chief's e-mail for leads."

"Well done," Lee said. "I'm supposed to meet with Jenkins now—but I'll see you at eleven."

As Lee entered Jenkins's office, she saw that he looked tired. Lee suspected that he'd been up for more than twenty-four hours by then. "Close the door behind you," Jenkins instructed.

Lee did so. "It's like that, is it?"

"Yeah, it is. Mayor Getty named Assistant Chief Yessum to serve as acting police chief until Corso recovers. I will announce the appointment at the presser."

"So Corso's going to recover?"

Jenkins shrugged. "No one knows for sure. But so long as there is a chance, it would be unseemly to replace him."

"That means we have some time."

"Not really," Jenkins replied. "Yessum may be the acting chief, but he's still in charge, and he's tight with Getty."

"How tight?"

"The mayor is godmother to Yessum's son."

"Shit."

"Yup," Jenkins said wearily. "So, it's like I told you on the phone, get the shooter. And do it quickly." The phone rang at that point. Jenkins looked at the readout and made a face. "I've got to take this, Cassandra . . . Keep me informed."

After leaving Jenkins, Lee returned to her desk, where she waded through some e-mails prior to getting a large coffee and making her way to Conference Room B. The crew from the Criminalistics Lab had arrived and were settling in.

Mary Solby was in charge of the group, and Lee had done business with her before. Solby was thirtysomething, and her perfectly cut bangs ended at her eyebrows. She had big brown eyes, pink lipstick, and lots of tattoos. She smiled. "Good morning, Cassandra . . . You're a busy lady these days. Have you met Mark and June? No? Well, Mark is with the field-investigation unit—and June is here on behalf of the firearms-analyis team. Mark, June, meet Detective Lee."

There were handshakes all around, and June Summers's hand felt so fragile that Lee feared she might break it. "I know all about the weapons you carry," the firearms expert said intently. "May I ask why you chose a Smith & Wesson 627 as a backup?"

Lee thought Summers was putting her on at first. But the look in the other woman's eyes said otherwise. "Revolvers don't jam," Lee answered. "And the 627 holds eight rounds. That's two more than a regular .38. Oh, and it's made of stainless steel, so I can take a bath with it."

Summers's eyes were huge. "You do that?"

"Sometimes, yes."

Solby laughed. "June is something of a workaholic—not to mention a fan girl." Lee looked at Summers, who blushed.

"Then there's Mark," Solby continued. "He'd rather be at the beach."

Rogers had bleached blond hair and a deep tan. He looked up from his phone. "Huh?"

Yanty and Prospo entered the room at that point and, after some more introductions, the meeting got under way. Rogers delivered his report first, and in spite of his surfer-dude affect, clearly knew what he was talking about. He was careful to point out that only hours had passed since the raid, and investigators were still at the site, so the final reports weren't ready.

"But," Rogers said, "I can offer you some early impressions. First, based on the trophies we found, it's safe to say that the Bonebreaker lived there. We identified items belonging to all nine victims, including your father."

At that point, Rogers slid a printout across the table and Lee found herself looking at a photo of her father's badge. A lump formed in her throat, but she managed to swallow it. "Good. Can we say as much to the press without fear of having to take it back later?"

Rogers nodded. "Yes."

"Excellent. So what, if anything, did you find that would help us make an arrest?"

Rogers made a face. "Nothing so far. And believe me, we're on it. What we can tell you is that the Bonebreaker had a room full of carefully organized disguises, so it seems safe to assume that he's wearing one."

"And we found a .22 caliber cleaning kit," Summers put in. "Along with five boxes of ammo. But no weapon. Based on that we figure he's carrying a .22. It could be a rifle, but a pistol seems more likely."

"There was a scrapbook, too," Solby added, "filled with articles about *you*. So be careful."

"I will," Lee promised. "Thank you for the readout. Please keep Detective Prospo informed regarding any new developments. My team continues to have responsibility for the Bonebreaker case—but we've been told to work the Corso shooting, too. What, if anything, do you have on that?"

"It's very early in the process," Solby reminded them, "but by looking at the security footage, we were able to get a license-plate number off the car. It was stolen one day prior to the shooting. So it's safe to say that the crime was premeditated.

"Based on the hotel's video, it appears that the suspect is either male, or a large woman. And the cowboy clothing appears to be new. That suggests a disguise and would seem to confirm premeditation. It's also possible that the cowboy persona constitutes an attempt to manipulate the media. If so, it's working because some reporters are referring to the perp as 'the cowboy killer.' And that's in spite of the fact that the chief is alive. June has something to report as well."

Summers was so skinny, she reminded Lee of a bird. A jerky nod served to reinforce that impression. "The shooter's weapon was a single-shot Contender pistol. If you aren't familiar with them, Contenders can be fitted with a wide variety of barrels, including a .45 caliber tube. And that's consistent with the slug that flattened itself against the chief's vest."

"That's weird," Yanty put in. "You're saying that the perp had to reload?"

"Yes," Summers replied. "And that makes the Contender a strange weapon to use for a hit. But I have a theory about that."

"Okay," Lee acknowledged. "Give."

"Well," Summers replied eagerly, "even though it's easier to hunt game with a rifle, there are people who prefer to use pistols. They pride themselves on getting in close and scoring a kill with one bullet. Many of them own Contenders. Maybe the suspect is trying to mess with our heads or, and this is my theory, he's the real deal. Meaning a hunter who owns a Contender and feels comfortable with it."

"That's interesting," Lee responded. "Especially since your theory runs counter to the possibility of a professional hit man."

"We should keep the double tap in mind however," Solby put in. "One in the head and one in the chest. That's the sign of a pro."

There was more, about half an hour's worth, all of which served to provide the detectives with a base of information to work from. After the specialists departed, Lee held a follow-up meeting with Yanty and Prospo.

She told the detectives about Yessum, his connection with Getty, and what that could mean for the investigation. "We've got to move quickly," she said. "I think it safe to say that Silverman has spoken with Getty by now—and the others may be in the know as well.

"So unless we get a lead on someone with a grudge, or a whacko with a Contender, we're going to focus on Getty and her coconspirators. Let's use the Corso attack to scare the crap out of them. Be sure to ask questions like why would someone shoot Corso? That kind of stuff. Maybe one of them will point a finger. We have four people to interview," Lee continued. "If you have a preference, speak up."

"I want Ma," Yanty said.

"I'll take Stryker," Prospo put in.

"Okay, I'll talk to Moss," Lee said. "We'll worry about Jones later. Let's get to work."

It was well past noon by that time, and Lee had a lot of administrative work to do, so she ate a sandwich at her desk. Time passed quickly, and suddenly it was time to attend the prepress-conference scrum.

As Lee entered the conference room where the presser was scheduled to be held, she saw that Jenkins and Yessum were present, along with Molly from Public Affairs. She had a mop of brown hair, wide-set eyes, and a pointy chin. "Here you go," Molly said as she gave Lee an outline. "Let me know if you have questions."

Jenkins turned to greet her. "Cassandra, have you been introduced to Chief Yessum? No? Well it's about time. Chief, this is Detective Lee."

Even though Lee hadn't met the man before, she certainly knew who he was. Up to that point, Yessum had been in charge of Operations—which was to say about ten thousand people across twenty-one police stations. That made him a heavy hitter and a natural for the top slot. So much so that the department's critics would be hard-pressed to question the mayor's choice.

Yessum was shorter than Jenkins, built like a fireplug, and bald except for a halo of very short hair. Caterpillar-like eyebrows were perched over eyes separated by a fist-flattened nose. The latter was an important part of Yessum's street-cop mystique. "It's a pleasure to meet you," Yessum said as he shook Lee's hand. "Congratulations on finding the hole that bastard was living in. Here's hoping we nail his ass soon."

Yessum could be charming, no doubt about that, and Lee found herself struggling to stay neutral as she allowed herself to smile. "Yes, sir . . . Nothing would please me more."

"Okay," Jenkins said as he scanned the piece of paper in his hand. "Let's go over the outline. I will update the press on Corso's condition and take a few questions."

Jenkins looked up at Yessum. "Then I will announce the fact that you're going to serve as chief until Corso recovers. Are you willing to answer questions?"

Yessum shrugged. "Sure . . . Why not?"

"Good," Jenkins said. "Toss it to me when you want to break it off. I'll make the announcement regarding Operation Mole Hole, and Lee will take a couple of questions. Once that's over, Molly will shut the session down. Are both of you good with that?"

Both of them were, and the subsequent press conference went smoothly for the most part, the only glitch being the moment when Lee's TV nemesis Carla Zumin chose to ask a question. "Detective Lee," Zumin began. "What do you have to say about your boyfriend's upcoming murder trial? Will he get off?"

Molly was quick to jump in. "That has nothing to do with the subject of this press conference."

"Oh, but it does," Zumin said serenely. "It's my understanding that Mr. Deon Eddy was killed by a bullet from a .45 semiautomatic pistol that originally belonged to Detective Lee's father . . . And he was the Bonebreaker's *eighth* victim."

That caused something of a stir, and there wasn't much that Lee could say other than, "I have no comment. Questions like that one should be directed to Dr. Kane's attorney."

"That will be all for today," Molly said hurriedly. "We'll release an update regarding Chief Corso's condition at nine tomorrow morning."

Lee looked at Yessum to see how he had reacted to Zumin's question but the chief was chatting with one of the reporters. So all she could do was go back to her desk and return to work. Even though Lee had been able to empty her in-box earlier in the day, *another* load of stuff had arrived while she was gone. And an eight-inch-by-eleven-inch manila mailer was sitting atop the pile. She knew it had been scanned, opened, and cleared by internal security prior to being delivered to her desk. It was a process put in place *after* the package the Bonebreaker had sent her the month before.

Lee picked it up and looked at the return address. The envelope was from Dr. Alan Penn. And judging from the address, he lived in the West Adams section of Los Angeles. Had she met him? No, Lee didn't think so. But the mailer was heavy. She dumped the contents onto her desk, and a bound journal hit with a thud. The loose sheet of paper was wrinkled but still legible.

Dear Detective Lee,

My name is Dr. Alan Penn. I am a semiretired criminologist and profiler. I worked for the FBI prior to the plague and taught criminal psychology at the University of Maryland. Fortunately, my wife and I moved to LA just before the outbreak. Edith is gone now, but I'm writing what will probably be my final book, the subject of which is the Bonebreaker.

I mention these things in order to establish my bona fides and

*explain why the Bonebreaker sent his journal to me. Assuming that
it was he rather than a deranged wannabe. But you're an authority
where the Bonebreaker is concerned—and can command the
resources required to determine if the diary is genuine. Assuming
it is, the journal will provide you with valuable insights into
the Bonebreaker's character and give me the opportunity to use
excerpts in my book.*

*Finally, please accept my condolences regarding your father's
death.*

Sincerely yours,
Dr. Alan Penn

Lee put the letter aside and took a moment to flip pages. The
journal was written diary style and packed with marginalia,
unbound inserts, and newspaper clippings. All of which was
especially interesting since it had been vetted by a trained
criminologist. Or so it seemed. Lee made a note to run a search
on Penn. Still, the journal was or could be a very exciting
development, and Lee planned to read it soon.

That task would have to wait, however. Lee had a different
priority at the moment . . . She was going to put Kane first instead
of last and visit him. And, if a TV crew jumped her, Lee planned
to flip them off. She placed the journal in her briefcase, grabbed
her bag, and left. A short drive took her to an overpriced parking
lot located two blocks from the MDC. By that time the sun was
low in the sky, and dark shadows pointed at the jail.

As before, Lee had to show ID, surrender her weapons, and
fill out a form prior to being admitted. Because people were off
work by then, the waiting room was packed with friends and
relatives, all there to see one of the inmates. Lee felt a kinship with
them now—and a lot more sympathy than she had earlier.

Twenty minutes passed before her number was called and
Lee could enter a booth. Kane was there, handset to his ear,
smiling at her through scratched Plexiglas. "Hi, hon," Lee said,
as she picked up her phone. "It's good to see you."

"You, too," Kane replied. "Congratulations! You found the
Bonebreaker's hideout . . . That's awesome."

"You get to watch the news?"

"Not often," Kane admitted. "Most of the guys prefer sports. But I lucked out."

Then he frowned. "You shouldn't be here. I heard the question Zumin asked you . . . The bitch could be out there lying in wait."

Lee shrugged. "I don't care. I wanted to see you."

Both were silent for a moment as they eyed each other through the barrier. There was so much to say—and no way to say it. Not with jailers listening in. "I can't go into details," Lee said finally, "but there is a promising lead where your case is concerned."

Kane's expression brightened. "Really? That's wonderful."

"It could be," Lee replied cautiously. "But there's more work to do. Just remember that I love you, and people are working to get you out of here."

Kane nodded. "I know . . . Thank you."

"Okay," Lee said, "I can't come here often, but we'll talk on the phone."

"I love you."

"And I love you," Lee replied. And with that, the conversation came to an end.

Lee rose, blew him a kiss, and turned to go. Was Zumin waiting outside? Lee steeled herself for a possible confrontation as she paused to collect her weapons. Then, with her jaw clenched, she left the MDC. The only person waiting for her was a homeless man who wanted a handout. Lee gave him a five-nu bill and returned to her car.

Lee had plenty to think about as she drove home, parked the car, and took the elevator up to Kane's condo. It was dark, and turning the lights on did very little to make the place seem less lonely. *Don't be silly*, Lee told herself. *You lived alone for years.*

Yeah, the other her responded, *and I didn't know what I was missing.*

Lee dumped her bag and briefcase on the couch prior to heading for the bedroom and a quick shower. Then it was time to microwave her dinner, pour herself a glass of wine, and curl up with a good book. Or what could be a *bad* book in this case.

The journal was strange in a number of ways, not the least of which was the fact that, while most of it was written in the first person, certain sections had been penned in the *third* person. Especially those that described violence. It was almost as if the author wanted to distance himself from what he'd done—and Lee wondered what Kane would think of those passages. For her part, Lee wasn't ready to dive in yet.

After sampling sections of the book Lee poured herself another glass of wine and went back to page one.

I was five years old when the plague broke out, and like most ~~kids~~ children of that age, had only a limited understanding of what was happening around me. But I'm older now . . . Old enough to read up on the subject—and put my memories down on paper.

I know my parents worked at LAX because they took me there . . . Daddy took me up into the control tower so I could look out at the planes—and mommy let me spin her chair around. Looking back, I realized they were good jobs, or would have been except for *B. Nosilla*. But it was an airborne disease. And, since people had been sent to LAX to spread it around, my parents were vulnerable. Why? Because the government was incompytent that's why . . . Because they didn't care. Mommy got sick first. I remember how pale she looked—and the way the bathroom smelled when she was done in there.

Daddy did the best he could to take care of her but he got sick ~~also~~ to. Then the people in white suits came. I didn't know why. But now, based on the ressearch I've done, the answer is obvious. The neighbors turned us in. To pertect themselves? Maybe. But the city health department was paying a fifty dollar per head bounty for "positives" by that time.

So the pigs came. They were dressed in white suits with stick-on badges and name tags. I could see their faces through the foggy plastic and they looked like monsters. I was scared of them, but daddy said they were scared of *me*, and maybe that was true because they didn't want to touch me. They made daddy carry mommy to the bus. He fell down once and they yelled at him to get up. I was crying, and trying to help, as he got to his feet.

Daddy managed to carry mommy to the bus where a passenger helped him. There were other people to... Sick people and the air smelled like vomit. I had to sit on a woman's lap and she thought I was her son.

Later, much later, I wondered what happened to our house. And to our belongings. So I did some reesearch. And sure enough... It was common for neighbors to turn positives in and take all of their possessions. May they burn in hell.

Eventually, when I turned twenty-one, the government gave me fifty thousand nu as "compensation." Fuck them. No-body can compensate me for the ride to the quarantine center. It was hell on earth. Tens of thousands of sick people were dumped into a tent city filled with people to sick to take care of themselves. There were sanikans, but not enough of them, so people went to the bathroom outside their tents. That led to the spread of callera, which killed hundreds of people who weren't BN positive—but had been sent to the camp because they might be carriers. But God was smiling down on me, and I didn't catch so much as a cold.

Fresh water arrived in tankers each morning. Those who could took the bottles they'd been given and got in line. Daddy and I went there together. Then, when he got to sick to do it, I took over. The bottles were heavy and it was hard for me to carry them. And sometimes people who were to lazy to wait in line took my water. Then I had to find new jugs and start over.

All of this was detailed in the factual manner that Lee might use to write a police report. But the facts were so horrible that no exaggeration was required to make her cry. And, while the Bonebreaker had caused her to weep before, it had never been for *him*. She continued to read.

Oddly enough there was plenty to eat. Military rations not only arrived on trucks, they fell out of the sky on parachutes, and some of them landed on tents. But because most of the people in the camp were nazeous, and suffering from diherea, pallets of MREs sat untouched. I was hungry. So it didn't take me long to open meals and pick through the contents. The candy and cookies were my favorites.

Mommy died three days after we arrived. I watched the police in the white suits throw her body onto an already heavily loaded truck. I screamed, and begged a policeman to let me go with her, and he told me to "shut up." Years later I learned that tens of thousands of such bodies were dumped into mass graves—and there was no way to know which one my mother was buried in.

A picture of the vast ditch called CBP-314 had been inserted into the journal and it was filled with rag-doll corpses. Lee winced and hurried past it.

Daddy got even sicker and it was hard for him to talk. But somehow he managed to say goodbye. And I remember every word he said. "You're going to servive," he croaked. "That's because you're immune. 'Immune' means you won't get sick like mommy and daddy did. I wish I could tell you who will take care of you but I don't know. But god loves you—and he will watch over you.

"Now take this piece of paper and never let it go. It's a list of the policemen who were mean to us. When you grow up all big and strong I want you to find the men on this list and kill them for mommy and daddy. Will you do that son? *Will* you? And not just them . . . But their children too. Because bad people don't deserve to have children."

"Yes, Daddy," I told him and took the piece of paper. And I kept that piece of paper all through the years in the orphanage and beyond. I still have the original but here's a copy.

Lee felt something akin to ice water trickle through her veins as she read the list of murdered policemen. And there, scrawled next to the number "8," was her father's name.

ELEVEN

ee rose two hours earlier than usual, showered, and got ready
for work. Breakfast consisted of coffee and a stale blueberry
muffin from a drive-thru restaurant.

Lee's heart was beating a little faster than usual as she
approached the Street Services Garage and for good reason. She
was about to risk her career for Kane by using her position to
run a records check she shouldn't run. Would someone notice it?
Probably not . . . But if they did, Internal Affairs would nail her.
Who had the opportunity to access the records on that particular
morning? Answer: Detective Lee. And who had the motive to
help accused murderer Dr. Lawrence Kane? Answer: Detective
Lee. Case closed. Next.

With that in mind, Lee parked the car, entered the building,
and went straight to her desk. Other people were present but
very few compared to the number who would arrive when the
day watch started at 7:00 A.M.

Should someone ask, Lee planned to tell them that she'd come
in early in order to work through her in-box. To support that story
she logged on to her computer and opened her e-mail. Then she
removed a thumb drive from her bag, put the bag in a drawer,
and pushed it closed.

Lee said "Hi" to a homicide detective as they passed each
other in the main corridor, took a left, and made her way back
past some cubicles to the cramped space where records clerk

Misty Gammon did her job. Gammon was employed by the LAPD's Records and Identification Division. It ran a stand-alone computer system that was isolated from the Internet, and because of that, it was virtually impossible to hack.

That was no defense against someone's making unauthorized use of it from the *inside*, however, which Lee was about to do, thanks to the fact that Misty had her log-on written on a slip of paper in her lap drawer. A fact known to at least a dozen detectives as well as various clerks who took over when Misty was ill or on vacation. It wasn't right, of course, but like so many workarounds, it solved a problem, and higher-ups had chosen to ignore it.

After a quick glance over her shoulder, Lee sat down on the thick cushion that Misty kept on her chair, pulled the lap drawer open, and eyed the slip of paper that was taped to the beige-colored metal. Keys rattled as Lee entered the alphanumeric code and hit ENTER.

When the Records Division interface appeared, Lee chose "Motor Vehicle Licenses," and entered "Janice Olin." Bingo! There it was: Olin's name, birth date, and address. It took only seconds to transfer the data to the thumb drive and slip that into a pocket.

Then, conscious of the seconds that were ticking away, Lee exited the system. The moment the screen went dark, Lee left the area and returned to her desk, where she heaved a sigh of relief. She was in the clear, for the moment at least, since Misty had no reason to check recent activity on her terminal, and even if she did, the clerk would assume Olin was under investigation by one of the detectives.

No, there wouldn't be any trouble unless IA got wind of what she'd been up to, and Lee planned to avoid that. As for the information itself, Lee would follow up on that later. But first it was necessary to get through the day.

Lee wanted to have one of the department's experts look at the Bonebreaker journal and give her an opinion as to whether it had actually been written by him. So she placed a call to a forensic document examiner named Alvin Soltis. She'd dealt with the specialist before—and wasn't looking forward to doing so again.

But like most of the people on the day watch, Soltis hadn't arrived yet. So she left a message and went to work on clearing the backlog of e-mails. And she was working on her weekly activity report when the phone rang. "Detective Lee."

"This is Alvin," Soltis said. "Long time no see. What can I do for you?"

Lee gave him a general idea of what she wanted and Soltis agreed. "Thanks to all of the material recovered from the Bonebreaker's hideout, plus the notes he sent in after some of the murders, we have lots of handwriting samples to work with. When can I expect the most beautiful detective in the department to arrive?"

"I don't know," Lee said. "You'll have to ask her. I'll be there at eight thirty." Then she hung up. Some people change over time—Soltis wasn't one of them.

Just prior to roll call, Lee managed to corral Yanty and Prospo long enough to show them the journal—and tell them about the appointment with Soltis. "Providing this thing is real, and it fits with the evidence collected in the cemetery, it could help us create an accurate profile. But remember . . . We've got to focus on the Corso shooting at the moment. I'm scheduled to meet with Carolina Moss at noon."

"I'm trying to get a one-on-one with Ma," Yanty put in. "But he doesn't seem all that eager to talk."

"I have an appointment to see Stryker at his gym," Prospo added. "He's a fitness freak."

"You should try it," Yanty suggested. "Before your blood turns to gravy."

Prospo looked hurt. "Let he without brains throw the first stone."

Lee laughed. "Okay, you two . . . Let's go to roll call. And, Dick, if you fall asleep, do it with your eyes open."

Roll call was a routine affair for the most part. According to Jenkins, Corso was not only stable but able to speak. A good sign indeed.

The team working on the Halvo kidnapping had very little progress to report, the detective in charge of Operation Roundup announced that her group was about to be disbanded, and Prospo gave a brief presentation regarding the Bonebreaker case.

So far, all of the evidence gathered from the underground hideout was consistent with the theory that the killer had lived there for a long period of time. And based on items collected there, a long-standing question had been answered: By what means was the Bonebreaker able to incapacitate so many armed policemen? And then abduct them?

The answer was one of the many disguises at his disposal, combined with a long barreled CO_2-powered pistol, and a dart loaded with Ketamine—an anesthetic that was widely available on the street. "Once an individual was subdued," Prospo told them, "the Bonebreaker could load him or her into a stolen vehicle and wait for night to fall. Then he would drive to a spot on the west side of the cemetery, where a section of fence had been loosened.

"Once inside, the Bonebreaker could open the trapdoor located nearby and lower his victim into the tunnel below. Maybe he left the vehicle to be towed, or maybe he took it somewhere, that isn't clear yet. But a handcart was found in an alcove near the entry point and might have been used to move prisoners from the point below the trapdoor to the so-called lab area, where they were tortured and killed."

Lee fought to suppress the images that the words conjured up and was glad when Prospo's report came to an end. He made no mention of the journal, which was just as well since Alvin Soltis hadn't had a chance to look at it yet.

When roll call was over, Lee returned to her desk to get the journal. Then, just as she was about to leave for the appointment with Soltis, her phone rang. "Detective Lee."

"This is Carla," the voice on the other end of the line said. "Carla Zumin with Channel 7 News."

Alarm bells went off in Lee's head. Was Zumin recording the conversation? Possibly, so it was important to choose her words with care. "Good morning, Carla . . . What can I do for you?"

"I'm calling about the Getty investigation," Zumin replied. "I understand that you're in charge of it. What can you tell me about the nature of the charges?"

The investigation hadn't been made public. So how did Zumin know? The obvious answer was a leak. But who would do that? The question seemed to answer itself. Deputy Chief Jenkins, that's who ... By leaking the news, he was trying to make it more difficult for Getty to quash the investigation—and put additional pressure on the mayor. How much information had Zumin been given? Lee had no way to know but figured that the reporter was attempting to verify what she had and get more if possible. There was a pause as all of that flashed through Lee's mind. "Are you still there?" Zumin inquired.

"Yes, I'm still here," Lee responded. "I can neither confirm nor deny that such an investigation is under way."

"Which, translated into real speak, means it's true," Zumin said confidently.

"I suggest that you call Molly in Public Affairs," Lee said. "If there is an investigation, and if it's public, she'll know about it."

"Sure," Zumin said sarcastically, "I'll get right on that. You'll have to talk eventually, Cassandra, and when you do, remember that you owe me."

"For what?"

"For watching you leave the MDC last night and keeping it off the air," Zumin responded. Then she hung up. Lee swore and put the phone down. There had been lots of pressure to begin with. There would be even more now.

Since the Criminalistics Laboratory occupied rented space about a block away from the garage, it made sense to walk there. It was going to be a hot day, but the air was still cool, and Lee enjoyed the opportunity to get outside.

There was no sign on the storefront. Just an address. As Lee opened the door, she found herself in a dingy lobby so small, there was room for only two chairs and a tired plant. After showing her ID to the woman behind the counter, and signing a log, Lee had to wait. Soltis made his appearance a few minutes later.

The specialist was of average height, had carefully tousled hair, and was reasonably good-looking. That didn't keep him from being a pain in the ass, however. The smile came on as if a switch had been thrown. "Cassandra! You look lovely as always."

"And you are full of shit as always," Lee replied.

The receptionist giggled, but Soltis didn't seem to notice as he ushered Lee through a pair of swinging doors. "I get it," he said. "No hanky-panky at work. So let's get together this evening and get something going."

"You should watch the news more often," Lee replied, as they walked down a hallway. "If you did, you'd know that I'm dating an accused murderer . . . He's locked up in the MDC at the moment—but we hope to get him out soon."

The expression on Soltis's face was priceless. Lee was pretty sure that she saw elements of surprise, disapproval, *and* fear in the way he looked at her. It was difficult not to laugh.

Although the lab was clean and well lit, it had a make-do quality about it. Worktables consisted of pieces of plywood that rested on sawhorses, wires dangled snakelike from the ceiling, and the filing cabinets were various hues, including tan, green, and black. On the way back, they passed two white-coated technicians, both of whom were engrossed in whatever they were doing. "Okay," Soltis said, as they arrived at his workstation. "Let's see what you have."

Lee gave him the journal, and Soltis paused to pull gloves on prior to opening the cover. She watched him flip through the book. He paused every once in a while to examine a page under a powerful magnifier. Then he looked up at her. "That's some interesting stuff."

"So?" Lee inquired. "I know you'll need time in order to carry out a complete evaluation, but I need a preliminary opinion. Should we take this thing seriously?"

"Hold your horses," Soltis said, "I'm getting there. Let me do some comparisons. Then I'll give you my initial impressions."

Lee had to stand around and wait for the better part of half an hour while Soltis compared journal entries to handwriting samples that the Bonebreaker had "donated" over the years, along with documents gathered from his underground bunker. Finally, the document examiner turned to look at Lee.

"Okay, here's what I think. The Bonebreaker tried to alter his handwriting on the notes he sent in after some of the murders. But there are still lots of similarities to the handwriting in the journal. And, given the age of the paper, variations in ink, and the inclusion of contemporaneous clippings, I'd say there is a high degree of likelihood that the diary is genuine. Will that impression hold up under an in-depth analysis? We'll see."

"Thanks, Alvin," Lee said. "That's a huge help. Please let me know as soon as the final report is ready."

"Will do," Soltis assured her. "I hope your boyfriend gets out of jail soon."

"Me, too," Lee told him. "Who knows? Maybe the three of us could go out for drinks." She could feel his eyes on her back as she left and felt sure he wouldn't come on to her again. Victory was hers.

After returning to the office, Lee went looking for Jenkins and discovered that he wasn't in his office. "He's with Chief Yessum," a clerk informed her.

Lee wasn't surprised. Chances were that Zumin or some other reporter had called the mayor's office in an attempt to get more information about the investigation, which caused Getty to call Yessum, who called Jenkins.

Lee glanced at her watch and saw that she had only forty-five minutes to reach the shopping center where she was to meet with Carolina Moss. So she grabbed the recorder, slipped the device into her bag, and went out to the parking lot.

Because the Taj Mahal Shopping Complex was located in Hollywood Hills, and traffic was heavy, she barely made it in time. Everyone knew the story of how Carolina Moss and her husband had purchased a small strip mall, acquired the land around it during the depression that followed the plague, and borrowed money to construct the sprawling shopping complex laid out in front of her.

After parking the sedan, Lee hurried across a large parking lot. There were clusters of palm trees to provide a vaguely tropical feel, recirculating pools of water here and there, and festive-looking tents where shoppers could buy food and drink.

But the centerpiece of the complex was the transparent cap that sat atop the Taj Mahal's considerable dome. Sunlight glinted off glass, and Lee could see tiny figures working up there. To clean it? That seemed likely.

Lee followed a steady flow of foot traffic inside, where she could smell the carefully scented air and hear the soothing music. The mood was one of restrained opulence, and the beautifully dressed shoppers were clearly well-off. Lee spotted a kiosk and went over to speak with a woman dressed in a sarilike garment. Her name was Margo according to the name tag that she wore. "Hello, how can I help you?"

"I'm here for an appointment with Mrs. Moss."

"And you are?"

Lee showed her ID, and the woman nodded. "Hold on, hon . . . I'll let them know you're here." At that point, Margo picked up a phone and made a call. "This is Margo down by the north entrance. Detective Lee is here to see Mrs. Moss."

Margo nodded, said "Thanks," and hung up. "Ken is coming down to get you. There are some chairs over there . . . Please have a seat."

Lee preferred to stand, and her eyes were drawn inevitably upward. There were at least twenty circular galleries, each smaller than the last, with the glass dome at the very top. Rays of golden sunshine streamed down through the glass, and Lee got the impression that God might speak at any moment.

"Detective Lee?" The voice came from behind her, and Lee turned to find that a young man was standing there. He was something of a dandy, judging from the artfully combed hair, the pink bow tie, and the blue shirt. His suit was tight, as if to emphasize a slim figure, and Lee could smell the cloud of cologne that surrounded him. "My name is Ken," he said. "It's a pleasure to meet you. Mrs. Moss asked me to accompany you to the eighteenth floor."

Ken led Lee over to an escalator that spiraled upward. It would be an uncomfortable ride for anyone who was afraid of heights. As Lee looked down, she could see the central pool, the lush greenery that surrounded it, and places for tired shoppers to sit. "Here we are," Ken said, as they got off on eighteen.

Lee followed Ken along a walkway. There were expensive stores on the left and a vast, open space on the right. Then the path curved away from the center of the building to make way for a large restaurant. There were lots of linen-covered tables, gleaming silverware, and well-watered plants. They served to separate the booths and provide diners with an illusion of privacy. "Mrs. Moss eats here every day," Ken explained. "It's just one of the things she does to stay in touch with the Taj Mahal's customers and employees."

Lee couldn't see how eating lunch there would keep Moss in touch with anyone other than her waiter, but Ken seemed to believe it, and that was fine. Ken waved to a receptionist as they breezed past—and led Lee to a large booth protected by vegetation on three sides. The dome's transparent cap was only fifty feet above the restaurant. So when Lee looked up, she could see a couple of workmen and the sky beyond.

A woman who Lee assumed to be Carolina Moss was already seated on a curved banquette. She was flanked by two nearly identical Pomeranians—both of which had fancy collars and shiny eyes. Moss looked up from a pink data pad as Ken cleared his throat. "Excuse me, Mrs. Moss, but Detective Lee is here."

Moss had shoulder-length black hair that was heavily streaked with gray. She was wearing glasses with oval lenses and gold-leaf earrings. Lee figured that the gray-and-black animal-print top that Moss was wearing would cost her a month's salary. Moss smiled. "It's a pleasure, Detective Lee . . . Or I hope it will be, anyway. Please forgive me for remaining seated. I sprained an ankle a few days ago, and it still hurts. Have a seat."

Lee sat down on the banquette with a dog on her left. It growled deep in its throat. "Don't worry about Mr. Bigels," Moss said. "He's a sweetheart."

"I'm glad to hear that," Lee replied as she placed the recorder on the table. "As you know, I'm here to talk about your relationship with Mayor Getty. If you have no objection, I'm going to record the conversation."

"I suppose my attorney would object," Moss said. "But screw him . . . He objects to *everything*. And I have nothing to hide. What's this about anyway? I like Melissa. She's a nice person and a good mayor."

"I'm in charge of a team looking into allegations that Mayor Getty traded favors in return for support from people such as yourself."

"Like *what*?" Moss demanded.

"It's my understanding that you are in the process of expanding this shopping center—and in order to do that, you need more land. But, until the mayor threw her weight behind your push for the necessary zoning changes, the plan was dead in the water. So her support was worth a great deal to you."

"So? Melissa made the right choice on behalf of the city. This mall employs more than a thousand people, produces millions in tax revenue, and supports the local community in a variety of ways. What's wrong with that?"

"Nothing on the face of it," Lee replied. "But we have evidence that you offered to make an extremely large donation to the Fortuna Foundation in return for the mayor's support. That would be illegal."

Moss threw back her head and laughed. The dogs looked alarmed. "That's a hoot, it really is," Moss said. "Prior to my husband's death, we donated money to the Fortuna Foundation on a regular basis, and I continue to do so, as does Melissa. Hell, we serve on the board of advisors together . . . So, as the saying goes, there's no there-there."

At that point Lee realized why Moss's attorney wasn't present. The two of them had discussed the situation and agreed on a story. A story that would seem more genuine if Moss pitched it alone. What they didn't realize was that the DA had a videotape in which Moss could be seen cutting the deal with Getty.

But Lee didn't want Moss to realize that . . . Not yet. And what she did want to do was put some pressure on. Maybe Moss would turn on Getty, and maybe she wouldn't, but it was worth a try. "Okay," Lee said. "But just to be clear, were the DA to prove the existence of a quid pro quo, the arrangement would still be illegal regardless of donations made in the past."

Moss frowned and opened her mouth to say something. But the words were never said. A charge went off, the dome shattered, and shards of glass rained down on the unsuspecting shoppers below. Lee could hear screams as she jumped up and rushed to peer over the wall. There was pandemonium as some people fled, and others stayed to help the injured.

Lee was still struggling to understand what had taken place when the answer dropped from above. The man was dressed in black, armed with a submachine gun, and dangling at the end of a rope. Lee was in the process of drawing the Glock when he opened fire. Lamps shattered, and there were *more* screams as bullets sprayed the inside of the restaurant.

That forced Lee to duck. And by the time she stuck her head up, the first terrorist had dropped down past the eighteenth floor. Lee was about to fire at him when more killers dropped from above. And that was when Lee remembered the people she'd seen earlier. Not working, as it turned out—but preparing to attack the shopping center!

Lee began to track one of the perps. He was still in motion, which made for a tricky shot. *Lead him,* Lee thought to herself as she allowed her talent to kick in. The Glock seemed to fire itself. The first shot missed but the rest didn't. The man jerked and went limp.

Then someone cut the rope high above and the body plummeted to the floor below. When it hit there was a flash of light and a BOOM that sounded even louder inside the dome. *Bombs!* The bastards had bombs strapped to their bodies— explosives that could be detonated on command by someone up above.

More people were being lowered into the shopping center by that time, but Lee chose to ignore them as she squinted her eyes. It was difficult to see through the swirling smoke, but she saw a shadowy figure standing near the edge of the shattered dome. Was that their leader? The person who could detonate their explosive vests? Maybe.

Lee took careful aim and fired six shots. She thought she'd missed until her target toppled forward. What had been a blob turned into a body as it fell past her. Lee looked down to see it splash into the pool.

But the battle wasn't over. Far from it. Two terrorists were dangling inside the dome, each at a different level. Lee dropped a magazine onto the floor and shoved a fresh one into the Glock as she leaned out to look. One of the shooters was firing a machine pistol, and the recoil was causing him to spin. Empty brass arced away from him to fall into the abyss as glass shattered and people on the thirteenth floor screamed.

Lee took aim and was about to shoot the bastard when a bullet whizzed by her ear. She looked up to see a figure in black pointing a pistol at her. Lee ducked, heard two shots, and came up firing. That was when she saw a flash of light followed by a clap of thunder.

The force of the blast threw Lee back onto the floor. She hit hard, lay there for a second, and struggled to her feet. A chorus of sirens could be heard from outside. For the first time since the attack began, Lee had time to check on Carolina Moss. The businesswoman was facedown on the table, and the formerly pristine tablecloth was stained with blood. Mr. Bigels was whining and licking Moss's arm. The other dog was nowhere to be seen.

Lee went over to check for a pulse and was unable to find one. The recorder was where she'd left it. Lee picked the device up, turned it off, and put it in her bag. The interview was over. But a long, exhausting afternoon had just begun.

After doing what she could to help patrol officers organize the response to the shopping center attack and checking to make sure that all of the injured were being treated, Lee drove back to the office. As Lee listened to her police radio and civilian news coverage, a picture began to emerge. Aztec terrorists had carried out eight highly coordinated attacks on the city in addition to the one at the Taj Mahal shopping center. The other targets included the airport, the metro, and a freeway interchange that had been destroyed by a massive truck bomb.

Up until then, Lee had been too busy to pay much attention to the war but, according to the newscasters, the attack on LA was just the latest in a string of such incidents in other cities. They included Phoenix, Arizona, McAllen, Texas, and Corpus Christi. Lee thought about her friend, Deputy Ras Omo, and hoped he was okay.

The first thing Lee noticed as she approached the Street Services Garage was that security had been doubled. She had to show ID *three* times before being allowed to enter the parking lot.

Once in the building, Lee went looking for Jenkins and found him in a makeshift war room. Phones were ringing, a Channel 4 newsperson could be seen on the wall screen, and the whiteboard was covered with lists of things that needed to be accomplished.

"There you are," Jenkins said, as Lee entered. "According to what we heard, you capped two or three of the bastards at the Taj Mahal! Well done. Based on preliminary estimates, sixty-eight people were killed there—and about a hundred and fifty were wounded. Some of them are listed as critical, so the death toll is likely to rise."

"What about the rest of LA?"

Jenkins scowled. "At least a thousand people are dead—and three times that many were wounded. It looks like the terrorists spent weeks filtering into the city, choosing targets, and getting ready. All of them were passers . . . So that made their job a lot easier."

"Passers" were mutants who looked normal but were BN positive and could be communicable. This meant that there was a *second* element to the assault. During the weeks leading up to the attacks, the mutants could have infected hundreds or even thousands of people with *B. nosilla*. That would scare the hell out of an already terrorized population. "So they're using germ warfare, too."

"Yeah," Jenkins said disgustedly.

"So what's the deal, Boss? I shot some of the bastards . . . Does that mean I have to sit at my desk?"

"No, you don't," a third voice interjected. Lee turned to find that Chief Yessum had entered the room. "Taken together, our people shot twenty-seven terrorists today," Yessum said. "And I can't spare that many cops—not to mention the people required to investigate all those incidents. So I asked the police commission to suspend the shooting-review requirement for twenty-four hours. But it will be back in force at midnight. So no time off for you."

The last was said with a grin, and even though Lee wasn't sure she could trust Yessum where the Getty case was concerned, she liked his cut-through-the-crap style. "Yes, sir. I'm glad to hear it."

Yessum turned to look at Jenkins. "Can I borrow the detective for a few minutes?"

Jenkins nodded. "Of course."

"Thanks," Yessum said. "Follow me, young lady . . . Let's get some coffee."

After getting some coffee from the break room, Yessum

led Lee into what had been Corso's office. She was beginning to worry by then. Did Yessum know she was working to free Kane? If so, she was in deep trouble.

"Have a seat," Yessum said, as he closed the door behind her. Then, rather than put the desk between them, he sat in one of four guest chairs. "So," the chief said, as their eyes met. "This morning, before the attacks began, I saw a news story about the Getty investigation. Tell me something . . . Were you the one who leaked it?"

Lee opened her mouth to reply but stopped when Yessum raised a hand. "Hold on. We're getting acquainted . . . But I know you're something of a legend around here. A street cop's street cop. And you have a rep as a straight shooter in more ways than one. So don't bullshit me, Detective . . . Are you responsible for the leak?"

Lee looked into Yessum's gun-barrel eyes. "No, sir."

Yessum nodded. "I believe you . . . And I'm not stupid enough to ask you who did. I was sorry to hear about Mrs. Moss. Tell me about the interview."

Lee told him, and when she was done, he leaned back in the chair. "So you don't have much of anything."

"That isn't true," Lee replied. "*I*, that is *we*, have the tape, and it shows Moss cutting a deal with the mayor. I assume you've seen it. Moss was guilty as hell."

Yessum eyed her. "Are you aware that the mayor and I are friends?"

"Sir, yes, sir."

"So if I tell you to back off, and to help the police department protect the city from Aztec terrorists, you'll assume I'm doing her a favor."

The last thing Lee expected was for Yessum to be so direct. There was only one answer she could give. "Yes, sir. I will. And so will my team."

Yessum took a sip of coffee and made a face. "This stuff tastes like shit."

"Yes, sir, it does."

"Okay, here's what I want you to do . . . Put your foot on the gas and find out who shot Chief Corso. Maybe that will have a bearing on the Getty investigation, and maybe it won't. If it's relevant, follow the evidence wherever it leads, no matter how high that may be . . . But keep the focus on that shooter. I want that bastard. Do you read me?"

"Yes, sir. Five-by-five."

"Good. Tell your team what I said."

"I will."

Yessum smiled. "It's half past six . . . Go home, Detective Lee. Get some rest and go after it tomorrow."

Lee knew she'd been dismissed and left. Thanks to the talk with Yessum, she felt as if a heavy load had been lifted off her shoulders—and she planned to follow his orders to the letter. She couldn't go home, though . . . Not until she paid a visit to a woman named Janice Olin.

So she took Olin's address off the USB drive, wrote it down, and left the office. Once in the car, Lee read the address to the sedan's nav system. It thanked her and threw a map onto the screen. The address was in Sherman Oaks, which meant a half-hour drive under good conditions, and the worst part of rush hour was over. Lee took 101 into the general vicinity, got off, and followed the map into a nice, middle-class neighborhood. The house she was looking for was well kept and had clearly been built prior to the plague. Lee got out, locked the car, and crossed the street. It was dark by then, and she could see that the lights were on. A short flight of stairs took her up to a tidy porch with a single chair on it. There was a button next to the entrance, and Lee pushed it. The better part of a minute passed before the door opened a little and a middle-aged woman peered through the gap. Her hair was pulled back, and she was wearing glasses. "Yes? How can I help you?"

"My name is Cassandra Lee . . . I'm looking for Janice. Is she in?"

"No, she isn't."

"I see . . . And you are?"

The woman blinked rapidly. "I'm her mother. Is there a problem of some sort?"

Lee couldn't flash her badge since that would make things even worse if the IA people came after her. All she could rely on was charm. "A friend of mine is in jail charged with a crime he didn't commit," Lee replied. "And I have reason to believe that your daughter witnessed the incident. If so, her testimony could be very helpful. When will she return?"

"Janice doesn't live here," Mrs. Olin replied. "And she travels a great deal."

I'll bet she does, Lee thought to herself. "Could I have her phone number?" Lee inquired. "I'll give her a call."

"I can't provide that," Mrs. Olin replied. "Not without my daughter's permission."

"I understand," Lee said as she wrote in a small notebook. "This is my number . . . Please ask Janice to call me."

"Okay," Mrs. Olin said doubtfully. "But she's very busy. I can't promise."

"Understood," Lee said. "But please tell her that the man who tried to protect her on the night that the Aztecs shelled the city has been accused of murder."

Mrs. Olin's eyes grew wider. "Murder?"

"Yes. My friend shot a man who was attacking your daughter."

"Oh, my! That's terrible. I'll tell her."

"Thank you," Lee said, and went back to the car. After performing a 360, she drove away. When she was a block away, Lee pulled over to the curb to make a phone call.

Codicil answered after three rings. "Hello, this is Marvin Codicil."

"Cassandra here . . . I need some help."

"I'm not surprised. You never call to say 'Hi.'"

"Sorry about that . . . But I have some information regarding the mystery woman."

"Really? Shoot."

Lee told Codicil about the research Keyes had performed and their conclusions. "So," she said, "I went to the address listed on Olin's license. She doesn't live there, but I spoke with her mother."

"I won't ask how you got that information," Codicil said.

"Good. Don't. Anyway, Mrs. Olin refused to supply her daughter's phone number."

"Which supports your theory regarding what Janice does for a living."

"Yes. And, assuming she doesn't know about Kane's situation, she'll want to help. I left my phone number."

"And if she *does* know? And fails to call you?"

"Then she's a bitch. So, just to cover all the bases, I'm hoping your investigator can watch Mrs. Olin. Maybe she'll lead us to Janice."

"Give me the address," Codicil said. "I'll take care of it. By the way, I saw the news coverage regarding the Bonebreaker's hideout. Congratulations."

"Thanks."

"A word of caution, though . . ."

"Yes?"

"He's still out there."

TWELVE

It was early in the morning. Much earlier than Dr. Mark Holby liked to get up. Unfortunately, he had no choice in the matter because George Ma wanted to see him. And since Holby owed Ma two hundred and fifty thousand nu, and since his wife was unaware of the debt, he had to do Ma's bidding. And it was important to be on time.

Traffic came to a halt, and Holby hit the horn in frustration. That produced a rude gesture from the driver in front of him. The moment was emblematic of the way things had gone for Holby. Looking back, he could see that his parents were at fault. They were rich, so he'd been rich, and that led to bad habits.

At his mother's insistence, Holby had applied to dental school, and thanks to a hefty endowment from his father, he made the cut. But it was more fun to chase girls, play golf, and go hunting than it was to study. So his grades suffered. He graduated, but his dental practice was a failure for all of the same reasons that he'd done poorly in school.

Girls, women by then, took up a great deal of Holby's time and resources. As did his favorite sports. But when he met Melissa at a cocktail party, things clicked. The physical chemistry was there—and she had the ambition that he lacked. As Melissa made her mark in politics, Holby supported her with money and the good-old-boy personality that her supporters loved. His job was to play golf, go hunting, and learn the family business.

Unfortunately, there hadn't been enough time for the third activity. So when his father died, and Holby took charge of the company, it floundered. And as profits fell, Holby sought to recoup his losses in Ma's casinos. Looking back, it was clear that his parents should have established a trust fund for him—and hired a professional to run the company.

Could he tell Melissa? Yes, but the look of disappointment in her eyes would be hard to take, and the last thing Holby wanted to do was add something more to her considerable burdens.

Holby put his foot on the gas as the car in front of him pulled away. He wasn't a complete loser though . . . Unbeknownst to Melissa, he'd been able to slow if not stop the investigation into her relationship with people like Silverman and Ma, the latter being the individual who had ordered Holby to either kill Chief Corso or pay off his gambling debt. And, since Holby didn't have enough money, the choice was no choice at all.

The lights on top of a cop car stuttered as Holby passed a three-car accident, and traffic began to flow. Holby couldn't refuse Ma, but he could negotiate his fee, and he'd done a good job of it. In return for shooting Corso, fifty thou had been deducted from his debt. And although Corso was still alive, Ma's goal had been achieved. Corso wasn't pushing the investigation anymore. So what did Ma want now? Holby didn't know. But one thing was for sure . . . It was going to cost the casino owner fifty thousand nu.

Lee had been at work for an hour when the e-mail from Alvin Soltis arrived. It was ten paragraphs long and loaded with qualifiers. But after wading through all of the CYA bullshit, the document examiner's conclusions were clear: The Bonebreaker journal was for real. And that was enough to get her going on a task she'd been putting off. It was time to check on Dr. Penn.

After e-mailing an official request to records clerk Misty Gammon, Lee performed an Internet search on the criminologist, and came up with 76,923 hits. And he was, by all accounts, the real deal. Unlike many academics, Penn had worked in the field, most notably for the preplague F.B.I. Then he'd gone back to school to get his doctorate before accepting a teaching position at the University of Maryland. During the years that followed, Penn served as a consultant on some very-high-profile murder cases and was credited with solving a couple of them. Finally, after a successful career in teaching, Penn retired. That was when he and his wife departed the Northeast for sunny California. And their timing was excellent since the plague was released on the world shortly thereafter, and Maryland fell inside a red zone.

Mentions of Penn began to dwindle subsequent to that, but he had published an updated version of an existing textbook and had told a crime blogger that he was writing a book on the subject of serial killers. All of which was consistent with the letter that came with the journal. The records check came back shortly after Lee completed her online search. There was no way to check with the authorities in Maryland anymore but, with the exception of a minor fender bender in LA, Penn's record was clean.

That was good enough for Lee, who got the letter out, found Penn's number, and dialed the phone. Three rings were followed by a cheerful "Hello."

"Is this Dr. Penn?"

"Yes, it is," the man answered. "What can I do for you?" The voice had a raspy quality, similar to one Lee had heard in the past, but she couldn't place it.

"This is Detective Lee with the Los Angeles Police Department. I'm calling in regards to the journal that you sent me."

"Ah yes," Penn replied. "What did you think of it?"

"It's very interesting," Lee replied. "And, according to one of our document examiners, it's genuine."

"I thought it was," Penn replied. "Although there's the possibility of an imposter. It's hard to imagine a wannabe with the skills and patience required to create something so realistic, however. And to what end?"

"I agree," Lee replied. "And I'd like to meet with you. I imagine you have some theories about the Bonebreaker, and I'd like to hear them."

"I have some opinions," Penn allowed, "and I'd be happy to discuss them."

"How does tomorrow look?" Lee inquired. "Say ten o'clock?"

"That would be fine," Penn replied. "You have my address?"
"I do," Lee said. "I'll see you there."

There was a click followed by a dial tone. The Bonebreaker put the receiver down. *It worked!* Lee had taken the bait. Just when he'd been ready to give up. *Thank you, God . . . Thank you for answering my prayers.*

The first part of his plan was complete, and twenty-four hours would be plenty of time in which to prepare his backup residence and set the trap that would kill Cassandra Lee. The Bonebreaker whistled while he worked.

Mayor Getty's office was located in the Los Angeles City Hall. It was a little after eleven in the morning, and she was seated with her back to a wall-sized painting of Los Angeles in which city hall loomed larger than everything else. Her desk, like the rest of the furniture, was made of mahogany and had been donated to the city by a wealthy supporter.

Sunlight poured in through the tall windows on her right, and matching cabinets dominated the wall on the left. The shelves were loaded with photos of Getty standing next to VIPs of every possible stripe which, taken together, symbolized how far a lower-middle-class girl could go. And how far she could fall. It was something very much on Getty's mind as she waited for Chief Yessum to arrive.

Suddenly, out of nowhere, stories had appeared in the press. All based on statements made by an unidentified police official who claimed that she was being investigated. But for *what*? Things she'd done, or things she *hadn't* done? The second was better than the first but a problem nevertheless. Her first instinct had been to chat with the DA. But his response was a chilly, "I have no comment at this time."

That was enough to confirm that something was going on, however . . . And, according to back-channel sources, Chief Corso was behind whatever it was. Then Corso had been shot. By whom? And for what reason? Not that Getty wasn't grateful . . .

The shooting had the effect of dividing the press corps' attention and slowing the investigation.

But Getty needed more than that . . . She needed to have the whole thing go away. And now that Yessum was in charge of the police department, that was a real possibility. Getty's thoughts were interrupted when her secretary appeared in the doorway. "Chief Yessum is here."

"Send him in," Getty said. "And could we have some fresh coffee, please?"

"Of course," Chloe replied, and disappeared.

Getty was up out of her chair by the time Yessum entered—and she went over to accept a hug. "Good morning, Sam. Thanks for coming by. How's it going? Did you get all of the terrorists?"

Yessum shrugged. "Interrogations are still under way . . . But according to preliminary estimates, we nailed about 90 percent of the bastards. As for the possibility of a second wave? That's anyone's guess. The fact that the 'tecs are using passers makes our job that much harder."

"Of course it does," Getty said sympathetically. "Please . . . Have a seat."

An oval-shaped coffee table surrounded by six chairs occupied the center of the room. Chloe entered, carrying a tray just as they sat down. "Thank you, Chloe," Getty said as she reached for the thermos. "This will fix you up, Sam . . . I know how much you like your coffee."

"I do like coffee," Yessum admitted, as the mayor filled his cup. "And, since most of it comes from the Aztec Empire, it's getting more expensive every day."

After serving herself, Getty eyed Yessum over the edge of her cup. "I won't dance around it Sam, I need your advice, *and* your help."

Yessum met her gaze. "Regarding the investigation?"

"Yes."

"I figured that would come up," Yessum told her. "So I brought you a present. Just a sec . . . I'm going to load something into your player."

A flat screen was mounted on the wall next to the display cabinets—and a universal player was sitting on the console table below it. Getty watched Yessum insert a thumb drive into one of the ports and wondered what he planned to show her.

Yessum took his seat, took the remote off the coffee table, and waited for the directory to appear. Then he selected an item titled "Getty Video" and pressed play.

Video swirled, and Getty wasn't sure what she was looking at until the picture locked up. Then she saw herself sitting across from Syd Silverman in Maxim's apartment! Getty felt a chasm open at the pit of her stomach as the audio came up, and Syd began to pitch the *Oceana* project. Damn Maxim! The bastard was *still* screwing her, albeit in a different way. Getty looked at Yessum to get his reaction, but his face was blank. "So how many conversations are there?"

"Five," Yessum answered. "There's this one, plus vignettes with Carolina Moss, Jack Stryker, Herman Jones, and George Ma."

Getty felt nauseous. "How bad are they?"

Yessum thumbed a button, and the video froze. "They're pretty bad."

Getty's mind was churning. The tape was Maxim's insurance policy—a way to make sure she couldn't dump him. Not without a financial settlement. That much was clear. But Maxim was dead—so how had the tape come to light?

The answer was obvious. Detective Cassandra Lee! She'd been part of the rescue team, she'd been to Maxim's home, and she was in charge of the investigation. Or so the reporter on Channel 5 claimed. Assuming that chain of logic was correct, Lee had been able to get her grubby hands on the tape and had given it to Corso, who wanted her job. The bastard.

Yessum was sipping coffee and waiting for her to absorb the full import of what she'd seen. As Getty put her cup down, she discovered that her hand was shaking. "I want to speak in my own defense," she said. "Yes, I cut deals, but not to make myself rich . . . Not a single penny went to me or my family. Everything I did was aimed at winning reelection, so I could continue to serve the people of Los Angeles."

Yessum nodded. "I believe you, Melissa. That's why I brought the tape over."

Getty looked at him and remembered what she'd been taught.

"Never let them see you sweat." She forced a smile. "Thank you, Sam. I appreciate that . . . And believe me—I won't forget. So, given the nature of my motivation, can you help me?"

The moment the words came out of her mouth, Getty regretted them. What if Yessum was wearing a wire? *He isn't,* her inner voice told her, *but even if he is what difference will it make? Things are about as bad as they can get.*

Yessum frowned. "'Help you,' as in put a stop to the investigation?"

"Yes."

"I'm sorry, Melissa, but that's impossible. There are too many people involved—and too many copies of the tape floating around. Not to mention the fact that the DA has the bit in his teeth—and believes the investigation will get him reelected. All I can do is what I've done . . . And providing you with early access to evidence will cost me my job if it comes out."

Getty swallowed. "I won't tell . . . You can count on that. What advice, if any, can you offer?"

"Beat the DA to it," Yessum replied. "Put the videos out there yourself, spin them up as best you can, and let the voters decide."

Getty was silent for a moment. Then she sighed. "That makes sense, Sam. Thank you. Can I keep the thumb drive?"

"Yes, you'll need it. But please protect my identity."

"I will," Getty promised. "And one more thing . . ."

"Yes?"

"Push Detective Cassandra Lee in front of a bus."

It was 7:36 P.M., and Marvin Codicil was sitting in a van two car lengths north of the Olin residence. *Why? Because I'm an idiot, that's why,* Codicil thought to himself. *And because I'm a sucker for a cause. In this case, Cassandra Lee and Dr. Lawrence Kane. Both of whom deserve something good.*

So rather than pay for around-the-clock surveillance out of Kane's quickly dwindling bank account, Codicil had assigned the six-to-midnight shift to himself. That left the midnight-to-six slot uncovered, but that was okay since it seemed unlikely that Mrs. Olin would visit her daughter during the early-morning hours.

Time dragged by. Neighbors came and went. Codicil listened to classical music, grew weary of it, and switched to a news channel. The city was still recovering from the terrorist attacks and prepping for more. Armed forces from Pacifica and the Republic of Texas were involved in joint exercises in Arizona. Could that mean they were getting ready to invade the Aztec Empire? It would be a bloody business if they did so—but what else could the two countries do? And who knew? Maybe an alliance between the red and green zones would lead to a better relationship in the future.

Codicil's thoughts were interrupted as the front door opened and light spilled out onto the porch. He jerked the earbuds out and tossed them aside as a silhouette appeared, turned, and pulled the door closed. Mrs. Olin? Yes, it must be. Where was she headed? To the store for a quart of milk? Or to a meeting with her daughter? Codicil would have prayed for the second possibility but why bother? He was an atheist, and if God existed, he or she was unlikely to grant him any favors.

Mrs. Olin, if that's who she was, made her way down off the porch and walked to the street. Lights blinked on and off as the *especiale* answered to her remote. As the woman entered her car, Codicil got ready to start his engine. Though no expert on stakeouts, the attorney figured that his vehicle would be less noticeable if he started the engine *after* she pulled out.

Once the sedan pulled away from the curb, Codicil started the engine and followed. If the woman in the car was alarmed, he saw no signs of it as she turned onto an arterial and entered the flow of traffic. They passed a supermarket not long thereafter, and Codicil felt a rising sense of excitement. She wasn't after a quart of milk then . . . Although there were still plenty of possibilities other than a meeting with her daughter.

Even though Codicil hadn't had much experience tailing people, he knew it was important to hang back, but not too far back, lest he lose Mrs. Olin at a light. So Codicil had reason to worry until the woman he was following made a series of turns and pulled into the parking lot outside a restaurant called Nero's Steakhouse. She parked, and he did likewise.

After giving Mrs. Olin a head start, Codicil followed her into the restaurant. It was a dark, gloomy place, much given to black leather booths, dim lighting, and shadowy corners. Was that what Mrs. Olin preferred? Or was it a place her daughter was familiar with? Assuming Janice Olin was there. Codicil watched Mrs. Olin walk to a booth where a younger woman was seated. Bingo! "Can I help you?" The receptionist was a plump woman in a black dress.

"Yes," Codicil said. "One for dinner. I would like to sit over there please . . . It's my favorite booth."

Codicil pointed, and the woman nodded. "Certainly . . . Please follow me."

The two women were already deep in conversation by the time Codicil sat down across from them. The attorney wasn't close enough to hear what was being said—but he recognized Janice Olin right away! Was Mrs. Olin telling her about Kane? Codicil hoped so.

"Good evening," the waiter said. "My name is Pedro . . . And I'll be serving you tonight. Can I get you something to drink?" Pedro was twentysomething and had his hair pulled back into a neat ponytail.

"Yes," Codicil replied. "A gin and tonic would be nice."

"Excellent. And an appetizer?"

"No, thank you."

"I'll be back with water and your gin and tonic," Pedro promised, and left for the bar.

Codicil was hungry and didn't want to order something that would take a long time to prepare lest Janice Olin get up and leave before he was finished. So he settled for a French Dip sandwich. And as he put in the order, he asked for the check. Pedro was clearly surprised but took the request in stride.

As the waiter left, Codicil took a sip of the gin and tonic and winced. The house gin had a medicinal flavor. Rather than stare at the women, Codicil pretended to surf the Internet on his phone while watching them from the corner of his eye. It appeared that they were arguing about something. Time passed, their food arrived, and Pedro brought the French Dip two minutes later. Codicil tackled the sandwich as Pedro went off to run his credit card.

Pedro returned, Codicil signed, and put the card away. He was halfway through the second half of the sandwich when the women got up to leave. Codicil wiped his mouth with his napkin and followed them out. He was focused on Janice Olin now—and cognizant of the fact that she was an experienced law-enforcement officer. Tailing her was likely to be more difficult than following her mother had been.

The women hugged prior to parting ways. Codicil watched Janice Olin head for a sports car and hurried to enter the van. There was a bad moment when a customer backed out of a slot to block him, but Codicil managed to go around, and was there to follow Olin out of the lot.

What ensued was a stressful fifteen minutes' worth of driving as Olin switched lanes, ran a yellow light, and made a lot of turns. Was she trying to lose him? Or simply driving the way she always did? The way she'd been trained to. Codicil hoped for the latter.

In any case, he was still on the woman's tail as she pulled into a decidedly downscale apartment complex. It appeared to consist of three identical concrete buildings with a common area between them. That wasn't what Codicil expected of a federal agent, so he figured that Olin was working undercover.

Olin parked her car, so Codicil did the same and managed to exit quickly enough to follow her. Pole-mounted lights threw a harsh glare down onto the path. Codicil passed a rickety-looking play set, a trash-filled wading pool, and a dead tree on his way to the second apartment building. Even though it was well past nine, people were lounging around the main entrance, smoking weed and drinking beer. Most were men, and Codicil heard one of them shout, "Hola, chica! You look hot, baby . . . I have what you need."

The coarse come-on produced a variety of ribald comments and laughter as Olin entered the building. The merriment gave Codicil an opportunity to slip through without being harassed. The lobby smelled like stale cooking, and bare bulbs lit the hallway. Olin had already passed the elevator with the OUT OF SERVICE sign taped to it, and was headed for the back stairs as Codicil hurried to catch up. An encounter in the hallway wasn't ideal. But since Codicil had no way to know who might be waiting for Olin, it seemed like a good idea to approach the agent before she arrived at her destination. Plus, assuming she was working a case, Codicil didn't want to blow her cover.

"Miss Olin!" the attorney said, as he caught up with her. "My name is Marvin Codicil . . . I'm Dr. Lawrence Kane's attorney. As you may or may not be aware, he shot the man who attacked you the night that the Aztecs shelled the city. The police put him in jail for that. Could I speak with you please?"

As Olin turned, her right hand slipped into her jacket. To access a weapon? Yes, that's the way it appeared, and Codicil raised both hands. "There's no need for a gun. All I want is your account of what took place. In person, if possible. But I could arrange for taped testimony as well—and protect your identity if that's necessary."

Now, in the harsh glare of the overhead light, Codicil thought Olin looked older than she had at Nero's. And older than she actually was. There were deep circles under Olin's eyes, her skin was bad, and he could see a cold sore on her lower lip. Her hand remained where it was. "How did you find me?" she demanded.

"It wasn't easy," Codicil said, "but I did. The fact is that my client may have saved your life. The least you can do is tell authorities what happened."

"*Nothing* happened," Olin said coldly. "Now leave me alone. And if I ever see you again, you'll be sorry."

And with that, Olin turned away. Codicil could hear her heels clicking on concrete as she climbed the stairs. He felt his spirits slump. Olin knew about Kane . . . He felt sure of it. And she didn't care. All he could do was rerun the gauntlet that was waiting outside, and return home.

After receiving Marvin Codicil's phone call, Lee had gone to bed feeling depressed, and as she drove to work the following day, she was still in the dumps. Why had Janice Olin refused to cooperate? Was she working undercover? Or was she a dyed-in-the-wool bitch? Lee was inclined to believe the latter since there were a number of ways that a law-enforcement officer could testify without being publicly identified. *So what are you going to do?* Lee asked herself. *Give up?*

Hell no, came the reply. *I'll find a way,* Lee thought to herself as she joined the line of cars waiting to enter the Street Services Garage parking lot. The city was still on edge in the wake of recent attacks—and the police department had put even more security in place.

After passing through security, Lee entered the building and went straight to her desk. Roll call was scheduled to start in fifteen minutes—and she was supposed to visit Dr. Penn at ten. That didn't leave much time for e-mail. She was working on it when Prospo came in for a landing on her guest chair. "Good morning."

"You, too," Lee said. "What's up?"

"What time are we leaving?"

"Leaving? I have to attend a ten o'clock meeting with Dr. Penn."

"Right," Prospo replied. "That's what I'm talking about. I'm going with you."

Lee's eyebrows floated upwards. "Okay, *why?*"

Prospo looked offended. "Because I've been working on the case for a million years—and because I'd like to hear what Penn has to say. That's why."

"I see," Lee said. "And that's all?"

"It always makes sense to have backup," Prospo said evasively.

"So, you're afraid that Penn will attack me?"

"No, but someone shot Corso ... And you're leading the Getty investigation."

"Speaking of which ... How did the conversation with Stryker go?"

"I think I got his attention," Prospo answered. "In spite of the fact that he did a deal with Getty, I don't think they're that tight. So as things stand right now, I have him pegged as the guy most likely to roll over."

"Okay," Lee said. "You're welcome to come. We'll leave at nine thirty."

Roll call was primarily focused on activities related to preventing another terrorist attack. There was one bit of good news though . . . Chief Corso was up and walking around. That announcement produced a round of applause.

Lee was back at her desk when nine fifteen rolled around, and Prospo appeared. "It will be lunchtime once we clear Dr. Penn's house," he said. "And you're buying."

"Works for me," Lee agreed as she logged out. "But if I'm buying, you're going to have a salad."

"Sure," Prospo replied. "A salad *and* fried chicken. That sounds good."

Lee groaned as she grabbed her bag. "You're hopeless . . . Come on. Let's see what Dr. Penn has to say. This could be interesting."

There were backups on the freeway, some of which were caused by random checkpoints intended to catch terrorists. That forced Lee to take an exit and travel on arterials in order to reach the West Adams section of LA. The delays meant that the detectives were five minutes late when they pulled into a slot two houses down from Penn's bungalow.

Lee made her way to the point where a poorly maintained walk led to a shabby porch and a door covered with peeling paint. That was when she saw the yellow sticky on the door: "Detective Lee, Please come in . . . I'll be back in a minute. Alan."

Lee turned to look around, but other than Prospo, there was no one in sight. So she put her thumb on the latch and pushed. Lee felt the door give and knew it was unlocked. A hinge squeaked as she pushed it open. "Dr. Penn? Are you here?"

There was no answer. So Lee went inside. Prospo followed. Judging from the worn furnishings, Penn didn't have much money. Or, if he did, the academic chose not to spend it.

They were standing there, waiting for Penn to arrive, when Lee noticed the heavy odor of cinnamon in the air. Some sort of deodorizer perhaps? Probably . . . And that was when Prospo grabbed hold of her arm. "Gas! I smell gas! Run!"

Prospo turned toward the front entrance, and as he ran, Lee was right behind him. Fortunately, the door was wide open, which meant that Prospo could charge through without pausing. Lee was two steps back and closing on him when she felt the force of the blast. The explosion threw her forward, and both of them collapsed in a tangle of arms and legs as a loud BOOM shook the surrounding houses. Lee rolled over onto her back in time to see pieces of flaming debris climb high into the blue sky and trail smoke as they fell. Then Prospo grabbed the back of her collar and towed her down the path toward the sidewalk.

Car alarms were shrieking by then, and a siren could be heard in the distance as Lee struggled to stand and look at the blazing inferno that had been Penn's house. "It was a trap," Prospo said thickly, "and the journal was bait."

Lee's mind was reeling. The journal appeared to be real because it *was* real. But Penn wasn't Penn, he was the Bonebreaker! And the criminologist was buried somewhere. "The Bonebreaker is *here*," Lee said as she turned in a circle. "After flooding the house with gas, he used some sort of remote to trigger the blast."

"What you mean is that he *was* here," Prospo said disgustedly. "He's long gone by now."

Lee looked at him. "All I could smell was cinnamon."

Prospo grinned and tapped his generously proportioned nose. "See *this*? It can detect a taco from a hundred feet away."

Lee laughed, the first fire engine arrived on the scene, and a news helicopter appeared overhead. It was going to be a very long day.

Mayor Melissa Getty entered the wood-paneled press conference room at precisely 3:00 P.M. It was crammed with reporters of every possible stripe. Lights strobed as the still photographers clicked away, camera operators jostled each other for position, and reporters tried to elbow their way to the front of the crowd. None of them knew what Getty was going to say—but all of them had a feeling that she was about to drop some sort of bombshell. The result was a feeding frenzy. As Getty stepped up to a thicket of prepositioned microphones, she was having something akin to an out-of-body experience. It felt as if she were looking down on herself the way a spectator would while analyzing what was about to take place.

Getty had been an English major before making the switch to political science in college. As such, she'd been entranced by the perfection of the poem "If—" by Rudyard Kipling. And there was one passage that seemed especially apt given what she was about to do.

"If you can make one heap of all your winnings and risk it on one turn of pitch-and-toss, and lose, and start again at your beginnings and never breathe a word about your loss," Kipling had written, and that described what she was about to do. Because consistent with Yessum's advice, Getty had decided to release the incriminating tape herself rather than wait for someone to leak it.

That would give her the opportunity to put her own spin on the content. And if she lost the next election, then so what? She was happily married, her husband had a lot of money, and she'd be free to do whatever she wanted. As for Silverman, Jones, and the rest, they'd have to fend for themselves. But if they were smart, they'd fall in line and back her narrative.

Getty turned to make eye contact with Press Secretary Marv Barker. He was vehemently opposed to the "let it all hang out" plan. Was he right? *No second thoughts,* Getty told herself as she gave him the nod. *You have a plan. Stick to it.*

Barker addressed the room. "Okay, everybody . . . You can go to our Web site for the press release and the video that the mayor is going to tell you about. She won't be taking questions . . . But there will be a follow-up press availability within the next couple of days. Thank you."

At that point all eyes and cameras turned to focus on Getty. She smiled. "Good afternoon. Thank you for coming on such short notice. As most if not all of you know, rumors about me have been circulating of late. And given all of the problems that face this city, I thought it would be a good idea to clear the air so we can focus our energies on terrorism and *real,* rather than contrived, issues.

"Marv told you that a video has been posted to the city's Web site. It consists of vignettes, clips really, from five different conversations all captured by a security camera located in a friend's apartment. Unfortunately, he was killed during the Aztec assault on our city, but it seems that some of his belongings, including security videos, were stolen by parties unknown."

Getty paused at that point, and as her eyes swept the room, she saw that she had their full attention. *Secret tapes!* The press was enthralled—and some were trying to access the Internet. "So," Getty continued, "since we don't know *who* took what must have been a number of tapes, we don't know *why*. Not for sure.

"But it seems safe to assume that one of my political rivals was involved. Especially since they went to great lengths to edit the videos in a way that would make it appear that I, along with prominent people including Syd Silverman, Carolina Moss, George Ma, Jack Stryker, and Herman Jones, was plotting to win the next election."

Getty smiled. "Well, guess what . . . ? We *were* plotting to win the next election! That's how politics works. And I need to win if I'm going to build on the successes we've had so far. But as you watch the vignettes, here's something you *won't* see . . . You *won't* see me accepting anything that would benefit me personally. What you *will* see is a cynical attempt to win the next election through the use of doctored security videos. So if you want answers regarding the tape, I suggest that you take your questions to the people who have the motive to publish lies about me. Thank you."

And, with that, Getty left the room. At least a dozen reporters shouted questions at her back, all of which went unanswered. Channel 7's Carla Zumin was one of those people—and she was looking forward to viewing the tape. Was Getty correct? Was the tape part of a plot to discredit her? Or had she and the rest of the press corps been witness to a bullshit blizzard? Time would tell.

THIRTEEN

Lee and Prospo had been forced to remain at the scene of the blast all afternoon and into the evening in order to make sure that potential evidence was properly gathered and preserved. That was especially important in light of the fact that the house might have been the scene of a murder. It was too early to say for sure, but the *real* Dr. Penn was missing and presumed dead.

Everyone involved in the investigation assumed that the Bonebreaker had set the trap and triggered the blast, but there was no proof of that. And there wouldn't be unless fingerprints found in the Bonebreaker's underground hideout could be matched to those on one or more pieces of debris. And that search was going to take a lot of time and effort.

Because of this, the police had not released any information regarding a potential connection to the serial killer. So while noteworthy, not to mention scary, the incident didn't generate the kind of news coverage it would have had the press been aware of the Bonebreaker connection. And Mayor Getty's afternoon press conference overshadowed the explosion, relegating it to page two in the *Times*. The press was fixated on it. And they weren't alone. When Lee dragged herself into the office the following morning, she found that her fellow police officers were talking about little else. And there was a note taped to her computer screen. "My office, 8:00, Sean."

So Lee barely had time to eyeball her e-mail and grab a cup of coffee before making her way to Jenkins's office. As Lee entered, she discovered that Chief Yessum and Assistant Chief Wolfe were already there. "Close the door," Jenkins instructed, "and take a seat."

Lee did as she was told. The only available chair was located next to Wolfe. The other woman winked at her as if to say "I'm in the same boat you are."

"Okay," Yessum began, "all of you know why we're here. Someone gave a copy of the Maxim tape to the mayor, and rather than wait for the DA to drop charges on her, she went public. I ordered the IA folks to investigate, and once they find the culprit, I will bring them up on charges." Yessum's gun-barrel eyes roamed from face to face. "That includes the people in this room should the evidence point your way."

No one said anything—so Yessum continued. "As you can imagine, my phone is ringing off the hook. Most of the questions are the same. Will the investigation continue? And will I, as a friend of Mayor Getty's, cut her some slack?

"The answer to the first question is an emphatic 'yes.' The DA looks at it this way . . . The mayor came very close to confessing during her press conference. So he's confident of scoring a win there. But what else is she hiding? That's what he wants to know.

"As for the second question, the answer is an equally emphatic 'no,'" Yessum added. "I won't back off—and neither will *you*." His eyes swung over to Lee. "Tell your team that . . . And put more pressure on Getty's coconspirators. They're facing a clear choice now. They can sing *her* tune, and stick to *her* story, or they can go their separate ways.

"Emphasize the obvious," Yessum said. "Point out that the first person to roll is likely to get the best deal. Especially if they have new information to offer . . . stuff that isn't on the Maxim tape. Understood?"

Lee nodded. "Yes, sir. But what about the Bonebreaker? It looks like he murdered a civilian—and he blew up a house yesterday."

Jenkins offered a wry smile. "Because *you* were in it!"

"I'm glad that you and Detective Prospo survived," Yessum put in. "And Wolfe here will push for hard evidence linking the Bonebreaker to the explosion. But I want you and your team to stay focused on the Getty thing."

Lee had mixed emotions about that—but all she could do was agree. There was more, but it was relatively trivial, and the meeting came to an end fifteen minutes later.

Lee caught Yanty and Prospo just as they cleared roll call and led them to a vacant conference room for an impromptu meeting. After Lee brought them up to speed on the meeting, she asked for status reports. Yanty spoke first. "You remember what I said earlier? That George Ma didn't *want* to meet with me? Well, I think I know why . . . Not only did he cut a deal with Getty—there's a possibility that he's working with the Aztecs."

Prospo frowned. "Say *what*?"

"Since Ma wouldn't talk to me," Yanty said, "I went looking for someone who would. And that person turned out to be Ma's personal assistant. A woman named Lora Millich. She was a cocktail waitress in one of Ma's casinos before he hired her to take care of his personal needs."

Lee frowned. "So you walked up to Ma's personal assistant, ordered her to spill her guts, and she obeyed."

"Hell no," Yanty responded. "I had Misty run her name and guess what? The *real* Lora Millich is eighty-two years old, and lives in Medford, Oregon!"

"So I'll bite," Lee said. "Who *is* this woman?"

"Misty ran her driver's license photo through the Facial Recognition System and came up with one Anna Kolak," Yanty replied. "She's wanted for embezzlement, fraud, and identity theft in Oregon."

"Well I'll be damned," Prospo said. "Yanty did some work."

"Somebody has to," Yanty replied smugly.

"All right, you two," Lee said, "save it for your nightclub act. Nice job, Dick . . . You blackmailed her."

"That would be unprofessional," Yanty objected. "I merely suggested that she tell me everything there is to know about Ma, or I'd send her to jail."

Lee grinned. "Right . . . That's completely different. And?"

"The border is reasonably secure at the moment," Yanty said, "and Ma went down there. While he was there, he met with a woman known as Senora Avilar. The name didn't mean anything to me, and the records check that Misty ran didn't produce anything, so I made a call to a friend who works for the Federal Counterintelligence Agency. He told me that Avilar is the *nom de guerre* used by a high-ranking Aztec agent . . . And he wants to be copied on anything that we come up with."

"Wow," Lee said, "that's interesting. So what did Ma and Avilar talk about?"

"Kolak didn't know," Yanty confessed. "She wasn't present when the two of them met."

"But she's going to try to find out," Lee said. "Or take a trip to Oregon. Right?"

"Right."

"Okay . . . Let's keep this to ourselves for the moment. Some asshole leaked info to the mayor—so it's hard to know whom to trust. How 'bout you, Milo? Did you have any luck with Stryker?"

"We're dancing the dance," Prospo replied. "But I'm getting together with Stryker and his attorney this afternoon."

"His attorney? Maybe he's about to roll."

"Or clam up," Yanty said cynically.

Prospo shrugged. "Let's hope for the best. I'll let you know."

After the meeting with Yanty and Prospo, Lee returned to her desk. In addition to the Bonebreaker and Getty cases, Lee had a *third* investigation to worry about because Kane was still in jail.

Things had been looking up for a while. But now, in the wake of Olin's refusal to cooperate, the effort to help Kane was stalled. And for the life of her, Lee couldn't see how to get things off dead center without taking yet another trip over the ethical line. Because good cops follow the rules. *But a good cop wouldn't let an innocent man be convicted of a crime he didn't commit,* Lee told herself.

That's nothing but self-serving spin, the other her countered. *If you're going to step over the line, then do it. But spare me the bullshit.*

Lee sat there for the better part of five minutes, staring at an e-mail without seeing it. Finally, with an empty feeling at the pit of her stomach, she got up and went looking for Detective Harmon Sloan. The obvious starting place was the bull pen.

After getting directions from a clerk, Lee entered a confusing maze of cubicles, stacks of cardboard evidence boxes, and water-starved plants. And it was deep inside the bull pen that Lee found Sloan. He was well past middle age, balding, and dressed in an outfit that consisted of a white shirt, a bow tie, and an argyle sweater. A pair of brown cords and hush puppies completed the look.

Sloan was on the phone, and when he saw her, he pointed at his guest chair. Lee had to remove a well-worn leather briefcase in order to sit on it. As his conversation came to an end, Sloan turned in her direction. "Hi," Lee said, "I'm . . ."

"I know who you are," Sloan said. "Everyone does. I wondered when you'd show up."

"You did?"

"Of course I did. You're in a relationship with Dr. Kane, he's in jail, and you want to get him out. Plus you think you're a big deal. So it was only a matter of time before you came to see me."

Lee wasn't sure what to make of Sloan's attitude. His eyes were like black buttons, and they never blinked. "Well, you're right," she said. "About the Kane part. Here I am."

"Yes," Sloan said peevishly. "Here you are. But you shouldn't be. Not if you plan to interfere."

"That isn't my intention," Lee assured him. "I want to alert you to some new information regarding Dr. Kane's case."

"This isn't about the missing woman is it?" Sloan demanded. "I can't begin to tell you how many times I've heard about her from Dr. Kane and his attorney. And I looked for her, I really did, but without success."

"As a matter of fact, it *is* about her," Lee told him. "Mr. Codicil hired private investigators to learn the woman's identity—and to find out where her mother lives." That was only part of the story of course—but Lee wasn't about to reveal her role in finding Olin.

Lee went on to tell Sloan about the fact that Olin was a fed who might or might not be working undercover, and wasn't willing to cooperate. Finally, when she was finished, Sloan blinked for the first time. "So why are *you* here? Mr. Codicil has my phone number."

It was a good question and one Lee should have been ready

to answer. All she could do was try to spin it. "There's a law-enforcement angle to this . . . What if Olin *is* undercover? That isn't the sort of thing that Codicil's likely to worry about."

Sloan nodded as if that was a reasonable reply. "I'll have a talk with Mr. Codicil," he said. "I'd like to hear all of that information directly from him. In the meantime, I want you to back off."

"By all means," Lee said meekly. "I will." And with that she left. Sloan hadn't mentioned Internal Affairs, thank God. Did that mean he wouldn't call them? No. All Lee could do was hope that he wouldn't.

Having done what she could, Lee returned to her desk where she retrieved her bag and the recorder she used to conduct interviews. Five people had been taped cutting deals with Getty in her boyfriend's apartment—and one of them hadn't received any attention as yet. His name was Bishop Herman Jones. And, as head of the Church of Human Purity, Jones had been willing to support Getty's reelection effort if she promised to leave LA's stringent antimutant ordinances in place.

Lee thought it was a weak case since the argument could be made that Getty was doing what politicians were supposed to do . . . And that was to talk to constituents and represent their interests. But Lee thought it was important to interview *all* of the coconspirators, Jones included.

Lee made her way onto the Harbor Freeway and followed it for a while before exiting onto West Pico Boulevard. The complex that housed the church consisted of four buildings, all of which were located on the site of the old convention center. Because they were of different heights, and "stair-stepped" up from the smallest to the largest, media wags had taken to calling them the "staircase to heaven."

Lee had been there before and knew the drill. In order to enter the well-groomed compound, Lee had to show her ID. Then she was allowed to cross the moatlike "water feature" and pass through a gate in the twelve-foot-high "peace wall" that was intended to protect the church's buildings from the sort of unrest that had taken place back in 2038.

During the days immediately after the release of the plague, hundreds of thousands of people had entered Los Angeles, attempting to get the kind of medical attention that wasn't available in the suburbs or rural areas. In a matter of days, all hotels were full, and people were sleeping in parks. In an effort to house and control them, large numbers of refugees were sent to the city's convention center. But in a short period of time, *that* facility was filled to overflowing. So it wasn't long before food ran out, sanitation broke down, and *B. nosilla* began to spread.

More than a thousand brave volunteers went to help and thanks to their efforts the situation was brought under control. But half of those in the convention center were dead by then—and it took convoys of trucks to remove the bodies.

What happened thereafter was still in question. Some people believed that an accidental blaze destroyed the convention center; others claimed that the fire had been set, but the result was the same either way. The convention center had been reduced to a pile of rubble and might still be that way had it not been for the previous bishop, who offered to lease the land from the city in 2040. There had been lots of more urgent projects for the mayor and city council to fund, so they agreed to a hundred-year lease. The project took three years to complete. The final result was a church housed within a fortress.

In keeping with a sign that ordered her to do so, Lee stopped next to a glass-enclosed shack and handed her ID to a uniformed security guard. His smooth-shaven face was professionally blank, and his words were stilted. "Your name is on the list. Please surrender your weapon. I will return it when you leave."

"Dream on," Lee said sweetly. "I can't do that. But what I *can* do is radio in and ask for backup. Then the SWAT team will arrive, we'll shut the complex down, and request a search warrant. Once we have that, we'll go to Bishop Jones's office and take a look around. *You* decide."

The guard wasn't allowed to make decisions. Especially ones that involved the bishop. "I need to check with my supervisor," he said, and entered the shed, where Lee could see him talking on a phone. He was back moments later. "Please follow the signs to the visitor parking area and use slot three. Have a nice day."

"You, too," Lee said as she removed her foot from the brake. From there she followed the signs to slot three, where a young woman was waiting. She had shoulder-length blond hair, blue eyes, and was dressed in what looked like a sailor suit. "Good morning, Detective Lee," the woman said, as Lee exited the car. "My name is Sharon—and I'll be your guide."

"Thanks," Lee said, as she closed the door. "I have an appointment with Mr. Jones."

"Yes," Cindy acknowledged. "I know. Mr. Jones is in his office. Please take a seat on the cart, and I'll drive you to building one."

The golf cart was so well maintained that it appeared to be brand-new. A paved two-lane path led them past the first three buildings in the so-called "staircase" to the twenty-story building where, according to Sharon, "Bishop Jones is leading the effort to purify Pacifica."

Lee knew that Sharon, like the rest of the church's followers, believed that *Bacillus nosilla* had been sent by God to cleanse the planet of evil. And, since mutants were infected with BN, they were ipso facto evil . . . And evil should be eliminated. That included men, women, and children. The cart came to a stop in a small parking lot. "Please follow me," Sharon said. "Bishop Jones's office is located on the top floor."

Of course it is, Lee thought to herself, as she followed Sharon through a security checkpoint and into the gleaming lobby beyond. A steady stream of people were coming and going. The men were dressed in snowy white shirts, blue blazers, and khakis, while the women wore Puritan-style blouses, knee-length skirts, and high heels. The latter were a mystery to Lee, who sought to avoid them whenever possible.

Sharon led Lee onto an elevator, which paused occasionally so that people could get on and off. A pair of stainless-steel doors parted to let them out on the twentieth floor. And as Lee followed Sharon into an expansive lobby, she saw that the domed ceiling and the surrounding walls were covered with beautifully executed murals.

The ones above her were replete with fluffy clouds, angelic beings, and joyful people, while those on the surrounding walls featured all manner of monsters. The heaven-and-hell motif had clearly been borrowed from traditional Christianity, with mutants standing in for demons. Never mind the fact that mutants were victims of a disease—not people who had chosen to be evil. The whole thing was massively screwed-up.

Sharon led Lee over to a huge desk, where she spoke with a prim-looking secretary who, like all of the other secretaries Lee had seen, was female. "You're three minutes early," the woman pointed out. "Please have a seat."

Sharon apologized for the error and led Lee over to a nicely furnished sitting area. "We'll wait here," she said brightly. "Can I get you something to drink?"

"No, thanks," Lee responded as she glanced at her watch. "I'm fine."

Exactly two minutes and forty-five seconds later, the secretary waved them over. "Bishop Jones will see you now."

"I'll wait for you," Sharon told Lee. "Have a nice meeting."

Lee thanked her and had to circle the secretary's desk in order to pass through a doorway. A privacy wall prevented her from going straight ahead, so it was necessary to turn left or right. Lee chose left and emerged in a brightly lit room. The windows along the south wall offered a sweeping view. Rather than the desk and credenza setup that Lee expected to see—a table large enough to seat a dozen people was located at the center of the space.

A shaft of light angled down through a skylight to splash a man in a gray business suit. A halo of fuzzy white hair circled his mostly bald pate, his skin was brown like hers, and when he stood, Lee saw that he was about five-five. As the bishop came around the table to greet her, Lee was struck by the stern expression on his jowly face. He had a deep basso voice and a firm handshake. "Good afternoon, Detective Lee . . . I'm Herman Jones."

"It's a pleasure to meet you," Lee replied. "Thanks for slotting me into what must be a very busy schedule."

"I didn't have much choice, now did I?" Jones said. "But I'm glad you came. I have nothing to hide. Please have a seat."

Although most of the table was bare, Jones had clearly been working at it because there was a laptop and a scattering of printouts in front of what Lee imagined to be his favorite chair. Once they were seated, Lee placed the recorder in front of her and asked for permission to use it. "Absolutely," Jones said.

"And please be aware that I plan to record our conversation as well. In fact, I may decide to broadcast our conversation over the church's radio station so that all of our members can hear it."

"That's up to you," Lee replied, and wondered where the microphone was. Not that it mattered. "So," she began. "You know why I'm here."

"Of course," Jones answered. "And if trying to protect the church's members, not to mention the rest of Los Angeles, from mutants is a crime, then I'm guilty."

"So you admit to cutting a deal with Mayor Getty."

"Of course I admit it. You've seen the tape. More than that, I'm proud of it—and Mayor Getty should be as well. I hope that the DA indicts me. That would give me an opportunity to tell people how dangerous the mutants are. Many of them already know, of course . . . Church attendance is up thanks to the Aztec attacks and so are donations!"

Lee could tell that Jones was serious. The DA didn't have much leverage where he was concerned. "I see," she said, noncommittally. "And the deals with other people? Do you approve of those as well?"

Jones shrugged. "I don't know anything about them, so I'm not qualified to say."

That was a dodge but one Lee couldn't counter. The trip had been a complete waste of time. She thumbed the stop button and put the recorder in her bag. Then she stood. "Thanks for your time, Bishop . . . I'll show myself out."

Jones smiled for the first time since they'd met. And why not? He'd won. "Stop by any time, Detective Lee," Jones said. "It was a pleasure."

Sharon was waiting for Lee in the lobby and took her back to the sedan. Then she waved like a princess as Lee drove away. So far, including her last run-in with the Church of Human Purity, the score was one–one. Could she go one up? Time would tell.

Lee glanced at the readout on the dash. It was midafternoon by then, and she hadn't had lunch. But rather than eat, she decided to visit Kane. Then she'd go back to the office.

It took more than half an hour to reach the MDC, fill out the same form all over again, and pass through security. The crowd in the waiting room was smaller than it had been during the last visit, and it was only ten minutes before her number was called.

Lee crossed the room and sat down in a grubby cubicle where thousands of painful conversations had taken place over the years. She was staring through scratched Plexiglas when Kane appeared. Her heart fell as she caught sight of the black eye, the white bandage across his nose, and the purplish lips. He'd been beaten and beaten badly. "Hey, hon," Kane said, as he picked up the receiver and sat down opposite her. "This is a nice surprise. It's good to see you."

Lee frowned. "What happened?"

Kane tried to smile and winced instead. "There's this guy . . . His name is Teddy Rexall—but the guys call him T-Rex. And when he began to pound on my buddy Tom—I decided to attack his fist with my face. How bad *is* it?"

"Your modeling career is over," Lee informed him. "Fortunately, I'm more interested in your cooking than your good looks."

"That's a relief," Kane replied. "I was worried."

Lee pressed the palm of her right hand against the Plexiglas, and he did the same. "I'm sorry, baby," Lee said. "Hang in there. We're going to get you of here . . . I promise."

"There's no hurry," Kane assured her. "I like the bologna sandwiches. With mustard."

Lee laughed in spite of herself. "You're crazy. You know that."

"Of course I know that. I'm a psychologist."

Lee smiled. "I love you."

"And I love you."

That was followed by a long moment during which they stared at each other . . . As if to drink the images in and save them. Lee blew him a kiss. "I have to get back to work, babe . . . Call me."

"I will," Kane promised, and the visit came to an end. Lee could still see Kane's battered face in her mind's eye as she left the building—and felt a renewed sense of urgency about the need to get him out of there.

Once back in the office, Lee booted up her computer and scanned the list of e-mails that had accumulated during her absence. There were messages from Jenkins, Yanty, and Prospo.

But it was the e-mail from Harmon Sloan that captured her attention. "Urgent—Call me." The message consisted of a phone number.

Lee dialed it, and Sloan answered right away. He was grumpy as usual. "It's about time . . . I spoke with Codicil. He verified what you told me. So, based on the new information, I'm going to interview Mr. Jarvis in half an hour. You can watch if you're willing to keep your mouth shut. Can you handle that?"

Lee knew that Jarvis, AKA Tufenuf, was one of the men who had attacked Olin, and she was very eager to hear what he had to say. And, even if Sloan wasn't very tactful, Lee knew he was being nice to her in his own way. Sloan could get into trouble for allowing her to be present. "No problem," she said. "And thank you."

Lee left the office in a hurry, got in the sedan, and drove to the LA County Jail. Sloan was waiting for her when she arrived, and they went through security together. After handing over their weapons, they were shown into one of the jail's interview rooms. It was little more than a box with green walls, mismatched plastic furniture, and ceiling-mounted cameras.

There was a long, somewhat awkward silence. Sloan was a mystery to Lee. He didn't like her, or anybody else so far as she could discern, yet he had chosen to help. And at some risk to himself. *Why?* The question went unanswered as the door opened and a man wearing a dark blue jumpsuit entered the room. He had close-cut hair, a smoothly handsome face, and his expression brightened when he saw Lee. "All right! That's what I'm talking about. You're fine, girl . . . What's your name?"

"Her name is none of your business," Sloan said sternly. "Sit down and shut up."

Jarvis winked at Lee and took one of the two remaining chairs.

A guard had entered the room by then. He had a paunch and was clearly bored. "What'll it be? Cuffs on? Or cuffs off?"

"Leave 'em on," Sloan replied.

The guard nodded to the phone. "Dial five when you're finished." Then he left.

"Maybe my lawyer should be here," Jarvis said hesitantly.

"Maybe so," Sloan agreed. "It's up to you. Or, maybe you'd like to have a chat without her. This has to do with the night D-Eddy got shot. We have a photo of you with your arm around a woman's throat . . . A jury would love *that*. But what if I told you that we're more interested in the woman than we are in you?"

Jarvis was a master of cool. But Lee could see the wheels turning as his eyes flicked to her and back to Sloan. "What's in it for me?"

"I can't promise you anything," Sloan replied. "Only the prosecutor can do that. But if you're helpful, I'll ask him to reduce the charge to a misdemeanor. You could be back on the street by tomorrow night."

Jarvis perked up. "Now you're talking."

"Good," Sloan said. "So why did you and D-Eddy attack the woman? So you could rob her?"

Jarvis shook his head. "Hell, no . . . That bitch is a crackhead . . . And D-Eddy let her run a tab. He said she was somebody important but wouldn't tell me who. Then, when the bill came due, the skank stiffed him. So we went out to teach her a lesson." Jarvis shrugged. "That's when D-Eddy got shot."

"Did D-Eddy have a gun?"

"Yeah . . . He was pointing it at her."

"What happened to it?"

"I took it."

"And what did you do with it?"

"I sold it for twenty nu."

Sloan looked at Lee to gauge her reaction. Her mind was racing. Olin was a drug addict! Maybe she got hooked while working undercover or maybe anything . . . The process didn't matter. The point was that she couldn't come forward to help Kane without running the risk that her connection with D-Eddy would be revealed. And then she'd lose her badge. The whole thing made sense now—and Lee felt a sudden surge of hope. According to Jarvis, D-Eddy *had* been armed. Just like Kane said he was. She gave a nod, and Sloan turned to Jarvis.

"Okay, that's more like it. I'm going to contact your attorney *and* the prosecutor . . . Then we'll see what they can work out."

Jarvis did a very good imitation of someone who didn't have a care in the world. "Okay . . . Whatever."

Once Jarvis had been taken away, and the detectives were outside the building and away from the cameras, they paused. Sloan eyed her. "I know where she is . . . It's time for you to butt out."

Lee nodded. "Yeah . . . You're right. This is going to get real complicated, what with the feds and everything. I know you were doing your job," Lee added. "But you didn't have to keep me in the loop. Why did you?"

"I did it for your father," Sloan replied. "We were partners for a few months immediately after you were born. We responded to a biker brawl . . . Two gangs were going at it. But when we arrived, both groups turned on us! I went down in the melee, and your dad pulled me out. He was cut, and it took eight stitches to close the wound. So I owed him . . . But not anymore."

"No," Lee agreed soberly. "Not anymore."

They parted company after that . . . And Lee called Codicil to let him know about the new development. He was very excited and promised to get in touch with all the right people first thing in the morning—his hope being to get Kane out on bail pending a final resolution to the case. But rather than risk getting Kane's hopes up only to have them dashed, they agreed to leave him out of the loop. For the first time in a long time, Lee went home feeling happy, had a glass of wine out on the deck, and watched the sun dip into the ocean. Kane would be home soon. She could feel it . . . And life was good.

The morning drive was a routine activity. A task so mundane that Lee could do it while thinking about other things, in this case Lawrence Kane and the vacation they would take once the murder charge was dropped. Where should they go? The San Juan Islands perhaps? That would be nice. Traffic was heavy, but not unusually so, and the sun was peeking over the horizon when a traffic light turned red. The bus in front of Lee came to a stop, forcing her to do likewise.

A pair of headlights appeared in Lee's rearview mirror and caused her to take a second look. The garbage truck, like the bus in front of her, was a normal part of the early-morning scenery.

But something was different. Lee couldn't put her finger on it at first. Then she realized that the front-loading truck was holding a Dumpster out in front of it! That wouldn't be unusual in a parking lot or an alley, but on a major arterial? *Perhaps the driver is taking the container somewhere,* Lee thought to herself. Then the Dumpster fell on her car.

Holby was out playing golf. That's what his wife believed anyway. Wouldn't she be surprised to know the truth? On orders from George Ma, Holby was about to kill Detective Cassandra Lee! Everybody knew that Lee was a crack shot. So, if Holby got into a shootout with her, he'd be toast. That's where the garbage truck came in. It was big, it was powerful, and it would give him an all-important edge.

He pulled the control lever back, realized his mistake, and pushed it forward. That brought the so-called "can" down onto Lee's car. It would have been nice to crush her then and there, but the lift arms weren't long enough. So the plan was to immobilize the sedan while he got out and shot Lee through the driver's side window.

The trunk of the car collapsed but, before Holby could apply the full weight of the Dumpster to the sedan, the light changed, and the bus pulled away. Rubber screeched as Lee stomped on the accelerator.

Lee did her best to shove her foot down through the floor in a desperate attempt to get out from under the descending Dumpster. Then she had to dynamite the brakes to avoid slamming into the back of the bus. But it wasn't going to be enough. The truck was closing in. Lee was forced out into oncoming traffic. A horn blared as an oncoming delivery van barely got out of the way and smashed into a parked car. A sedan plowed into it, and steam billowed out of the engine compartment.

Lee had the mike in her fist by that time and was driving left-handed. "This is 1-William-3 . . . I am being pursued by some yo-yo in a garbage truck and I'm eastbound on Santa Monica

Boulevard. There are multiple accidents at my location. Officer needs assistance."

Then Lee was forced to drop the mike in order to veer back in front of the bus. That was when she glanced at the outside mirror and saw that the garbage truck had pulled out and was chasing her! The Dumpster had been left behind—and the behemoth was headed *into* westbound traffic! Lee hit the lights and siren in hopes of warning oncoming motorists. There was an intersection up ahead . . . Maybe she could use it to escape.

Holby should have been frightened. He knew that. But chasing the police car was like going after big game, only a hundred times more exciting. His head was clear, his heart was racing, and he was conscious of the sickly-sweet stench of garbage that permeated the cab. If only he'd known! Killing people was so much more stimulating than shooting a grizzly . . . And he was getting paid for it!

Holby uttered a whoop of joy as the truck's front left fender nicked an old *especiale* and sent it careening into a fire hydrant. A geyser of water shot up into the air and came raining down behind him. Plan A was in the shitter . . . But Plan B was ready to go.

Lee knew the dispatcher was talking to her—but didn't have time to chat. She saw the light turn yellow, braked, and took a left. There was no way in hell that the truck could corner like a car. There was a problem however . . . Black smoke was pouring out from the back of the sedan! A fire? No, Lee decided . . . Not yet. Crushed metal was pressing against one of her tires—and she could feel the drag as she pressed on the accelerator.

The truck was going too fast as Holby entered the turn. He felt the big vehicle tilt and thought it was going to roll, before he was able to regain control. Some practice sessions would have been nice . . . But lacking those, he'd have to learn on the job.

The enormous steering wheel was sticky with the original driver's blood, and the brain matter splattered across the lower part of the windshield made it hard to see, but Holby could peer over the mess. Smoke was pouring out of Detective Lee's car—and Holby could see that the sedan was beginning to slow down. That was good because she had almost certainly called for help by that point, and it would arrive soon.

Lee was unaware of the mistake that she'd made until the sedan crashed through a sawhorse and sent wooden daggers flying in every direction. The street was closed ahead! She could see barriers with the diagonal stripes on them and stood on the brakes. There was a screech of rubber as the creeper slewed sideways, came left again, and slammed into the concrete wall.

That was when Lee heard two shotgun blasts, or what *sounded* like shotgun blasts, as the car's air bags deployed and pinned her in place. She could smell the acrid odor of gunpowder as the bags started to deflate. She couldn't move though . . . Not yet. And that was when something rammed the car.

Holby was ecstatic! He had the bitch now . . . Machinery whined as he hit the wrong switch, corrected the mistake, and took hold of the control lever. It worked the same way a joystick would. He used it to move the truck's insectlike arms forward. Once they penetrated the car, Holby pulled back. He could feel the cab dip as the sedan came off the ground, rose into the air, and disappeared over his head. Everything shook as the car fell into the hopper.

The truck was equipped with a wall-like trash compactor. All Holby had to do was flip a switch to turn it on. He heard a whining noise followed by snapping sounds as the hydraulic ram made contact with the sedan and began the process of converting the car into a cube.

Sirens sounded in the distance as Holby opened the door, jumped to the ground, and strolled away. He was wearing a spit mask, latex gloves, and was carrying the Contender in a custom-made holster under his coat. It took less than a minute to remove the gloves and leave the area. Then it was time to hail a cab for the trip to his car. After that? Well, there was still plenty of time for nine holes of golf.

FOURTEEN

Lee was upside down and struggling to free herself from the car's seat belt. And when she unlatched, precious seconds were lost as Lee battled to right herself and exit the vehicle. The air bags had released their grip on her by then, but it was difficult to maneuver.

Lee's fingers scrabbled at the door latch, felt it give, and pushed. The door collided with something solid. The inside surface of the truck's hopper? Yes, and the gap was no more than a foot wide! But she had to get through, and do so quickly, because she could tell that the compactor was on and pushing the front of the car in on her.

As Lee forced her body through the narrow opening, there were creaking sounds, the siren continued to yelp, and the dispatcher demanded to know what was going on. "I'm trying to escape from the fucking car!" Lee yelled. But the mike wasn't on—so the dispatcher couldn't hear her.

Lee felt a moment of pain as something clawed at her arm followed by a sudden sense of freedom when she cleared the car. Then it was time to scramble upward as the steadily advancing wall of steel crushed the front of the car, and the siren produced a final burp of sound. Once on the roof, Lee was able to step over onto the edge of the hopper. A patrol officer was below and staring up at her. Lee flashed her badge.

"Are you all right?" the officer wanted to know.

Lee took a quick inventory and decided that she was although her hands were shaking, and her stomach felt queasy. "Yes, I think so."

"Can I give you a hand?"

"No. I can get down by myself . . . But what you can do is turn the compactor off and help me locate my bag. I left it on the front seat of the car."

The police officer stared up at her. "Seriously," Lee said. "Get in the cab and turn that thing off."

Lee jumped to the ground as the patrol officer went forward to do her bidding. Lee's legs felt shaky, and it took a moment to recover. Someone had attempted to kill her. The reality of that was still sinking in. How many reports would she have to fill out anyway? Too many . . . The truck smelled like rotting garbage, and Lee did, too. But she was alive. And that felt good.

The sanitarium was a sprawling affair that occupied more than five acres of land near the city of Walnut. Prior to the plague, the site had been home to a junior college. Then, as thousands fell ill, the school was fenced off and converted into a medical treatment center for those who had been infected but were expected to recover.

Two years later, the government closed the facility. At that point, some of the locals urged authorities to restore the land to its original purpose. But even though the complex was classified as BN-free, many people wouldn't go near it. Nor were they willing to send their children to the campus.

As a result, some two dozen buildings baked under the hot California sun, weeds grew up through cracks in the pavement, and the central fountain filled with sand. Teenagers climbed over the fence occasionally, as did homeless people, so the once-pristine brick walls were covered with graffiti. But no one stayed inside the brooding buildings for very long. No one except the Bonebreaker, that is, who had established a backup hideout there and was now forced to use it.

What the Bonebreaker thought of as the Bolt Hole was

located in a remote corner of the administration building's basement in a former storage room. When he found it, the steel door was equipped with a special box that was supposed to protect a heavy-duty padlock, an arrangement which, judging from the tool marks, had been enough to prevent other people from gaining entry. But after two days of hard work, the Bonebreaker had been able to access the lock and cut it off. Then he replaced it with one of his own plus the means to lock the door from within.

Now the room was equipped with a cot, lights he could recharge from a solar panel up on the roof, and a wall-to-wall storage system loaded with supplies. Water was a problem however, since the Bonebreaker had to haul it in during the hours of darkness. It was a labor-intensive process that he didn't enjoy.

But the storage room was primarily used for sleeping. During daylight hours, the Bonebreaker spent most of his time up in the clock tower, where he could look out over the campus and listen to a battery-powered radio. It was a comfortable perch and one that allowed the Bonebreaker to enjoy the occasional breeze and think. And there was plenty to think about. His privacy had been violated, his home had been ravaged, and his trophies had been stolen. Then, in spite of all the work he'd done, Cassandra Lee had been able to escape his trap. That should have been impossible—but the woman was like a cat with nine lives.

So what to do? That question was very much on the Bonebreaker's mind as he watched a hawk ride a thermal. The original plan was to kill the police who'd been involved in murdering his parents, and to eliminate their children, starting with Cassandra Lee. But the Bonebreaker had come to realize that wasn't possible anymore. The police were closing in. Which was to say that Lee was closing in, because she, more than all the rest, was responsible for the situation he was in. The Bonebreaker watched the hawk spot something, stoop, dive, and hit its prey. A pigeon most likely—which the larger bird carried away.

That's what I need to do, the Bonebreaker mused. *I need to watch and wait for the perfect opportunity. Then, when Lee least expects it, I will swoop in and kill her. After that, I will leave Los Angeles for good. I'd go to San Diego, except that's too close to the Aztecs. Some little town up north would be better. I'll find a place to live and go fishing every day. Surely, God will grant me that after all my years of service.*

The sun had been hidden behind a cloud until then. Suddenly it was revealed, and the entire campus was bathed in a golden glow. The Bonebreaker had his answer.

By the time Lee was able to leave the location where the garbage-truck attack had taken place, and catch a ride to the Street Services Garage, it was almost eleven o'clock. Word had spread by then and the heckling began as she entered the building. "Hey, Lee," a detective said, "what's the name of that perfume you're wearing? Eau du gar-bage?"

"A garbageman tried to kill you?" another inquired. "What did you do? Leave your can too far from the curb?"

"You parked your creeper inside a garbage truck?" a narc inquired. "Send me a copy of the report . . . I want to see how you write that up."

Lee gave him the finger and arrived at her desk sixty seconds later. Fortunately, the patrol officer *had* managed to extricate her bag from the car, and, after putting it away, Lee went looking for her team. She ran into Prospo as he was headed out to lunch.

Prospo opened his mouth to speak, and Lee raised a hand. "Careful, Milo . . . If you were about to try a garbage-truck joke, I wouldn't advise it."

Prospo grinned. "Who, *me*? Never!"

"Good. So you're working on Stryker . . . And he's the president of the Sanitation Workers Union. Could there be a connection between that and the attempt to cube me?"

Prospo was about to reply when Yanty arrived. "Good morning, boss . . . It's good to see that you're all in one piece. Come on . . . Let's find an empty conference room. I have some news to share."

They had to check a couple of rooms before locating one that was empty. The chairs sat every which way, empty coffee cups littered the table, and a diagram took up most of the whiteboard. Yanty closed the door. "Someone leaked the Maxim tape to the mayor," he reminded them, "so it's best to be careful."

"I agree," Lee said. "What's up?"

"I think I know who tried to kill you," Yanty said.

"Someone who works for Stryker?" Lee inquired.

"Nope," Yanty replied. "I put some pressure on Anna Kolak, AKA Lora Millich, and she came through. Senora Avilar paid a visit to George Ma yesterday. That's the same Senora Avilar he met with near the border—and the same Senora Avilar who works for the Aztecs. But this time Kolak managed to listen in on their conversation. And guess what? Ma *is* working for the Aztecs . . . And when Avilar told Ma to have you killed, he went along with it."

"Why would Avilar want to kill Lee?" Prospo inquired.

"To punish her for what she did to the terrorists in the Taj Mahal Shopping Complex," Yanty replied. "The Aztecs want to make an example of her. If you're a police officer, and you kill an Aztec terrorist, you're going to die. That's the message they hope to send."

"So Ma paid a sanitation worker to assassinate me?" Lee inquired.

"No," Yanty said. "That's what's so surprising . . . After getting his marching orders from Avilar, Ma ordered Mark Holby to do it for him."

"Holby?" Lee asked. "The name sounds familiar, but I can't place it."

"Dr. Mark Holby is Mayor Getty's husband," Yanty reminded her, "and it turns out that he owes Ma money. A quarter mil according to Kolak. So it looks like Holby shot the driver, stole the garbage truck, and tried to kill you with it."

"Holy shit!" Prospo said. "The mayor's *husband*? Do you think she knows?"

"There's no telling," Yanty answered. "But my guess is no. I have a feeling she doesn't know about his debts *or* the type of work he's doing for Ma.

"By the way . . . What I'm about to say is pure conjecture . . . But I hear that Holby is an avid hunter. What if he has a Contender? That would raise the possibility that he shot Corso."

"For Ma?" Prospo inquired.

"Possibly," Yanty said cautiously. "But he might have done it for himself. As a means to protect his wife's career. So I'm running a check to see what kind of weapons he owns."

"Good work, Dick," Lee said. "We need to get Kolak off the street and into protective custody pronto. If Ma finds out what she's been up to, he'll kill her."

"I'm on it," Yanty assured her. "Based on the same info I gave you, the DA agreed to put her in protective custody. By now, Kolak is in a safe house watching daytime TV with some deputies."

"That's outstanding," Lee said. "So where's Ma? Let's bring him in."

"He dropped out of sight right about the time we took Kolak off the street," Yanty replied. "Maybe that was enough to spook him—or maybe he's on a low-key business trip. Jenkins agreed to put out an APB so there's a good chance that a patrol unit will spot him."

"That's perfect," Lee responded. "And Holby? What about *him*?"

"Same thing," Yanty answered. "The men and women in blue are looking for him as well."

"I'm glad to hear it," Lee replied. "The sooner we put him on ice, the sooner I can feel comfortable around garbage trucks again."

Both detectives chuckled. "I have some news, too," Prospo said. "It isn't as sexy as what Dick dragged in—but I think you'll like it. Stryker's attorney is busy cutting a deal with the DA. Stryker claims that there's more to his relationship with Getty than what we saw on the tape. He says that Getty promised to hire him when he retires next year in return for the union's support."

Yanty produced a low whistle. "Wow . . . That's like icing on the cake."

"Way to go Milo," Lee put in. "Good job. Feel free to leave at three thirty."

Prospo frowned. "That's when my shift ends anyway."

Lee smiled. "I know . . . The Bonebreaker is still out there. We need to find him."

Getty was sitting at her desk reading the results of a snap poll conducted by her campaign organization. Her numbers were down, and how could it be otherwise given the Maxim tape, and all the negative publicity? According to the summary of results 52 percent of the city's registered voters disapproved of her performance as mayor, 44 percent approved, and 4 percent were undecided. That was bad . . . But not as bad as Getty had feared. Not "it's the end of the road" bad. With months to go before the next election, there was still time to turn the situation around. That's what Getty was thinking when her secretary stepped into the office. "Chief Yessum is here, Mayor."

"Send him in," Getty said. "And you know how he likes his coffee."

"I'm on it," Chloe said cheerfully, and disappeared. Like most of the members of Getty's staff, Chloe was doing the best she could to keep a stiff upper lip even though *her* job was on the line, too . . . *Which is all the more reason to battle on,* Getty thought to herself.

Getty was up and circling her desk by the time Yessum entered the room. "Good afternoon, Chief . . . How's it going?"

Yessum gave her the usual hug before he answered. His expression was glum. "Things are going poorly I'm afraid."

Getty felt her spirits plummet. "Have a seat, Sam. What's wrong?"

Yessum was sitting across from her. "You know that the DA is putting the squeeze on your friends."

Getty noted that Yessum had chosen to use the word "friends" rather than "coconspirators." It was another reason why she liked him. "Yes, I believe that's SOP in a situation like mine."

"Yes, it is," Yessum agreed. "And I'm sorry to say that Mr. Stryker's attorney is in the process of cutting a deal with the DA."

Getty felt the walls closing in on her. "What kind of deal?"

"He's going to testify that you agreed to give him a job in exchange for support from the Sanitation Workers Union."

Getty looked away. Moss was dead, Silverman was her rock, and the Jones case was extremely weak. That left Ma and Stryker. She'd been hoping that they would hang tough. But now, based on the news regarding Stryker, things had just gone from bad to worse. She forced herself to make eye contact.

"Okay, thanks for letting me know. Is that all of the bad news? I sure as hell hope so."

Yessum shook his head. "I'm sorry to say that there's more."

"What? Is Ma going to roll over, too?"

"Not that I know of," Yessum replied. "But this involves him."

Getty listened in shocked silence as Yessum told her about her husband's gambling debts, the way Ma had used that leverage to turn her husband into a hit man, and what appeared to be his failed attempt on Detective Lee's life. It was a shocking allegation. But a credible one. Mark was a weak man . . . That, plus his wealth, was why Getty had chosen him. She was strong enough for two people. "So what's going to happen to him?" she inquired.

"We'll find Mark," Yessum predicted. "And we'll charge him with murder. At this point, it looks as though he killed a sanitation worker in order to go after Lee. And, while we hold him on that charge, we'll examine the possibility that he shot Chief Corso as well."

Getty sat up straight. "*Corso?* Why would Mark do that?"

"There are two possibilities," Yessum answered. "Maybe Ma ordered him to do it as a way to slow if not halt the investigation. Or maybe he took a shot at Corso as part of a misguided effort to protect *you*. Maybe he figured that once Corso was dead, you'd be able to choose a chief who would kill the investigation."

Getty stared at him. "And I chose you."

"Yes, you did. But the situation was too far gone by then. Tell me something, Melissa . . . How much does Mark know about *our* relationship? When we catch him, is he going to blab about it? If so I'm about to have problems of my own."

Getty shook her head. "No, Sam, he doesn't know anything about that part of our relationship. And I won't tell."

"Here's your coffee," Chloe said as she entered, carrying a tray. "But be careful . . . It's very hot."

Yessum thanked her and waited for the secretary to leave before picking up where they'd left off. "So what are you going to do now?"

"Does the press know about Mark?"

"Not yet," Yessum replied. "But they will soon."

"I think that closes the door," Getty said. "I'll discuss the situation with my staff, but it would be silly to stay on."

"So you'll resign?"

"Probably, yes."

"And if Mark contacts you?"

A single tear rolled down Getty's cheek. Was it for her? Or was it for *him*? Getty wasn't sure. "If Mark contacts me, I'll dial 911," she said. "It's the right thing to do."

Even though the garbage-truck attack seemed like ancient history by that time, it had occurred earlier *that* day, and after receiving a late-afternoon call from Marvin Codicil, Lee left work early. And now she was on her way to get Kane. The feds had been notified about Olin and promised to investigate, but there wasn't much doubt as to what they would find. Then, within a matter of days, the murder charge would be dropped. And that was why Kane had been able to make bail. Lee felt nervous and didn't know why. She knew Kane, after all . . . But what if things had changed? For him, yes, but for her as well. Lee had put Kane's marriage behind her, as well as his failure to tell her about it, or *had* she? Lee would know the answer soon.

The sedan was a beater that the folks in the motor pool referred to as "the garage queen" because that's where the ancient car spent most of its time. But it was the best vehicle they'd been able to come up with on short notice. One of the belts was screeching as Lee turned into the parking lot. Then, as she guided the sedan into one of the slots, Lee had to stand on the brake pedal to keep from hitting a waist-high concrete wall.

Once the car stopped, Lee got out, locked the doors, and began the short walk to the MDC and the side door through which prisoners were released. And that was where Marvin Codicil, Carla Zumin, and her camera operator were waiting.

"Hi," Zumin said. "Fancy meeting *you* here."

Lee made a face. "Someone tipped you off."

"Of course someone tipped me off," Zumin said shamelessly, as the camera operator turned to capture the conversation. "So let's catch up," Zumin said. "Is it true that the Mayor's husband, Dr. Mark Holby, tried to kill you with a garbage truck?"

Lee sighed. "It's true that *someone* murdered a sanitation worker, stole his truck, and tried to kill me with it. But I didn't see the driver."

"But the department issued an APB on Holby," Zumin insisted. "What does that suggest?"

"I think you should contact our Public Affairs office for information on that," Lee replied. "I have no comment."

"Okay, let's change subjects," Zumin said. "I understand that Dr. Kane is about to get out on bail. How do you feel about that?"

"It's long overdue," Lee replied carefully.

"Why is he being released *now*?" Zumin demanded. "What happened?"

"New information has come to light regarding the case," Codicil put in. "We can't share the details yet, but suffice it to say that Dr. Kane is innocent, and we're confident that the charge against him will be dropped soon."

Zumin was about to follow up, but the door opened, and a young man in his twenties emerged. He saw the camera, pulled his sweatshirt up over his head, and hurried away.

Kane appeared next. He blinked as if unused to the sunlight, and Lee was shocked by how pale he was. The black eye was better but still in the process of healing. His trademark grin was firmly in place, however—and his sense of humor was intact. "Really? Only *one* camera? My feelings are hurt."

"Carla Zumin, Channel Seven News," the reporter said as she shoved a mike in his face. "You're a well-known psychologist . . . What was it like to spend weeks in jail?"

"The food was execrable, I had to watch a lot of daytime television, and it's noisy at night. But I got my first tattoo . . . Would you like to see it?"

Of course Zumin wanted to see it. And as Kane rolled up his sleeve the camera zoomed in. And there, on his slightly reddened bicep, was a well-executed likeness of Lee's face. "She's beautiful, isn't she?" Kane said proudly. "The guy who did it is a pro . . . His name is Nicky, and he's waiting to be arraigned."

All three of the other people turned to look at Lee. "I think the tattoo says it all," Zumin said. "Don't *you*?"

The truth was that Lee didn't like tattoos, not most of them anyway, but she had to admit that this one was special. She wasn't looking at Zumin *or* the camera. Her eyes were on Kane. "Yes," she said simply. "I think it does."

The sun had started to set as Holby drove north. And as the orb went down, so did his spirits. What had begun as a promising day had been transformed into a rolling disaster. The attempt to kill Detective Lee had been an abject failure. And somehow, by means that weren't clear to him, the police had successfully ID'd him. A fact made clear by the fact that the public had been urged to be on the lookout for Dr. Mark Holby.

As a result, he'd been forced to ditch his car and steal another from an old lady in a supermarket parking lot. Had the police been able to connect him with carjacking? He didn't know . . . But even if they hadn't, he was still in trouble.

But that wasn't the worst of it. Melissa was in hot water, too . . . And partly because of *him*. That made his heart ache because he was in love with his wife. Unfortunately now, when they needed each other most, they couldn't communicate. Were the police monitoring Melissa's phone calls? And watching their home? Of course they were.

That left Holby with only one person that he could turn to: George Ma. Which was why he was headed north on I-5. He was supposed to meet the businessman at a truck stop called Joe's Travel Plaza up in Castaic. *Why* Ma wanted to meet him there wasn't clear, but the trip would get Holby out of LA, which was a good thing.

So when Holby saw the brightly lit sign for Joe's Travel Plaza, he followed a sixteen-wheeler off the freeway. It led him straight to the truck stop. Joe's was *huge*, with what seemed like acres of parking, and lines to buy fuel. There was a restaurant, too . . . And according to the brightly illuminated signs, truckers could get a haircut there, take a shower, and watch sports on a big-screen TV. But that was the last thing on Holby's mind.

He wanted to find Ma—and to do that, he had to make a call.

Though no expert on such things, Holby knew that the police could track cell phones. So after throwing his phone away, Holby purchased a disposable plus some tacos at a convenience store. And that's what he used to call Ma. The phone rang three times before a male voice answered. "Yeah?"

"This is Mark Holby. I just arrived."

"Go to the northwest corner of the lot and look for the trailer with the name Dobson Logistics printed on it." Click.

Holby followed the directions he'd been given, spotted the truck, and parked the car fifty feet away. As Holby got out and began to approach the big rig he saw that two men were busy working on a tire. Or were they? As the men stood and turned to face him Holby got the feeling that they were muscle. *Paid* muscle. One of them spoke. He was built like a fire hydrant— short and strong. "You need something, pal?"

"Yes," Holby replied. "I'm here to see Mr. Ma."

"Your name?"

"Holby."

The man nodded. "Follow me."

Holby could hear the persistent purr of a generator as the man led him to the back of the trailer and some fold-down stairs. That was when Holby realized that Ma was *inside* the trailer. And he wondered why. "Go on up," the man instructed. "Knock on the door."

Holby did as he was told. He had to back down one step as the right-hand door swung out and threatened to hit him. A man was waiting to greet him. There was a smile on his face. "Sorry about that," he said. "Come in . . . Mr. Ma is expecting you."

Holby stepped up and in. Much to his surprise, the interior was nicely lit and tastefully furnished. He was taking that in when two thugs stepped in to grab his arms. "Search him," Smiley ordered. One of the men put a pistol to Holby's head while the other patted him down. "Holy shit," the second man said, as he jerked the Contender out of its holster. "What the hell is *this*?"

"Keep looking," Smiley said, as he accepted the pistol. "He might have a backup."

The search continued but didn't turn up anything more than

a wallet, some change, and a pocketful of loose .45 cartridges. "Okay," the second man said. "He's clean."

"Good," Smiley said, as he stepped into position. The blow hit Holby in the gut and was enough to bring the tacos up. Smiley took a step back. "Hurt him, but leave his face alone."

The beating lasted for less than a minute but seemed to last forever. And if it hadn't been for the man who was holding him, Holby would have fallen face-first into his own vomit. "That's enough," a voice that Holby recognized as belonging to George Ma said. "Clean up the mess and bring him here. Dr. Holby and I are going to have a chat."

Holby wanted to throw up again but didn't have anything left to give as they escorted him back to a nicely furnished lounge and ordered him to sit on what looked like a kitchen chair. A coffee table separated them, and Ma was seated on a couch. "So, Dr. Holby . . . You want my help."

Holby wiped the last of the vomit off his lips. "Yes," he said weakly. "The police are after me."

"Yes, they are," Ma agreed. "You were given a mission and failed. Why should I help *you*?"

"I almost killed her," Holby said defensively. "But she managed to escape."

"Just like you *almost* killed Chief Corso," Ma observed. "Almost isn't good enough. Let me explain something to you, Doctor . . . Because your wife was stupid enough to let someone tape our conversations, and because you are a grade-A fuck-up, *I* have to leave the country. But the only place I can go is the Aztec Empire—and they won't grant me asylum until Detective Lee is dead.

"Now, I could send a professional after her . . . And maybe I will. But that would cost money, and I need to conserve my capital. So I'm going to give you another chance. If you kill her, *really* kill her, I'll arrange for you to cross the border with me. You won't be rich, but I will take fifty thou off what you owe me, and the freaks can use a dentist. In fact, I'll bet some of them have extra teeth! So get out there and kill Detective Lee or die here . . . It's up to you."

Holby's mouth was dry and when he tried to speak, all that emerged was a croak. So he tried again. "I'll need some expense money, a different car, and a way to contact you when it's over."

Ma was silent for a moment. Then he nodded. "Okay, Doctor . . . But don't disappoint me again. We'll kill your wife if you do."

Holby was horrified. *Melissa!* If they killed Melissa, it would be his fault! "Don't do that," he said. "I won't let you down."

When Lee awoke, it was to the feeling that something was different. But *what*? Then she heard the rasp of Kane's breathing and knew . . . He was back! And the knowledge filled her with joy. His homecoming had been enjoyable to say the least. Lee didn't like to cook but could get the job done when she had to, and was determined to stage a warm welcome. So they had steaks, grilled veggies, and a bottle of Shiraz. But good though the meal was, Lee barely noticed the food. Both of them had a lot to share—and the conversation lasted for hours.

Then they went to bed. The lovemaking was tentative at first, but it wasn't long before the awkwardness vanished, and chemistry took over. There was a long slow build followed by a spectacular conclusion. And, like most men, Kane was asleep five minutes later.

Not Lee, however. She was thinking about all of the changes in her life and what they might mean. For many years Lee hadn't been sure what happiness would consist of. But finally, just before sleep overtook her, Lee discovered the truth: Happiness was what she had.

So as Lee got out of bed and showered she was in a good mood. To celebrate, Lee had a breakfast burrito at her favorite Mexican restaurant before heading off to work. As far as she knew, Holby was still on the loose, as was the Bonebreaker, so she kept a sharp eye out until she reached the safety of the headquarters parking lot.

As soon as Lee arrived at her desk, she checked to see if there were any new developments regarding Holby, Ma, and the Bonebreaker. But there weren't any, and that meant she was free to tackle the administrative work that had piled up. Time passed quickly, and it was well into the afternoon when the phone rang for what might have been the twentieth time. "Detective Lee."

"This is Carla Zumin," the voice on the other end of the line said.

"If you're calling about Dr. Holby, I don't have anything new to share," Lee replied.

"No, I'm not," Zumin replied. "This is about the Bonebreaker. I may have a lead."

There was something different about Zumin's manner. The normally self-confident reporter sounded hesitant. As if unsure of herself. "What kind of a lead?" Lee wanted to know.

"The Bonebreaker has to be hiding somewhere, right? Well, a source tipped me off to a suspicious man who matches the pictures you put out."

Lee knew Zumin was referring to art that the LAPD had commissioned to show what the serial killer *might* look like . . . Realizing that he was a master of disguise. Still, a sighting would be a big deal. "So why did your source call you instead of me?"

"Because he knows I'll give him fifty bucks, and you won't," Zumin replied. "So how 'bout it? Would you like to see what might or might not be the Bonebreaker's latest hideout? He isn't there anymore . . . But who knows? Maybe he left some evidence lying around."

"Okay," Lee said. "We'll take a look . . . What's the address?"

"There isn't going to be any 'we,'" Zumin replied. "I want this scoop for myself . . . And if you roll in with an army of forensic geeks, the competition will be there in minutes. You come, tell me if you think the place is *worth* bringing the tech heads in, and I'll have what I need."

Lee sighed. Zumin was predictable if nothing else. "Okay, what's the address?"

In spite of Zumin's insistence that Lee come alone she figured it would be a good idea to bring backup. Who knew? Maybe Holby would attack her with a bus.

Unfortunately, neither Yanty nor Prospo were available. So Lee was determined to be extravigilant as she drove the car out of the parking lot. According to the information displayed on the nav screen, Lee's destination was deep within the old industrial area in the southeast part of downtown. That put it inside the zone slated for redevelopment under Mayor Getty's "Flash Forward" urban development program. Would the initiative go down with her? Time would tell.

There wasn't a whole lot of traffic inside the warehouse district. The area was in the midst of a slow-motion transition from shabby to chic and had been for a long time. Some of the buildings stood tall, but others were slumped under the weight of time, and waiting for the wrecking crews to arrive.

"You have arrived at your destination," the nav system announced cheerfully. Lee brought the car to a stop in front of what had been the Caldwell Bottling Company's main plant. The white letters were barely legible over the arched entryway—and the street address was spray painted on a wall to the right. The building was six stories tall, made of red brick, and seemed to radiate gloom. Dozens of empty-eyed windows stared down at Lee as she pulled in next to one of Channel 7's brightly colored vans.

It was strangely quiet for a neighborhood in the heart of the city . . . And if it hadn't been for the van Lee would have called for a black-and-white before venturing inside. Even so, she drew the .38, removed her waist-length jacket, and draped it over the pistol. The Glock was visible under her right arm. But the Smith & Wesson was hidden—and that could give her an edge.

With her bag hanging from her left hand, Lee entered the complex through a high-arched gate. It was wide enough to allow two trucks to pass each other—and a sure sign of how busy the complex had been. A pigeon flapped its wings as it took to the air, and Lee had to resist the temptation to shoot it. She was in the arch's shadow at that point—but emerged into sunlight as she entered the open area beyond. Zumin was standing near the center of the courtyard and looking her way.

Lee felt silly at that point . . . What would Zumin think of the .38? It was too late to retreat however—so Lee planted a smile on her face and kept walking. But as Lee neared the reporter she could see fear on Zumin's face. And where was the camera operator? Lee felt something cold trickle into her veins as she stopped a few feet away. "Carla? Are you okay?"

By then Lee could see the sheen of perspiration on Zumin's forehead. Her lips formed a single word: "Holby."

Lee let go of the bag, threw herself to the left, and heard the crack of a rifle shot. There was no impact, so Lee knew that Holby had missed. Lee rolled over and let the jacket fall as she came to her feet. The central loading area was surrounded by at least fifty windows, and Holby could be firing from any one of them. She turned and ran.

There was a *second* report but Lee didn't look back as she sprinted across rough cobblestones to an open door. Darkness took Lee in, and she hadn't gone more than a few feet when she came across a body. A TV camera lay two feet away from it, and now Lee knew the answer to her question. Zumin's cameraman had been shot.

She knelt to check his pulse. There was none. Lee stood and returned to the door where she took a peek outside. Zumin was nowhere to be seen. The reporter was no dummy and, when Holby fired, had taken the opportunity to run. Was she hiding somewhere? Could she call for help? Lee hoped so . . . And would have made the call herself had it not been for the fact that her phone was in her bag, and it was lying in the middle of the courtyard.

Something blew a chunk out of the masonry next to Lee's head, and the sound of a report followed. So she stepped back, put the .38 away, and drew the Glock. But while the semiauto was more accurate than the revolver, it was still no match for Holby's rifle. That meant she'd have to get in close, and thanks to the most recent shot, Lee knew the killer was on the opposite side of the complex.

As Lee ran, she was conscious of the fact that she was passing doors and windows to her right. Could Holby see in? And fire on her? It quickly became apparent that he could. Because as she rounded the closed end of the U-shaped building, bullets pinged around her. *Keep going,* she told herself. *Don't give the bastard time to aim.*

And the strategy worked at first. But as Lee passed an open loading dock, a bullet slammed into her right leg and dumped her onto the cement floor. Rather than continue to play catch-up, Holby had sighted in on a spot out in *front* of the detective and waited for her to cross it.

Lee rolled into the shadows where she went to work removing her tee shirt while swearing a blue streak. But all the F-bombs in the world weren't going to help. She had to get pressure on the entry and exit wounds, and she had to do it fast, because Holby was in motion and coming fast! The .38 fell to the floor as Lee pulled her belt loose and made use of it to cinch the makeshift bandage in place. She paused long enough to pick the weapon up and stuff it into a back pocket before limping away. There were tanks to the left and right, and Lee passed between them. Cover, she needed cover, and they fit the bill.

A bullet made a spanging sound and threw sparks as it glanced off steel. Holby was close, *very* close, and the thump of Lee's heart was so loud she feared he might hear it. "Detective Lee?" Holby said. "I know you're wounded. But don't worry, 'cause I'm going to put you out of your misery. Unless you'd prefer to shoot yourself, that is . . . And that's fine with me."

Lee was circling a tank and moving with great care lest she give herself away. As she edged around it, Lee saw Holby silhouetted against the outside sunshine. "LAPD! Drop the weapon!"

Holby responded by swinging the rifle around and pulling the trigger. His bullet went wide but Lee's didn't. It hit Holby in the chest and knocked him down. Lee heard him say, "Shit," as the long gun hit the ground. He was reaching for it when she put a boot on his wrist. "Hold it right there . . . You're under arrest."

Holby stared up at her. "It wasn't supposed to end this way."

"Bullshit," Lee replied. Her head felt light, and it was difficult to maintain her balance. "This is the best way for it to end. Asshole."

But Holby didn't hear her. His eyes were open, but they were blank, and a pool of black blood was expanding around him. That was when Zumin appeared to wrap an arm around Lee's waist. Tears were flowing down her cheeks. "I'm sorry," the reporter said. "He called and offered to surrender on camera . . . But only to me. I couldn't resist. And once we arrived, he threatened to shoot Hal if I refused to make the call . . . So I did. Then he shot Hal anyway and forced me to help with the body. Cops are on the way, though . . . So hang on."

Lee couldn't hang on. She was falling by then. The concrete

came up to hit her, a deep well opened under her body, and Lee fell into it. The pain disappeared.

FIFTEEN

The siren made a bleating sound as the aid unit continued to thread its way through heavy traffic. "Her blood pressure has improved," an EMT named Brady said, "and I think she's coming to."

"Good," the ER doctor said over the radio. "We're ready for her. I'll see you shortly."

Lee opened her eyes. Everything appeared fuzzy at first. Then a man with a moon-shaped face rolled into focus. "Hi," he said. "My name's Brady. And not just Brady, but Brady Brady. My parents thought it was funny."

It was the medic's icebreaker. The time-tested line he used to introduce himself and put patients at ease. Lee tried to reward him with a grin but produced a grimace instead. "I'm sorry," Brady said. "We'll arrive at the hospital soon, and the doctor will give you something for the pain." Lee nodded and closed her eyes.

She was floating in a nowhere land as the vehicle came to a halt, the siren died in midyelp, and Lee heard voices. She saw light through her eyelids and opened them long enough to catch a glimpse of the blue sky. Then it was gone as the EMTs rolled her into the emergency room.

There was a stab of pain as they transferred her from the stretcher to a gurney. That was followed by a flurry of activity as one person took her vital signs and someone else examined her leg. A face appeared. The man had dark skin, ears that stuck out, and was wearing wire-rimmed glasses. "Hello there . . . I'm Dr. Wold. The bad news is that you were shot in the right thigh . . . The good news is that it looks as though the bullet went through without hitting bone. But we'll confirm that with an X-ray. There's some bleeding, though . . . So once the pictures have been taken, I'm sending you up to surgery. If there's a bleeder, Dr. Gomez will find and seal it off. Do you have any questions?"

Lee knew she should have questions but couldn't figure out what they were, so she shook her head. The X-ray was followed by a mishmash of impressions. Lee was aware of being wheeled through a hallway, passing through double doors, and entering an operating room. A voice murmured something about going to sleep as a mask came down over her face. Then came a cessation of being, followed by a gradual return to consciousness. Lee's eyes were closed but she could hear voices. "I'm sorry, sir . . . But you can't enter the room without hospital ID."

The man had a raspy voice. "I guess I left it in my locker . . . How 'bout cutting me some slack? All I have to do is draw some blood, and I'll be out of here."

Lee had heard that voice before, she was sure of it, but *where*? Her eyes felt gummy, but she forced them open. She was in bed and her head was elevated. A man in green scrubs stood next to the door where he was face-to-face with a uniformed police officer. "Why don't you go get your ID?" the cop suggested. "Then I can let you in."

"Okay," the man with the raspy voice said, "you win." And that was when Lee recognized the voice. It belonged to Dr. Penn! No, the Bonebreaker *pretending* to be Dr. Penn . . . And as he whipped a towel off a roll-around cart, she knew what would happen next. Lee tried to shout a warning but heard what sounded like a croak. "He has a gun!"

But it was too late. Lee heard a pop and saw the police officer's head jerk as the Bonebreaker shot her. Lee ripped the IV out of her arm as the body crumpled to the floor. A momentary spurt of blood stained the sheets.

The Bonebreaker had climbed up over the foot of the bed by then and was crawling up Lee's body. *Why?* Lee knew the answer. To see the fear in her eyes, to make the killing last longer, and to savor the moment he'd been looking forward to for so long.

She felt a stab of pain as the serial killer sat astride her thighs. "It was on the radio," the Bonebreaker explained. "How you'd been shot and which hospital they were taking you to . . . So I came to say 'Hi' and send you straight to hell."

That was when Lee brought her left hand up and stabbed the Bonebreaker in the neck. The 22-gauge needle went in all the way. "God damn you!" the Bonebreaker screamed shrilly, as he reached up to jerk the IV needle out. "I'm going to kill you with my bare hands!"

Wires connected Lee to the machines stationed next to her bed. There was a chorus of alarms as she ripped them free. Then Lee tried to capture the killer by sitting up and wrapping her arms around his waist. Her strategy failed. The Bonebreaker knew that the beep, beep, beep would bring people on the run and managed to break free. So he stood and made use of a side rail to vault over onto the floor. The door opened as he landed.

A nurse entered, saw the body on the floor, and began to back out of the room. The Bonebreaker was on her in an instant. He grabbed the RN's hair, brought his right knee up into her stomach, and used both hands to club the back of her head. She collapsed in a heap.

It was impossible to roll off the bed because of the side rails. So Lee was forced to wiggle her way down. Each inch of progress incurred a stab of pain.

The Bonebreaker had recovered his pistol by then and fired a shot at Lee as he backed out into the hall. Lee heard the bullet zing past her left ear as she cleared the foot of the bed. Her leg was on fire, but she had to put weight on it in order to reach the spot where the policewoman lay, to see if she could help. Lee winced when she saw the blue-edged hole at the center of the woman's forehead. There was no need to check the woman's pulse.

Lee bent over to jerk the Glock out of the cop's holster. A pant leg was pulled up, exposing the policewoman's ankle holster. The backup gun was a Tarus .25 semiauto. Not the weapon Lee would have chosen but better than nothing.

There was no time for holsters, so Lee left the room holding a pistol in each hand. She was wearing a patient gown and one of the ties had come undone. Fabric flared around as she limped down the hall. "Police!" she shouted. "The man with the pistol . . . Where did he go?"

A middle-aged male stood frozen in place. He was holding a bouquet of flowers. "That way," he said, and pointed to his right. Lee thanked him as she shuffled past, butt exposed.

The Bonebreaker was no longer trying to kill Cassandra Lee. All he wanted to do was to escape the hospital. Now, having descended to the second floor via a stairwell, he opened a fire door and stepped out onto the walkway that opened up onto the lobby below. Two policemen, both with weapons drawn, looked up at him.

The Bonebreaker turned and began to hurry toward the bank of elevators. A woman with a little girl blocked his way. The Bonebreaker gave the woman a shove and scooped the girl off the floor. She was a prop . . . A way to change his appearance as he forced his way onto an open elevator. "Sorry," he said, as the other passengers stared at him. "We're late for an appointment." But they were still staring at him. That was when the Bonebreaker saw that drops of *his* blood were dripping down onto the little girl's face! The doors opened, and he stepped out.

There were spots of blood on the floor . . . And Lee followed them to a stairwell, down to the second floor, and out onto the walkway that looked out over the lobby. Her leg ached, and a single glance was enough to confirm that she was bleeding through her dressing.

The commotion in the lobby should have claimed Lee's attention, but she was distracted by the woman who was beating on an elevator door and screaming at the top of her lungs. "He took my baby!"

Lee didn't have to ask who "he" was as she limped down to

the elevators. "LAPD, ma'am. Did he go up or down?"

"Up!" the woman said urgently, apparently oblivious to the way Lee was dressed.

Lee looked, spotted another exit sign, and limped toward it. It was necessary to shove the .25 in a side pocket in order to open the fire door. It seemed to weigh a ton. And that was the first sign of a larger problem. The initial surge of adrenaline had worn off, and Lee was losing strength.

Climb, she told herself. *Climb*. And she did. Step by painful step, using the metal handrail to pull herself up. A fire door slammed up above, and Lee caught a brief glimpse of a man carrying a child. Then the Bonebreaker was gone as he turned and continued up the stairs.

Lee swore under her breath. He had a hostage, and that would make an already difficult situation even worse. She redoubled her efforts. There was a sign. It said, roof, and an arrow pointed upward. *Got ya*, Lee thought to herself, as she dragged herself upward. Her feet felt as if they were lumps of lead, her vision was blurred, and Lee was dizzy as she arrived on the top platform.

A steel door blocked the way, and it took every bit of her remaining strength to push it open. Bright light stabbed her eyes as she stumbled out onto the flat roof. A helicopter was hovering above, which gave Lee reason to hope. Maybe the SWAT team was going to fast-rope down! But no, she was looking at a Channel 7 News copter, and its rotors were blowing dust in every direction. It swirled around the Bonebreaker, who was holding the child in front of him. "The Lord is with *me*!" he shouted. "And the devil is waiting for you in hell."

Lee squinted into the glare, and was about to raise her weapon, when the Bonebreaker fired. The bullet hit her right bicep and lodged there. The .22 didn't pack much punch, but it hurt like hell. The Glock fell free and hit the roof. The Bonebreaker laughed gleefully. "How does it feel, bitch? How does it feel to be the one who takes a bullet?" Then he shot Lee in the left leg.

Lee heard herself cry out in pain as the roof came up to meet her. She could feel the heat radiating up off the asphalt and blinked her eyes in an attempt to see. Time seemed to slow. The long-barreled pistol was up and aimed Lee's way as she felt for the .25. What kind of woman had the dead cop been? Did she keep one up the spout? Or did she figure that safety was more important than speed?

Lee prayed for the first possibility as she thumbed the safety and brought the weapon up. Her head was swimming, the child was blocking the Bonebreaker's chest, and she would have to fire left-handed. But Lee had a talent . . . She could "see" in a way that others couldn't . . . And the talent *knew* when to fire. Lee pulled the trigger, felt the recoil, and let the darkness engulf her.

The Channel 7 cameraman got it all—and the station carried the confrontation live. That meant people all over the city saw the way Detective Cassandra Lee was gunned down. And then, lying in a pool of her own blood, fired one last shot. It could have gone wide. Or, worse yet, killed little Cindy Miller. But somehow, by the grace of God according to some, the .25 caliber bullet pulped the Bonebreaker's right eye and traveled up into his brain.

The Bonebreaker swayed like a drunk struggling to maintain his balance before toppling over backwards. That was the scene as the chopper circled above. Two bodies lying on the roof, with a distraught child sitting between them. Cindy was crying when a policeman dashed out to snatch her up, and medical personnel entered the swirling dust. And that was when Channel 7 cut to a commercial.

Lee was afloat on an ocean of pain. Her eyes were closed, but she could see light through her lids and hear voices. One of them belonged to Jenkins. "How is she?"

"She's fine for someone with multiple gunshot wounds," a woman answered.

"Don't bullshit me, Doctor . . . Is she going to make it?"

There was a pause followed by, "Yes, she's going to make it."

It felt as if her eyes were glued shut, but Lee forced them to open. She could see Jenkins standing at the foot of her bed talking to a woman in green scrubs. Lee's mouth was dry, and her voice emerged as a croak. "What happened? Did I kill the little girl?"

There was no mistaking the look of pleasure on Jenkins's face as he came to stand next to her. "She's fine, Cassandra . . . Thanks to you."

"And the Bonebreaker?"

"You killed him. One bullet through the right eye. The whole thing was on TV."

Something gave way inside her. It was as if a dam broke, resulting in a flood of emotion. All of the pain, and all of the sorrow, was released at once. Lee began to cry. A series of sobs racked her body as she remembered her father and the rest of the Bonebreaker's victims.

"This isn't good for her," the doctor said firmly, as she injected something into Lee's IV. "She needs to rest."

Lee said, "No, I don't want . . ." Then her vision began to fade, and darkness rose to envelop her. The Bonebreaker case was closed.

EPILOGUE

The sailboat wallowed slightly as a northerly breeze swept across Sucia Island to nudge the boats anchored in Echo Bay. Something rattled up in the rigging, and Lee could hear water sloshing around the stern. She knew next to nothing about boats. But Kane did and had been able to sail the twenty-seven-foot sloop up from Bellingham with very little help from Lee. And that was good because even after a month of painful rehabilitation she still felt creaky. But now, sitting on a cushion in the stern, Lee was nearly pain-free. And judging from the sounds coming from below, Kane was preparing dinner.

Meanwhile, back in LA, a lot of things had changed. Mayor Getty had been forced to resign and would be going to trial in six months, along with Syd Silverman. As for Jack Stryker, he'd agreed to testify against the pair of them and was likely to stay on as president of the Sanitation Workers Union.

George Ma did not fare as well. In a last-ditch attempt to flee prosecution, he ordered his thugs to crash the big semi through the border crossing in Tijuana. But having failed to kill Lee, he wasn't welcome there. So Ma died in a fiery inferno when *two* RPGs struck the tractor-trailer rig. That was fine with Lee.

The good news was that Chief Corso was back on the job and widely expected to run for mayor. So Acting Chief Yessum had returned to his previous duties, which, according to him, was just fine.

As for the dead, including the sanitation worker, Zumin's cameraman, Dr. Penn, *and* the policewoman who had died trying to protect Lee . . . All of them had been memorialized. And Lee was present for every funeral. In a wheelchair at first, then on crutches. There had been a lot of tears—so many it felt like she had none left to give.

That's over now, Lee told herself. *You've got to live in the moment, not the past.*

"Here you go," Kane said cheerfully, as he carried a tray up the ladder from the cabin below. "A crab salad with French bread and a bottle of Yakima Riesling. Prepare to be amazed!" Dinner was served on the tiny table in the boat's cockpit just aft of the wheel. And it *was* amazing . . . The crab was delicious, the crunchy bread was a delight, and the white wine made a perfect accompaniment.

Better yet were the changes that had come over Kane during the weeks since his imprisonment. The prison pallor was gone, his practice was back on track, and he was happy again. And Lee had discovered that when *he* was happy, *she* was happy. She looked him in the eye. "Thank you."

"For what?"

"For being you."

Kane smiled and lifted his glass. "To all the years ahead."

Glasses clinked, a gull circled above, and sunlight glittered on the water. The worst was behind them—and the best had begun.

ABOUT THE AUTHOR

William C. **Dietz** is an American writer best known for military science fiction. He spent time in the US Navy and the US Marine Corps, and has worked as a surgical technician, news writer, television producer, and director of public relations. He has written more than 40 novels, as well as tie-in novels for *Halo, Mass Effect, Resistance, Starcraft, Star Wars,* and *Hitman.*

williamcdietz.com

ANDROMEDA

William C. Dietz

When a bloodthirsty power grab on Earth results in the murder of her entire family, wealthy socialite Cat Carletto is forced into hiding. On the run from the ruthless Empress Ophelia, and seeking revenge against the woman who destroyed her family, Cat enlists in the Legion—an elite cyborg fighting force made up of society's most dangerous misfits. On the battlefield, Cat Carletto vanishes, and in her place stands Legion recruit Andromeda McKee. As she rises through the ranks, Andromeda has one mission: bring down Empress Ophelia—or die trying.

ANDROMEDA'S FALL
ANDROMEDA'S CHOICE
ANDROMEDA'S WAR

"Nail-biting military action adventure."—*The Guardian*

"The action rarely lets up… A page turner."—*Kirkus Reviews*

"A likeable protagonist, a ruthless villain, and pounding action."—SF Signal

"The battle scenes are numerous and thrilling; the world feels immersive and authentic; and our heroine is a tough-as-nails badass."—RT Book Reviews

TITANBOOKS.COM

AMERICA RISING

William C. Dietz

On May Day, 2018, sixty meteors entered Earth's atmosphere and exploded around the globe with a force greater than a nuclear blast. Earthquakes and tsunamis followed. Then China attacked Europe, Asia, and the United States in the belief the disaster was an act of war.

Washington D.C. was a casualty of the meteor onslaught that decimated the nation's leadership and left the surviving elements of the armed forces to try and restore order as American society fell apart. As refugees across America band together and engage in open warfare with the military over scarce resources, a select group of individuals representing the surviving corporate structure make a power play to rebuild the country in a free market image as The New Confederacy...

INTO THE GUNS
(AUGUST 2016)

SEEK AND DESTROY
(AUGUST 2017)

BATTLE HYMN
(AUGUST 2018)

For more fantastic fiction, author events, exclusive excerpts, competitions, limited editions and more

Visit our website

titanbooks.com

Like us on Facebook

facebook.com / titanbooks

Follow us on Twitter

@TitanBooks

Email us

readerfeedback@titanemail.com